D0950003

AFTER IMAGE

KATHLEEN GEORGE

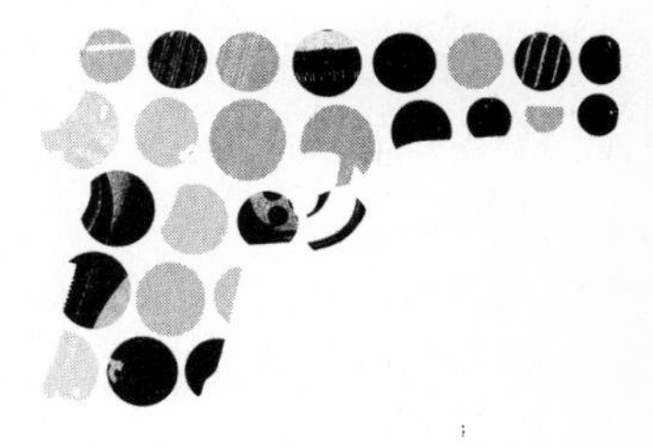

THOMAS DUNNE BOOKS
ST. MARTIN'S MINOTAUR
NEW YORK

This is a work of fiction. No characters are meant to represent real people. The Pittsburgh setting of *Afterimage* includes both real and fictional businesses, streets, and organizations; all of the real businesses and organizations are used fictitiously.

THOMAS DUNNE BOOKS.
An imprint of St. Martin's Press.

AFTERIMAGE. Copyright © 2007 by Kathleen George. All rights reserved. Printed in the United States of America. No part of this book may be used or reproduced in any manner whatsoever without written permission except in the case of brief quotations embodied in critical articles or reviews. For information, address St. Martin's Press, 175 Fifth Avenue, New York, N.Y. 10010.

www.thomasdunnebooks.com
www.minotaurbooks.com

Design by Dylan Rosal Greif

Library of Congress Cataloging-in-Publication Data

George, Kathleen, 1943–
Afterimage / Kathleen George.—1st U.S. ed.
p. cm.
ISBN-13: 978-0-312-37249-1
ISBN-10: 0-312-37249-3
1. Women detectives—Fiction. 2. Murder—investigation—Fiction. 3. Imagery (Psychology)—Fiction. 4. Pittsburgh (Pa.) Fiction. I. Title.
PS3557.E487A69 2007
813'.54—dc22

2007032082

First Edition: December 2007

10 9 8 7 6 5 4 3 2 1

For Hilary

ACKNOWLEDGMENTS

Thanks to retired Commander Ronald B. Freeman of the Pittsburgh Police Major Crimes Division for a great deal of detailed information; to Commander Thomas Stangrecki for a tour of Police Headquarters; to the Allegheny County Coroner's Office for a tour of that facility; to research assistants Alexandra Zamorski, Eliza Farrell, and Jasmine Fannell for much of the library work involved; to the Richard D. and Mary Jane Edwards Endowed Publication Fund for financial help; to my husband, my family, and the University of Pittsburgh for understanding and support.

AFTERIMAGE

ONE

IT WAS THE THREE OF THEM from the beginning.

One Friday in mid-July, Commander Christie was in the outer office, pacing in a relaxed way, chatting up Artie Dolan, his best detective, who had his feet up on his desk, a stack of papers in his lap. Both were avoiding the grunt of paperwork. Colleen Greer, the rookie on Homicide, sat at her desk, trying to do her own reports and form filling. The others on the evening shift were all away from their desks with one thing or another.

"You talked to James Picarelli lately?" Dolan asked.

"Nah, they retire and they leave us behind. He was tired of it."

"He was tired before he left. He was blowing cases left and right."

"There but for the grace," Christie said. He looked over at Greer. He was her mentor.

"Don't make me nervous," she said. "I have a lot of years before retirement."

"You'll make mistakes," Christie said. "Hopefully not too many of them while I'm your boss." He chuckled.

"Hopefully."

"Hey, Boss," Dolan said, "did you bring in your dinner tonight?"

"No, I have to order something. Marina was going out with some friends. You ordering out?"

"I was thinking maybe Quik-It chicken."

Fried, fatty, salty—all the causes for indigestion, to which Christie was prone. Artie's stomach was a steel drum. Christie needed takeout like what Greer had in front of her. Looked like a salad of some sort, pretty much finished.

"Or"—Dolan hefted the stack of papers onto his desk, looking hopeful—"we could go out?"

"We could," Christie said distractedly. "Hey, Greer, I ever tell you about the serial killer we had? Accountant from Zelienople?"

"No."

"Oh, that's a good one," Dolan said.

"A true legitimate cannibal. Cooked and ate his victims."

"No way."

"Yeah way. You think it's only in the movies, but he did it. Finally—I was wondering this all along—somebody finally asked him what human beings tasted like."

"Right."

"Know what he said?"

"Huh uh."

"Chicken."

"No joke?"

Christie shook his head. "No joke, that's what he said. Chicken."

Greer shook her head.

"He was the most ordinary guy. Had everything going for him. Crazy, huh?"

"So you don't want Quik-It," Dolan murmured.

"Ah! I don't know. I'm going to try to do something," Christie said, heading back to his office. He sat, imitating Dolan, put his feet up and stacked the files he needed to brush up on for court on his lap. He felt sleepy from the afternoon delight he and Marina had indulged in.

The case he needed to brush up on for Wednesday was kids, everybody lying, bullets, illegal guns, one poor slob very dead of the mess. Only three motives for crime, they always said at the station. It was going to be love or money or revenge, and sometimes on a good day, two or even all three at once. Little lesson to pass on to Greer.

And brains maybe helped a little, but the real secret of solving crimes was *luck,* nine times out of ten. Mostly, the police didn't advertise that fact.

He was bored with the case he was boning up on.

After ten minutes of study—ah, a detective had to cram at the last minute anyway, right, like a student?—he tossed the papers onto his desk and went back out to where Dolan was now chatting up Greer. Dolan was telling the one about the two dumb guys he'd interrogated who told him how they planned to rob a nice old couple and of course didn't want to be identified as the robbers, so they decided to kill the old folks, as a by-the-way.

"*Did* they kill them?" she asked.

"Oh yeah. It never occurred to the idiots to use masks, stockings, hats, something." Dolan chuckled. "When I was questioning them, I asked them straight out, '*Why* didn't you guys use masks?' They looked surprised, like, *what a good idea.*"

Christie, who wasn't a particularly apt actor, joined in, put the heel of his hand to his head. "Oops, didn't think of that."

Dolan chuckled. "They were keeping it simple."

"Jeez," Greer said appreciatively.

"Hey, let's go out," Christie said to Dolan. "I'll go if we can sit down someplace."

"Okay, then how about Atria's?" Dolan suggested.

"I don't think they have fried chicken."

"That's okay."

"No game tonight?"

"Pirates're in Cincy."

Colleen Greer went back to her paperwork, looking for all the world as if she wanted to be one of the boys and didn't want to—equally. Christie liked her. She worked hard. She was pretty, took care of herself. Sometimes, when she wasn't so worried about being professional, she was fun. And she had that edge of uncertainty that made her sweet. Dolan liked her, too.

"Hey, Greer, come with us."

She suddenly looked superhappy about dropping the pencils and papers.

They went in one car over to Federal, near the new ballpark, several blocks away from Headquarters. The detectives had had their favorite restaurants over in East Liberty, and they still went across town sometimes for a Tessaro's fix, but now that the offices had been moved to the North Side, they'd had to pick a whole new series of favorites. Christie secretly missed the old offices. He'd been used to the dirt and grime and squalor of them. Now he came to work and felt he was entering the front offices of NASA or an airport or something.

It was a short hop over to Atria's, a matter of twelve, fifteen blocks, past the park, around the post office, and they were there. They even lucked out and found street parking. The place was jumping with Friday-night after-work gatherings. All the outside tables were taken. They decided air conditioning was going to feel better anyway, and, in spite of the fact that the inside was crowded, too, they snagged a table.

Christie ordered only iced tea to drink. Dolan got a beer and Greer got herself a glass of wine. They ordered. When the chop with mashed potatoes, a chicken blackened, and the salmon were put before them, the two guys were telling Greer of some of the wildest cases, watching to see if she blanched, but she started on her blackened chicken, no problem. No, they weren't the usual ticket, people who went into police work. More like the young doctors on that TV show who always wanted to be at the most grisly surgeries. *Show me the brain. Show me the blood. Show me the disease. I want to see the worst you can give me. I want to put my hands around the tumor, pluck out the enlarged heart, claw through some fat guy's guts.*

Christie's phone rang. "Yeah?" he said into it, swallowing down a bite of the salmon.

He heard the trill of anxiety in the voice of the patrol cop they put on the line with him. The cop asked for a detective car, said it was definitely a murder and it was very very messy. Messy was also usually interesting.

"We got what sounds like a good one," Christie told the others. "Regent Square." Raised his eyebrows. "Boyfriend called it in. I'll have someone bring us some supplies so we don't lose any time."

"Damn," Dolan said, cutting himself one last big bite of chop. "We tempted fate." But he didn't look exactly unhappy.

Christie motioned to the waiter and showing his ID, said, "We'll be back to settle up. You want my card?"

The waiter looked uncertain.

Christie dropped his card on the table. "Keep that safe for me. Take a tip."

He said for the second time that evening to Greer, "Come with us."

She looked eager enough. She wouldn't be official. Because of red tape and court costs, only two on a case were official, the first two there, usually, but she could come, she could learn.

He had Dolan call Forensics while they were sirening their way through the streets onto the parkway. Friday night, so the guy on call made the usual moans about finding people.

Seven minutes later, the three detectives tumbled out of their unmarked car. There were already neighbors scattered on the private road, a cruiser with lights on, rolling out the amber signals, a cop stringing out yellow tape.

"You touched anything?"

"Nothing."

"Body's in the kitchen?"

"Yes."

"You went past the kitchen?"

"No, Commander."

"You think anybody's in there?"

"I don't think so, but there's all kinds of rooms, like basement and upstairs, to check."

"Point of entry? You see anything?"

"Nothing obvious."

"You checked the backyard?"

"I checked the backyard going around from the front. Nothing. I mean nobody."

"What door did the boyfriend use?"

"Front."

"And you?"

"Front."

So the three detectives ducked under the yellow tape to get the first look at the victim and to do the walk-through. Greer looked at her heeled sandals and winced. Christie didn't say anything. No booties at the scene yet. Well, he hated booties anyway. He and Dolan never used them. Got blood on things when they had to, washed it off, ruined certain pieces of clothing and footwear from time to time. As they entered the house through the front door, they drew their guns. The living room showed no evidence of violence. Christie swung back to take a quick look at the front door. Right, no signs of a break-in. The dining room looked clean. But the kitchen, that was something else. There was blood everywhere—on the kitchen cabinets, the table, the floor, the slatted blinds, the dishcloth, pot holders, hanging frying pans, loaf of bread on the counter.

On the floor, twisted in her last attempt to fight someone, was a woman, slender, with wavy brown hair. She wore a conservative pair of pants, some kind of linen blend, dark brown, and what had been a white shirt, sandals with small heels. Her clothes were of a good quality. She'd put a little makeup on. And she was truly, absolutely dead. Her throat was severed and she had what looked like six, seven stab wounds.

Greer gasped and turned away for a second. Ha, still green, Christie thought.

First, they needed to make sure there was nobody hiding in the house, so they started the walk-through. "Move. Nice and easy. Make sure we check points of entry and exit, windows, that stuff." Mostly, he was talking for Greer, even though she'd been trained well, passed the tests, interviewed well.

She tried the back door. "Locked," she said. She wasn't looking at the body, he noticed. She'd been a counselor before this, just a master's degree counselor, though some of the guys teased her and called her a shrink.

They passed back through the dining room and living room into the hallway. Then down the hall, up the steps, bedroom, spare room, bathroom—closets, under beds. Windows. All still. They went back down the stairs to another set of stairs to the basement. The light was dim, but they covered the corners, checked the basement door. Locked. Nobody in the house. Most everything seemed untouched outside the kitchen, where the murder clearly took place.

"Somebody she knew," Dolan said. "Somebody she let in."

"What do you think?" he asked Greer.

"Same."

They stood in the kitchen, doing an intense study of the scene.

The woman had really fought.

Good. Better to go down fighting.

They studied the position of the body, the amount of blood, the apparent orderliness of the kitchen before the blood. There was a partial print of something on the table, a glass—no, *two* glasses, but neither of them in sight. That meant, or seemed to mean, somebody had removed them. Greer was stooping and studying the woman's face.

"Better hear what that boyfriend has to say," Dolan urged.

Christie was eager to hear it, too. As they trooped out front, Forensics called, saying they were still trying to round people up. "We need blood, fingerprints, shoes," Christie said into the phone as he listened to Dolan tell Greer, "Friday night, they're going to try to crimp or combine."

She smiled indulgently. "In the old days, one person did everything."

"In small towns, they still do," Dolan admitted, "but we have experts, and in a case like this, we want 'em."

Christie stopped on the front sidewalk and beckoned the patrol cop over. About twenty neighbors had gathered in roughly three clumps. He gave them a slight nod of acknowledgment. He was going to need them soon enough. Sitting in the cruiser in the driveway was the boyfriend. Even looking past the driver's seat to the passenger seat, where the man sat, it was clear he was sobbing.

"You suspect him?" Christie asked.

Patrol cop shook his head. "The guy is falling apart."

"What's his story?"

"Came here because he couldn't get an answer on the phone. Thought they were supposed to go to dinner together and a movie later. Couldn't get an answer. Came over. Found this."

"Let me talk to him." He looked around for a place.

The garage was open. It was clearly a new one, clean, no blood that he could see, good lights, even some heating elements along the floor, though they wouldn't want them in this season. "Set me up in there."

The patrol cop hurried to move a couple of outdoor chairs into the garage.

Dolan was looking for blood spots on his dapper, perfect clothes, a nice light suit and shirt, all in shades of khaki.

"Artie, would you talk to those people who are watching us, see if anyone wants to come forward with anything. And when Forensics gets here, call me. Greer, help me question this guy." But she was clearly distracted, looking back toward the house.

"Boss. I think I might know something. What is the name of the deceased? Do we have her name?"

Christie didn't need to look at the notes the patrolman had handed him. It was an ordinary name, but he remembered it. "Laura McCall." He looked at her questioningly.

"She—it's hard to see her very well," Greer said in a low voice. "It's hard to be sure, but she looks like the wife of someone I knew. Laura Hoffman was her name. The first name is the same."

"Who was the husband?"

"He was the head at the Family Counseling Center on the North Side where I worked. Over on Arch. David Hoffman."

"You think she is Hoffman?"

"I think so."

"I'll check on the name. Anything we need to talk about now?"

Greer shook her head.

Christie took in the neighborhood, the neighbors, the yard, the park in the near distance, wondering if some park stranger with a good-enough story might have been let into the house. Then he helped the boyfriend out of the cruiser.

The man was thin, with dark hair, a little long, and gentle blue eyes. He looked like someone who would sing folk songs badly, accompanying himself on guitar with three overused chords. He wore jeans, a plaid cotton shirt in light browns, and a jacket that looked like a summer version of tweed. He and the victim "matched." Christie's wife, Marina, an actress, had taught him how costume designers tied people together with color and fabric. Now he noticed this odd detail, that the man's clothes matched his girlfriend's. Christie helped hold the man up. He guided him into the garage and gently lowered him into a seat. "Sorry this isn't a pretty place. We have to keep the house as it was. Give me a second." He opened the patrol cop's notebook and studied it while Greer took a seat next to where he stood. Then he sat.

"I'm very sorry for your loss. I know you're upset, but if you can just answer a couple of questions. Information is what we need right now. You're . . . What's your name?"

"David Shoemaker."

"David. You dated her?"

"Yes."

"She was married, divorced, separated—what?"

"Separated," he replied.

"From? Husband's name?"

"David Hoffman."

Christie didn't look over at Greer, but he sensed her adjusting her position with this confirmation.

"She used to comment on that."

"What?"

"That it kind of freaked her out. Another David."

"But now she goes by McCall."

"McCall, yes, it's her maiden name. She was in the process of changing it officially."

"She was close to being divorced, then?"

"She felt so. They'd been separated for more than two years. We . . . I hoped we were going to be married eventually. I wanted that." He looked about vaguely, as if he still thought there might be hope of such a thing.

" 'Hoped'? Things weren't settled between you?"

"We talked about it. Imagined it. But she still wanted time. She said she was sorting things out."

"What kinds of things?"

"I don't know. Feelings, I guess."

"When was the last time you saw her alive?"

"Yesterday evening. Night. I left about midnight."

"Did you talk to her since?"

"This morning. And then about three."

"She didn't sound different? Frightened?"

"Nooo. . . . But she sounded far away, busy with something."

"She has a job?"

"She works—worked—in marketing for the symphony."

"Why was she home on a Friday afternoon?"

"This was her vacation week. She said she was getting to things she'd been meaning to do for a long time."

"What were those things?"

Shoemaker shook his head. "She was a little bit private about it. I had the feeling I should leave her be."

"Was she seeing anyone else?"

"No! She wouldn't. She wasn't like that. It was something else on her mind."

"Did you have any inkling of what was making her quiet about this thing?"

"Well, I thought it might have something to do with her ex. Finances or something. Maybe."

"How long had you been in a relationship with her?"

"About a year."

"How often did you see her?"

"Lately, couple of times a week. At first, not so much."

"And how did you meet her?"

"There was this jazz event in the park. Mellon Park. I went alone. She went with her best friend, Amy Rosenstein. We all just started talking. I offered them a place on my blanket. The attraction between me and Laura was just there, right away. We connected."

"Have you been married?"

"Was. Divorced five years ago."

"Reason?"

Shoemaker looked puzzled. "It didn't work out."

"Tell me about your first marriage. Just briefly. Give us her name and address, your address, too." He pushed a legal pad toward Shoemaker. "When you have a second."

Shoemaker looked confusedly from the blank legal pad to Christie's face. "She didn't love me. She sure didn't love what I did. She thought academic life was full of nothing but nerds and that I was one of them. Which is true enough. I was a loner for a long time, until I met Laura."

"Then you dated for a year and it was serious."

"Yes. We were both serious people."

"She had no other boyfriends?"

Shoemaker looked completely amazed by the question. "No!"

"So what was holding up the divorce?"

"Her husband didn't want it. He kept asking to work things out, and so it was taking time. She felt kind of bad for him, I think. Do . . . do her parents know?"

"No."

"This . . . this is going to kill them."

"Did she ever tell you she was afraid of her husband?"

"No. Uncomfortable around him, but not . . ."

"Tell me how you found her."

"I was coming over to see why I wasn't getting an answer. I wanted to go to dinner and a movie. I thought she might be in the backyard or something or her phone was out of order."

"You spend much time here?"

"Pretty much. But I still have my own apartment because, you know, her husband was looking for roadblocks—although I can't believe any judge is so dense these days that he wouldn't understand how things really are—"

"Right. I need your ages."

"I'm thirty-six. Laura was thirty-three."

"And Hoffman?"

"Hoffman is a bit older. I think maybe thirty-eight or just under forty."

"You're saying—tell me if this is what I'm hearing—that she was still hooked into him in some way?"

Shoemaker paused. Christie studied him while he answered. There was little blood on him, only the amount that corresponded with his finding the body. Shoes. The cuffs of his jacket. No scratches on his hands or face.

"These things are so complicated," Shoemaker said. "She wanted to get away from him, but she wanted to understand him, too. . . . Something about him bothered her."

Christie looked up. Colleen Greer had moved forward a few inches.

"What did she want to understand?"

"How he ticked. She said she didn't love him, but she wanted to know how he ticked."

"Why did she marry him?"

"He pressed it. Apparently."

"He loved her?"

"He thought so, I guess. She got pregnant and he liked the idea. He didn't want her to get rid of it, so they got married. He wanted a family, she said."

"What happened to the baby?"

"They lost it."

"On purpose or naturally?"

Shoemaker looked shocked again. "Naturally. The way she talked about it, I never thought the other. But there was a lot of unhappiness between them, if that's what you're asking. She was sweet and good. He wasn't a very happy guy. She made a bad marriage."

Christie said, "I have to ask you to be absolutely forthright here. Are you saying you think he killed her?"

A sob escaped him. "I keep thinking she didn't have trouble with anybody else. But how could anyone do such a—"

"Did she ever say she feared her husband might kill her?"

"No. No." Shoemaker looked confused. "Maybe it was a stranger. But why would a stranger . . ."

Exactly. Why would a stranger slit her throat, fight her to the death, not rape her (it looked like), and not rob her (it looked like), at least not of anything very obvious?

Christie waited for a while. "Give me a picture of her. Personality, you know. Volatile, quiet, complicated, emotional?"

"Quiet. And straightforward. But a very determined woman, once she got an idea about something, very persistent."

"Thanks. I know this is hard, but you're doing very well. Can you tell me how I can contact her parents?"

"Yes."

Christie tapped the legal pad. "Put it all there. That would be helpful. Thanks." He got up and looked outside to where Dolan was talking with neighbors. He turned back to Shoemaker. "If you know how I can contact Hoffman, put it down."

"He runs a center on the North Side, a counseling center."

"Who does he counsel?"

"Mothers, fathers, kids."

"Is he good at his job?"

"Very good, I hear. Even Laura said he was good at it."

"All right. We'll talk to him. Just one more thing. Routine question. Where were you today between, say, three and when you came to pick her up—what was it, six?"

"Home."

"You live alone?"

"Yes."

Christie said kindly, "I have to ask these questions. Did anyone see you?"

"No. I was reading. Oh, well, I got a UPS package. Some books from Amazon. The deliveryman saw me. Does that count?"

"It counts. What time was that?"

"About five."

"Anything else? Any phone calls?"

"I talked to my department chair."

"When was that?"

"Maybe four, four-thirty."

"Good, write down the details for us and we can check it all out." Shoemaker nodded and began sobbing. Christie patted him on the shoulder. "We can talk again."

He told Colleen, "Stay with him for a few minutes. Make sure he's all right. Get him something to eat or drink if he needs it. I'll have you and Dolan switch in a little bit so you can see what we're up to inside."

Two TV news cars pulled up, two rival stations at one time.

His stomach was already dyspeptic without the media people to help it along. He held up a hand. "We just got here moments ago. I'll give you a statement as soon as we know something."

He made a sign to Dolan to turn over the questioning of neighbors to someone else. Coleson and McGranahan had just driven up, that'd be okay. There were police radios going, but otherwise there was a kind of hush outside.

He and Dolan went back into the kitchen and it was quiet in there, too, possibly because the house was close to Frick Park.

They donned gloves, tiptoed around the rest of the house.

The place Laura McCall had bought herself when she left her husband was one of the more modest houses on the street—but it was a wonderful street, because it wound right up into Frick Park, as good a city park as you could find anywhere in the country, very woodsy, very . . . natural, isolated-feeling. So it was possible, completely possible, that a maniac had emerged from the woods and talked his way into Laura McCall's house. No weapon in sight. It had been removed.

No handbag in sight so far.

A handbag—the thing every woman carried with wallet and keys and tissues and probably a lipstick and comb inside—had not been in sight during the first sweep through the house. Christie figured maybe she was the type of careful woman who tucked it in a drawer somewhere until she went out. This second time, as he moved more carefully with Dolan, he didn't see it, either. But all the stereo equipment was still there, jewelry on the bureau still there.

Slit a throat to take a handbag? Not likely.

Christie and Dolan stopped moving.

"I still say someone she knew."

"Yeah."

There were plenty of photos in the upstairs hallway, a whole wall of them, artfully arranged. And easy to read. There was the deceased at age ten or so with her parents, presumably. Traditional types, they looked like. House with painted siding. Buick in the driveway. Neat plants. They seemed, as a family, earnest and a little shy. Then the deceased with some friends in her high school days. Then the marriage. Looked like. Husband reminded Christie of somebody on the news. Who? Light brown hair receding slightly, cut short, combed backward, eyes hidden behind glasses, body getting a little fleshy. Cross between senator and minister.

"Greer knew the husband." Christie pointed. "Worked with him."

"Get out," Dolan said.

"Yeah."

"Ought to be something she can tell us, huh? He's very pale-looking," Dolan observed.

"Could use a little sun."

Christie and Dolan moved down the hall and checked out what looked like a spare bedroom. It didn't yield anything.

Dolan was looking around the place with a detective's lust for something physical, a clue. "This is a very clean house," Dolan remarked. "She must have just moved in. Nothing's collected, no debris."

"Let's check the bathroom," Christie said. He and Dolan went in. "Wet shower," Christie said levelly, and a hopeful note crept into his voice. "Shouldn't there be a wet towel in here somewhere?"

"Yeah. Should be," Dolan said excitedly.

"Her hair wasn't wet. Towels don't look wet."

"Shower curtain is still *very* wet."

"I like this all right."

"He washed the blood off! Hot damn."

"Forensics can do the drains, everything. Unless she got ready to go out, changed the towels, used a hair dryer, and did the laundry, there's something going on here."

Very carefully, they lifted the hamper lid. Bunch of stuff, not towels.

"I'll check the basement again," Dolan said.

But they stopped first at the room that served as a home office. There was nothing startling in the room and nothing out of order. In one drawer were copies of recent letters to and from the lawyer, not yet filed.

As soon as they powered up the computer, they could see that the letters had been written on it and were available in that nontactile form as well. "We'll have to see what else is on here." Christie tapped the aqua casing. "We'll have to print this room, too, but if the guy was in here, he was mighty neat."

"He wasn't here. He was in a hurry, cleaned up, got out, that's what I say."

"You go out and switch with Greer for a while. See if Shoemaker has a user name and password for this thing. Do your magic on him. Tell Greer to meet me outside. I'll check the basement for laundry."

There were no towels anywhere in the basement.

Greer came up to him on the lawn, handing him a piece of paper from her legal pad. One line said "lauhofmcc@aol.com." Another line said "union3."

"Boyfriend knew it," she said.

"Tell me everything you knew about the wife, the marriage, the husband."

"Well, he was a good counselor."

"Like how?"

"Helped people to get off drugs and alcohol. He'd get them to AA and NA."

"Did he seem like a violent man?"

"No . . . no, a *nervous* man, and there was an ego that was bruised."

"Clients liked him?"

"Yes. Well enough."

"And his wife? You'd met her?"

"Couple of times, parties, gatherings. I didn't know her. Just traded party talk."

"And what did you think of her?"

Colleen blanched. "She was nice."

"You hadn't expected her to be?"

She paused. "Hoffman alluded to trouble between them. I was picturing a difficult person. Then she seemed anything but. She was very quiet, didn't say much, but I had the impression of a person who was . . . warm, sympathetic."

"You liked him?"

She hesitated. "I respected him. Then I got nervous because he seemed to want more friendliness from me than I could give him. That got in the way."

"Did he seem possessive of his wife?"

"Yes."

"Devoted to the marriage?"

"Yes, well, no, more worried about it."

"A womanizer?"

"Not a very successful one. I think he thought the marriage was falling apart and he was looking around to see if anything else might work for him. But nothing else did because he seemed so uncertain and needy. I always felt a bit of sympathy for him." She shivered. "Maybe that was nuts."

"He came on to you?"

"Yes."

"And how far did it go?"

"It didn't go anywhere. I said no a couple of different polite ways."

Christie smiled. "What are the polite ways?"

"Always being busy or distracted or not quite understanding his intention."

"You played dumb?"

"When I had to."

"That must rankle."

"Thank you. It does."

"Well. I'm sure I'll want to talk to you again about him. Under the circumstances. You understand?"

"Fine with me."

Forensics arrived in one car and the mobile crime unit in another. "Let's go," Christie said.

Two of the specialists pointed to a third. "He's what took so long," they said good-naturedly.

A squat, chubby man blushed. "I was at a play with my wife. Had my phone on vibrate. The play had just got started when the call came in."

"I'm sorry," Christie said.

"Oh, don't be sorry. It didn't look like I was going to like it. This way, my wife can watch it and not be angry with me for fidgeting." He looked at his watch. "With luck, I'll pick her up when it's over or after she has a cappuccino somewhere."

Christie looked at his own watch. "She's going to need a couple of slow cappuccinos. Possibly a vodka after."

"It's a biggie, huh?"

"Yeah."

The men from the mobile crime unit had joined them. The photographer tipped his digital camera to Greer and Christie in hello.

"Okay." Christie sighed. "Let's get started. Careful of the scene. Delicate with the evidence."

They went inside, where he gave a series of directions, but he also let them look. They were experts. They were good.

Again, Christie and Greer studied the victim, her body now being submitted to photographs. Around them, the staff tiptoed, joking among themselves.

The burly playgoer said, "He kinda wanted to be sure, huh?"

The photographer, snapping the counter, said, "Ruined a real nice loaf of bread."

Greer looked as if she might be sick.

Christie thought she could use a break. "Greer, I want you to look through her makeup, medicine chest, personal items. Try to find a handbag. Meet me in her study."

Only ten minutes after he'd logged on to Laura Hoffman McCall's E-mail and seen the most usual of messages, including chain letters meant to spread humor, Colleen Greer joined him. She seemed self-possessed again.

"Her makeup and medicines couldn't be more ordinary. Couldn't find a handbag, though. No wallet anywhere, either. Somebody lifted those."

"Primary objective, or cover-up?"

"I'd vote cover-up."

He nodded. "What happened when you sat with the boyfriend?"

"Nothing new. He's stunned. He thought his life had turned around for the good, and now it's as bad as it can be. He's not getting past that. Sounds like he was more committed than she was, though."

"Because?"

"Her secrets. Things she had to do. He doesn't know what they were."

"The computer isn't telling me what they were, either. I'm not finding evidence of another lover. I'll put Potocki on it tomorrow. We're all working tomorrow, in case you wondered."

"I didn't wonder."

They both looked at their watches. Almost eight forty-five. They had a lot of night ahead of them yet. "We want to beat the media to the parents and the husband," Christie said, shutting down the computer. "I'm going to let McGranahan and Coleson watch over the scene here. I think it's under control. Let's tell them."

Christie was writing a list of instructions as he walked down the stairs and out the front door to find the two detectives he wanted.

"Uh-oh," he heard Greer say from a step behind him. He looked up from the list he was compiling.

Coming up the front walk was a familiar-looking man, the ten years older version of the husband in the photos. David Hoffman. Was this going to turn out to be easy after all?

Or. Someone had called him?

No. What would explain the *puzzled* look on the man's face?

The patrolman on duty put an arm out. "You can't come any further, sir."

"What happened? What is this? What happened?" Hoffman tried again to move forward. "I have a right to know."

"Stop where you are, please." Christie moved down the steps. "You can see this is a crime scene. Nobody passes."

"I'm David Hoffman. What happened here? My wife lives here. Is she all right?"

Christie shook his head. "I'm sorry. I have sad news for you. Your wife passed away."

"Oh my God. Oh my God." David Hoffman moved in a figure eight, hunched over, his arms cradling his stomach. "How . . . how did it happen?"

"I'm sure we'll find that out in time." Christie looked toward the garage, where Dolan was still ministering to and at the same time covertly grilling the boyfriend. He couldn't very well put the husband in the garage, too. He said, "Mr. Hoffman. David?" And when he was sure he had the man's attention, he asked, "Why did you come to the house just now?"

"She's my wife. What happened in there?"

"We're trying to find out."

"Are you saying she was killed?"

"Her death is definitely a police matter."

"Oh my God. I have to know what happened. She was my wife."

The detectives exchanged quick looks. "But separated. Correct?" Christie asked.

"Yes." Hoffman let out a groan, closed his eyes. He didn't appear to care that he was being studied. Or he did care and was natural in the limelight.

"Did someone call you to tell you?"

"No. Laura called earlier. She asked me to come over."

"So you were still in touch? You saw each other?"

Hoffman looked at the sidewalk. "Sometimes. We weren't enemies.... *She* called *me* today. She said she needed to see me tonight. I had other plans, but I came because she asked me to. I would have anyway, but she sounded a little funny."

"In what way?"

"Just . . . worried, or maybe scared."

"Scared? Did she frighten easily?"

"I don't know. Yes, I guess so. Yes, but it doesn't mean it wasn't real."

"No, it doesn't. We're going to ask you to go back to the office with us, try to help us out a little more on this. It won't take long."

"I want to go in there."

"No. It's absolutely not allowed."

"Is there any chance she's—"

"No chance."

David Hoffman made another rebellious start toward the house and came face-to-face with Greer, who put an arm out, much as the patrolman had, a gesture mimicked by those mechanical arms installed in parking lots. *Stop. Pass.* "Oh," he said. And he was clearly nonplussed. "Colleen! What are you doing here?"

She showed her badge. "I was on duty when this was called in. I'm sorry for your loss."

"Of course, of course, you're police now. I'm glad to see a friend," he murmured. He moved a step toward her. "They don't know me."

"I'm sorry. We can't let anyone in. It's not you. It's procedure." She softened her tone. "Are you okay? You'll have to answer questions."

He looked at her for a while, nodded, then turned and went back down the steps to Christie. He said, "All right. Whatever I need to do." But his face had changed and his eyes were more guarded than they had been.

"Why don't we talk over at the station now. You can see her at the coroner's office—say nine tomorrow morning—to make a formal identification." He wasn't needed to make the ID, but Christie wanted to watch him in that setting. Unless, of course, he confessed tonight.

Dolan rode in Hoffman's car, no doubt doing his magic, easing the guy up, while Colleen rode with Christie back to Headquarters.

"There are no scratches on his hands or face," Christie said.

"Right," she said quickly. "I looked as well as I could, too."

Christie was using the parkway, expertly weaving in and out of traffic. "He looked pretty distressed, didn't he?"

"He did. But if not him, who?"

"That's the question. And he didn't ask it."

"I noticed."

"Good."

"He said *what* but he didn't say *who*."

THEY GOT TO HEADQUARTERS, and as they strode down the corridor, Christie watched Hoffman walking ahead with Dolan. The man was alert, looking around at everything. "Greer, I want you to get the friend, Amy Rosenstein, scheduled for an interview, tonight if possible, check on any priors for Shoemaker and Hoffman, try to contact Shoemaker's ex." She looked disappointed, but he didn't want to complicate matters by putting her in a room with Hoffman, who'd been her boss at one point.

He went into one of the small interview rooms with Hoffman and Dolan.

Hoffman had meanwhile worked up a little anger. "Am I being held? What is this? She called me and asked me to come over."

The claustrophobia of the room alone tended to make people angry. Windowless, maybe seven by eight, small metal table, three hard chairs, a fitting on the floor for leg irons, the interview room made a person's mind leap ahead to the discomforts of prison, although the truth was, the newest prisons now rivaled boys' camps. Minus the frogs and pond and tennis courts, of course.

Christie seated himself. Dolan followed. "We asked for your help. Are you going to help us?"

"Yes."

"All right. Now, what do you need—water, coffee, soda?"

Dolan stood back up. "We could get you food if you haven't eaten."

"I couldn't eat if my life depended on it. Water, though. Water."

Dolan went out for it. With the door open, Christie and Hoffman could see him put some coins in a machine. Hoffman leaned forward in his seat, looking out into the hallway until Dolan returned with a cold bottle of water and closed the door. Hoffman reached toward his pocket.

"No," Dolan said. "It's just a bottle of water. Let me know if you get hungry." Dolan sat. "Okay." He put his hands on the table. "Okay now."

Christie did the routine part, very formally, legal pad in front of him, another pushed over to Hoffman. "Address, phone number at home, at work, cell, E-mail address." Hoffman wrote rapidly. "Now we simply need to know your whereabouts from say noon on today. Or if you can, give us the whole day."

"I was at work. Meetings. Clients. All day. Then dinner with a friend."

"Can you reconstruct the day?" He indicated the legal pad. "Jot down what you remember. Names."

Hoffman wrote down names of people who'd had appointments from eight in the morning until five o'clock. Some were solo appointments; most were family sessions with several people."

"Who else saw these people?"

"We have a receptionist. She shows them in and sees them on the way out."

"Write down her name and any phone numbers you know."

Hoffman was able to do that with a phone book, locating the woman's home number.

Christie and Dolan exchanged a look as Hoffman wrote. It had clearly been a busy day at the center. The hours were completely filled. The man bore no scratches and he could account for his time until five. Alibi was going to be tight. Yet the man's legs were shaking as he wrote. Once he stopped writing, he was practically sitting on his hands.

"Who was the dinner with?"

"A woman I met through a dating service. First date."

"Can you give us her name?"

He wrote it down and the name of the restaurant. "It wasn't anything. I could hardly concentrate because I knew I was supposed to go see Laura."

"How long were you separated?" Christie asked mildly.

"Two and a half years."

"Pretty long time. And the divorce?"

"Well, we were on the way to it. But we were becoming friendly again, talking. I wasn't sure where we would end up."

"You initiated the divorce? The separation, I should say."

"No, she did."

"And you accepted it?"

Hoffman hesitated slightly before nodding. This is where Dolan knew to come in. His turn.

"You don't need to be embarrassed. It almost always happens this way, this direction. The woman makes the decision; then things get very dicey. I don't know about your case, but just to tell you, you don't need to hold back anything. We've heard it all. When women get angry, they are very very vulnerable in a million ways."

Hoffman made a face, but his eyes were alive. He was interested. "You sound like a shrink."

Dolan shrugged. "It's the work. I don't have the language, maybe, but I've seen a lot of relationships fall apart. Whatever you have to say, we won't be shocked. Honestly."

"What you say about anger becoming vulnerability, I'd agree with that. I used to think, she's going to have an accident or she's going to get sick or something."

Dolan nodded. "Was there any particular thing triggered the separation? The boyfriend?" His voice gave a critical slant to the last word.

"I think he came after."

"What did it, then?"

"She got tired of me, I guess. I work hard. I'm not the most romantic man."

"Had you been having sexual relations with your wife?" Dolan somehow made this sound sympathetic.

"Not that often."

"How often? Or when did it end?"

"I don't know."

"I thought everybody counted. Trying to do their twice a week national average. Did you manage twice a week?"

"Nothing like it."

"Twice a month?"

Hoffman shook his head.

"Twice a year?"

"More like it."

"That could be rough going on a guy," Dolan said evenly. "Whose choice was that?"

"Hers. She was off me."

"Do you think she was seeing anyone else in this time—if not the boyfriend?"

"I don't think she was."

"And you? This is confidential. It wouldn't be surprising if you were having relations with someone else. Under the circumstances."

"Not really."

"You went all that time without pursuing more intimacy?"

"I had one or two lunches, dinners with women I met. I guess I was rehearsing for possible separation."

"Any of those other relationships come to anything?"

"No. I saw the women one or two times in each case. My heart wasn't in it. But I felt like I had a right to try. The relationship at home was not good."

"Yet you didn't want it to end."

"I didn't say that."

"I thought you did. Sorry. It seemed . . ." Dolan began looking back through his notepad.

"I didn't think we'd worked hard enough to keep it together."

"That's what made me put it the way I did. It seemed she was more keen on ending it *completely* than you were. Is that fair?"

Hoffman nodded. "But look, I'm no dummy. I know about these things. I know how these things go."

"What things?"

"Murder. People look at the husband first. But I didn't do it. I didn't do anything to her." He looked back and forth at the two detectives, who remained impassive. "I should have a lawyer, shouldn't I? You think I did something."

Christie said, "Of course you can have a lawyer if you need one. I'm just trying to make this investigation happen now, without delays, as fast as possible, to find the person who killed Laura."

Silence.

"Killed." Hoffman let the word sink in, as if he hadn't used the word *murder* a second ago. "How?"

Christie and Dolan looked at each other. Still no *who.*

Christie performed a little, looking at the door, appearing thoughtful, murmuring, "We aren't supposed to . . . There are a lot of rules."

"Shot?"

They didn't answer.

Hoffman groaned. "I hope not beaten or strangled. Please. Say no."

Dolan shook his head ever so slightly. "I'm afraid it was very brutal."

"A knife?"

The detectives didn't answer. They allowed themselves to wince slightly. Hoffman looked as if he would faint.

Christie said, "Who do you think did this to your wife?"

"I don't know."

"If you had to guess."

"I don't know. Some maniac."

"Maybe. Who was *that* angry with her?"

"I don't know."

"Anyone at work?"

"Not that I know of."

"Family?"

"Her family adored her. I don't know. You have to look at the guy she was dating, don't you?"

Christie nodded. "You pointing a finger at him?"

"I don't know. Yes, unless . . . Was anything taken?"

"Like what?"

"Money. Her purse. Jewelry. Was it robbery?"

"Of course we're looking into that. It could turn out something is missing."

Hoffman looked relieved. Violence for the sake of fifty bucks was preferable.

There. They could say they'd told him little, but they'd had a chance to watch him as he guessed.

Christie needed to move onto McCall's parents, so he ushered him out, past Colleen, toward the exit. "Stay put. We'll be in touch."

Hoffman, turning back to Colleen, said, "Thank you."

"I'm not sure what for. . . ." She managed to smile.

"For being here. Just for being." His eyes welled up. He looked around at offices, at the people who looked up from what they were doing to register his presence, at Dolan, coming up behind Christie.

Christie and Dolan saw him out as far as the stairway and then watched him from the windows as he went to his car. It was dark now, except for the city streetlights, ten o'clock. The man sagged. He moved slowly. He cast a long look back at the building before he got into his car and drove off.

Colleen gazed inquisitively at the other two.

"Alibi the size of Texas," said Dolan.

"I broke the news to Amy Rosenstein. She's coming to the office at midnight. She's pretty broken up. She wanted to come right away, but I figured you'd want to go to Butler first—unless you want to assign me to question her."

"Midnight. Works. You did fine." He thought for a moment. "Come with us to the parents."

Then the three were on their way to the parking lot, walking fast.

Christie said, "We can swing by Atria's for a second. It's on the way to Butler. I want to get my charge card back."

"I wonder if he boxed my half a chop."

"Probably not."

They approached one of the fleet cars. Dolan insisted Colleen sit in front. "I'll take the front seat on the way back. Trying to be fair here. Equal rights to the death seat."

Christie punched an automatic dial on his cell as he started out. "It's me," he said. He laughed when Marina said, "It's a big one and you're staying past midnight, not a lot past, but a bit."

"All that in my voice?"

"Yeah. I miss you. And that's just on regular hours."

"I'm going to get out of this lousy work."

Dolan favored him with a laugh that meant "And do what?"

"Like I believe you," Marina said. "I heard someone laughing. Artie?"

"Yeah."

"Oh, well, you warned me." Her voice was silky, warm. She'd go to bed early, but when he climbed in, hours from now, she'd roll over and hold him. No matter how quiet he was—and sometimes he couldn't hear a thing, not even his own breathing—she caught the vibrations.

"You got the kids?" he asked.

"Yeah. They're excited about tomorrow."

Police picnic. He'd forgotten. Now he wondered if he'd get to it at all, even for a couple of minutes. But he didn't say that to Marina.

When the call ended, he turned to Colleen. "Hanging in there?"

"Yes."

"Long hours tonight and tomorrow. I was just reminded we have the police picnic tomorrow. You were going?" He directed this to Greer again, since he knew Dolan was always up for a party.

"I was. We'll have time for that?"

"Use it as our lunchtime," Christie said. "Take a break if we can."

"We have to eat," Dolan said from the backseat. "Couple of burgers and dogs have my name on them."

Christie chuckled. "God, I'd give a lot to be able to eat the way this one does. And no indigestion. Anyway, Greer, I'm probably going to need you most of the weekend. Say eight tomorrow morning? Or nine, if we go superlate tonight."

"Whatever. It's fine."

"You have to make any calls? Your fellow?"

"Yeah. Yeah, I think I will."

"Good."

Just then they pulled up outside Atria's. Christie said, "I'll run in."

Dolan said, "I want to hit the can. Hold the fort, Greer."

The two of them got out of the car. They were aware Colleen had waited to punch in her call until they were gone.

"What goes on there?" Christie asked on the way into the restaurant.

"They don't live together, but they spend most nights together, from what I can tell."

"It's serious?"

"I guess. One time she told me she gets frustrated because she has her own house she has to take care of and she feels like she's neglecting it. She gave the desk sergeant the address and phone of the boyfriend's place. You know, just in case. 'Cause she's there a lot."

"Right. You always get information out of people, even when they haven't committed a crime. You ever met him?"

"Nope."

The waiter handed Christie his charge card *and* three small boxes of leftovers while Dolan made a streak for the john. The stop took them, altogether, about ninety seconds. Sometimes things worked out.

When they got back to the car, Greer was just closing her cell phone. She had the car window cracked.

"Your guy understands?" Dolan asked.

"Sure." She wiped sweat from her brow. "What is it? Ten at night and still ninety-six degrees?"

While Dolan was arranging his seat belt, he said, "Make sure to bring your guy to the picnic tomorrow."

"I mentioned it, actually. He's going to try."

"He has to come. We make our spouses come to commiserate with each other. And, of course, *we* want to get a look at him."

Colleen smiled. "I'll do my best. I don't think he's working tomorrow."

Christie said, "Greer, you ever done this before? Telling the family of a victim?"

"No."

"Well, there has to be a first time. It's hard. If they're normal, they're falling apart, and you want to respect that, but all the while you have to be grilling them."

"I get it," she said.

Dolan opened and handed out their Styrofoam containers. They ate in the car with their fingers on the way to Butler, where they were not surprised to find a different, newer, but not new, Buick in the driveway; a neat, clean porch; two puzzled people in robes peering at them through a screen door.

TWO

HE WALKS INTO HIS HOUSE, trembling, picks up the phone, puts it down again. Phones are dangerous, traceable. He paces, living room to kitchen, back and forth.

Before he has exactly decided to do so, he rushes out of the house, drops into his Honda CR-V, much too big, more than he needs in a car, and yet he liked it, bought it, thinking, Something for me, for once. Its power, the way it starts up quickly and purrs under him, is a comfort. He drives to Shady and takes the long street the whole way to the parkway ramp, wondering where to go next, and is about to change his mind, make a U-turn, go back home, when he sees it's too late, there's someone right behind him, he's got to get on the ramp.

Pay phone, pay phone, pay phone. Where are they these days?

If only he could call Colleen, find out what she and the police are thinking, *seeing*. She was always nice to him; a friendly face right now would help him get himself under control. He checks his watch. Would 411 give him her number? He punches in the three numbers. The sound of his voice using his clearest diction to tell a mechanical operator "Colleen Greer" jolts him. He doesn't talk to himself. He doesn't usually *hear* his own voice. He sounds scared, breathy.

"I'm sorry. That number is unlisted."

He hangs up, keeps driving along the parkway, past Oakland.

He could go to his office. They didn't tell him he couldn't. But he decides on downtown, taking the Second Avenue exit. The streets right past the exit are deserted because there isn't much downtown life, a couple of theaters and clubs down near Penn Avenue, but mostly empty streets. With turns right and left, he's in front of the big Kaufmann's department store building, which, glorious history notwithstanding, is about to become Macy's. No more Horne's, Gimbels, Lazarus, Lord & Taylor in town, either. Will Macy's, the interloper, also have a "sale" every weekend, as if the customers don't know that's the real price and you'd be an idiot to buy midweek?

What seemed indomitable, with its big sign, will have a new name. Will it change inside, too?

It's still now, quiet. A sleeping building.

There on the corner is a pay phone.

He parks, exits the big silver SUV, looking around to be sure no one is watching him, fumbles for change. A quarter and a bunch of dimes come up in his hand. Ought to do it. He punches in numbers he can almost not remember in his nervousness.

An abrupt "Yeah?"

"It's me. What do you know about what's going on?"

"You shouldn't call me. I heard. I don't know *no*thing," the gruff voice says, making a point of the ungrammatical, just a smart man joking. "I'm looking into it."

"It was you, wasn't it?"

"I was going to ask you that question."

"Something happened, didn't it?"

"Like I said, I'm going to look into it. You told them about me, huh, when they had you in? Did you?"

"I didn't mention you."

There is a long silence. "I'm glad you told me that. That's the better way right now. Tomorrow, next day, I'll call you. How much did *she* talk to you?"

"Laura?"

"Who else?"

"She said she wanted to talk to me. She sounded funny. She said she was talking to you. What's going on?"

"I'm not sure. I'll call you when I know something. If I hang up, you just wait by the phone until I call you again. Don't call me. Where are you now?"

"Downtown. Pay phone."

"Good. Don't do it again."

"Okay, but if it wasn't you—"

"I don't know. We'll talk." The line goes dead. Hoffman puts the phone back. He takes a handkerchief from his pocket, wipes the receiver several times, then the square phone buttons. He looks around. Nobody.

He feels a familiar vertigo. His thoughts won't cohere. He hates this spinning, spinning, spinning.

Trying to steady himself, one hand on the roof of the van, one on the car door, he manages to get the door open, get himself seated again. He thinks, It isn't true. I'm in one of those bad dreams. He thinks about the fact that the detectives wouldn't let him inside the house Laura bought for herself. Now, looking back, he isn't quite sure anymore what they said to him and which part is his imagination.

He is supposed to meet Christie at the coroner's office at nine o'clock to formally identify the body. *The body.* His wife. His chest heaves. She's gone.

The new boyfriend? A stranger? Someone he knows nothing about?

No. No. He knows who did it.

Driving again, just driving, he thinks he remembers Colleen's old phone number. Worst that can happen is he wakes someone up. Best is that she's home, willing to talk to him. The phone is answered by a recorded voice. Hers. He can't think what to say, so he hangs up.

IT IS EXACTLY TWO WHEN Colleen leaves the office. Sleepy, wired up at the same time, she wants to go to John's place to talk, unwind, but she drives to her place in Squirrel Hill to pick up a change of clothes.

It's been a long night. She can still feel the fragile bones, the heartbeat of Laura McCall's father, who collapsed into her arms. He's not all right; the mother is not all right, either. Laura was their life, that's clear, and it's as if the news sucked the life out of them. It was cruel to grill them when they were stunned by grief, but Christie did it and did it well—cleanly, crisply, one question after another. Did they know of anyone who wished their daughter ill? Did she have any enemies? Had she behaved oddly or differently lately? What did they think of her current boyfriend? How had they felt about her marriage and her estranged husband?

Colleen has the unwelcome, horribly selfish thought that Laura McCall was loved in a way she herself will never know. Parents doted, husband wanted her back, boyfriend said he found his life when he found her, best friend is distraught beyond belief. Would anybody care that much if she died? Selfish thought. She, after all, is alive. And life is precious.

Her cell phone rings.

"You're on your way. I hear the car."

"I'm going home first. I need clothes for the police picnic tomorrow."

"Couldn't you get them in the morning?"

"I'm due in at eight tomorrow."

"Jeez."

"Christie runs a tight ship. I hope I can sleep. It's been busy, so my mind—"

"You must be hungry."

"I am."

"Good. I'll see what I have."

"If Lindo's were open right now, I'd get the one-armed bandit."

Lindo's is a greasy spoon near where John lives and near the Police Headquarters. Their one-armed bandit is enough food for two people, and it's the *small* breakfast, only costs about three bucks. One buttermilk pancake, one egg, one sausage, one piece of toast, one small bowl of grits, coffee. But Lindo's isn't going to be open yet.

The sounds of cupboards opening and closing come through the phone. "I think it's going to be tuna salad on toast."

She gets an immediate cooperative hankering for tuna salad on toast.

"I've already got two plates on the table."

He's waiting up for her. That's good, isn't it? He'll listen to what part of her work evening she can tell him about.

"I saw your case on the news. Your commander."

"Yeah, he gave them about two minutes early on. Nobody leaked anything else? No details?"

"No."

"That's to the good." Colleen won't even tell John that Laura McCall's throat was slashed first.

To quiet her probably. The Nicole Simpson treatment. Eliminate screaming.

"I'm home." She hits the button to end the call.

There it is, the house she hardly ever spends time in, a cozy nest, lots of cloth, soft woven fabrics. She enters. Her house in the dim light of lamps on timers looks soft. Calm. A bit dusty with neglect. What a waste of real estate. And all because John is not at all flexible. Cannot sleep unless in his own bed.

She rushes about, gathering things.

Hoffman, alibi big as Texas notwithstanding, is the classic solution. "He gets my vote," Dolan said after they interviewed Amy Rosenstein and were wrapping up. "Only why am I always on the wrong side in every election?"

Christie chortled that he liked the idea of electing the murderer, that it beat working for a living.

She shivers. She knows Hoffman. He's been to her house, came there when she had a group from work over. He couldn't have, could he?

She sits at the edge of her bed, remembering how Hoffman made her uncomfortable, wanting more than she wanted to give. "Go somewhere for lunch?" he would say, pretending casualness. And in that same tone, as if just chatting, he'd question her about her private life, her time away from the office, asking, "What did you do this weekend? How do your spend your evenings? Did you ever date anyone you met at a bar? Did you ever use an Internet dating service?"

She always answered his questions truthfully, briskly, as if they weren't intrusive: "Reading. Reading, running, cooking, shopping. Yes. Yes." She brought up his wife whenever she could. And when there was any sort of party that included spouses, she made a point to connect, if briefly, with Laura Hoffman and talk about clothes, diets, whatever came to mind. Laura was a shy person, not terribly secure.

Colleen rouses herself, tugs a pair of capris and a shirt off the hanger, grabs a set of underwear from the top drawer of her bureau, tosses everything into a bag, and throws a pair of sandals on top.

She remembers a couple of dates with Arthur Leland, a tall, elegant, *hurt* sort of man who headed up one of the other city facilities. He told her, "You know, Hoffman has a case on you."

"He just values me." She knew men could be terrible gossips and anything she said one evening after a couple of glasses of wine might be quoted in bright daylight someday when boys were ganging up on girls.

Yet she knew what Leland said was true.

Even thinking about it now makes her fidgety. Her cell phone rings. "I'm almost there," she tells John, "five minutes."

Truth is, it will be exactly twelve minutes. Police could time just about any drive in the city to within fifteen seconds. She rushes through the rest of her packing up and doesn't bother to check her land line for messages or caller ID.

IT IS THREE A.M. HOFFMAN is so tired, he can hardly move. When he was a child, he used to fall asleep standing up. It would come on him suddenly, like in the old movies when someone got a chloroform handkerchief over his face. His mother worried about that instant fatigue, the way he got lost, just gave up consciousness.

He tries to drive home now, but sleep overtakes him, as powerful as a sleeping potion, as old and powerful as a chloroform hankie. Still downtown, he manages to pull over to a spot in front of a breakfast joint with a 2-2-2 sign in the window. Two eggs, two bacon, two pancakes. Two of everything. He lets his head fall back against the headrest, hardly noticing it's uncomfortable, the angle working a pain into his neck. A second later, he is asleep.

It is a little past five when a tap on the window wakes him. A uniformed policeman stands there, looking nervous—perhaps nervous that the knock *wouldn't* rouse him, then possibly nervous that it has.

"You okay, buddy?"

"I'm okay. Waiting for breakfast. They open at six."

"You coulda gone to an all-nighter. Ritters."

"I like this place."

"I do, too. You had a rough night?"

"Kinda. Do I have to move?"

"There's no parking here from seven on. Morning traffic has to get through."

"I'll be gone by then."

"Okay." The cop raps twice on his windshield and leaves, looking relieved.

David Hoffman looks at the city waking up. Way up the street, he sees in his rearview mirror, is a woman, probably a hooker, getting into a car. The car moves slowly. Maybe she isn't being paid for it. Maybe some innocent explanation. Everybody hooks up, one way or another. Mean people, depressed people, all kinds. Ugly, horrible people get hooked up. Everywhere he looks.

Traffic has started to appear; he becomes aware of the hum of motors around him. A homeless man carrying about seven grocery bags of clothing, it looks like, ambles along. He probably has someone somewhere he drinks with. A bus discharges two people who then walk purposefully down a side street.

A lone car horn toots, and a little later, a few more horns, as if they've been awakened by the first, punctuate the morning.

Some things he knows start crowding in on him. He weeps a little.

After a while, he thinks he smells bacon. He consults his watch. Too early. Imagination, the bacon was, more in his mind than in the world. It's happened before. The way the mind works, looking for pleasure, comfort, even in the midst of despair.

Oh, poor Laura. Most days, he hated her for leaving him and then for her sharp inquisitions, then for thriving without him, but today he thinks kindly of her, imagines her asking him in a gentle voice what is wrong with him, imagines himself accepting her hand on his shoulder, and then, even then, in his imagination, he's still himself, unable to tell her the things he knows, on the verge of telling her, and still unable.

THREE

THE FIRST HINT OF SUN SLIPPED through the blinds. Christie kissed Marina, said, "Don't get up. Sleep. Meet you at Schenley, okay?"

"Umm."

"The Vietnam Veteran's Pavilion. You can get the kids' bathing suits and whatever else they want?"

"Umm."

"Sleep."

For a while, he just looked at her. When they disagreed about something, he gritted his teeth, walked out of the house, took a drive, or yelled, and then went out to the garden and dug something up, usually an ailing azalea, and replanted it where the sun or the soil or something was different. He'd go back into the house and she'd be drying her hair or putting dinner on the table, and he would wonder how anything had seemed to come between them. You had to be feeling significant hatred to grab a knife and stab again and again, significant something—fear, fury?—to slash a throat.

Chinos, tan plaid sport shirt, khaki jacket. He would feel overdressed and uncomfortable at the picnic. So be it.

He made enough coffee for Marina to have some when she got up, and as he sat at the kitchen table with a mug of it in front of him, he ticked off what he hoped to accomplish before lunchtime, before the picnic. Second round with Hoffman, talk with coroner's office long before it was time for any official autopsy report. Assign Greer to the Counseling Center, then to follow up on Hoffman's alibi. Let Dolan sniff around about the boyfriend, check out his alibi, canvass the neighborhood around Laura's place again, see what he could dig up a day later.

Christie put two pieces of bread in the toaster and took out butter and jelly. He found it interesting that breakfast was a matter of serial love affairs. He'd been through stages where nothing but oatmeal appealed. There was a sausage period. He remembered a youthful addiction to cinnamon toast. A doughnut phase gripped him a couple of years ago, until he noticed the ten extra pounds; he'd fought to get through that phase, but he could always be tempted back to it if doughnuts were right in front of him. What next? Bacon, farina, granola? These days, toast with butter and jelly seemed just exactly right.

There was a hole in the case, but he didn't know what it was. Most murders were simple. Everybody—neighbors, family, friends—knew who did it and the evidence pointed just that way, so it was a matter of rounding up the suspect and letting someone like Dolan go at the guy until he confessed. This was trickier. Somebody had been furious with Laura McCall, but Christie wasn't picking up spent fury from either the husband *or* the boyfriend. Secret lover? Strong motive had to be there somewhere. Love, money, revenge.

All that blood. He was immune to it one moment. A second later, he was not. He had to hold it at a distance, not think of his own leaking out, not think of pain, but call up the objective mind and examine the event. He could do that. He could detach from his own body. But if he thought of harm to Marina or his kids, his insides went ballistic. This was a bad thing, he understood, a Nazi thing, a criminal thing, to be able to detach and separate, but he wouldn't be able to work if he couldn't do it.

He sat there, adding blackberry jelly to his buttered toast. He had heard the thump of the paper arriving at 5:30. In fact, it's what woke him when he'd just managed to drift off for the second time. Carrying the toast in his hand, he went to the front porch and picked up the green-sleeved *Post-Gazette.*

Yep. There it was. The story that wasn't a story yet. Just the bare facts. A woman who was thought well of (and a picture to show how unassuming, nice-looking, and clean she was—not to mention white) was found dead in her home. Neighbors expressed shock. Police were investigating. Woman was in the process of divorcing her husband and had begun seeing another man. Well, there, the crime reporter had put all the usual ingredients in, and it looked like an easy-enough case, didn't it?

But the husband showing up at the house like that . . . Was it some kind of bravura performance? And if it wasn't, why that night, why just then?

Christie crunched through his toast and read his horoscope. "Do not engage in large financial transactions today." Fat chance. "Pay attention to family and friends and smell the roses." For an hour, maybe.

He checked his watch and got up abruptly. He had to meet Hoffman at the coroner's office at nine. Had to get the squad in order before that.

Hoffman seemed to like Colleen Greer, trust her. She could be useful somehow, he suspected. How exactly to work it, he wasn't sure.

JOHN MURMURED SOMETHING, still asleep. He turned away from her. She studied the back of his neck, where he had one of those indistinct hairlines, all growth, the way lots of dark-haired men were put together. He pulled the sheet partway over his face.

She let him be, showered quickly, and went back to his bedroom. Her hair was wet. She toweled it dry, not wanting the fuss and noise of the dryer. Her hairdresser referred to the cut as "the Meg Ryan special." Quirky hair is how Colleen thought of it, wavy and wedgy.

John murmured more clearly now, "Do you need breakfast?"

"I'll get it."

"I'll help." He swung his legs out of bed before actually sitting up. His upper body bobbed up like a balloon.

Colleen laughed. She always liked physical humor. "I don't have much time."

He sat on the edge of the bed then, frowning. *What is so desirable about being awake? Don't much like it.*

"Really, it's okay."

"I'm helping."

He hauled himself up and went down to the kitchen. Naked. He liked naked. Felt covered, perhaps, by some of that dark body hair. Some people would see him, in that game of impressions, as a bear, she was sure. She liked the solidity of him.

Christie and Dolan sounded as if they were going to grill him about his intentions. It made her laugh. A nice old-fashioned bring-the-guy-home-to-Papa kind of thing. Put the fear of God in him.

Colleen used the dryer briefly, put on a little makeup, put on the simple shirred white shirt and pair of trim navy pants she kept there, then slipped the clothes she had chosen last night for the picnic into a plastic bag. It was going to be a scorcher, ninety-two degrees at least, so it was silly to sit at a picnic table and sweat through the clothes she needed to work in later in the afternoon. She topped her work outfit with the light beige jacket that helped make anything she put on read as professional. Navy sandals. Good thing they were here. It was hard living in two places.

Behind her, John, who had come back upstairs, crossed to get a pair of boxers. Going outdoors for the paper required some clothing. He always joked he didn't want to get too many neighborhood women excited by showing it all.

John was smart. It was important to her that he was smart. He'd done well in college and had Greek and Roman history (his major and then a master's degree) at his fingertips. Watch *Rome* or *Gladiator* with John and you'd get running footnotes. He talked a lot when they first met about going back to school for a doctorate, just because he loved the study of history, no matter that Ph.D.'s couldn't get jobs in the field. His real job didn't challenge him at all. He was a ticketing agent for the wounded, beleaguered US Airways. How he could bear to spend his days putting people on flights to Boston, changing their seats, checking their IDs, she couldn't imagine. Didn't he die of boredom?

He looked a bit like a Roman gladiator himself. He didn't exactly comb his dark hair forward, but it fell that way when wet. He had a thick jaw and neck, a wrestler's body, muscular and square. Large brown eyes and rich olive skin. When he got on his motorcycle on his days off, a Vincent, one of the two bikes he owned, it seemed he was going to do something gladiatorial, whatever the contemporary equivalent might be, to bring his life into correspondence with his physical self. Save someone. Fight evil. But no, most days, he got into his car, drove to the airport in nice pants and a polo shirt, changed into his uniform shirt there, drove home, ate heartily, watched TV, read, and crashed.

She was the gladiator. She was the cop. She'd gone into the home of a murder suspect only two days ago, gun drawn, praying she would not need to use it. The idea of shooting someone was still, even after the training, even after exercises of imagination, foreign, a dream.

At the kitchen table, she found a bowl of granola with milk already in it, a cup of coffee, and a paper opened to the article about the Laura McCall murder. She began to eat and read at the same time, while John, sitting across from her, sipped at a half cup of coffee. Partly, she felt off center because she'd missed her run this morning.

"Are you sure I'm going to like this picnic?" John asked.

"Think hot dogs."

"I like hot dogs. I don't know about people."

She shot him a look.

"I don't know anybody."

"That's kind of the idea." She looked at her watch and ate more hurriedly. He had lost confidence lately or something. "Come on. You have this very good *mind*."

"Maybe my mind isn't as good as you think it is. And maybe that's not what you need to trot out at a picnic. Okay, okay, I'll go."

"One hour. I'll call you to tell you exactly when. Okay?"

He nodded, even smiled.

Truth was, she felt nervous about showing him off, having him tested.

COLLEEN GOT TO HEADQUARTERS a few minutes before eight and signed out a fleet car even before she signed in. Christie was already there, too, standing in the meeting room, studying his notes on a legal pad. He said, "I have you down to interview Mindy Cooper, the secretary at the Family Counseling Center. Did you know her when you worked there?"

"No. She must have been hired after I left."

"I thought so. She agreed to come in at eight-thirty. How about you take this"—he handed over Hoffman's handwritten alibi—"and check him out."

"Yes."

"Every which way you can and then some. Including the clients."

"Right, Boss. I understand."

Colleen sat with the other detectives, who were filtering in, each one more groggy than the one before. Christie came over to where she sat. "You can go. We'll catch you up later."

THERE WAS HARDLY ANY TRAFFIC on Saturday morning, so she got there before Hoffman's secretary did. She studied the piece of paper in her hand until it was almost memorized. Mindy Cooper drove up at exactly eight-thirty in, of all things, a red Mini Cooper. It was like a joke—a now you hear it, now you don't. The woman must have chosen the car for its name, since her own name had presumably been with her for a much longer time.

Colleen watched her get out of her sporty little vehicle. She was fifty or so, a tidy, rounded black woman, who didn't look like someone who would choose a red car with sports suspension that jostled the spine. But it was a cute car all right.

"Love your car."

"Me, too." And that was all there was to it.

They introduced themselves and Mindy Cooper opened the door to the offices.

"You have keys. Are you always here first on a workday?"

"Usually. Unless there's a traffic accident or snowstorm or something." She moved about routinely, putting several lights on.

Colleen experienced a dash of familiarity. The place looked the same. The cube puzzles and bead puzzles and magazines—*Jack and Jill, Nickelodeon,* and *Family Circle*—on the end tables might in fact have been the same ones that were there five years ago. "Mind if I use the bathroom?" she asked.

"Be my guest. Right down the hall."

Guest wasn't exactly the word, but Colleen refamiliarized herself with the place—Hoffman's office, two smaller offices, the two larger family therapy rooms with lots of chairs. Those rooms were also used for individual therapy when they were needed. The bathroom.

If they got an intern, the intern squeezed into the area behind the secretary, no privacy at all.

The same. Everything was the same so far.

The place needed a paint job. New furniture wouldn't have hurt.

Colleen smelled coffee. She went to the bathroom just to stay honest and then walked back to the reception area.

Mindy Cooper was carrying a tray with two cups of coffee in aqua mugs, a generic cylinder of powdered creamer, and a bowl holding packets of sugar and sugar substitutes. She put the tray on a small square table in the waiting room. "I always come right in and make coffee, so I thought I might as well today. I'm not sure I can think real clear without it."

Colleen sat, got out her notebook. "Thanks. I appreciate the hospitality."

"We don't keep real milk here." Mindy Cooper smiled and sat across from Colleen, handing her a mug. "I hope that's okay."

"It's fine. Just black for me."

The woman looked at Colleen's notebook. "You have questions for me?"

"I'll need the complete schedule for yesterday, who saw whom, all that."

"That's easy."

"Then I'll need to know how long they stayed, and if you saw them come in and leave and if you saw your boss actually go in the room with them."

A frown. A pause. A flicker. "I'll get you the book. Are you saying you think he—"

"We don't think anything yet, Mrs. Cooper. It's very early in the investigation, so we're just making the most common inquiries. Just routine. But he was here yesterday, right?"

"Oh yes. He put in a whole day. Eight to five." Mindy shifted and balanced her way to behind the counter, touching things along the way, and when she returned to the small table, she made the same physical adjustments, exhibiting the balance problems that came with age and body type. Colleen beat down her impatience. Cooper was probably a wonderful grandma, a clucking, cooing, mesmerizing, soothing one.

"And you were here?"

"I got here ten to eight and I left at five."

"And stayed the whole time?"

"Yes."

"Out to lunch? Other breaks when you were away from your desk?"

"I brought my lunch," she said proudly. "Ate at the desk. I . . . well, I go to the bathroom, say, two times in the morning, two times in the afternoon."

"Do you mind if I just study the appointment book for a second?"

"No. Go right ahead."

Colleen compared the piece of paper Christie had given her with the book. Dead-on, a match.

"Did you see Mr. Hoffman leave at any time?"

"No. How could he?"

Colleen nodded. She remembered what a full day at the Center felt like: one client after the other, and the dance you did was between pulling teeth with some and damming the flow of words with the next. "I'd like to make a Xerox of this page and a few other pages for our records."

"Go ahead. The machine is on. I put it on automatically when I came in."

"Did all of these people show?" Colleen asked as she stood up.

"Yesterday, yeah, they did. And we were busy with the phone ringing off the hook, too. You want me to make the copies for you?"

"No. I can do it." Same Xerox machine. Colleen ended up doing eight pages altogether, two months. While she worked, she asked casually, "Could you get me addresses and phone numbers for yesterday's people?"

What if Hoffman hired someone? Stayed put at work with an unassailable alibi while someone else—

But that didn't account for the fury of the multiple stabbings.

"Any of these people new clients?" Colleen asked.

"A couple." Cooper looked, pointed at three names, all women.

"Do you remember them at all?"

"Sure. Single mothers. All three."

Not likely to be a hit man among them. "Does he lock his computer?"

"No. Leaves it on most of the time. I turn it off on weekends."

"I'll take a quick look," Colleen murmured, as if it were perfectly all right to go into Hoffman's office, into his files. While Mindy wrote down addresses and phone numbers, Colleen got on Hoffman's computer. Her heart was beating. She was really pushing it, what she was allowed to do. Mindy didn't stop her, but anything she did would have to hold up in court.

By the time the secretary handed over a sheaf of papers with neatly written phone numbers and addresses, Colleen had quickly scanned the files on the computer. They looked ordinary enough, and she didn't have a warrant to take the computer yet. Still, she hated to shut it down.

She could hear Mindy moving about, getting out car keys and shutting off the coffeepot. Then she saw the secretary move past Hoffman's office to the bathroom to rinse the pot. Colleen hurriedly opened Hoffman's desk drawers. She rummaged through stray files marked "Meetings" and "Grants" and "Community Volunteers." She pushed aside bent paper clips and half-expended tablets of Post-it notes.

When she looked up, Mindy was standing at the door. "They said on the news it was afternoon," Mindy murmured apologetically. "He was here. I'm not trying to defend him. I'm just telling you."

"Right. Thanks. Help me on something. I'm supposed to be getting a full picture of him." Not mentioning, of course, that she knew him. She tipped her head toward the desk drawers. "Right now, he seems hardworking—"

"Yes."

"Competent."

"Yes."

"How about interpersonally? How does he treat you?"

"Sometimes he seems to need something. More like I'm a mother to him. I've always just sort of felt bad for him."

It didn't necessarily make him a killer. She continued, "And just a bit awkward, clumsy, in interpersonal terms."

"Yes. Yes, that's right."

At 9:30, Colleen and Mindy left the office and parted. Colleen drove up the hill. She had to locate seven people to find out if David Hoffman had done exactly what he and Mindy said he'd done the day before. After that, she could go to Schenley Park and the police picnic and the men in her life: John, Artie Dolan, Richard Christie.

FOUR

JAMILLA ANSWERED THE PHONE. It was ten in the morning. Her jaw clenched when she heard the familiar voice, the rhythm of the words, the breathiness that didn't go with the voice.

"I called to tell you you're going to have to come in. I can give you an appointment today at five."

She turned. Across the room, her baby sister, whom she'd put on the blue blanket, was trying to crawl toward her. "The thing is," she said, "today is kind of hard because—"

"No, you know what I told you. If we need to go over things, you have to come in."

"All right." She kept her eye on Soleil because she had to. Kameen was bad enough at watching the baby, and now he was "laid up," which was the expression the doctor had used day before yesterday—"This boy is going to be laid up for a while." She doesn't want to go through a day like that again. Her mother and father not to be found and Kameen hurt and nobody to watch Soleil, so all of them in danger. The police being called to the hospital to find out why the kids were left alone with a thirteen-year-old in charge. Jamilla making every sort of explanation and then suddenly the police taking them home and letting them go.

On the phone he said, "I helped you out the other day. Didn't I? Didn't I?"

"Yes."

"We have to talk about what happened."

"Okay."

"We have to get things straight. How you need to handle things."

"Okay."

"Five o'clock. It's your job to get there."

"I know." I know, I know, she said to herself. It was what she wanted to say to him, but she never talked to him like that. Five o'clock was going to be hard because there was nobody to take care of Soleil. Sunshine. Her mom said it meant sunshine.

As always, she tried to keep hold of a lot of things at once. She had to feed the baby. There was one jar of applesauce left and a little bit of hot cereal. Her parents said they would come up with some groceries today, but she never knew whether they were going to remember. Kameen was watching TV—what else?—with his bandaged foot up on a snack table. Jamilla had taken him to the hospital herself, pushing him along on an old bike, his one foot wrapped in a towel, the other foot doing the pedaling, her helping with the balancing, and all the while she was holding the baby. How had she done that? At the emergency room, they'd told her it was very smart, the way she'd figured how to get him there. She told them it wasn't that far but that she was worried about his foot bleeding so much. He'd dropped the knife right straight through it, right into the floor. You could still see where in the kitchen.

Now Kameen was supposed to "take it easy" and be "laid up." He sure liked that advice.

The phone rang again. A feeling of dread kept her from answering right away. When she finally answered after about ten rings, she was relieved to hear it was only her friend Malika, wanting to come over.

"I don't know," she said. "I have to clean house today."

"I could help you."

"You kidding me?"

"No, I'll help."

Jamilla knew Malika really just wanted to talk to her, but she was glad to have company, even if Malika's talk slowed her down some. She was lucky, *blessed,* one of her teachers told her, because people liked her so much.

"Okay," she said to Malika.

While she assembled the broom, mop, rags, cleanser, and looked unsuccessfully for some liquid cleaner, she kept Soleil in her arms. Soleil was a little bit late walking, but she wanted to crawl all right. And a kid who wanted to crawl was a squirmer, always trying to get down. Jamilla had to spend a lot of time beguiling her away from the floor when she didn't have time to run after her. Now she cajoled, "Hey now, help me out okay? We're going to clean this tub, okay? We'll do a good job. I'm going to show you how, c'mon, do it with me." She wet a cloth, put some cleanser on, and let Soleil hold it. The baby took a few halfhearted swipes at the tub and Jamilla cheered her on. "You are soooo smart, yes, you are. Good girl."

But soon enough, and she knew it would happen, her stomach started to tumble up in her. The smell of everything bothered Jamilla, cleanser, coffee, everything, and that was normal, she knew these things because she'd helped her mother out when she got like this a couple of years ago. But man, oh, man, what was going to happen if her mother saw and figured it out?

Suddenly, in the heat of the bathroom, with the sun coming straight in, breaking a window pattern over Soleil's curls, Jamilla got a wave of nausea she couldn't ignore. It came and grabbed her. She just managed to get the baby down on the floor before she upchucked—and it wasn't much but it was everything she'd eaten, toast and a piece of cheese. She felt sad to lose it, nutrition gone.

Soleil started to cry.

"No, don't! Everything's okay. Hey, sweetie!"

Soleil hesitated, her face showing that she was considering not crying.

"It's okay."

Jamilla knows she will have to figure out all by herself how to live for the next seven months. She always finds a way to keep the peace. She doesn't tell secrets, but holds them in, tight to her heart. She is not supposed to tell *anyone* about *anything*; so she doesn't. Now she has to work out for herself what she is going to do when it shows. She lies awake at night and thinks about the possibilities. She must be strong enough not to tell, no matter what anybody asks her.

Except. She told that woman. She didn't *tell,* exactly, but she didn't say no hard enough. The woman guessed when she began to walk fast, saying she felt sick. But *how* did the woman find her and why did she care? And why did she promise to come find her again?

Jamilla has decided she won't talk at all next time. She wipes her mouth and begins to cry.

Soleil is up in her arms again, with arms and legs wrapped around her. They both turn and watch breakfast disappear in the swirling water.

The sun is hitting them both. In the bathroom mirror they look like a framed photograph. Two sisters. Isn't Soleil beautiful? "You are beautiful," Jamilla tells her. She bounces her in the picture frame of the mirror. "See. There you are." When do babies first understand mirrors? Soleil reaches forward eagerly, hand touching to image of hand.

They look alike. Even Jamilla, who gets embarrassed when people make a fuss over her, can see what it is they find beautiful in her when she sees it in Soleil—the large bright eyes, a startling green, smooth, coppery skin. How do you catalog these things? Her mother brings home magazines; in the magazines, beauty is analyzed; do people agree on what it is?

He talks about beautiful bones, but what are beautiful bones? He says there is nothing like braided hair to show off a fine skull and that she has beautiful bones. She told him it was just easier to keep her hair out of her face and that's why her hair was braided. He nodded, listening. He makes her talk. He gives her money.

His breathing is bad. He doesn't breathe right. His breath going in and out makes a scraping sound. Maybe it means he'll have a heart attack and die. She hates herself for wishing it, but she does wish it.

Jamilla knows everything has to be very *careful*. The woman couldn't understand how it all falls apart if you do *anything*. Like the big risk she took getting Kameen to the hospital where people asked all kinds of questions. But in the end, the doctor said she was right to bring him in.

"I'll help you tell," the lady said.

"Who would I tell? You mean my parents?"

"We could start there. With your mother."

But her mother is in no shape to deal with this. She is either out of the house, or up at Doc's or over at Bigg's, or sick, or sleeping, or working, or arguing with her father, or the two of them are locked in their room, doing what they do, groaning and creaking, forgetting about food, school, everything. Her mother is in no shape.

She told him last week her parents need therapy help again and he said he would see what he could do.

"We're going to mop the floor," she tells Soleil now. "Kameen is a lazy bum. He doesn't do anything."

Kameen, glassy-eyed, looks at them, waves, goes back to the TV. Is he really all right, she wonders. Will she have to take him back to the ER? It was nice there. With everybody busy and humming around. The cot. White sheets. She wished she could lie down there and just think.

She'd been sitting in the treatment room with Kameen, her little sister across her lap, asleep, and just there, on the wall, near the door, was a sign, as if somebody had put it there for her. She'd read it slowly and then read it again and again.

> PREGNANT? PEOPLE URGING YOU TO TERMINATE? DON'T DO IT. SAVE A LIFE. WE ACCEPT NEWBORN BABIES FROM MOTHERS WHO CANNOT CARE FOR THEM. NO QUESTIONS ASKED, NO LEGAL HASSLES. SEE SOMEONE ON OUR STAFF.

Jamilla stared at the sign a long time, so long her brother asked her what she was looking at.

"Nothing," she said.

What she really wanted was to take her family somewhere far away, where nobody asked questions, and live with the new baby. What was inside her was hers, wasn't it, a little miniature version of herself that she could take care of. She pictured the baby as a combination of herself and Kameen and Soleil. She knew how she'd gotten it, but it really had nothing to do with him.

Now, she thinks again about that sign at the hospital. A place to put the miniature version of herself where it will be safe, cared for, and nobody mad at her. And it won't be killed—the lady's solution.

She rinses out the tub.

"Foor."

"Right. Now we clean the floor."

There is so much to do.

She's finally found a trace of Lysol in a bottle and pours it into the bucket. But before she gets any water in the bucket, the smell of the chemical comes and gets her. The Lysol stings her nose, her throat, and there it is—the nothing in her stomach she has to throw up again. She tries to hold on to the mop, drops it, puts Soleil down on the floor, leans over the toilet.

"It's okay," Jamilla says. "I'm okay."

Soleil peers worriedly into the toilet even before Jamilla empties her stomach.

There is a tap at the front door, then a more insistent knocking. Moments later, it's clear Malika has let herself in, calling, "I'm here."

"She's upstairs in the bathroom," Kameen says.

Jamilla gets herself up off the floor. She can hear her friend asking Kameen, "So, how's your foot?"

"Hurts."

Then Malika is at the bathroom door. Jamilla, hanging over the sink, looks up, waves, rinses out her mouth.

"Hey, what's with you, girl? You ain't pregnant on me?"

"No. Just feel sick. Maybe the flu."

"Yuck. Well, don't give it to me, okay? Hey, I brung some bagels and shit. My mother had too many. They gave 'em to her at the church after she got done cleaning. From their freezer. They gotta be thawed some."

When she's careful, things turn out okay. Now, food when they need food.

Jamilla opens the bag. There's raisin! She'll toast it. There might be some butter in the house. But, oh, the smell is twisting her stomach again. It just kills her that she can be holding something she likes, loves, and not be able to enjoy it.

FIVE

WHEN COLLEEN GOT TO THE picnic at a little after one, she found John sitting at a picnic table on the periphery, leafing through the newspaper. She leaned over and kissed him.

"How was it?" he asked.

"Okay. Puzzling. I did what I had to." She pointed over to where Christie and Dolan were talking. "See the guy, right there, brown hair, suntanned, taking his jacket off? Right there. That's Christie," she said. "And that's Artie Dolan with him."

"Um." John looked obediently at the well-set square figure of Christie and at the crisply dressed black man he was talking to. Dolan was much smaller, but built like a bursting action figure, triangular torso. He was written up all the time, known as the detective who could get confessions from anyone, including the hardened smart ones who had sworn themselves to eternal silence.

When Colleen had a moment to look around, she was actually surprised at how many police and their families had shown up. There were hundreds of people. Little kids everywhere, darting in and out, looking frantic with excitement.

"I'm starved. Let's get some grub." She took John's hand and led him toward the line at the food table.

She had to stop for one little boy, about four, who had his swimming trunks in his fist. He appeared to be running toward a softball game.

This was what she wanted. A family. Excited kids. That brand of fun.

The boy paused.

"Son. Son?" A man with a British accent was trotting after the boy. "Here, let me carry those for you." The man's voice was so wonderful, it put Colleen in mind of living with a great recording of *Winnie-the-Pooh*.

The boy seemed uncertain.

"Would you like to go swimming later?" the man asked.

The boy nodded.

"But first we're going to watch the softball game, right?"

"I want to play."

"Well, the boys are older. Let's go over there and see what's going on, okay?"

The son nodded. He let go of the swimsuit.

"And let's go tell Mummy where we are so she doesn't worry."

Colleen looked at John, who was also watching and listening as the man led his son off. "I'm in love," she said.

John said, "I think I am, too."

Colleen watched the father and son lope along until they were out of sight. She and John moved forward to the food. Burgers, hot dogs, chicken, sausage. Which to have? Potato salad, fruit salad, chips, green salad. The green salad didn't look too good, but everything else did.

They decided to split a burger with everything on it, each have a hot dog and a piece of chicken, some chips, some potato salad, some fruit salad, and then, later, chocolate cake.

While they were stacking their plates, Christie came up to Colleen and said, "Squad meeting at two in that corner over there." He pointed to a section of the shelter. "No sense in going back to the office."

Colleen said, "Makes sense. Thanks. And Commander? If you have a second, this is John Brach. John, this is Commander Christie."

"Heard many good things about you," John said.

"Oh, well," Christie said. "They're afraid to say anything else." He shook John's hand. Then he noticed their plates. "Greer, you amaze me."

Colleen, flushing, said, "I heard a stellar appetite was one of the requirements of the Homicide squad." Then she couldn't think of what else to say, so she asked, "Did your family come?"

"I'll introduce you," Christie said. "Eat first, then come over. We're on and around that red blanket." He pointed.

Colleen saw what looked from a distance to be a beautiful woman with a mass of dark hair sitting with two kids, a girl and boy. Cripes. Talk about the perfect family. "I'll be over in a few minutes," she said.

She and John went back to the table he'd chosen on the periphery and sat across from each other on the attached benches to dig into their food. The table was a little remote, but it was good for people-watching. It caught lots of picnickers traipsing from the road where they'd parked to the food or games.

A big burly lumberjack of a guy, whom Colleen remembered from the training center, walked past. He had a kind of waddle. A few feet behind him was a boy who walked just like he did, arms held out at his sides. This boy was only about two and a half, three years of age. Exploring. He poked his head underneath the picnic table where Colleen and John sat.

"Come on, little buddy. You don't want to hit your head under there." The father didn't fetch his son, though, just kept moving. "Yo," he said to Colleen in passing.

"Yo," she answered.

The boy emerged but soon found another table to put his head under.

"That's mighty low," the big bear said. "Watch your head."

The boy didn't listen. The father kept moving, but he was saying, "Come on, buddy. You don't want to get in under something that low. Didn't you want cake?" The boy cleared the table without incident and the two of them barged off toward the cake.

"What are you studying so hard?" John asked.

"That big guy. At first, I thought he wasn't paying attention, but he was. He didn't physically haul him out from under the table, just kind of let the son make his own mistakes. I thought it was interesting. I tend to run in and rescue, but that's probably more how *you'd* do it. And it works."

John said, "Sorry. I wasn't paying attention. You know the guy?"

"Peripherally. At the Academy. Nice guy."

Then Dolan came up to them. "Meeting at two. Did you know?"

"Commander told me. Artie, this is John Brach." Colleen searched for an appositional phrase—my boyfriend, my partner, my lover—but her mind didn't come up with one fast enough. "John, this is Detective Dolan. He generally partners with Christie, but they let me come along with them yesterday. Sit?" she asked Dolan.

"For a sec." Dolan sat. "Glad you could get a day off. Greer tells me you work for US Airways?"

"I do," John said. "In charge of a bunch of other agents."

"How is that? I mean, I keep reading they're getting rid of half their employees."

"I've weathered a couple of storms."

Colleen thought John sounded rude. She hated when he used that tone. She said as casually as possible, "If they don't appreciate him at the airline, he'd make a great teacher, I think. He has a graduate degree in history."

"School! Never did like it," Dolan said. "Now my kids, something altogether different." Colleen had heard him say that when his daughter was ten years old, she announced she wanted to go to Harvard. "They really *like* it."

John finally gave a little. "I liked school when I was there. But once you get out, you realize you have time for other things—you know? Hardware stores, changing the screen door, tennis."

"Don't you get free flights?"

"Oh, yeah. It's why I took the job."

"That has to be a nice perk. If I had that, I'd go exotic places. Chile, South America, various islands."

John looked thoughtful, nodding. Colleen had been having trouble getting him interested in anywhere lately. She said, "Maine and Nova Scotia he's mentioned. I've never been to either."

Dolan nodded. "Me, neither. Lots of fantastic places." He got up. "I'll leave you to your lunch. Good to meet you."

John stood and shook Dolan's hand, then sat back down and resumed work on his plate. "He seems to like you."

"I hope. I like him."

The half burger was especially good, smothered in onions and dark mustard.

A few minutes later, Colleen trotted over to the red blanket, where the beautiful woman and two very nice-looking kids were finishing their lunch. "Hi," she said. "Excuse me. Mrs. Christie? I'm Colleen Greer. I wanted to meet you. I work with your husband. Oh, don't get up. I just wanted to come over and introduce myself."

Christie's wife smiled warmly. "I'm Marina. I kept my own name, Benedict. Sit down, if you don't mind the blanket. Eric? Julie? This is Detective Greer."

Colleen sat down.

"The tables were so full, we decided to picnic on the ground."

Nobody was perfect—Colleen knew that, not the man with the British accent—and she saw him across the lawn with his son and one of the female officers—not the burly Academy man with his independent son, and not Christie's family, either. But in the sunshine, as they greeted her, they looked damn near perfect. The boy, about ten, maybe, didn't particularly resemble his father. He was light haired and had an upturned nose. The girl, maybe seven, eight, had dark hair and suntanned skin and she had Christie's features. Colleen knew Marina was a second wife, a stepmother to the children. Everybody on the force knew the story of how Christie and Marina had met on a case. He'd left his first wife for her. That, too, seemed romantic.

"How long have you been a detective?" Marina asked.

"A year. They bounced me around some. Then a month ago, I got assigned to Homicide, which is what I wanted."

Marina nodded. "That's what I would have chosen."

"Really?"

"Umm."

"I heard you're a teacher. And an actress."

"Kind of more like a teacher because there aren't enough roles to keep me going otherwise. I like it fine. I still somehow think of myself as an actress first."

"Are you in anything now?"

"In a couple of weeks, I go into rehearsal for a show at St. Vincent's. *Dinner with Friends.* Goes up the end of August."

"That's great. We'll come see it."

"Thanks."

"I used to want to be an actress."

"No kidding? When was tha—"

Eric pulled at Marina's sleeve, interrupting her. "They're starting the games."

"You can go."

Both kids ran off.

"I was in musicals in high school. My high school did the old-fashioned ones."

"Those are the ones I like."

"I got to sing 'I'm Gonna Wash That Man Right Outa My Hair.' "

"You played the lead."

"That time."

"You can sing a song, then."

"High school version of belting a song. It wouldn't be considered much anywhere else."

"You know, if you liked it, you might be good undercover. It's what I'd want to do. If I were on the force, I mean."

"Oh. Do you actually think about police work?"

"Kind of a lot. But, well, two in one household, probably wouldn't work out."

"Hard on the kids."

"Hard on the kids." Marina sighed.

"I think I have to go to a meeting now." Colleen pointed to where the squad was gathering. "It was really nice talking to you. Your husband is a great boss."

Marina nodded. "He takes it seriously all right."

Colleen crossed the grounds, squeezing and ducking around clumps of people who were too busy with food or conversation to notice someone needing to get through. She saw John watching her. He gave her a mild wave. She felt sad, but she had no explanation for it.

And unsteady, too. The sun, she supposed. The humidity.

DOLAN HAD COME UP TO Christie before the others gathered to meet.

"Hey," Christie said. "Get enough to eat?"

"Almost."

"You meet Greer's guy?"

"I did."

"I did, too."

"Well, I guess that says it," Dolan cracked. "How long do you give it?"

"I don't know. She's a stick-to-it kind of gal."

"She was working hard to keep it going. He's not in it."

"That's what I'd say."

"You'd think she'd detect that."

"I think she's . . . loyal."

"Maybe we're wrong. Maybe it'll work." Dolan let it go, although gossip was one of their great pleasures.

Christie was studying his legal pad of notes. He'd met with Hoffman at nine in the morning, when he broke it to him on the street, before they even went inside the coroner's office, that he couldn't let him anywhere near Laura's body. Rules, rules, unbendable rules. Different places did it different ways, but Pittsburgh used a video camera for ID purposes. Word was, soon it would all be dental records, computer scans, completely technical.

Hoffman had been distraught.

When Christie took him to the viewing room, it seemed a long time before an image appeared on the screen, the only movement eerily what the camera made, scanning and focusing. Finally, a face.

"It's Laura."

Hoffman sat down. He held his hands over his face for a while and Christie let him.

All the while, Christie studied the man. Cataloged the red-rimmed eyes, the rumpled clothes, the head down, erratic conversation. Hoffman, in his opinion, was half out of his mind—nervous, sad, angry, all moiled and broiled together.

He'd watched Hoffman go to his car, and that was the end of his first interview of the day.

Dolan's canvassing of Laura McCall's neighbors had yielded nothing, either. Amazing, but it happened all the time. Because *most* days, nobody noticed who went in or out of a place. Let that kind of info out and people would be killing each other all the time. Some other place, police might be scraping a part of David Hoffman's cheek and planting it in the sink or bathtub just to get on with the thing.

All around him now was the din of the picnic, children yelling, mothers calling after them. A boy, maybe ten, ran through the meeting, another kid chasing him.

Christie waved to Marina and some of the others to take the children farther away from the meeting area. As the detectives gathered, they formed a silent pocket in the midst of the noise.

"This is the official squad meeting. I'm passing a pad around for you to sign in. You're getting paid for picnic time, too." Grunts of approval. "While you sign in, check your various phones for messages." He looked up and around. "Are we out of earshot? I think so. But keep it low in any case. Children aren't so good with boundaries."

A few detectives were checking cell phones. One was Colleen, and she was listening to something. Her hand went up. She walked toward Christie. "I just retrieved from my home phone. Hoffman wants to talk to me."

"What about?"

"Funeral arrangements."

"Play it again. Let me hear."

She punched in some numbers and handed over the phone.

"Colleen? David Hoffman. I . . . I have a problem. I went ahead—I mean, I was just starting to call a couple of funeral homes, when I got a call from a lawyer. Apparently, my wife's parents have hired a lawyer. They . . . they want to stop me. They're calling me a suspect. I didn't know who else to call and I thought maybe you could tell me what my options are. I could use some help in getting through this. I . . . I would value talking to you as a friend. Give a call if you can. I would be grateful." He left his number before hanging up.

Christie handed the phone over to her. "Don't delete it. Let me think."

"As a *friend,* though."

Christie nodded. "We'll keep contact with him. This could be useful. Anybody else?"

Nobody else had significant calls.

By the time Christie reported on his early meeting with Hoffman, Dolan told about his canvassing, Colleen confirmed Hoffman's alibi checking out completely, and Coleson verified much of the boyfriend's alibi, they realized they were nowhere.

Potocki gave the names of people who had been arrested for burglary in the area. It would take time to check on all of them.

The detectives looked irritable, wanting something. Christie had already explained in the morning meeting what he knew about the evidence so far—that some of the towels appeared to be missing, that Forensics had scraped the bath drains, the chain, the plug, and dug into the pipes. The pipes gave them preliminary presumptive positive for blood with the luminol test, but they warned it might be nothing but rust. They did lots of scrapings and swabs from the bathroom. But it was Saturday. And they weren't going to get to the rest of the testing for a while.

They all knew by now what the bloodstain patterns suggested. Laura McCall's throat had been slit from a standing position and then the stabbing occurred while she fought the killer. McCall had defensive wounds to her hands. She'd raised them to protect her neck before the killer got to the carotid, which did all the squirting. The last stabs happened after she was already down and near death, if not dead by then. Big-time anger.

The yard and porch of the McCall place yielded a couple of shoe prints. They thought they might have shoes going in that they did not have coming out.

It was strange—so many happy people cavorting in the park and them huddled, thinking, like some teenage gang ready to do something unsavory. Christie paced a little and his eye caught a kid trying to get a kite up. It was not a good day for kites.

"Tell me," Christie said, "how are we profiling our killer? What do you think? Organized or disorganized? Given the cleanup of the person and yet the chaos of the murder."

The squad loved profiling because it helped them eliminate certain people. If they were investigating an orderly, planned murder, going door-to-door, and saw, say, a guy living in a pigsty, scratching his crotch, didn't know his own name, they'd pretty much eliminate him.

"Organized," McGranahan volunteered. "Organized, male, white."

Hurwitz said, "Organized, male, black."

"What are you thinking of?" Christie asked Hurwitz. "What model?"

"Christa Worthington."

But that was a sexual murder. And took forever to solve. And finally got solved on the basis of DNA. There was no rape in this one. "Anyone think disorganized?" Christie asked. Suggesting not premeditated.

Colleen said, "Organized, but with supreme effort. A pool of disorganized behavior beneath it."

It's what he would have said. She was going to be okay.

"We're ruling out some bum from the park?" McGranahan asked.

"Not quite," Christie said. "Just keep the profile in mind. We could be wrong, though. Right now, it looks like someone got into the house, had a little social time, killed her, cleaned up. Now think, think. Her boyfriend didn't know what she was up to. Says she had some things she was working out on her own, private time. What could that be? And Hoffman said she *called* him and asked him to come over. They hadn't seen each other for a while. She had a secretive side. So, she might have wanted to get back with her husband. She might have had another lover. What were her secrets?"

"Financial? Something financial," McGranahan said.

A very predictable man, McGranahan was, giving a money answer whenever possible.

"Sexual," Potocki said, shaking his head. "It's always sexual in a stabbing like this."

Christie was inclined to agree with Potocki. There was no rape, but there was passion of the angry sort. He told Potocki, "Let's have you stick to her computer and financial records."

Just then, his phone rang. He listened quietly to the pathologist. Everyone went still, waiting. When he was finished, he turned to them. "We have the autopsy report. It's only preliminary, without some of the tests, but they're really working to help us out here. The stabbing was done with one of her own kitchen knives. She had no food in her stomach, but she did have a trace of alcohol in her bloodstream. Some of the splashes in the kitchen were brown, watery, and the early results on them suggest they're the same as what was in her stomach—bourbon probably. No bottle, no glasses left at the scene, but we saw what looked like rings from two glasses. So." They were listening, some nodding. "It definitely still looks like somebody she knew.

"They don't have anything yet from the fingernails. When they do, and if we find a glitch in Hoffman's alibi, and if we haven't already done so, we'll get a DNA sample from him. So—" He looked at his legal pad, getting ready to send them to their various posts and functions. "Questions?"

Dolan waved a hand. "I'd like to work the street, the prisons, see if there are any rumors of hit men hired for the job."

Christie nodded that Dolan should go ahead with it. He'd be good at that.

Colleen, he said, should call Hoffman back, keep a connection going. "Tell him the facts, which are, one, that the coroner's office will need the body until later today or tomorrow and, two, if there's no decision about where to have the funeral, he should know there are options for holding it off for a while. You don't have to tell him the option—they'll send Laura to the mortuary school to embalm her. It's not very dignified, all that carting around, so find some way to be vague about it. Three, tell him, yes, he might as well get a lawyer in case his in-laws persist, and let him know, four, they'll probably drop it when they understand any judge is going to rule in his favor given that he's the husband. Maybe let things cool for a day."

"What do I tell him about the fact that her family is calling him a suspect?"

"Well, he is, of course, but not officially so. The parents don't know what else to do with their grief. Stay friendly with him. Listen well."

"If he wants to meet?"

"Meet. Let me know time and place. I'll get a couple of people to show up wherever and watch out for you; you'll be okay."

She took a visible deep breath.

COLLEEN WALKED AWAY FROM the squad meeting and tried to find John. He'd moved. Unless *she* was turned around. Shading her eyes against the glaring sun, Colleen scanned the tables for him. Suddenly, she jumped. Her heart began pumping hard and her knees went weak under her.

Hoffman. What was he doing here?

Not.

Not Hoffman. Another man. Older.

Her mind was playing tricks on her. She thought about Hoffman, then she thought she saw him. Crazy. Very crazy. Not the sort of thing she wanted to admit. The other man, the man she'd mistaken for him, was laughing and holding forth with several other people, telling jokes, it looked liked. He had a raucous laugh and it made its way past the other noises to her. She realized slowly that he was another one of her former bosses, so to speak, not anybody she had had much direct contact with. He supervised the patrol officers.

She wiped sweat from her neck and tried to get hold of herself. Then she saw John, right where she'd left him, looking off into space, unaware of her. Chocolate cake in front of him. Coffee, probably cold by now. Frown on his face.

ONLY A FEW MINUTES AFTER finishing up the chocolate cake on his plate, John left the picnic, driving his new Camry. He hadn't been in the mood for one of his bikes, the Vincent or the Triumph. Most people with a motorcycle would have taken it to the park, but he'd gotten a reverse attraction to his bikes lately; maybe his image was changing. After all, he wasn't a kid. He was divorced—a very early marriage, lasted from the ages of twenty-two to twenty-eight—then he stayed single for a long time, in a second bid at youth. Last month he traded his old Jetta for a middle-aged person's car. Every time he got into the Camry, he thought of all those air bags that were going to envelop him from every which direction if he needed them, and hopefully not before he needed them. He had the routines down, the way his right arm adjusted the temperature, put in a CD. The new car smell still lingered. It had taken him a long time to decide what to buy, and then one day, he was ready and he just did.

That was his rhythm. A decision formed out of the muck of indecision, and once it did, he was swift.

It was going to be messy. But it was over. How to say it? He turned over phrases. The weak ones: *I need a few days to myself. We need to take a break from each other for just a little while.* Then the strongest, most honest: *You've meant a lot to me, but I'm not in love with you.*

The Camry hummed underneath U2 doing "Vertigo." He noticed his hands were shaking with the thought of the scene coming later. Breakups were never okay and there was never a good time for them and he didn't know why he hadn't just refused to go to the picnic. She had seemed to want it so much, and she was exhausted and keyed up with this big new case, so he told himself, Why not just see her through it? But sitting at that picnic, among people he didn't particularly want to get to know, he thought, Why bullshit any longer?

Colleen was a warmhearted type, always bringing him food, even gifts. But the gifts had embarrassed him from the start because he knew she was not the woman he was looking for, not *the one.*

He pounded the heel of his hand against the steering wheel. This was going to be hard, trying to work up some anger against her. Some outrage. It helped to be angry. He began to rehearse tougher phrases: *You don't really respect me. How do you think that makes me feel?* Kernel of truth there. He kept at it: *You keep pushing me to go back to school; you're not happy with me, either. You don't know who I am.* Man, he hoped she didn't apologize.

There weren't too many of her clothes at his place. A sign that even she knew their arrangement was temporary. Right?

By rolling over to his left hip, he was able to pull his cell phone out of his pants pocket. Driving time was dead time without a phone. He went to the SENT menu and scrolled down, tilting the phone in the sunlight to be sure he didn't choose a wrong number. There it was. He pressed SEND.

Answering machine. He spoke to it.

"Josie, hi. It's me. Look, are you on the desk tomorrow, Sunday? Morning and afternoon? I don't have my schedule with me, but I think you are. I was wondering if you could meet me for supper tomorrow. Call me on my cell if you can, or I'll call you back."

There, he'd set the breakup clock.

Tuesday night, Colleen had been working. And he'd called Josie then, too, asking would she be willing to go for a drink and talk.

She said she was playing tennis at seven, but that she would cut it short to meet him by eight-thirty. And she did.

She knew what was happening. After a couple of beers, he said, "Look, I keep thinking about you. You know that, right? But I've been in this other thing for over a year. I'm not really free, but I want to be."

"I understand," she said.

He'd followed her to her apartment.

Josie wasn't a major looker. She was *nice*-looking in a very brisk, clean, way. Sharp-featured. Very brisk voice. Fairly athletic, thin. What was it about her? She wasn't interested in his motorcycles, even said something condescending about his need for a shot of youth. Yet, she was *the one.*

"I don't want to wait. I want to get us to bed," he said as soon as they got to her place. They were walking up the sidewalk, kissing. "So long as you know I'm not out of the other thing yet."

She laughed a little, looking at him. "Oh, what the hell," she said. Very no-nonsense.

And so they went inside. And her place looked like his place. Same sofa. It was wild how many things were alike. He thought, This was meant to be.

They fell into bed. When she ushered him out the door a couple of hours later, she told him to be absolutely sure. She didn't want any haphazard breakup on her conscience. Four days he gave it. Even went to the picnic.

He now took the ramp past the football stadium. Soon, in a matter of weeks, football mania would be starting up—traffic clogged. In a quick lick of fantasy, he was moving himself out to Josie's apartment, much nearer the airport.

His phone rang. He tilted it to read the number. His heart jumped up.

"Hello!" she said. "Well, I was supposed to meet my mom for supper tomorrow, but I'll change it."

Colleen didn't love him. Josie—the way she always found a way—Josie was the real thing.

SIX

JAMILLA WAS HEADING FOR the door of the Family Counseling Center when she saw his car.

It was late. It was already almost midnight on Saturday. He had called when she didn't show up earlier, but she explained that she had to get the baby to sleep because Kameen was not supposed to be on his feet. She had to get both of the kids to sleep before she could leave the house, she told him, and he got angry, but she insisted.

He beckoned to her now. "Hop in. We're not going to meet in the office tonight."

She got into his car. It felt unfamiliar. She hoped it meant they would talk a little in the car and he would drive her home.

"They had a burst pipe in there. The floor's all wet. I have another place where we can meet."

It's weird, she thought, this late. "Maybe . . . tonight isn't good. I don't like leaving the kids alone."

"No, I have to talk to you. It won't take long."

He drove down the street a couple of blocks and then turned left and then left and then left again into a space with places to park and what looked like a row of garages. She held her hands tight together on her lap. Would he drive her home, then, after?

He was different tonight. "What's the matter?" he said as he parked. "You look like you want to say something and you're not saying it."

"I can't keep meeting you anymore," she told him. "See, I just can't." She didn't know she was going to say it, but she had—said it and not just thought it.

"What's going on, huh? Haven't I done everything for you?"

She didn't have an answer.

"Your parents could be arrested, you kids could get split up and taken away from them, you know that? Haven't I taken care of things? What's going on with you?" His eyes were squinted, but hard and glaring, like little stones.

She shrugged.

"Where are your parents tonight?"

She didn't answer. There was no right answer.

"Come," he said. "We'd better go inside to talk. Obviously, we need to talk."

"In there?"

"Yes, inside."

It didn't look like a house or an office. "How can we go in there? It's garages."

"I have an office in there, too. You'll see." And he pulled out a very large ring of keys, selecting one. "Just sit for a minute in the car," he said. "Let me make sure nobody else is around." He got out and opened a door and went in. Then he came back out and motioned to her. She got out of the car and went inside, and it *was* an office, right in the middle of all those garages. To her right and left she could see trucks and the kinds of carts that drove in the park.

"It's different," she said.

"But comfortable. Sit here. Let's talk. About this idea of yours. Please. Just sit."

And she did. She sat on the orange couch.

He was sweating; he was shaking. She hated to see that. She could tell when he was getting funny like that. He was saying, "How is the food supply at home? First things first." He smiled, but his eyes were all wrong. She could smell alcohol on him, strong.

"Low," she said. "Nothing much in the house. Bagels."

"You need more than that," he said. "Growing kids. Can you get something with this twenty?" He held up twenty dollars. She was happy to see that. She thought she could just go to the supermarket when he let her go tonight. Then he added another ten, holding up the two bills. "You should get juice, things like that. Okay?"

"Okay," she said. She could get some decent food with thirty. Lots of food. She was trying to remember when her father and mother got paid, so she could shop wisely. "I should go get the food now," she said, "because Kameen—"

"What?"

"Wakes up."

"So?"

"Well, he isn't too good at watching Soleil. If *she* wakes up, it's bad. So I have to get home. Soon."

"Where'd your mum and dad go again? Did you say?"

"They're out," she said. It was very hard to lie. He always knew.

"Where?"

"He's working. My mom said she deserved Saturday night to let loose."

"How do they let loose?"

"You know. Drink." She had to say it every time. He checked every time. He sat on a chair that looked uncomfortable. It was hard, but covered in fabric with a diamond-shaped pattern. She was still on the long orange sofa, not a nice one, but definitely better than his seat.

"I need to talk to you. I think you know that. I think you know why."

"No."

"Didn't a woman . . ."

He was shaking harder. Sometimes she felt so bad for him when he was suffering. He kept trying to be nice. She knew how it was to pause and try to be nice and then get mad anyway. He said, "There was a woman who talked to you and you told her some big story."

"I didn't tell her anything. She guessed things."

"What did she guess?"

Jamilla didn't answer him. Again, every answer was trouble, so her mouth wouldn't form the words.

"Tell me," he said. "Tell me she was wrong. Wasn't she wrong? Making it up to scare you."

She didn't answer.

"You aren't sick or anything? Throwing up. Are you?"

She didn't answer.

"If you are, we have to get rid of it."

"No," she said.

"What do you mean, 'No'?" His chin trembled. His eyes . . . he was almost crying. She wanted to cry, too, but she couldn't do anything when she talked to him. She always had to be careful, slow and careful.

"I won't tell," she said. "I won't say anything. To anybody." She always said that to make him calm.

"But you did tell."

"I didn't. She guessed."

"And what do you think people are going to do when you get big with it? You think they're going to guess or not?" He was not nice now; he was turning to the not nice part.

"Please let me go," she said.

"Stupid. You were going to what? Huh? What were you thinking?"

"I didn't tell and I won't tell. It's our secret, just being friends." She knew to say this, too. She didn't say, What's in me has nothing to do with you. It's just me, inside me. She tried to smile, because he thought she was pretty and he liked it when she smiled. But he wasn't smiling back this time. "It's late," she said.

"You don't leave until we get this straight."

She got up. "I don't like it in here."

He came after her and headed her off before she turned to the door.

"Maybe I could come to the other place on Thursday," she tried.

"Do you have a boyfriend? Somebody you fuck around with?"

The word bothered her. It went straight through her mind like a knife. "No. No." She tripped over a stack of magazines on the floor.

"Because people are going to ask you where you got that baby."

"I can go away. I can go stay with my aunt. I know I could stay with her."

"They'll make you tell. She'll make you tell."

"I won't tell."

"Don't be stupid, you little bitch."

Something flames up in her. "I'm not stupid. Don't keep calling me that." She never talked back to him, and she sees how much it surprises him. "I don't have to do everything you say. I know what you're doing. I mean, I know it's wrong." She tries to head for the door.

But he is at the door before she is, slapping both hands against it. When he swings back to her, he roars in anger, his eyes are wilder than ever before, and sweat pours down his forehead as he comes at her.

SEVEN

NOTHING SEEMED RIGHT IN A day until she got her run in. An addiction, but a good one.

John was asleep beside her, deep in, not a budge or a twitch when she turned restlessly. If she could get her run in now . . . It was only five-thirty and not very light out, but day would break in a few minutes, and two hours from now, the humidity would be unbearable. So she crept out of John's bed, rummaged in one of the two drawers in which she kept her things, found a pair of shorts—good ones, not the ones she preferred to exercise in, but okay—and a T-shirt. Shoes here, thank heavens. Should she make coffee before going? She decided no, but she killed a few minutes bringing in the paper and reading the headlines. News. Nothing new on Laura McCall, and certainly nothing she didn't know.

Suddenly, she did not feel like being alone. She bounded back up the stairs and sat on the bed next to John. Did he sense her? Had his eyes closed just a little tighter? "I'm going for a run," she said. No reaction. "You want to come? I'll wait."

"No," he said. His diction was very clear, not a groan.

She smoothed his hair. "Okay. Sleep."

She headed back down the stairs and out into the street. There was little sign of life. The light had not quite broken. Near but not *on* most stoops were newspapers sheathed in green plastic; she'd seen the delivery guy once in winter, driving up the street, both windows down, tossing papers carelessly left and right.

There were no cars moving now. It was too early to be out, still almost night. John should have said, No, don't go alone. Climb back in. He should have said, Wait. You're not going without me, not at this hour. But he hadn't said those things. Her feet started the jog. Keys in her pocket, tissue, and that was it—nothing to steal from her, that was for sure. She crossed the street and made her way into West Park. In the dim light, she saw bits of the colorful baggage that made bedding for the homeless men who preferred the park to the Light of Life Ministries. Usually, she ran later in the morning, when the men were waking—sitting up and groggily letting the day in.

The park was gently sloped and beautiful in its design. Except for the debris that collected, it might be a park in France.

She chugged along, past the statue of George Washington on his horse, past the path to St. Peter's. If this were Europe or even one of the small towns of her youth, there would be old women going to church now, but early-morning Masses were becoming a thing of the past.

One man sleeping, two men sleeping, two more, one more. One green quilt, one red something or other, two scrambled sets of rags. So colorful. Like India. Poverty and friendship. Whatever was at hand to cushion and wrap the body. Rain washed these bedclothes, sunshine dried them out. How did they feel? Have nothing, wait for a few bucks, get your drink or your drug, whatever you needed, and experience what the rest of us miss—the grass, the earth, the birds, the sound of traffic, the sky. Well, in summer anyway, it seemed a possible way to live.

She kept running. She could feel her heart rate accelerating, her body manufacturing sweat. Her thoughts turned to John. He never wanted to do anything anymore. She said last night when she got home late, "We need to get away somewhere, even if only for a weekend." But he said his work schedule was going to be tight for a while.

Early on, a year ago, they'd gone to Toronto for a weekend. Once he accompanied her to a wedding in Connecticut. That was about it. All those free flights going to waste, an unused perk.

She runs.

She and John look good together—her light and him dark, neither of them overly tall. They fit.

She runs. There is traffic moving on North Avenue now. One homeless man sits up. Still it's mostly quiet, peaceful, early, humid. Sweat is pouring down her face.

Then a funny thing happens. Inside, in the print of her eye, she's seen something, but she doesn't know what, something important. She shakes her head to figure out what it was—she looks around, can't figure it out. It's like when she's reading, knows she sees a particular word, and can't locate it again, but this is something she can't even define. She stops running. She feels dizzy. Is she overtired?

Her heart plummets. What if she turns out to be weak, bad at this work?

She starts running again.

Is she frightened?

It's her mind playing tricks again.

She turns, does her loops around sidewalks, looks up toward where Hoffman's office is. Maybe she saw Hoffman in her peripheral vision going to work. But if she did, there's no evidence of his car now.

At one point she thinks, there must be a couple under a bush far to her left, for she sees what looks like a woman's foot sticking out. Like something out of an Irish play, tinkers living, loving under a bush. Funny to think of women living so much on the edge of things.

Keep running. Clear the head.

She finishes with three laps around the pond. The ducks look at her with some interest, then go back to snoozing. They live a dangerous life. She's heard some of the neighborhood people steal the ducks from time to time, make dinner of them. There are a lot of poor people in the neighborhood. The park happens to be relatively clean today—no condoms, no needles. She's seen the cleanup crews some mornings slowly sweeping those things out of sight.

Back at John's place, she is surprised to hear his voice when she walks in the door. The phone light in the living room is lit, but as soon as she slams the door, the light goes out.

He's at the top of the stairs, naked. "Where the hell did you go?"

"For a run."

"It's not even light out."

"It is now. I told you. Listen, don't yell. I'm a bit shaken."

"What?"

She climbs the steps toward him. "Something funny happened."

He takes her hand. "What?"

"It could have been imagination, I don't know." He puts his arms around her and holds her, a nice tight wrestler's hold. "I'm really sweaty."

"It's okay. What's wrong?"

"I got the spooks in the park. I felt like I saw something in my peripheral vision, but I couldn't catch it."

"What kind of thing?"

"For a while, I thought maybe the guy we questioned the other night. Maybe he passed in his car, going to his office and I saw him without knowing I did? But I ran up that way to check, and nothing doing. I guess it was just the spooks."

"It's hardly light enough to see," he says. "No wonder. Come back to bed?"

"You think I'm losing it?"

"No."

She lies back, trying to calm down.

In the tangle of covers, these of light blue, she thinks briefly of the people living outdoors with nothing but friendship and some drug or other to keep them going. She's still got a bad case of the nerves. John had said they'd spend time this morning over a Lindo's breakfast, talking, debriefing about the picnic. She's curious what he thought of Christie, Dolan, and the others. He puts his arms around her and hugs. Arms. His last name, Brach, is wonderfully appropriate—he uses his arms well; he's a good hugger.

"Take your time. Breathe."

"How much wine did I have last night?"

"Couple of glasses."

"It's very unsettling. Very."

"You're okay," he says. "Just rest up for a few minutes and then we'll walk over to Lindo's. A little food—"

"Or a lot."

"You'll feel different—better."

She nods.

CHRISTIE WAS STARTING OUT for Headquarters early—he liked the quiet of the office on a Sunday morning. Last night, middle of the night, he got a call: A man had been found shot dead in his backyard in Homewood. It looked like a drug deal gone bad, the patrol cops said, so Christie put a couple of men on it overnight, orchestrating from the phone beside his bed. Marina didn't get much sleep with the phone going all night, but that case was moving along fast. Four men had named the same shooter and now the detectives could be very specific. The suspect couldn't hide forever. Hopefully.

The full moon had been two nights ago, but maybe there was some lunacy left over, with these two murders in two days—and on a weekend, as usual.

Christie left his house and took Fifth, then the parkway. He'd had only an hour with his kids at the picnic. Marina was being decent about it, but she ended up spending much more time with his kids than he did. His hope on this Sunday morning driving to work was to get in, get everybody assigned and organized, and somehow *sneak* a couple of hours with Eric and Julie before they had to go back to their mother.

So, in his mind, and occasionally at a red light, on paper, he was preparing the roster of assignments as they'd be split between the Homewood killing and the McCall killing. On the legal pad he grabbed from time to time, he put Coleson and McGranahan on canvassing, Potocki on computer records. What to do with Greer? On computer with Potocki? Or quiz people about Laura McCall?

Meanwhile, the DA was still leaning hard on the lab technicians to get backlogged evidence ready for a trial that would begin on Tuesday. Truth was, they didn't have enough analysts, they didn't have enough hours; new cases had to wait while old cases got their attention.

What a mess, to have the technology without the manpower.

Do it the old way, Christie's inner voice said. Before DNA, footprint analysis, chemical tricks. The old way. That meant thinking, observing. That meant Dolan sweet-talking a confession out of someone.

He was coming off the parkway and passing Heinz Field when his phone rang. "Commander. Looks like a homicide. I have the patrol car on the line."

Christie kept going past Heinz Field, dazed. Three, then, in thirty-six hours. He really wasn't young enough for this round-the-clock stuff. He heard the patrolman come onto the line to report the crime.

"Commander, we took a call this morning. A child, a girl, was found dead in West Park."

The park was only three blocks or so from where Christie sat at a light, phone to his ear. "How old?"

"I can't tell. Could be ten. Eleven. Older."

"I'll be right there," he said. "I mean *right there.*" The media was going to be all over this one. The assignment sheet next to him was definitely going to change unless someone was standing by, waiting to confess. He called the desk at Headquarters. "Start calling the Homicide detectives early," he said. Some were due at nine. He wanted all of them by eight. A dead kid meant no time with his own kids. He heaved a big sigh.

Driving toward the crime scene, he called for a mobile crime unit. He felt the craziness in the air, the oppressive humidity pressing his skull, making his brain clogged, foggy. The air conditioning in his car was on high and he could still feel the wetness in the air.

He got back on with the patrol cop even though he was only fifty yards from the site. "Who called it in?"

"Some guy walking his dog."

West Park, he thought. Our Greer runs there most days. He wondered if she'd run this morning yet.

"You're able to keep people away?"

"Yes, sir."

There was something already funereal about the scene in the park. People standing around. A body on the ground, half under the bushes. A gate made of yellow tape.

"Who found her?"

"I found her," a bespectacled, lean man volunteered. He'd been standing with a woman who kept pulling a dog, presumably theirs, away from the crime scene. The man took out of his wallet some ID that identified him as Anthony Thurston, a writer for the *Post-Gazette.* "I called my wife to come for the dog," he said.

"Did you touch anything?"

"Yes. I pushed the bush aside. I felt for a pulse, I felt her neck. I was sure she was dead. I called nine one one and waited until an ambulance came and a police car."

"What about the dog? What did the dog disturb?"

"I wrapped the leash around my hand until he had nothing more than a foot. I practically held him in my arms when I touched her. Did I do anything wrong? Oh, I'm so sorry." The man's eyes teared up, and his hands made a steeple over his mouth.

"You did okay. Stand back, please. Everybody, stand back." Christie went up to the body. A dainty foot, a pair of jeans. He also pushed aside the bush so he could see the rest of the girl. And he saw the sweet face of a beautiful child. He felt for a pulse, even though the paramedics watched him doing it. He felt her neck. A leaf from the bush fell on her face. He brushed it off gently. What a lovely child.

Her clothes were simple. She didn't look homeless. She was not lying on a mass of newspapers and bags or on a quilt as so many of the homeless were. There was, however, one neat plastic bag under her and one over her. Both looked new.

She was young. Twelve or so?

Christie rubbed his forehead. He put in a call to Forensics. Laura McCall's murder had given them as many spatters and fibers as they could handle for the next two months, and now he was going to give them a mess of footprints and dog hairs, too. "This is Christie here," he said.

"Commander. What can I do for you?"

"I have another homicide."

A breath. "These weekends."

"Yeah. I need a car with all your specialists."

"If it requires everybody . . ."

"Yeah it does, again. In West Park. A child—strangled, it looks like. The scene is highly corruptible and I want all the help I can get as soon as possible."

The man replied soberly, "Yes, I'm writing it all down."

"Your best people," he added, "if you would."

"I'll try," the guy was saying. "You'll need ground prints and scrapings—"

Christie looked up. Two vans were already starting to drive off the street and over the lawn. Television crews. Into the phone Christie said, "All that. Yes. Two news teams are here already. As I said, the site could be hard to maintain, so hurry."

He called Headquarters and dictated to the desk his revised assignment sheet.

He turned to the crowd. "Who saw something here? Can anybody come forth with information?" He studied the faces in the crowd. "Does anyone know who she is?"

He saw a few people shake their heads.

"Who was here in the park all night? Come forward. I need to talk to anyone who was in the park during the night." Slowly one, then another, then three more people came forward to tell him they had spent the night in the park, were sleeping, didn't notice, heard nothing unusual, saw nothing.

He tapped his foot for a moment and made a decision. He called Colleen Greer's cell. He didn't usually act on personal information, but he knew plenty well she stayed over in this neighborhood and ran in this park. She might be only minutes away. And if she was, he could put her to work.

LINDO'S WAS ALREADY STARTing to fill up before seven, when Colleen and John arrived. She was ravenous. She slid into a booth toward the back, and John slid in across from her. He patted her hand. "You'll be okay."

She wasn't much in the mood to take lukewarm comfort. If only she could replay the tape of her run in the park, slow it down, figure out what had triggered a reaction in her.

The man who cashiered and bused and hosted in this breakfast dive for as long as she had been coming here appeared at her elbow. He was East Indian and the gentlest of personalities. "Are you doing well, I hope? I haven't seen you in many weeks."

"I *know*. I skipped a couple of beats."

He put down two flimsy napkins, then silverware she didn't care to look at too closely. "I'll bring water," he said, rushing off, as if she were royalty.

"He likes you."

Colleen nodded. Already she was feeling better. She was a social creature, a lover of routine visits to this or that place. While water and menus arrived, John studied the other customers and she ran her mental tape. Gun to her head, she wouldn't know how to answer what she'd felt in the park.

"Hey," John said.

"Yeah."

The waitress, about twenty, had *hard night* written all over her face. She brought coffee right away without asking (as they all did here, and kept refilling cups from a bronze thermos). The house brew always had that chemical ting of an aftertaste you got with cheap restaurant coffee. Colleen could smell the chemistry even before she tasted the coffee. She drank it anyway.

She ordered her one-armed bandit. John ordered French toast and bacon.

She yawned and checked her watch, trying to remember what clothes she had available. John rapped the table, rearranged his napkin and silverware a few times. She became aware of his restlessness.

"God, you must have hated the picnic. Hit me with it. You wanted to vent, vent."

He shook his head. "It's not that."

"Oh."

"I'm . . . Look, I'm not abandoning you. I'm not a guy to let a friend down when she's going through a lot. I just want to back off for a while from the romantic part."

Colleen took a moment to bring her mind to the table. "I thought we were doing kind of okay lately. Did something happen? Is this about yesterday?"

"This . . . this feeling started before yesterday. We haven't been in the same place about this from the start. I think you know that. You wanted to get serious. I never did. I think it's better to . . . let it go."

" 'Let it go'? You're talking . . . completely?" Somehow, all the voices around her seemed upbeat this morning, happy. Silverware clanged and plates clumped.

John didn't answer right away. Then he said, "People never know how they're going to feel until they . . . try a separation."

"Something happened. We were bumping along. Why did you come to the picnic—and now you tell me it had nothing to do with anything yesterday? Why don't I believe you? Why would you bring me here and tell me here?"

Outside, a siren screamed, then another. Fire, police, ambulance—her world—emergencies and disasters. She ought to be able to get her mind around a surprise breakup. "Is this a breakup?"

"I've been trying to find a way to talk to you, but you're always in the midst of something. I think we need to date other people."

Her body slumped. "Speak for yourself."

"Look. Do you want me to sneak around, or do you want me to be honest?"

Something told her there had already been some sneaking around and now came the honest part. "Talk straight, please. What caused this?"

"It's not you. You're a wonderful person. It doesn't have anything to do with you. I just want to see other people."

"That's not the most flattering thing I've ever heard."

As she sat there studying him, if she'd been honest with herself, she would have noticed she didn't like him much. She cared about him, impossible for her not to, after being with him. In some way, she loved him. But she didn't *like* him and she didn't respect him. She wasn't ready to give that ground just yet.

"Okay. There's somebody I would like to start seeing."

Colleen nodded.

"But I don't necessarily want to rush . . . or make mistakes."

"Oh brother." She wasn't made for polygamy, sharing, if that's what he was talking about. It was bad enough when a thing started out that way, but to go from practically living together to several notches down on the relationship scale, she didn't think she had it in her.

She had a fleeting vision of getting into her own house again, making it sparkle, enjoying it. For a moment, everything lifted in her and she felt free, elated.

Then she thought, I'm going to be lonely again, bad lonely. She hated to blush. She blushed. She hated to cry, yet tears of anger were forming. How awful to be here at a restaurant, unable to express herself. How shitty of him to do this one day after she took him to meet her colleagues.

"Maybe I'd better get my breakfast to go."

"Please don't."

"I'd like to get my things and . . . not have them at your place under the circumstances."

"Please don't be like this. I like you enormously. I really do. I want to be your friend. Can't we just have breakfast?"

"When did you start seeing this other person?"

"There hasn't been much. We just both agree we'd like to try it together."

"I guess I haven't been noticing. You're right. It started when? She's from work?"

"Yes."

"You were talking to her this morning at six A.M. That sounds . . . developed."

"Why are you doing this?"

"I guess I want to know how out of it I am."

"This kind of thing happens all the time."

"I know. But what do you call our thing? I mean, what was it? For more than a year?"

"Off and on."

"Granted, off and on. You were marking time and I was handy?"

"Don't put it that way. There are lots of things I love about you."

The last couple of lines sounded like a song. Or like a speech he'd been rehearsing. Furious tears threatened again just as the Indian man brought their plates, and said, "I saw this was ready. I brought it myself so it does not get cold." He began to smile at Colleen, but when he saw her face, his expression changed. "Is something wrong? Is everything okay?"

"I'm fine," Colleen said, feeling like an idiot because his kindness made the tears well up rather than recede.

"Please call me if you want anything, please?"

"No. We're fine."

John was already pouring sticky syrup from a tin pot. He *was* fine.

Colleen's phone rang. She dug into her pocket for it and heard "Christie here. We have a homicide. Are you by any chance on the North Side?"

"Yes. I'm over on Western having breakfast."

"Well, I could use your help over in the park. Where you run, I think. Maybe knowing the area, you could think of something to check out that we're not coming up with."

"I'll be right there."

"I half-expected to see you running by the crime scene."

"I ran this morning. Early."

"You didn't see anything?"

"I . . . maybe. Maybe. I'll be right there."

"Thanks."

Colleen called the host over. "Could you box this up? I have to go to work."

"Work? Now?"

"Yeah." The man looked questioningly at John's plate. "No, just mine. He doesn't have to leave."

"My treat," John said.

Big fucking deal. She remembered with immense clarity that he was also a cheapskate.

It was amazing how good she was at eating while walking. It was astounding that with all that was happening to her, and a homicide three short blocks away, her stomach growled, demanding food, plenty of it. It took her about three minutes to get to the spot in the park where the yellow tape was, and she'd managed the grits and pancake and sausage on the way, leaving one piece of toast and the egg for after.

There were people standing around. Colleen realized the spot they were looking at was the one she had seen, the place that had made her think a homeless woman had been sleeping in the park. Had someone killed the woman before or after she ran by? She passed through the crowd, saying, "Excuse me, please. Police." Unfortunately, she didn't have any ID with her. She was still wearing shorts and carrying part of her breakfast, and had only her phone, a set of keys to John's place, and a twenty-dollar bill in her pocket.

Christie waved her through. "Thank you," he said. "The victim is a young girl. You may know if you've seen her around the park." Christie moved aside.

Colleen saw the legs, the feet. A child practically. A very young person. Her heart plummeted. What if she could have helped?

She said, "When I ran this morning, I saw her here. I thought it was just another person sleeping in the park. There are maybe ten, twelve people sleeping here most mornings. I wasn't close. I didn't run close by."

"Okay. I understand."

Was there a criticism in his tone?

Christie pulled the bush out of the way so Colleen could take a look at the victim's face. She stooped down to look closely, freezing at what she saw. Then she stood, backed up, holding her arms around herself. She hated it that her knees went weak. She said, "I knew her."

"Who is she?"

"Jamilla Washington. She and her family came to the center when I worked there." Memory flooded Colleen as she looked more closely at the beautiful young face. She had adored this child. Everyone had. The parents were like movie stars, they were so beautiful. And they drank, oh yes, Colleen remembered that perfectly well. Parents who drank and who left their kids alone, well, that hit home for her, she'd been there. She kept looking at the girl.

"You're sure?" Christie asked.

"It's Jamilla. She was memorable. Some people are simply special, and this one was. I could almost say—" She began to cry. She blinked away her tears and paused before finishing her sentence. "Angelic."

Even in death, the child commanded something. Nobody moved away. The people in the crowd murmured among themselves or just stood there, patiently waiting for the body to be taken away. The vigil for Jamilla Washington had begun.

EIGHT

THE MAN WHO KILLED JAMILLA does not know which patterns to keep, which patterns to break. Something's gone wrong in his head. He has lost his inner strength—the one thing he always had, always, every hour, day, year—the ability to think, plan ahead. He must get it back. He tightens his fist as if he can grab onto confidence, capture it, keep someone from stealing it. He must make no more mistakes. It's early Sunday morning. He pours half a glass of bourbon, drinks it down fast. Immediately, he feels better. No more mistakes. A moth flies close to his face. It's odd to see a moth in the morning; aren't they night creatures? He reaches out, grabs it, tightens his fist again, opens his hand to see nothing but powder.

COLLEEN DID A FIGURE EIGHT of a walk away from the body of the child and back again to where she could see her. There would almost certainly be a sexual aspect to this case, some sort of abuse. In that small figure eight, Colleen reminded herself of what it was to be twelve, thirteen, afraid, a girl who doesn't tell.

She knew about abuse, and not just from studying at school or working as a therapist. A lot of women knew. It happened all the time. In her case, she'd fought back. Why or how she *knew* to fight—that was a mystery. In spite of the fact that the man was clever enough to make her think it was her fault. She can still smell his rusty old car, the cigarette smoke. She can still see the neighborhood he drove through and the patch of woods he drove into. She didn't tell then, and didn't tell anyone for a long time after, either. Her parents have no idea. Telling. It still doesn't come easily.

"You okay?" Christie asked.

"Yes."

"What?"

"I'm just thinking. An older person did this."

"Why?"

"The orderliness. But also . . . back when Jamilla was a client—or her family was—I thought she might be a victim of abuse. She's a type of victim, one of the people who becomes loving and mature to compensate. There wasn't a hint of it in the talk, so if it happened, it never surfaced."

"You treated her?"

"No. No. I saw the family in the waiting room. She has a brother. I'd say a few words as I passed. They were pretty kids and the parents were intriguing. We had weekly meetings about our clients, so I knew *about* them. They were split up for individual counseling for a while, then they got family counseling."

"With Hoffman?"

"No. A guy named Jim Daniels. He moved on. To Wichita, I think."

"Can you get me a phone number?"

"I'll work on it."

"Do you know where her parents live?"

"Not offhand. I think I would recognize the address if I had a phone book."

"Back at your friend's house?"

"Yes," she said. He didn't need to hear about the complications.

"Call me when you get it. If you don't get it, I'll run it another way." She started to turn toward John's place. "Wait. Look. You were second on the scene. You have some knowledge of the girl, the area. . . ."

She held her breath.

"You ready to partner me on this case?"

"The two of us in charge of it?"

"Yes."

"You're on," she said.

In charge of the case! With Christie. She didn't want to bother him with being spooked earlier until she thought it through. She walked fast through the park, the same route she took when exercising, but this time, of course, everything was different. She dumped the take-out box with the rest of her breakfast in one of the overflowing trash cans. In her pocket was the set of keys to John's place. How she hoped he wouldn't be there yet. Knew he would be. Strange to think she was single again, just when she least expected it. Her mind was scrambling to redefine her life, but if anything could put a relationship mess into perspective, if anything could render John insignificant to her, this morning's scene in the park could.

Jamilla had bypassed childhood by the age of seven. She saw what needed to be done. Somebody's coffee was spilling over, somebody was harried, she quietly did the right thing—a napkin, a hand under a cup, a smile, a glance away—whatever preserved the dignity of the adults decompressing around her. Why did it have to be a kid like that who got hurt?

John was home. He was pacing the front hallway, talking on the phone. It wasn't difficult to guess to whom he was talking by the hurried way he hung up. "Hey," he said. "What happened? What's going on?" He looked sad. Or was it pitying?

"I have to get my things—my work, I mean. I don't have the time to pack up the other things now. I have to look something up."

"There's a homicide?"

"A child. I knew her."

"Oh, Col, I'm so sorry."

Tears stung her eyes. Was it for Jamilla or the awkwardness of feeling John's concern that prompted it? "I'll get my things later."

"It doesn't have to be like this. You can come back today or in a day or two, or we can talk again."

"Talk? About how your dating is going? Like good pals?" She was on the way upstairs, where her notebook and satchel were, her gun, her identity.

He was following her up. "Come on. I know you understand."

"I didn't see it coming." She grabbed her things. She couldn't visit the Washington family in her shorts. In the closet, she found the pants and jacket she'd worn yesterday. A tank. The day was stinko hot already. The tank would have to be acceptable when she was fainting and had to remove the jacket. "I have to change clothes," she explained. John looked away, then began a tiny pace of the small hallway outside the bedroom. There. Thirty seconds and she was more presentable. "I just need one more thing. I need to use your phone book."

"Sure. Sure. Of course." He let her pass him on the stairs; then he followed her downstairs and to the kitchen.

It was easy enough to find the address. There were several Washingtons, but the name Deon came back to her as she read through the list. The Washingtons lived at 967 Armandale. Colleen held a hand up to John, who looked as if he wanted to say something. She dialed Christie. "I have the parents' address."

"Can you handle it? I'd like to stay here with the girl. I could send Grafton with you if you need someone now. Or McGranahan in a little bit. You know what to do?"

"Break the news. Alert the mother or father to be ready to identify the body later at the morgue. Question them. Note everything down."

"Can you do it?"

"Yes."

Colleen was on her way to the front door, feeling like herself, a person who could do difficult things and do them quickly, while John stood, puzzled, in the dust she kicked up. "I'll be back in a couple of hours for the rest of my things," she said.

"Whenever. Anytime. So long as we talk. I don't want it to be ugly."

"Anytime" meant he didn't plan to bring the woman to his place, he'd go to hers. That was more than she wanted to know.

She was using her own car, an aging Accord. In it, she made her way up the hill to the brightly painted, sometimes derelict, houses of Armandale. The street was quiet except for a man with a shopping cart who was looking left and right with the practiced eye of a converter of junk to cash.

Colleen gave herself two seconds in the car to compose herself. Then she knocked at the door.

Deon Washington came to the door bare-chested, wearing boxers. The room behind him was sparsely furnished with a dilapidated couch and chair and a few tables. No carpet. A television. There were a few baby toys on the floor, but the place was not a mess and it was not dirty. Maybe the mother had stopped drinking. Colleen could hear a baby crying.

"What? What the hell?" He squinted, trying to remember who she was, why she looked familiar.

"Police." She showed her badge.

He put his hands up. "Whatever it is, I didn't do it."

"May I come in?"

"If you tell me what the hell this is about, come knocking on my door on a Sunday morning."

"It's about your daughter Jamilla."

He stopped dead. He shook his head. "She didn't do anything bad. I know that."

"May I come in?"

He opened the door. He smelled like alcohol gone sweaty; the house smelled of toast.

"If we could sit down for a moment."

He sat down, taking the sagging couch, a beige fabric couch with a green bedspread over it, tucked in fairly securely. He leaned forward with his elbows on his knees and his fingers laced, as if to show he was behaving. He was a handsome man, gorgeous still, even ravaged by alcohol. He kept his hair cropped short; his skin was a light café au lait, his eyes a brilliant green. And his body, as if defying what he did to it, was muscular and perfectly formed.

Colleen took the chair. She said carefully, "A child has been found in the park. We have reason to believe—"

His face registered the idea of the rest of the sentence. "No," he said. "No way. She's home." He looked behind him to the kitchen, as if his daughter might materialize. He looked upstairs, where the whimpering cries of the baby continued. "Still in bed, I guess."

Colleen's eyes closed for a second, a miniprayer. "I would be very happy to find that so. I once worked at the Family Counseling Center and—"

"That's it. I knew you looked familiar."

"I'm with the police now. There is a child in the park. I'm investigating. Could you show me to the bedroom?"

Anita Washington appeared at the top of the stairs in a threadbare kimono-style robe that she had to keep holding shut. She was beautiful, too, darker than her husband, with the distinct bone structure of a model's face. "What's going on?"

"We got to look at something," he told her.

"Who does? Who is this woman? What's going on?"

"This is the police. We got to look at something." His voice was cracking.

"Police? What for?"

Deon started up the stairs, motioning for Colleen to follow him. She addressed the mother as she approached her. "I'm trying to establish the whereabouts of your daughter Jamilla."

"Well, she must have left the fucking bedroom, else we wouldn't be hearing all this racket from the baby."

The mother was right, unfortunately. Jamilla was not in her room.

There was a boy asleep in the bottom of a bunk bed. He had a big bandage on his foot and two crutches in bed with him, his arm around one, as if it were a favorite toy. In the other corner of the small room was a crib with a baby standing in it, holding on to the railing, crying. The smell of a dirty diaper hung in the air. The room was otherwise fairly clean.

"When did you last see Jamilla?"

"Last night," Deon offered.

"What time did she go out?"

The parents looked at each other, puzzled. Colleen understood better than she wanted to. "Were you two out last night?"

"I work at night," Deon said, "and she wasn't out too long," he added, indicating his wife, but his wife was answering quickly at the same time. "I was just in bed most of the evening. I had a headache," she was saying. They paused, not untangling their excuses.

"What time did you see Jamilla? Please think carefully. This is important."

"What did she do?" Anita Washington asked, not caught up yet, not at all ready to guess, and definitely not wanting to know. In the pause that ensued, she looked to her husband for their story—who would blame whom for the problem, whatever it was. "Did you look in her room before you came to bed?" she asked him. She pulled the robe more tightly around her.

"I thought you did."

"What's this about?"

The boy in the bed stirred, but he didn't wake up. The baby wailed once loudly before her crying quieted a little, became more questioning.

"Could we talk back downstairs or at least move out to the hall?" Colleen asked. She fully expected one of the parents to lift up the baby, but they left the little girl crying and moved into the hall.

Where is she? Anita's face asked. And Colleen's face couldn't answer.

"Let me get some pants on." Washington went into the other bedroom.

His wife followed him in, asking, "What's going on?" But she was already crying.

"They found a body." Washington's voice came out low, slow, choked.

Colleen heard that distinctly. Then she heard Anita Washington's low groan, something like a hum, like music, and a repetition of the word *no.*

Deon said, "They found a kid in the park."

"Doing what?" she asked dumbly.

A silence answered: *Doing nothing. Nothing. Dead.*

"No!" Anita came into the hallway and faced Colleen. "It wasn't Jamilla. It wasn't. Couldn't be."

"We think it was."

She groaned again, that deep hum of a sound, like music, and the baby started crying again. "Think?" Anita called back to Deon, who emerged at that moment, startling his wife. "She said *think.* It might not be Jamilla."

He looked to Colleen.

"I knew her. I knew all of you a little at the Family Counseling Center. I suppose someone could look a lot like her. But, in that case, where is she?"

The humming sound again. It was eerie, and somehow beautiful. The baby kept crying.

"I'm very sorry for your loss. I want to do right by Jamilla. To do that, I need lists of her friends with phone numbers. I need a lot of information right now to help us solve this. Do you understand? Can you hold on long enough to help me solve this? I need to have all your family's movements for all day yesterday and last night. In a couple of hours, I'll need one of you to come down to the coroner's office with me to make an identification."

Deon nodded.

Maybe they did it, or one of them did, parents were often the killers, but the feeling Colleen had was that somebody hurt Jamilla precisely because her parents weren't paying attention.

The baby stopped crying now and looked to the hall, where Colleen stood. It took everything Colleen had not to go in, lift her up, change her diaper. The boy twitched and turned in the bed but still didn't fully wake up.

"We should go back downstairs, where we can talk. Do you have someone who can take care of the baby while we're talking?"

"No. Nobody. That was Jamilla's job." Anita looked around uncertainly. Her hands were shaking. "I should maybe feed her something while we talk."

"I understand."

Anita fetched her child, carried her in one arm. The baby looked floorward as if guilty of something. They all started downstairs. The heavy truth of what they were about to explore settled on them, settled in a silence as they moved. Anita held her daughter in the same way—on one hip—while she opened cabinets. "There isn't anything," she muttered. "Oh shit."

Colleen winced inside, kept an impassive face, and began writing. Christie urged them to fill up one or two legal pads in a morning—well, his handwriting was large, hers smaller, but still, she got down a lot of detail. She scribbled that the baby's diaper hadn't been changed and that there was no food in the house. You never knew what you would need in court.

Anita found a little cereal finally and, after giving up on finding milk, turned on the tap and wet the cereal down with water. She carried the bowl and spoon to the living room and kept her daughter on her lap. The baby made a face at the start, but after she got used to the taste, she ate eagerly.

Colleen looked at the legal pad in her hands. Then she addressed the mother. "When did you last see Jamilla?"

Anita touched her younger daughter's hair, smoothing it. "Six o'clock yesterday. Got home from work, took a shower."

"Where's work?"

Anita bit down some displeasure. "Making sandwiches."

"Where?"

"Peppi's, on Western." The baby reached for the cereal mixture with her hands and Anita let her, putting down the spoon on the small table in front of the couch.

"You didn't work the dinner hour?"

"Lunch hour."

"What time did you get off? At six?" The baby ate resignedly and studied Colleen. She was a gorgeous child and Colleen wanted to hold her.

"No. I got off at three. I spent some time with one of my girlfriends. She wanted to go out to Best Buy, so I went with her. She had a car."

"Can you give me her name, address, all that?" Colleen handed over a smaller notebook, one that she kept for these purposes. As Anita took the notebook awkwardly, her arms still around her daughter, Colleen noticed Deon didn't move to take over with his daughter. He stared into space. Colleen asked, "You came home exactly when?"

"Close to six. I didn't look at the clock when I came in." Anita cast her eyes down and kept them there.

"Did you call home when you were out?"

"Probably. Maybe."

"Do you remember calling?"

"No."

"And . . . and was Jamilla here when you came in?" When Colleen spoke Jamilla's name, the little girl came to attention. She twisted to look over her mother's shoulder toward the kitchen. Then she began to study Colleen.

"Yes. She was here. She was toasting bagels for the others."

"Did you talk to her?"

"Just this and that."

"Did she mention going out?"

Anita shook her head.

"Having anyone come over?"

Anita shook her head again.

But she did go out. The fact is, she was found outside. Colleen asked, "Was she rebelling? Giving you any trouble?"

Anita's lip trembled. "No, no, she was still good."

"She was the baby-sitter? For the others?"

"Yes. She took good care. She was very grown-up." The little girl twisted again and looked around, but she didn't try to say anything, made none of the little sounds a toddler usually made. How old? Two?

Colleen took the notebook from Jamilla's mother and turned to Deon, but she was aware that Anita had begun to rock back and forth and hug her child as one might hug a pillow. The little girl let out a small surprised sound every once in a while.

"I need a record of your movements for yesterday," Colleen told the father. "When you were here, when you saw her, everything. From the morning on."

He thought. "Went to check on my car. Sat with the guys at the shop some."

"What time was that?"

"Like nine in the morning."

Colleen handed over the notebook. "Where? Write it down. And who you talked to."

He took the notebook, telling her, "Way up on Federal," while she was asking, "You saw your daughter before you left?"

He stopped, untangled his answering rhythm, nodded. "She was up, sleepy, doing this and that. I don't remember what. Something in the kitchen."

"Did she say anything you can remember?"

"That she wanted to go shopping for food."

"And what did you say?"

"That I'd take her later."

"You set a time?"

"No. It slipped my mind."

"What hours did you sit around up at the car shop talking?"

He looked at the notebook and pen in his hands as if they were foreign and unfamiliar objects. "Ten to twelve or so. After we bullshitted, we watched some TV." He seemed to realize what his assignment was. "Say twelve to about one or a bit later, we watched the sports channel at a bar, Bucky's, not the bar I work at. We just watched. Then I came home for a bit and I took a nap, got up, went to work. Three o'clock yesterday."

"Where? Where is work?"

"I bartend over at Bigg's."

"Steady?"

"Yeah."

"Long hours," Anita said. "They put him there from like three in the afternoon until they close. It's long hours."

"And you were there last night?" she asked him.

"Yeah."

"Came home what time?"

"Maybe three-thirty. Could have been four."

"They don't close at two-thirty?"

"We usually squeak past a little."

"How much did you squeak last night?"

"Three. We stayed on some after I locked the door."

"Who?"

"Me and Anita."

"You were there? Working, too?"

"No, just keeping him company."

And drinking, Colleen knew all too well. Free booze for both of them, she guessed. "You allowed to drink on the job?" she asked Deon.

"One or two. Keep the customers happy. They buy drinks for me."

"I see. Make sure you write down the names and any contact for anyone who saw you during working hours."

"Lots of people."

"Get me some names. Did anybody besides your wife see you at closing time and after?"

"Sleepy Jones. This guy Sleepy Jones, we let him hang on because we give him a couple of quarters to sweep the floor. We kept the lights out so nobody else would think it was open."

"So you locked up? You have the key?"

Anita snorted.

Deon said levelly, "No, I lock up, then turn over the key to the owner's mailbox. Just up Atlanta. Slip it through the slot. He always wants it back."

Colleen nodded. So Deon worked for a bar owner who knew enough to be concerned about who had access to his place but was too lazy to be there himself. The man had to know the Washingtons could run to Keystone Plumbing before five o'clock any day to have a copy made—their own pass into the bar if they wanted. You put an alcoholic behind your bar, one who's married to an alcoholic, a part of you just doesn't want to know what's up. Probably have a few drinks yourself so you don't notice.

"Did you call, talk to Jamilla or your son in any of that work time?"

"No."

"Did you see her when you came home for a nap?"

"Yeah. She kept everyone quiet. She knew I needed to sleep. I can't sleep so good usually."

"Is your family still going to counseling over on Arch?" she asked.

"No, we quit that."

"How long ago?"

"Couple of years."

"Did you go back recently?"

"No," Anita said, while Deon said, "Once." He added, "We didn't need to go back after that once."

"I need for you to tell me about Jamilla. Everything you can think of. Who were her friends? Where did she go when she went out? Who did she spend time with? This is very important."

The Washingtons exchanged glances. They looked helpless.

"She went to the store for groceries. A lot."

"Where'd she tend to go?"

"Giant Eagle. Cedar."

"Did she ever go out at night for groceries?"

"Might have."

"You said there was no food in the house this morning. Might she have been going out to get something last night?" It made Colleen furious to think this child might have been killed for grocery money passing through the park. But if she got murdered last night, wouldn't the late walkers through the park have seen her long before morning? Was she out all night? Had she met someone she knew?

"I'm going to need to talk to your son. Will one of you go wake him?"

"I'll do it," Deon said. He sprang up, and once again Colleen saw the irony. He drank day and night, yet moved like a lithe, fit basketball player.

Anita watched him go up the stairs. She adjusted the child in her arms.

"She doesn't speak yet?"

"She's okay. Some kids just don't."

"What's her name?"

"Soleil is her name."

"Sun?"

"Yes."

"She's beautiful. Just beautiful."

Soleil squirmed and made a face that Colleen thought might be trying to say something about discomfort.

"If you want to change her, it's okay."

Anita nodded, sat her daughter on the couch, and went upstairs without noticing the little girl ended up half on, half off a throw pillow. Colleen concentrated on the sounds coming from above, to be sure the parents weren't pumping the boy with lines to say. She listened. The little girl tried to right herself to a better sitting position, then crawled off the sofa and came toward her. She came close up, unafraid, and touched Colleen's knee.

"Hi, Soleil. Here," Colleen said, and she reached out and lifted the toddler to her lap. She pressed her lips against the braided hair. "If only you could tell us," she murmured. "If only. If only."

Kameen, who looked to be nine or ten years old, came down the stairs, using a pair of crutches. He descended in front of his father, with his father both shooing him along and trying to help him, and his mother, carrying a diaper so triumphantly that Colleen felt sure it was the last one in the house. Kameen was a stunning boy, proportionate like his father. All those blessings, all those gifts . . .

"What's the matter?" Kameen asked.

"Sit down. You got to help us," Deon said. He took his daughter from Colleen's lap and put her down on the floor. The mother knelt to change the diaper. The boy sat himself on the sofa, looking around warily. Deon caught Colleen's eye. "We can't find Jamilla," he told his son. "We need for you to answer this lady's questions."

"Hi, Kameen. You do well on the crutches. What happened to your foot?"

"Knife fell."

"You were handling the knife? Or someone else was?"

"Me." He looked apologetic.

"You had it taken care of?" she asked all of them.

The parents nodded.

Kameen said, "Jamilla took me to the hospital. Couple days ago."

A little silence followed his words. The parents had not been there that day, either. Colleen made a note. "Where did Jamilla take you?"

"Allegheny."

"Emergency room?"

The boy nodded.

"Kameen. Tell me all about your sister yesterday or as far back as you want to go. We need to figure out where she went last night. Did she tell you?"

He shook his head. "Where is she?"

Colleen studied him. "How old are you?"

"Nine."

"Did she go out at night often?"

"No. I don't think. I never saw her go out, except maybe to Giant Eagle."

"What time did you go to bed?"

"Like maybe eleven or midnight."

"Midnight. That's pretty late. Do you always go to bed that time?"

He shrugged.

"She was here or not?"

"Here."

"And you don't have any idea who she would meet at midnight?"

The boy shook his head.

"Who called her? What phone calls did she take?"

Something. He hesitated. "You mean like her friends?"

"Who are they?"

"Malika Johnson. Jessa Jamal. That's about it."

"Only girlfriends? How about boys? Any boys call?"

"Nope."

"None at all?"

The hesitation again.

"Tell me. Someone else is in the picture. Even if she didn't tell you, I can tell you're smart. Somebody called her."

"Some guy."

"Who?"

"Just some guy."

"Okay. Any idea who he is?"

"No."

"A boy from school?"

"No."

"How do you know?"

"Too old. He was older."

Anita looked about to protest. Colleen put up a hand to silence her. "How did you know he was older?"

"Could just tell."

"His voice?"

"Yeah."

"What, you answered the phone?"

"Once he thought I was her," the boy said disgustedly.

"What did he say?"

"Just something about did she remember."

"Remember what?"

"To get something or . . . maybe to sign something."

Even Anita and Deon looked surprised at this. Sign something. What would a child need to sign? "You ever see him? This guy?"

"Nope."

"But you never saw her go out at night?"

"Nope."

"Okay, Kameen. The fact that you knew about the phone calls is very helpful. You're doing well. Did this person call often?"

He shook his head.

"I need to hear everything she did yesterday. You were here with her?"

"Yeah. She got me breakfast, helped me prop my leg up. She cleaned house. Malika came over, brought bagels. We ate bagels." He thought some more. "She was sick."

"Who was sick?"

"Jamilla. She was throwing up."

Colleen looked to the parents. "Did you know she was sick?"

They each said no. Colleen watched them. Something about Jamilla's illness caught them off guard or allowed in the sadness. Their movements became slower, *nicer,* the way Anita lifted her daughter from the floor, Soleil putting her head down as if to sleep on her mother's shoulder, Deon sitting beside his son, a hand on his knee.

"You know why she was sick?"

Kameen shook his head.

Colleen thought of two possibilities. She didn't like either of them. To solve the one, she wanted to get some food in this house. She made a note to call the Lutheran church.

"Where does Malika live?" she asked. As she got this information, there was a knock at the door. It was McGranahan, come to spend the rest of the eighteen-hour day with Colleen, following up leads. Colleen was sure he was going to say Christie had switched and made McGranahan second on the case, since he had been on the Homicide squad for fifteen years or so. But as she and McGranahan spoke quietly at the door, he said with a shade of bitterness, "How's it going? Tell me what you need from me."

She kept her speech to a low murmur. "We'll have to talk to the people the Washingtons say can account for them. And to the child's friends. We have to search her room first."

"And the rest of the house. Right? You know that?"

"Right. And the rest of the house." She needed to make sure she *said* everything.

She guessed the house search would take very little time. The place was spare.

McGranahan introduced himself and offered his hand in sympathy to the parents before Colleen could stop him. It was a mistake any number of detectives might have made—but it was horrible. With McGranahan's handshake and Deon's hesitation in taking the hand, there was a clear moment in which the boy saw and understood that Jamilla was not lost, not simply missing, but dead. Kameen yelled, "What is he saying? Dad? What's going on?"

Their worried faces told him. He scowled, or tried to, but he couldn't hold it. Soleil started crying when he did. "Jamilla," the little girl said. The sound was distorted, mumbled, but Colleen got it.

She went to Kameen and knelt in front of him. "I'm here to help," she said. "I'm on your side. I'm going to find out what happened. I promise."

Then she and McGranahan moved aside to confer. "I'm sorry I jumped the gun with the boy," he said edgily.

"The word was going to come sooner or later."

"Who made the ID?"

"I did. Not official, of course." If only she could be wrong. If only Jamilla could have been out with a boyfriend and this could turn out to be a mistake, some other kid in the park.

"Who do you want to come down to the coroner's office to make the official one?" McGranahan asked her.

"The father."

McGranahan nodded. "You looked at her room yet at all?"

"The boy was sleeping."

Colleen explained to Deon that she and her partner would need to do a search of the premises. And that in a couple of hours they would need him down at the coroner's office.

The search of the house took an hour. The detectives gathered pieces of paper, magazines, and wrote down phone numbers they found in the kitchen. But there was not a lot to see. Little clothing in the cupboards, three kids' beds in one room, no food except for one bagel in the kitchen, and only enough sitting places in the living room to watch the television.

Any money they had was burned up in alcohol. Yet it wasn't the whole story. Father and mother loved each other, it looked like. Deon loved Anita anyway.

Just one tiny ribbon of thought, just a trace of a ribbon, reminding her she was single again, went through Colleen's mind as she and McGranahan got into his car to go talk to Jamilla's friends. There'd be plenty of time for self-pity later.

MALIKA LIVED A COUPLE OF streets over. From the three mailboxes on the porch, the residence appeared to be a first-floor apartment in a converted house. Malika's mother, a large woman still wet from a shower, came to the door, tying a robe around herself. She moved with the burden of weight.

"Mrs. Johnson. Detective Greer. Detective McGranahan. Police. May we come in and talk?"

Malika Johnson's mother said she was getting ready to go to church.

Colleen explained their mission.

The woman clapped a hand over her mouth and stood frozen for a long time. "That little girl?"

"Yes."

"That fine little girl? Who done it?"

"We're going to find out. That's why we need to talk to your daughter, Mrs. Johnson. If you would allow us, we would prefer to break the news."

Malika had to be wakened. Moments later, the mother, looking terrified, came from a back room with her daughter in tow. The girl was slightly pudgy, pleasant-looking, with hair braided like Jamilla's, but a much shorter version, only to below her ears.

"Here she is," Mrs. Johnson said. She sat her daughter down and then sat next to her, an arm around her shoulder.

"Mom. What is it? Mom? What's the matter?"

Colleen began. "Malika. Your friend Jamilla has been hurt."

"Oh no."

"We are here to find out who hurt her. Will you help us? We need for you to tell us everything you can about her, her other acquaintances, anything that could help us. Please."

"But . . . how is she hurt? Like, what kind of hurt?"

"She was found this morning. In the park."

Colleen waited until Malika's mind could let in the truth.

"You mean—"

Colleen waited.

"You mean . . . dead?"

"Do you know anything that would help us explain that?

"Mom? What are they saying?"

"You know what they're saying. It's bad. Real bad news, honey, but you go ahead, answer everything. We'll talk later."

"Mom?"

"You answer the lady."

There was order here. This apartment was clean. Colleen guessed there was food in the house, lots more than a single bagel. "You visited Jamilla yesterday. You took bagels, is that right?"

"My mom said to take them over there. They never have enough food."

Mrs. Johnson made an angry, judgmental face. "I don't know what's with those people."

"You know the kids go hungry?"

"She tells me. I get an extra something, say from the church when I clean, I send it over."

"Very good of you," Colleen said. And the truth was, she was not sure what else this woman could have accomplished successfully. Calling the authorities usually came to nothing and made enemies of those who tried to help. She focused on Malika. "What did the two of you do yesterday when you visited? Specifically, did Jamilla tell you any plans she had? To go out? To meet someone?"

"No. Nothing about plans."

"What'd you talk about?"

"Nothing much. Cleaning house. She was sick."

"Her brother said she was throwing up. Right?"

"Yeah. She wanted a bagel real bad, but she couldn't keep it down. She likes when they have stuff in them, like raisins and stuff."

"Was something bothering her? Do you think the sickness was because she was upset about something?"

"Don't know."

"If you do know, it's important to tell us."

"Don't know."

"Did she have a boyfriend?"

Malika frowned. "Noooo. I mean boys liked her. But she would always brush them off."

Colleen said carefully, "We think she did have someone. We think she went out to meet someone who called her."

"Get out. No way. I would have known. She wouldn't keep it secret."

"Did she ever talk about being friends with a guy who was older?"

"You mean in high school?"

"Or older maybe."

"Ew. No." Malika appeared truly puzzled. "I think . . . there's no way. She would have told me. I would have talked her down from it." She let her mother pat her shoulder approvingly. "But I knew everything and . . ."

"Why did you hesitate just now? You thought of something."

"Cuz I was teasing her. About being pregnant. When she kept throwing up."

"Oh Lord," Malika's mother said. "Oh Lord."

Colleen said levelly, "Maybe she was."

"No. She would have talked to me."

"If she needed to talk to someone, I'm surprised it wasn't you. You sound like a good friend." Colleen moved far forward on the chessboard, risking everything. "Do you think she got help from counseling? I mean, she was going to the Family Counseling Center on Arch, wasn't she?"

"I don't know."

"What don't you know?"

"If they helped her. It was a long time ago."

"Not lately?"

"No."

"You're sure she didn't have appointments?" The girl shook her head. "You ever hear of her having to sign in anywhere?"

"No. Well, maybe back in fifth grade."

Colleen held her breath. "Where did she go to sign in?"

"Police station, I think."

"Police?"

"To say her parents were doing okay."

"Sure it wasn't the Counseling Center?"

"I don't think."

"When was it?"

"I don't know. Different times."

"Can you remember anything more?"

"Nuh-uh," Malika said sadly.

McGranahan's face showed he was scrambling to catch up to what was going on, but Colleen put out a hand to silence him.

When they left the Johnson place, he started up the car and asked evenly, but so evenly there was challenge in it, "You're going after Hoffman hard because he knew both victims?"

"It's a weird link, you have to admit. Fifth grade was three years ago.

I'll want to know if Jamilla had anything to do with the place lately. We have to find out about these appointments."

"You got a way?"

"Sometime today, I'm going to want to see Mindy Cooper again, the secretary at Family Counseling. Right now, I'm thinking more of Jamilla's friends. And checking the father's alibi."

"Hmm." McGranahan read the notebook on her lap. "Jessa Jamal. Emmet Speidman." He pronounced the names as if they were odd choices, some mistake she was making.

She didn't care about McGranahan's approval. She wanted Christie's. She pulled out her cell and called him.

TO SOMEONE WHO DIDN'T know how Christie worked, he might have appeared only to be looking sadly at the body of the murdered girl. But he was thinking, taking in his surroundings, looking at city streets, park, park lanes, apartment buildings, sidewalks, some unpaved paths. He was getting the lay of the land, trying to psych out who might have moved along these ways last night and who might have seen that person move.

Early on, he called the National Weather Service, where he'd made friends with the men who worked there. He had contacts everywhere. Needed friends in high, medium, and low places.

The guy at the weather service told him the weather would be humid but there should be no rain all day and no wind. This was good. It meant the mobile unit and the county people would have time to process the crime scene without having to rush things.

While he listened to his personal weather report, he looked at Jamilla's shoes. An inexpensive ballet slipper kind of thing, sad somehow in its delicacy.

He had twenty-five detectives altogether and thought yesterday that they'd all be working on the McCall case, then, this morning, that he'd have to release some for the Homestead murder; now everything was scrambled again with the third and most compelling of the cases.

He called the commander of the Robbery squad and filched two more men, making a case he didn't really believe for his two murders being motivated by robbery. But who knew? It could turn out to be true. Stranger things had happened. After a moment's thought, he dialed Bill Preekie, Chief of Police in Wilkinsburg. Man owed him at least three favors. "Sunday morning, can't be good," Preekie said. But he listened to Christie's argument and released two of his men. So he'd plumped up the squad by four.

All the while, he studied the body in the park. Next to it now was the large plastic bag that had been over her. The other was still under her. Nothing natural about that. Was the someone who killed her protecting her body or his? Trying to avoid getting fibers on her? Trying to make her look like a homeless person?

The position of the body suggested the murder had not happened here in the park. So. The girl was brought here, but how? Under cover of night, yes. Carried? Probably not. Car, yes. The killer parked on the other side of the bushes and then dragged the girl or carried her a couple of feet to this spot. That suggested familiarity. He stooped to examine the ground, aware that behind him a gaggle of people watched as if he were the television or, as Marina, his wife, would have it, the man onstage, a live theatrical event.

He hunkered down, reading the ground. The girl was dragged, he guessed, from the bricked car lane to the bushes. Maybe someone somewhere saw the car that brought the body.

Christie would ask Greer to keep running in the park to see if she could come up with any lead he was missing. Routine often unearthed what scrutiny didn't.

His phone rang. Colleen Greer.

"Catch me up," he said.

She told him everything that had happened so far. She read off the list of people she and McGranahan would continue to see. "I got hold of Mindy Cooper. I can see her this afternoon."

"Sounds good. The girl's father? You had a substantial talk with him?"

"Yes, I did. We still have to check his alibi. Anything is possible."

"Your opinion?"

"No. Not him."

"Keep going. Open mind."

Christie hung up and stood in the growing heat of the day, trying to think. He didn't feel as brisk as Greer sounded, but he tried to summon his best concentration. The fact that the body was not all that far from the Family Counseling Center and that the child had at one point gone to the Center was simply strange and it pointed to Hoffman again, but his brain rebelled. It was too easy—as if someone were trying to frame the guy, though that made no particular sense. So. Healthy skepticism.

Dolan arrived and stood beside him. "Shit."

His expletive substituted for a whole paragraph about youth, beauty, and race.

Day one of the Washington case and the Homestead case, day three of the McCall case. They were already in that altered state people got from jet lag or college finals—being wired, focused, sharp-minded, and hazy all at the same time. Quit sleeping, eat badly, drink too much coffee, you, too, could get high.

"How old?"

"Thirteen, we think."

Dolan pointed to the ground. "That looks like one good shoe print."

"It is. One good one." Some kind of sport shoe, large enough to be a man's, had pressed into the dirt near the body.

"You want me to go find the family?"

"Greer is partnering me on this one."

"Oh." Dolan frowned. "Oh."

"She's already seen the family. And some of the girl's friends."

Dolan scratched his forehead. He'd thought he was plenty early. And he liked this case better than the one he'd started on.

"She was here and you were waking up McCall's neighbors."

"Ninety minutes of nothing useful," Dolan said, miffed. "Where's your boy Darnell?" Dolan looked around for the kid who'd attached himself to Christie. Darnell Flowers lived in the neighborhood. "I thought for sure he'd be sniffing around."

"I could have found some use for him on this one. But I got him into a precollege summer program. He's not around."

Christie was doing some quick switching. If anyone could grill a witness on the racially mixed North Side, Dolan could, and this case was still fresh. And Dolan wanted it. "I could sure use you here for the morning, maybe for the day. Talk to these people in the park. Hit this neighborhood for us. And see if anybody remembers a car parking here in the middle of the night. The body was dragged and placed here."

Dolan brightened. "Shame that shoe print isn't distinctive-looking," he said as he took a few steps back to head for the gawkers. "Everybody's got treads." Several times in the past, they'd resorted to visiting one shoe store after another, trying to make a match. Talk about a haystack.

"Still, we'll print it."

"Got to." Dolan moved off.

Potocki pulled up next. He came walking across the park, hands in the pockets of his slouch, "relaxed," sport jacket. He smelled like coffee, like fruit. He looked at the body without saying anything.

"I need for you to go over to Zone One. Read all reports of assaults, attempted rapes, that kind of thing in the park."

"Six weeks?"

"Start with six weeks. Call me when you see what there is."

Potocki kept looking at the body. "She's a little kid."

"Practically."

The next call he got was from Headquarters. Janet Littlefield had come into the office. She had a bad summer cold, so bad he couldn't understand what she was saying when she tried to explain the almost absence of her voice. "You sound terrible," he said to Littlefield. "You need to go home, or can you manage to do some desk work?"

"Boss, I'm here. I got my pills with me. I'm taking lots of pills. I'll be okay. Just if I can breathe some."

"You go home when you need to."

Littlefield always teased him that he was like a papa to the rest of them. That's what people needed, she said, definitely what they wanted: mama and papa.

Well, he must have been born with the inclination to play papa, because it goes way back. He can remember being in that role with other kids when he was—what, five, six? It definitely kicked in when his father left his mother and he, just a preadolescent, took care of her. Oh, she was okay with the washing and ironing and getting food on the table. But emotionally, he took care of her. An only child was a strange beast. All that while, he wanted his father back, wanted *a* father, and his mother wasn't providing one, so he had simply become him, or acted the part, even when he secretly felt light-headed, vague, boyish, confused, not wanting to be in charge.

The mobile crime unit arrived next. The photographer yawned as he pulled out the digital camera and blinked at it, reading the screen. "You okay?" Christie asked. "You get any breakfast?"

Just take care of people and they assume you've got it together.

COLLEEN AND MCGRANAHAN descended the steps of yet another shabby house that held a teenager who had known Jamilla. They'd talked to the boy, a slightly heavyset white kid, a self-proclaimed computer geek, who, according to Jessa Jamal, had a crush on Jamilla.

The kid had been jealous enough to notice who Jamilla talked to. He gave a list of other boys he thought liked her. But nothing in his interview had rung alarm bells for her. The poor kid had frozen with incomprehension when Colleen told him why she was there.

McGranahan thought she'd been too easy on the kid. They got into his car, with him at the wheel, tapping at it restlessly. She thought, McGranahan is one of those thin guys, always hungry, always nervous, sure something has passed him by. "I want to have a crack at all the guys her age," he said.

"Absolutely. You'd be good at that. You can talk to the other boys this afternoon when I see Mindy Cooper," she offered. She was madly writing notes. There was a lot to record. The minister at the Lutheran church had promised to get food over to the Washington house by afternoon. Good guy.

His fingers rapped at the steering wheel. After a moment, he said, "I have a niece. God, is she a sexpot. I'm always afraid my daughter will idolize her and I'm telling you, these kids go around asking for it."

"They don't know what they're asking," Colleen said quietly. "And it's not to be murdered."

"Well, right. Of course. I forget to be PC sometimes."

Talk PC, he meant. Being went deeper.

"All I mean is, hey, I saw the pictures. She was pretty."

"Yeah."

Now he drove up Federal to find the body shop where Deon supposedly hung out. They left behind crowded inner-city hot dog shops, and not two minutes later they found themselves on a weedy, rutted, brambled, rural-looking road. Pittsburgh always amazed Colleen. Secret places. Bits of country in the middle of the city.

"I need to get some lunch," McGranahan said. "My stomach is chewing on itself."

"I'm hungry, too. How about after we talk to these guys Deon mentioned."

"Guys? Plural?"

"Might as well get it done. What do you want for lunch?"

"Anything. McD's is okay."

She shrugged. "McD's. Make it fast anyway." To distract him from his hunger, she asked, "How old is your daughter?"

"Twelve. Thirteen is the worst age, they say. I'm not looking forward."

"It's rough. It's a rough one." Thirteen was how old she'd been when she was assaulted. Aloud, she said, "Thirteen is that age that confuses the mind—"

"Whose mind? The kid's, you mean?"

"Everybody's, really. Sexual or not? Still a child or not?"

McGranahan made three faces in a row. "It didn't used to be like this. In olden times."

"Well, it kind of did. People got married very young. You know *Romeo and Juliet?*"

McGranahan shot her a look that said, *The play?* "Spare me. I'd say it has more to do with Britney Spears."

"There's the shop," she blurted, but too late. You could hardly see it behind so many overgrown bushes. They'd passed it and would have to find a place to turn around. She picked up the thread of her conversation and said firmly, "Therapists see thirteen as the borderline age. It's the question-mark time. It's dangerous."

"I'm going to keep my daughter in the house."

She nodded. He'd find out soon enough that that was impossible.

"Were you rebellious?"

"No."

"No?" He seemed distinctly disappointed.

She smiled at McGranahan. "I was kind of good and kind of dopey."

Her own secret—she's told it four or five times now, but it still rides around with her like a passenger in the backseat of the car—a week in which she grew up. At thirteen.

They parked on the narrow road and went into the body shop.

Emmet Speidman corroborated all Deon Washington had said about sitting around yesterday and he told them where Billy Vandergrift lived. They got back into the car and drove to Vandergrift's house. When Billy came to the door, he dittoed everything they had heard and he took them down the street to Bucky's Bar, where Frank Ferucci corroborated the previous two reports.

"Get me a bag of pretzels, peanuts, anything," McGranahan told Frank Ferucci. He offered no money. The man handed him two beef jerkies, which he tore into right away, before they even got to his car. Colleen got into the passenger seat and continued writing her notes. So far, Deon was not proving to be a liar. They still had to work on the Bigg's Bar alibi and they had to check out Anita's work schedule and her friend Bettina Butts, but so far, Butts wasn't answering her phone.

"Now we have to go get lunch," McGranahan told Colleen. "It's allowed, honestly."

She dialed up Christie, who preempted her by saying, "Get something to eat and meet back at Headquarters for a squad meeting. Twenty, twenty-five minutes."

"I need to get my car," she reminded McGranahan.

He returned her to the street where her car was parked in front of the Washingtons' house. When he left her off and turned the corner, going for his lunch, she drove her car to John's place. She parked, expecting

John to come to the window. Didn't he sense her presence? But he didn't show at the window or the door.

She dialed his number. No answer. Reaching into her bag for the key, she made a decision. Three minutes, tops. Clothes, makeup, lotions and potions, hair dryer.

"Hello," she called out, entering the house.

She smelled food. Something recently cooked. He'd eaten in, lunch, after the big breakfast.

The silence in the house caught her up with sadness. He might have the usual number of faults. All right, he did. But he was a regular Joe when it came to appetites, food and in the bedroom, and in the latter arena, he was gentle and considerate.

She could hear the kitchen clock ticking. She *detected* his meal. He'd eaten a tortilla with some leftover chicken in it, Mexican seasoning added, cheese. Nice. Better than what she was about to order. She wrote him a note saying she had come for her things. She grabbed a large black trash bag.

Now, this bag was deep black. Different from the one in the park, which had a sort of charcoal coloration. There must be thousands of manufacturers, types, brands. The bag was going to be important.

Hair dryer, bits and pieces of makeup, two drawers of clothing—everything went into the black bag.

She removed his key from her key ring and plunked it on the kitchen table. Then she left.

Pop of the trunk. Garbage bag flung in. Like a hobo, like a tramp, like one of the people in the park, necessaries in a plastic bag.

Once she was in her car and moving, she used her cell to check her home machine. When the series of beeps told her she had a call, she thought with an odd mixture of both joy and disappointment (she couldn't explain the disappointment) that it would be John, rethinking his stance. It took her a moment to come to the realization that the voice was David Hoffman's.

"I was hoping we could talk. I . . . really need a friend. Is it possible? Can you spare me some time? Meet for coffee or a meal?"

Her breath caught.

A thrill of both fear and hope went through her. Did he know they'd found Jamilla? Did he want to confess? Did he know something?

Her hands were trembling as she called Christie to report this newest development. She could hear children's voices in the background. "I popped home. Marina made me a lunch to go," he said apologetically. "Let's talk at the meeting. We'll take him up on it. I'm on my way. I'm in my car. Ten minutes."

Ten minutes to get something to eat and get herself to Headquarters.

NINE

HIS TV IS ON, AS USUAL. DRONing at a low volume. He uses it as a heartbeat, like the clock in the puppy's basket, comfort. He has been crying, off and on, ever since he made the identification at the coroner's office. His own lawyer has called him twice. Everybody's getting in on the act, apparently. Even the boyfriend thinks it's his call to make funeral plans. The lawyer has told him they can be heard in court on Tuesday or Wednesday and has assured him the judge will decide in his favor. There are laws. He's still the husband of record. End of the argument.

But it's Sunday. That's a long time to wait. Meanwhile, he's shut out, suspected, hated.

His television has been on since yesterday and some of the time, with a commentator murmuring about golf in one of those nice whispering voices, he managed to sleep on the sofa. The phone rang a few times. He let the machine pick up. Once it was a wrong number; once it was a funeral home he knew nothing about calling to offer its goods. He did not get the call he wanted.

No calls came from sympathizers. People were afraid of him because the case was still wide open, and what could they say? "Did you do it?" The silence made him feel lonelier than ever.

He ate a bowl of pasta around eight in the evening yesterday, then let baseball coverage at a very low volume put him to sleep again. It wasn't as soothing as the golf had been, but it did the trick. He found cake in the freezer at eleven at night, zapped it, ate it, and sat up, high on sugar, for a while. He read E-mails from Laura, thinking there was an answer to her death in there somewhere, but one message after another told him nothing, and he got sleepy again.

He dozed alternately and watched movies into the night. Around five he fell asleep for two hours. Now he's been fixed in front of the TV for a whole day, waiting for something to happen. Everything is on hold. He's afraid to move. He's almost afraid to talk to anyone, Greer included, but he called her, and if she calls back, he'll try to see her.

His life should not have ended up like this. He was not the worst. Not at all. He had the good qualities all his life that came with being a nervous workaholic—high grades in school, several degrees, a well-run office, a good rate of success with clients, fiscal responsibility at work and at home. Everybody preferred hearty sanguine types, but fate had burdened him with a nervous disposition and even in this day of medical miracles, you couldn't buy yourself a personality transplant.

In his heart, he is still sometimes that boy who couldn't do anything right outside of school. Nine, ten years old. Then eleven. Scared all the time. Wanting so badly to fit. Sensing that he didn't, the way Charlie looked at him, disappointed.

There were older boys he tried to hang around with, hoping they would lend him some of their bravado. They were thirteen, fourteen, smoking and laughing, talking sex all the time. Why they let him hang around with them, he never knew. They indulged him, so he wasn't about to reject them.

"You want to know stuff, don't you?" one of them asked him one day. "About girls? Fucking? Balling?"

He shrugged.

"Come with us tonight. We got us a hot one. Does it for money. Might as well learn your stuff, right?"

He was curious. His mother didn't notice him these days because she had Charlie in her life now and it made her happier when David was out of the house. Charlie and his mother kept having sex when they imagined he wasn't listening in (which he always was if he was in the house). So he started spending more time away.

The girl was older, maybe fifteen. She stood with one hip way out. He can picture her still, standing in the woods as if she were in her own living room, sipping from a small square bottle of booze, holding a blanket, asking them for money. Funny thing was, she was healthy-looking—very ruddy skin, rich hair hanging loose, rounded body. She wore a classic gauze Indian shirt and jeans and moccasins. She looked like everybody else her age, except better. "Ten bucks each," she said. For some reason, she kept looking at David. "You, too," she said.

He hadn't brought money. He really didn't want to.

The boys had their own bottle of booze. Theirs was large and rounded. They told David to drink some, too, and when he did, he choked and got dizzy. Mostly, he was looking for a time he could slip away from them. But one of the guys grabbed him and told him his job was to hold the girl down.

"Hey," she said. "Oh no you don't. Nobody holds me down."

And he didn't want to, but everything happened so fast. One of the boys hit him for trying to walk away. The two others got rough with the girl, pushing her to the ground. "Hold her," the first boy said, flinging him toward her.

He didn't want to, but he didn't want to be hit again. I need to get out of this, he thought. He pretended to hold down her shoulders. He didn't press very hard.

One of the boys was pulling off her jeans and she was thrashing, trying to kick the guy in the crotch, which only made him madder. The guy said, "What the—"

David let go of her shoulders. "Run," he said. Her jeans were only half up. She got up and started to run, grabbed the whiskey bottle and threw it at the other boy, who was coming at her. Got him right in the head. The girl ran, and David did, too. They didn't run together, but streaked through the woods, aware of each other.

The older boys let them go. They could have caught up if they'd wanted.

Next day at school, David got beaten up. Next day, the same.

Charlie asked him why. He had imagined all kinds of lies, but Charlie was too smart to lie to, so he gave up and told the whole truth. Charlie asked for the boys' names and where they lived. He wanted the girl's name, too. David's mother looked nervous when Charlie left the house after supper.

The boys never beat David again. The girl always looked at him with a measure of nervousness and alarm. He couldn't figure out what Charlie had said to them or why he felt both protected and doubly nervous after Charlie got involved. Later, when he knew more, he came up with imaginary scenarios. But the real answers, what happened in those conversations, he never knew.

"DON'T FORGET TO DRINK water," Marina had said, handing him a large bottle of it. "It's good for the brainworks."

He grunted. "I need gallons."

Then he drove fast, too fast, to Headquarters.

He'd indulged himself in two things his men might scoff at. Church and family. He'd stopped at St. Peter's for three minutes, sat in a pew while a man with muttonchops swept the floor. He sent up a quick prayer that he would do everything right on the case and not get himself entangled with Colleen Greer. Then he sped to his house where he hugged Eric and got the usual resistance that came with puberty, lifted Julie and wondered how much longer he would be able to hoist her, and grabbed the bag lunch Marina had made him. It sat on the passenger seat beside him.

So. Hoffman wanted to talk to Greer. There was some odd puzzle to be solved about Hoffman. He opened his water and drank a third of it, urging his brain to work the puzzle.

HOFFMAN SWITCHES THE CHANnel again. Tennis. Okay, anything that isn't news. Saturday night and again early, very early, on Sunday morning, the networks repeated the clip of him at Laura's house talking to detectives. To hear his name spoken each time was horrible. So, sports, movies, shopping channels if necessary.

He looks at his watch. It is early in the afternoon. He calls his lawyer and is assured again all will be taken care of, all will be well. Somewhere, Laura is being embalmed, stored. He shivers. He notches up the volume of the TV, waiting for his phone to ring.

Pull yourself together, man. Get a shower at least. He knows the signs of severe depression, knows that taking a first step toward normalcy can help. He listens for the phone, hoping.

TEN

IN THE CONFERENCE ROOM—too small for twenty men—the detectives were passing around pictures of the latest crime scene and of Jamilla; virtually all of them were eating. Christie went to the blackboard. While he drew a diagram, he took a bite of his thick sandwich. It was good. Marina had done it up with mayo, lettuce, tomato, and plenty of meat.

Across the room, Colleen stood in the corner, eating what looked like a fast-food chicken sandwich while she studied a legal pad and notebook. She looked up, caught his eye, put down her lunch, squeezed past people to come over to him.

"Talked to your Wichita man," he said while she punched a few buttons on her cell phone, listened, and handed it over. "He agrees with you that Jamilla might have been a victim of abuse. He described her as the kind of person who always managed to please everyone."

"Yep." Colleen sighed. "That was Jamilla."

Christie listened to the message and handed the phone back to her. "We're going to go for it."

"Fine."

"Let me catch everybody up quickly first. Then we need to meet the girl's father at the coroner's office. After this meeting. You and me."

"I have Washington on call for that. I gave him every reason under the sun for the delay. Or else he would have bolted to the park."

"Good. Well, finish up your lunch. We'll make this speedy." He took a couple of quick bites of his sandwich, swallowed, then shouted, "Okay, everybody. Eat while we talk. Attention this way. Let's get started."

A couple of chairs got scraped around.

"This meeting is about the two cases where we have a puzzle. We have good information that the killer in the Homestead case is holing up in McKeesport, so McKeesport police are looking and I've released two of our men to continue on that. The rest of us are on either McCall or Washington. Welcome two from the Robbery squad and two from Wilkinsburg who were lent to us. Go ahead, introduce yourselves."

Greco and Drzleski from Robbery identified themselves, stood, said their names; Peterson and de Fillippo from Wilkinsburg followed with theirs. Christie slugged another drink of water to hammer their names into his crowded brain.

"Last case first." He drew quickly on the blackboard, finishing a ground plan of the park. His drawings were always primitive and they were always going to be that way—he had no talent in the visual arts.

While he drew the Aviary and some public buildings, he said, "Greer was first on the scene after me. She was having breakfast two blocks away and she got there right away. So she's partnering me on this one." There, established—why he chose her.

He made a list on the left side of the board: *Victim's family, park workers, boys her age, a stranger.*

"You've seen photos of the body. We happened to notice the plastic bags around the girl's body look a lot like the ones the Park Service is using. Size is the same, weight of the plastic felt the same, and both have this kind of gray-black look. So Forensics has agreed to study them. We're hoping for something on that right away. In case."

"Are there clean bags kept under the dirty ones in the garbage cans? Like in hotels?" Coleson asked, meaning anyone could access them.

Coleson was a scrubbed-up guy and reliable on subjects to do with cleanliness. He had overcorrected good posture—he curved the other way, shoulders and backside aiming for each other. Even now, he was folding his sandwich wrapper to get rid of the wrinkles. Chubby good boy in school.

"No. The Park Service doesn't do that *generally.* But you never know where the bags might end up. I mean, the park workers might leave a truck sitting any one day, go on a break. People will take any damn thing. Well, anyway, we know the lab can get very specific with the bags. There are ream marks from the rollers when they're made. They can be matched—lot number, that kind of thing. So we'll be able to find out if they were Park Service bags, and lot numbers could tell us roughly *when* they were taken, and that might suggest roughly *where.*"

"Lab has time for this?" Dolan asked impishly.

"Well, no."

"Used your charm again."

"I think it might be wearing thin," Christie said. "So, help me theorize about the general story here. What ideas?" he asked.

"The girl had a boyfriend who worked for the county? Met him in the park, you know. Last night, things go badly. Guy loses his temper." It was one of the Wilkinsburg men answering. Greco. Yes. No. Peterson.

Christie paused. "Maybe. Good. Do those bags look like forethought?"

Colleen raised a hand gently. "Something not completely hasty in that part of it."

He grabbed another bite of his sandwich. "So. How do you all profile this killer?"

"Organized. Not premeditated," they answered, most of them with their mouths full. Some said, "Black, male." Most others said "White, male." Some thought young; some thought old.

Christie scratched his head, thinking, listening. He heard Greer say quietly, "Organized and disorganized. Older male."

"Tell them what the girl's brother said," he ordered Colleen.

"Jamilla's brother thinks some of the phone calls she got were from an older man. And one of her friends talked about her needing to go sign in someplace to establish her family was okay, years ago this was, but the girl thought Jamilla signed in with the police."

"That's interesting," Potocki said. "Isn't it? A little kid's notion that we police families?" He waved a hand in apology that he'd interrupted, went back, without enthusiasm, to a pile of fries on his lap.

"Does the boy, the brother, know more than he's saying?" Coleson asked, addressing McGranahan instead of Colleen. No matter what private squabbles Coleson and McGranahan had, they were going to buddy up against the rookie.

McGranahan responded quickly, "Maybe."

"We're going to have to go back to the boy," Greer said. There was a silence. "He's a shy kid. We'll try again. Maybe today, when we get the father to go to the coroner's office."

"Don't forget boys Jamilla's age," McGranahan piped up. "I'm doing that population this afternoon. Can't ignore that possibility."

Christie said, "Right. So." He pointed to the board. "The victim's family. The Park Service. Boys her age." He tapped his head, added the word *neighbors* to his list. "We've got Gibson and Leroy canvassing in Washington's neighborhood. What?" he asked.

Gibson and Leroy were women. Leroy volunteered, "So far, nobody sees the parents as violent, but they do see them as neglectful."

"And they all knew Jamilla," Gibson said. "Liked her."

"The father is a bartender," McGranahan added. "Alcoholic."

Colleen said quickly, "He's . . . yes, he's an alcoholic, but so far everything he said checks out. We still have his late-night alibi to do."

Christie said, "Sounds good. Detective Greer and I will go to the school tomorrow morning—some of the admin people work in summer—see who knows what about the kids. We're hoping to get into the Park Service *tonight.* I'm not going to wait to find out if the lab thinks those bags are theirs. I think they are and I want to see what I can see."

The detectives nodded, took notes.

"Now, one thing I held back so as not to prejudice you. I need your thinking on this. It's important. Okay. Here it is. We're working two cases, McCall and Washington. Unconnected, so far as we know. But.

There's an odd fact that makes no clear sense. I'm inviting you to help me think it through." The detectives got more alert.

Christie erased the list and added a square representing a building to the far left of the board. "The Washingtons went to family counseling a few years ago. At the Center here. There're two people who knew *both* victims. David Hoffman, husband to Laura McCall. *Estranged* husband. Runs the Counseling Center. And our own Detective Greer, who"—he paused to make sure they were all following—"used to work with Hoffman. What do we make of this? Anything?"

They all needed a joke. Christie hoped she could handle it.

"Colleen did it," almost everyone said. Then they started adding other lines that he could make out bits and pieces of. "Serial killer." . . . "She looks innocent, but she's got one crazy mind." . . . "Surveillance on her."

She blushed furiously. When things calmed down, Christie said, "Okay, now, here's a biggie. Hoffman called Greer again."

He felt the hopefulness in the room build.

"We don't know *what* he wants. Support, friendship is what he said, but long enough at this business and you know you never can tell what's in someone's mind. This is an opportunity, as far as I see it. She talks to him off the record and, hey, no Mirandas, nothing."

The detectives erupted with talk. A confession would get them home Sunday night and some time off, too, for the extra hours. Somehow, Christie didn't believe it was going to be that easy.

"Where was he last night?" the first Wilkinsburg man said to no one in particular.

And the other one added, "The Washington girl was seeing someone older; Hoffman and the wife were on the outs—"

Christie cautioned, " 'Someone older' is a large category to a nine-year-old boy. Anyway, maybe we should see if Greer can set up this meet."

"Okay with Greer?" Potocki asked.

"Yes," she said. "I thought I'd suggest Legends for dinner, since it's near here and—"

"Aren't you going to wear a wire? The place is too noisy, all hard surfaces," McGranahan said.

"European trendy," Potocki murmured. Others looked at him with amusement.

Coleson said, "For a wire, you need indoor/outdoor carpeting and padded booths."

"Are you comfortable with that?" Christie asked. "He'll suspect it, of course."

"The truth is, I'd be more comfortable without a wire. I'd just operate better."

"I take that seriously," Christie said. "Don't force it."

"I'll go make the call," she said.

As she started to the doorway, Christie said, "See if Hoffman has a suggestion. Give him the feeling that he has something to say about it, you know, let him believe in his own freedom and . . ." He searched for a word.

"Invulnerability," Colleen said.

How funny, Christie thought. Marina would have filled in the word that way, exactly.

"I'll have a car outside the restaurant, whatever restaurant it turns out to be."

She walked to the hall just outside the squad room; a few of the men turned to watch her calling Hoffman.

Potocki asked, "Is there any indication how the two victims might have been connected?"

"Not so far."

Coleson raised a hand. "It would make sense if the kid saw something like the killing of McCall. And had to be silenced. Although that's unlikely geographically."

Christie said, "I agree."

Potocki said, "We don't have the why."

The detectives started to roll up their lunch bags, pick up their paper cartons. Christie finished his sandwich, washed it down with a large swallow of water.

Greer came back into the room, saying, "Six o'clock. Alexander's. I said I absolutely had to have veal parm. And I told him I was on duty and had to be on my own wheels. Alexander's was his suggestion. It works. You can park easily around there."

"And if you change your mind about a wire," McGranahan said, "that place is nice and cushy, with those high-back chairs and carpets."

"I don't think I'm going to change my mind."

Christie said, "That's okay. I trust you on this one." He looked at the others. "Greer and I will see the girl's father at the coroner's office soon as this meeting is over, I hope. Then Greer will go see Mindy Cooper from the Counseling Center this afternoon."

"You're the only one with a dinner date tonight," Coleson said to Colleen. He tried to make it jovial, but envy crept through.

"Spare me," she retorted. She sounded a little like Nancy Grace on CNN. When he and Marina were watching the news, Marina did a great imitation of Nancy Grace going around in life dismissing everyone with contempt—*Get a life, get off my back, spare me, don't go there.* Canned, quick, hip. And forever pissed. They'd had a good laugh, he and Marina. He liked Nancy Grace, though, couldn't say exactly why.

Christie looked at his watch.

He tapped his legal pad. "Notes. Detailed notes on everything. You'll be glad later." He tried not to look directly at the Wilkinsburg men, who grabbed up pens. "Okay, go to your assignments."

Dolan, he noticed, was uncharacteristically quiet. Ah, being boss was not fun, not if you read people's expressions.

His phone rang. It was the coroner's office reporting the forensic pathologist, Morris Dean Cooke, was leaving and could not start the autopsy on Jamilla Washington until tomorrow. *Would* not, that is.

Christie rolled his eyes. Death was an interruption, as they said, but not much of one for some people.

Almost two-thirty. Deon Washington probably wondered what was taking so long. Red tape, red tape, red tape.

"I understand your position," he said to Cooke, who'd finally come to the phone himself.

Cooke said, "Look, I've been cutting all day, we have ten in the storage cooler, I have a golf game at three-thirty and a dinner scheduled at seven. I won't do another one today."

"I understand. I'm on my way," Christie said, "but do me a favor and check me on the means of death. Quick look."

"You don't miss these things," Cooke said. "You're a champ."

"Well, I'd hate to be wrong."

"When?"

"We'll be right there."

He triggered a finger at Colleen. "Coroner," he said. "One car. We'll go together."

ELEVEN

THANKFULLY, THE HOUSE WHERE Deon Washington lived was only a couple of minutes away from Police Headquarters, because as soon as Colleen buckled up, Christie peeled out.

"You holding up okay?" he asked her.

"Yes."

"Washington didn't try to get down to the park?"

"I lied. I told him she was already taken away."

"You did right. You think Washington is okay?"

"Hard to tell with an alcoholic, but I think so. You'll tell me what you see beyond neglectfulness. He wanted everything to be handled and he let his daughter handle everything. Whether he had a motive . . . I can't say yet."

"You treated a lot of alcoholics when you were a counselor?"

"A lot. Lot of druggies, too. Counselors wouldn't have jobs without them."

"Neither would police. Eighty percent."

"Eighty percent," she replied. Police Academy taught them that alcohol was involved in eighty percent of crimes committed. It was interesting, for sure. And no surprise that some alcohol was probably mixed with the blood splattering Laura McCall's kitchen.

"You ever know any alcoholics up close?"

"Yes, up very close." She tried not to be embarrassed by this. It was a fact, nothing she had done. "My parents."

"Both?"

"Yep."

"Still?"

"Yes. Moderated, but a part of their lives for sure."

"Moderated, less. I always find that *very* interesting. The way people change. What would take them the rest of the way, do you think, to stopping?"

"I don't know." She looked out the window, thinking answers she didn't say. God, illness. Letting the specter of death in rather than keeping it at bay. Maybe. The specter was hovering in her father's case. He hadn't been well for a while.

"Washington will be ready?"

"He said so. I called." They all but screeched to a stop.

Jamilla's father was standing on the front stoop. He had on clean pants and a shirt, open at the collar, and a sports jacket. Closer up, getting out of the car, Colleen saw the clothes were of a decent quality, maybe not expensive, but he made them look good. She thought about money in this family—not enough of it, and what there was didn't go to food.

Deon's face was distorted with tension. He stood erect, like a man waiting for the firing squad, determined to go down well.

"This is Commander Christie," she said.

Deon reached out to shake Christie's hand.

"Does your wife have someone to stay with her?" Christie asked.

"Her friend came over."

"The woman she went to Best Buy with?" Colleen asked.

He nodded.

She made a sign to Christie. The woman needed to be added to their list for the afternoon.

Autopsies and dead people were part of the training. She'd seen them before, but it still stung to think of a child like Jamilla sliced up, her skull cut, pulled apart, fitted back together. She hoped Deon hadn't seen the TV shows that now featured autopsies. Had Deon taken a few drinks? She couldn't tell. As they pulled out, she saw Kameen on crutches at the door, watching them.

The forensic pathologist on duty was a white-haired, white-coated old-fashioned Anglo doctor who looked like he belonged in a retro ad for the best-possible medical insurance in the world. He had a fresh pair of scrubs on.

Christie pointed Washington to what was known as the family room—same room Hoffman had waited in yesterday. It looked like it belonged in an old hospital in a very poor town of few inhabitants. There was a bathroom attached, and mounted high up on the wall was the small TV.

"Where is she?" Washington asked.

Christie caught Colleen's eye as he said, "I'll go see. Just wait here. These things sometimes take a little time." He hadn't yet told Washington the part about not being allowed anywhere near his daughter so as not to contaminate evidence.

He and Colleen went out past the front door, past reception, past the four tired-looking intake and investigative clerks at computers and phones, to the locker room.

There they found the pathologist, pulling on a thick pair of yellow plastic gloves.

He indicated with his arms up in saint position why he could not shake Colleen's hand. "Pleased to meet you." Almost a flirtatious smile, automatic. Then he addressed both of them. "I'll do your victim first thing tomorrow morning," he said. "And honestly, that means bumping a lot of other people out of the way. I'm cutting you a break."

"Thanks," Christie said politely.

As they passed into the hallway, Colleen became aware suddenly of the smell of the place, a sickening mix of formaldehyde and rot. All the chemicals in the world couldn't erase the smell of death here. Her stomach began to turn on her because she hadn't remembered soon enough the basic lesson: *Breathe through your mouth.*

A deputy materialized and opened the meat locker–style cooler. The smell deepened. Mouth breathing wasn't killing it. Inside the large room—a living room–size refrigerator—were ten or so body bags on gurneys. Blue bags and white bags. Cooke's mood made sense when you realized the four pathologists had to do all the county suicides, accidental deaths, homicides, deaths of undetermined causes, including the natural deaths of people with no prior histories of disease. So the corpses did pile up. The deputy wheeled out the gurney with the smallest bag, a white one, and unzipped it.

There she was again. Colleen saw bruising around the eyes.

Cooke was studying the girl's face, her neck. "Strangled. Smothered. Both. I'd say strangled, and when that wasn't enough something went over her face. What did you think?"

"Same," Christie said. "Same."

"I told you you'd nail it." Cooke nodded to the deputy, who slid the gurney under a camera mounted on the ceiling. He focused the camera. Cooke said, "You guys get over to the family room. I'll give you two minutes and then I'll put it on the monitor over there." He was already pulling off the yellow gloves. But as they were going out the door, he added, "What did you think for time?"

"I thought she was maybe six hours dead when I saw her," Christie said.

"Fits. Right now I'd say midnight last night. Give or take a few hours till we get further into it. I'll know more after I go in. That's it. For now. I'll have lots more for you tomorrow. Shall we let the father do the ID?"

And two minutes later in the waiting room with the blue couches, Deon Washington was asked to look up at the TV, where his daughter came into focus, bruised and far way. He nodded.

Christie took him by the elbow and turned him from the TV. "I'm sorry," he said.

Tears filled Washington's eyes. "She never hurt anybody," he said. "Never hurt anybody."

Should have, Colleen thought. How many people had failed Jamilla along the line?

"When will we be able to have the funeral?"

"They should be able to release her tomorrow, say early afternoon. It would be okay to call a funeral home and have them prepared to come and get her. You could go ahead and make the other arrangements."

Washington nodded numbly.

"I'm very sorry for your loss," Christie said again.

Colleen, walking behind the two men as they left the building and went to the car, heard Christie begin to question Washington in an even, sympathetic voice. "Tell me about her. What did you think of her friends?"

"Why don't you take the front seat," she said when they reached the car. "You can talk a bit easier that way."

She rode in the back, watched Christie work, the way he seemed to be offering sympathy while he moved to more and more pointed questions. But the questions were the ones she had asked. Did he know she'd done well? She had the childish wish to tug at his shoulder and tell him.

They pulled up to the Washington house. "I'd like to meet your wife and son," Christie said.

"They should be in there."

The two detectives followed Washington to the house.

The son, on crutches, stood at the door, waiting. Inside, Anita was dressed, sitting on the couch, holding Soleil. Her friend sat beside her, sipping coffee.

Colleen approached the friend, saying, "I'm Detective Greer. Could we talk for a moment. In the kitchen, maybe?"

"Yes, ma'am." Bettina Butts had a naturally pugnacious face.

There was food on the kitchen table.

A big bag of bagels—probably Malika's mom again.

Boxes of cereal, a gallon of milk, some cheese, and a package of sliced deli ham—the first installment from the Lutheran church.

Colleen took it upon herself to refrigerate the ham and milk. She asked Bettina Butts, "Did you see Anita Washington yesterday?"

"Yeah. We work together."

"Yesterday?"

Butts nodded in answer.

"And anything else?"

"We went shopping together."

"Would you write down where and how long?"

The woman paused. "Sure."

"I wanted to ask if you noticed any trouble between your friend and her husband lately, anything different?"

"Nope."

"Anything come up in terms of issues with the kids? Jamilla's responsibilities?" The woman shook her head no. "Financial situation changed in any way?"

Bettina Butts had been rehearsed. She said, "Man, there was just the usual, you know—not enough money for baby-sitters, lousy jobs. But hey, they weren't on welfare, and sure, it got on their nerves from time to time, but that was it. Just regular life. If you're asking sneaky like about that accident with the boy's foot, believe me, it was an accident. Nothing else. These are not parents who would hurt their kids. Kameen is a boy, you know what that is? Always into something. Course, it had to happen on one of the few times a parent was not at home. That was just plain old bad luck."

Colleen tapped on her notebook and asked Bettina Butts for a series of contact numbers.

Out of the corner of her eye, she could see a little of the living room—Christie stooping down to make friends with Soleil, then talking to Kameen, Anita, and again to Deon. She watched Butts write. It was slow going.

When she got her notebook back, she went into the front room and let Christie know with a nod she was ready to go.

"We'll be in touch," Christie said as he headed to the front door. "Detective Greer or me. You call us if you think of anything, I mean *anything* that comes to you that could help. Okay? Even a very small thing."

Deon answered, "I will."

"Sad man," Christie said as they walked to the car. "I mean before this."

"I know."

"He has—what would you say?"

"Dignity? Star quality?"

"Yeah. Both those things."

"Well, Boss, what do you think? Could he have? Or she?"

"Guessing is no good. I don't like him for it, or her, but unfortunately, I have been surprised in the past. The only lesson I learned is that it ain't over till it's over."

"I thought that was baseball."

"And homicide investigation."

They took fifteen minutes to sit in the car, air conditioning on high, and write. During the three-minute drive back to Headquarters, Colleen was going over her questions for Mindy Cooper and for the dinner with Hoffman.

"Were your parents that bad?" Christie asked, surprising her.

"No. Far from it. We always had food on the table. My father was proud of bringing home the bacon." There had been food, but sometimes she wondered if she'd feared there wouldn't be. Or was it just her own peculiar metabolism making her always ravenous? "There are all levels and kinds of alcoholics," she said.

"I know."

"I know you know. Sorry. I don't talk about them much."

"Why not? You don't feel close?"

"I feel very close." She had to think how to explain. "I feel close. I . . . we don't really *talk.* I accept that. Alcohol buffers the emotions, so they have that shield. They're very sweet people and they are sweet to me. Nobody would notice, really, what I mean without living it."

"But they were there in the house?"

"Physically, yes. Most of the time, but just . . ."

"Emotionally absent."

"Vague."

"I'm sorry you had that."

"Oh well, we all have something. That's mine. You know, 'Nobody ever loved anybody the way everybody wants to be loved.' "

"But you loved them?"

"Still do."

"Good. Better than the other way." They pulled up at Headquarters. "You take this car. I'll tell Jack." He got out and waited, door open, to let Colleen get into the driver's seat. He rapped the hood of the car in friendly farewell. "You call. Tell me what's up at each stage along the way. You see Mindy Cooper next."

"Right, Boss."

The way he'd just asked her questions—sympathetic, curious, seemingly unjudgmental—was the way he talked to others inside and outside of the formal interrogation room. So she'd had a taste of it.

She started out, checking the address of Mindy Cooper's house. Glancing in the rearview mirror, she saw Christie walking back toward the building, looking thoughtful.

ALL AFTERNOON, HE ACHES for what he has done. There are few people in the world who would understand the feelings he has, the control he has exercised all these years. He is a good man, he has done quite a lot of good, and now he must keep holding on until he finds his strength again. His fist is still closed tight.

When people talk about the terrible case of the child found in the park, he shakes his head and says the appropriate things.

TWELVE

ALEXANDER'S WAS BLESSEDLY quiet. A large family gathering, it looked like, had taken up three tables in back and otherwise there was only one couple sitting at a table at an early stage of their meal, dipping bread in olive oil.

Up front at one of the tables flanked by a banquette and a huge wing back chair was Hoffman. He had taken the banquette.

All was in order. The unmarked car was across the street in the Honda lot. After she'd seen Mindy Cooper, she ran home and showered quickly. Now she was wearing a gauze skirt and T-shirt, thin enough to suggest she wasn't wired—which was true.

She leaned forward and took his hand briefly. It wasn't much, but he was grateful enough for it.

Would he bring up Jamilla, or would it fall to her? Hold on to that card, she told herself. "How are you?" she asked simply. "This has to be horrible."

"It is horrible. I saw myself on the news all day yesterday." Now his face was angry. "Why do they have to come down like vultures? It makes me look like a suspect, people won't know any better, and how do I undo that?"

Nothing about Jamilla. Slow. Slow. "The clip is just because you were at the house. . . ."

"Yeah. But the way they report it . . . No wonder Laura's family thinks I'm the prime suspect and . . ." He grabbed his water glass, drank it all in a gulp, and put it back down. The glass hit hard; his hands were shaking. She reminded herself he'd always been a nervous person.

"Well, let's have something decent to eat. You haven't ordered?"

"No, I waited."

"Thanks. I know the pasta is the feature here, but I'm still up for veal parmigiana. I've been craving it."

He said helplessly, "What am I going to do?"

Just then her phone rang. "I'm sorry. I'm so sorry. Excuse me. I should get it." She expected it to be Christie checking on her, but the number reading out on the small screen surprised her. It was John. Strange as it seemed, only ten hours had gone by since they'd last spoken. Let the call go, she thought, but she couldn't persuade herself to do that. When the phone stopped ringing, she stared at the number, then pressed SEND twice. He picked up right away.

"Are you busy?" he asked. "Working?"

In case the voice was loud enough for David to hear, she said, "I'm on a break. I'm out to dinner."

"I don't want us to be enemies."

"That's a strong word. I can't really talk now. Can I call later?"

"I saw you stopped by. I want to be sure we have a meal together, slow it down, talk nicely."

Blood rushed to her face, making her curse the fact that she had such a telltale complexion. "I can't talk now. I'm sorry. I'll call you." She looked up. David watched, alert, as she pushed the END button. "Cripes," she said, "I shouldn't have bothered."

"Boyfriend," he said.

"Yeah."

"You're breaking up with him?"

"Yeah. So."

His face registered several expressions in quick succession—curiosity, pique, self-pity. He had always been interested in other lives because he never thought his own measured up. A hard way to live. Still, awkward as it was, the phone call had provided a sidebar, a buffer.

"How long were you with this guy?" He motioned toward her phone.

"A year. A little over."

"And it's not working out?"

"No. Not." Since, in Hoffman's scenario, she was doing the terminating, she added, "I don't know, maybe I'm being hasty."

"Breakups are awful no matter how smart you get."

"They are."

He folded the menu and put it aside. "I don't think I'm doing too well."

"I'm very sorry for you. For the loss and then the whole problem with the news, like you said."

"Thank you. I haven't been doing well for a long time, though," he said dreamily. "I wanted to ask a favor of you."

"If I can."

"It seems wrong to leave Laura's body wherever . . . Would you call her family? Would you see if you can get them to cooperate?"

"I could try. If they don't listen to me, what's the worst that can happen?"

"A judge will decide it on Wednesday."

"I'll try," she said again. She, too, thought it sad that Laura's body would be held at the mortuary school for three more days. Police were irreverent enough. Mortuary students were worse.

A million things she wanted to ask. She kept biting her tongue. Indirect was the way to go. It was torture, being indirect.

She felt her foot tapping and tried to convey that any jumpiness he might see had to do with searching for the waiter. "Ah, there he is," she said when the young man emerged from the kitchen with two steaming plates of pasta for the table with the couple dipping bread.

The waiter started toward them several times and finally made it.

With a quizzical leaning of his head, he asked if they wanted something to drink.

"Yes," Colleen answered. "I'll have a scotch, rocks."

"Cutty okay?"

"Yep. And could we see a wine list, please?"

"Oh, I thought there was one here. Sorry. I'll get it. You, sir?"

"Um. Go ahead and bring me the same. Cutty on the rocks."

When the waiter left, Hoffman asked, "You done for the day after all?"

She winced. "Nooooo. I'm due back. Why? You thought I should abstain?"

"I'm only curious—if cops drink and how much they drink and whether there's a consequence if anybody knows."

"Plenty of consequence if it gets in the way or you can't hold it or someone smells it when you're in a professional setting. It's just a scotch, though."

"And wine."

"And maybe some wine. I can drink. I can hold it."

"What about tonight, then? Workwise?"

"Organizing my notes, paperwork, typing."

"On my case? I mean, Laura's death."

She cast her eyes up as if calculating the workload. "Some. Some old, some new. I'm behind on notes."

"How did you manage a relationship on police hours? I mean you did, right?"

"It's hard. Really hard."

"I think it would be." The waiter deposited a basket of bread on the table and went off for the drinks.

"Police get passionate about work and there isn't any feeling left over."

"Is that why you're dumping him?"

Being the dumper rather than dumpee made anything she said an interesting exercise in revising her inner life. As she spoke what she thought was a lie, she noticed it sounded terribly like the truth. "That, and when it came down to it, we didn't have a lot in common."

"How so?"

"Well, for one thing, I would make a joke or a reference and he wouldn't get it. He's smart, but his education was so focused—well, maybe his mind is focused—on history and politics, and he's not much for humor."

"He's an academic?"

"Well, no, that's another issue. He *ought* to be." She explained that he was underemployed for his abilities.

The drinks arrived, but the waiter didn't stick around to take the food order. It was okay. Gave them time.

"I hope you can find something that will feel just right on your stomach," she said. "When I'm upset, my stomach goes berserk. Hence the word *upset,* I guess. Pasta can help."

Hoffman laughed bitterly. "That's what I've been eating for days, and the thing is, I think I'm going to order it again." He looked at his drink almost in puzzlement, as if he couldn't figure out how it got there. He sipped and resumed his questioning, not nearly so eager for food and drink as for distraction. "How did you meet him? This guy you've been seeing?"

She took a sip of her drink. "Oh, it was just . . . I'd been working a double shift and I was tired. I was done for the night and I decided to go to Home Depot to look at the gas grills. He was looking at gas grills."

"Well, I asked."

"You did. Kind of silly, I know, like some chick flick."

"You trusted him just like that?"

"No, no, it took a long time. Phone calls, coffee, met for lunch. Then after about a month, we started dating."

Hoffman sighed. "Uh. I always wonder how people meet each other."

"I do, too. I've been to dinner parties where everybody had to tell how they met. It's the question to ask at social events these days."

"People say the Internet is the current way. I haven't tried it. I've tried another service. . . ."

There it was, a link to nudge him. "How did you meet Laura?"

He paused. His face flickered nervously. "It was just ordinary. Friend of a friend set us up."

"Her friend?"

"Mine. Why?"

"Just curious. Men don't do the matchmaking thing as often as women do. This was in college?"

"No. After. When I was in grad school. That was a good time for me. Lots of things were coming together."

"I know that feeling." It was hard to know how much she could push him. He was pale, shaky. She smiled expectantly.

"She fell out of love with me," he said. "I guess I wasn't very exciting."

Unfortunately, the waiter arrived then and said, almost huffily, as if they'd been waffling on a decision, "Ready to order yet?"

Colleen handed her folded menu to him. "Veal parmigiana for me."

Hoffman handed his menu over. "I'll have pasta with sausage and cream sauce."

"Thank you. I'll be back with your salads."

When the waiter was out of earshot, she said carefully, "About Laura . . ."

His face went into a pained frown.

"I know you need to talk. You have to."

"Mostly, I'm angry. Somebody wiped her out, just like that. I don't get the chance to talk, to try to reconcile. That's never a possibility again."

"That's very sad."

Soon the salads were on their way. The waiter held them up high and out of reach. You'd have thought active eight-year-olds were trying to snatch them away. He had to be an out-of-work actor, playing his own quirky scenes, not particularly well, but with flourishes.

She squirmed, performing a little, and lowered her voice. "We probably shouldn't be talking about this, you know, but I'm really wondering . . . *was* she very serious with her boyfriend? Shoemaker?"

"I don't know a thing about him. Teaches math, I do know that. I can't help hoping you guys find his prints all over the place after all." Slightly different from his hope on Friday night that a burglar did it.

She didn't bother to point out they *would* find Shoemaker's prints everywhere, since Shoemaker lived with Laura much of the time.

"What's he like?"

"He seems quiet, ordinary. I've probably said too much already. It's early in the investigation. Lots more to do."

"Will you talk to people who work with him, that kind of thing?"

"Sure. Everybody knows that. Cop shows. That's what we do. Without the luck." She smiled.

"You don't like those shows?"

She smiled, shrugged. "Everybody is beautiful. Not to mention brilliant. Crime scenes yield wonderful clues. Labs operate like one-hour photo huts—instant results."

"Laura told me she met him at a concert in the park. I don't know if that's any safer than Home Depot."

"Hm," Colleen said. "People meet all kinds of ways." And because she knew what he was searching for, beyond the subject of his wife's death, she added, "And as the saying goes, mostly when they're not looking."

So far, Hoffman had not said anything he wouldn't want included on a tape recording. This interview is going to be a failure, she thought. I'll go back with nothing good, nothing helpful. She toyed with her salad, making a pattern of small bits of arugula while deciding to put the rest of the salad aside to have with the meal.

They didn't say much of anything except to order wine and scoff about cop shows until their meals arrived. "Hurray," she said. "The food." The waiter put down their plates. Hoffman smiled at her enthusiasm and they both began eating.

"You were a good counselor," he said after a while. "Why did you leave?"

"One day, I realized I could use some of the same skills in police work and it was more . . . extroverted? Right for me."

He nodded.

Then just trying to keep talk afloat, she asked what she thought was an arbitrary question. "Did you ever consider police work?"

He stopped bringing his forkful of pasta to his mouth, dropped his arm. His hand visibly shook again. He looked almost terrified. "What—what made you ask that?"

"Just . . ." She scrambled to keep it light. "Well, *I* did both, and they *are* two sides of the coin. You know? I mean, we're all pretty much in the business of child rescue. In my case, the child was me. Big surprise."

He appeared rapt.

"The basic police fantasy—okay, so you have to crack a few cocaine rings along the way—is to rescue a child."

His shoulders were up; he was frozen by her words. She had to keep talking. "You think I'm wrong?"

"No, you have a point."

"So, *did* you ever think of police work?"

"No. No, I never did." He struggled up from whatever depths he was tangled in to ask, "Your parents were bad to you?"

Colleen took a minute to formulate her reply. "They just weren't ever *looking.*"

"You got into trouble?"

Again she attempted accuracy. "I was lonely. When bad things happened, I didn't feel I could talk to them."

"You never mentioned that in all the time you worked with me."

"I know. But I knew it." She tapped her head. "You had good parents, then, or good parenting?"

His face blanched again. "Yes," he said. But his voice was almost a whisper.

"Good." Damn, what was it she was digging at? She couldn't tell where to go with it. He'd resumed eating and seemed to be forcing himself to look up at her.

She felt she was betraying her parents to talk about them so nakedly, and yet she continued because the talk was promising to reveal something about him. "I guess it was because my parents were hippie types. They were smart, but they never pushed themselves to compete or excel. They . . . believed in smelling roses, even if the roses smelled like whiskey."

"I would have guessed marijuana."

"Well, that, too. They didn't push me, either, but now they seem kind of proud of my degrees. They're a little nervous about the police work, but they're coming around. Do your folks like what you do?"

He swallowed hard and shrugged a weak yes.

Should she push it? Had to. "I can't remember you ever talking about your parents when we worked together, either. I mean, I don't know if I ever knew anything about your life. Did you grow up around here?"

"My mother lives in West Virginia. She raised me there. She was a single mother."

"Oh. Hard job." She suspected it was time for a U-turn. She cut a forkful of her meat. "This veal is a little dry. Your pasta okay?"

"Yes."

"Good. Let's not let this food get any colder."

The waiter came to ask them if everything was okay. "Another glass," Colleen said, tapping her wineglass. "You?" She pointed to Hoffman's.

He looked surprised. He hesitated, then said, "Yes." He was a follower. Socially imitated others. Yes, it was coming back to her. She tucked the fact away, unsure what to do with it.

"Do you have any brothers and sisters?" she asked.

"No."

"Can your mother help you through this loss? Are you close?"

"Not so close. I called her to tell her, though. She liked Laura a lot."

"Will she come up to be with you at least? You need someone. Just to talk."

"I know. That's why I'm talking to you."

"I can't be the one. I mean, I've probably broken some rule I don't know about just to have dinner."

He looked at her for a long time. "Are you wearing a wire? I think that's the expression."

"No." She breathed freely that she was not. She stood in the booth, patted at her skirt, sat back down, handed over her purse. "Look if you want. I came as a friend. I'm taking a risk here of getting myself in trouble."

"If you're a friend, tell me what they're finding."

"I can't. It's completely unethical."

"My God, I'm suffering here. And I'm scared. There are innocent people in jail. Maybe not many of them, but some. I'm worried something's going to be pinned on me."

"I won't let that happen."

"How can you stop it?"

"Because I'm good at what I do. And I'm a friend. It's going to be an honest investigation."

"Okay."

"Honest has to come from you, too." Again, her words hit him hard. He slumped visibly. She looked at him, trying to gauge her moment. "I assume you saw the news today."

"Yes."

"You did?"

"I guess. This morning. You mean the clip of me? They can't get enough of that clip."

"You watched later? Listened to the radio? Somebody called you? About the other?" She wasn't sure *what* was on the news. Jamilla's body hadn't been formally identified until two in the afternoon, but she had to play it safe. "You know about what happened in the park?"

"What park?" He was either a good actor or he didn't know.

"West Park."

Across the street from his office.

His eyes showed he got the connection. "What? What happened?"

"Jamilla Washington was found dead."

He was either a brilliant actor or her news stabbed him in the gut. He buckled, buckled again, moaned. "Jamilla? You're sure? How?"

"I can't talk about it. I really can't. You have to understand that. I thought maybe somebody'd already called you and that was why you wanted to see me."

He looked truly, truly surprised. "Jamilla?"

"Yes, Jamilla Washington. Now, peril of your soul, do you know anything about it?"

"No," he said. Then something crossed his mind. His eyes changed. He blanched again. "No."

HOFFMAN STANDS NEXT TO HIS car.

His world will not stay still. His feet are on a moving dock, a moving boat, an ocean tumbling.

He's not used to drinking three drinks at dinner. It's no help that he added drink to his already-moving world. He must drive carefully.

He slides into his car. What did he say? What did she say? One time, he had to give a speech to a large audience, and when it was over, when the stage fright subsided, he couldn't remember having given it. He knew he had. The rest was a blank.

He doesn't know if he trusts her. Trust no one, he tells himself.

If he goes home, he will turn on the news. He starts up and drives through Bloomfield, small residential streets, trying to figure out where to go. Downtown. He changes his mind and starts for home. Then he changes his mind again and drives aimlessly from street to street, with no idea of when he'll know where he's going.

Is someone following him, watching him? He looks into the rear-view mirror, studying the other cars on the road.

How do people disappear? Money in the pocket, a bus, a car, a bus, a plane, one method of transport after another in some hard-to-catch, random order, plenty of places in this country and elsewhere to land—cash, cash, not credit cards, paying for any of the above. A new name.

Start over taking menial jobs?

He'd need identity cards. And he knows where he could get them, too. It's a fantasy, and foolish, but it keeps coming to him.

Freedom.

He drives.

Jamilla. How old? Thirteen, it would be. A child.

He drives up and over Bloomfield, East Liberty, skirting the old police station that used to be Headquarters; he drives through Lawrenceville, hitting every stoplight there is to hit; he studies gas prices, station to station. It's more expensive to drive around these days than it used to be. Cheaper to go to a therapist. But he keeps going, remembering.

He was thirteen and the man he called Charlie said, "Come on, get in the car, let's go downtown, buy you some new clothes."

"I don't need anything," he told Charlie.

"Sure you do," Charlie said.

"Kids don't dress up. I'm already dressed like a dork."

"That's what we're going to change."

The car was hot from the shut windows. They drove for about five minutes and soon the air was cooler. When they got downtown, the car came to an abrupt stop. The driver-side window was down now. "Burn my eyes!" Charlie shouted.

"Charlie! Hey, you old bastard!" A jolly red-faced man came up to the car. "Where you been? Haven't seen you in ages."

"Ferris! You old son of a dog. Missed me, did you?"

"Oh, you know it. Poker loser is always in demand."

"You wish. How does that faulty memory serve you? Pretty well, looks like. When's another game?"

"Tonight, you believe? I can't get over it. We were just talking about you. Can you come?"

"Yeah, yeah, I could. Where?"

"Upstairs at the Old Dog Blues."

"What's that?"

"The old Siggie's Tavern. Fancy name now."

Charlie made a face. "Old Dog Blues. What time?"

"Nine, ten, tonight."

"Going to be a late one, then."

"With certain benefits." The red-faced man dipped his head to look into the car and nodded to confirm that he'd seen the boy there and would say no more. "See you then." He rapped on the car and Charlie drove off.

It was always like this. People liked meeting up with Charlie, but at home, it was another story. Charlie was not cheerful. He was often depressed, sullen, far away, unreachable. David had seen his mother crying repeatedly.

One day, he said to his mother, "It was better before you met him, wasn't it?"

She looked up at him, surprised to see him. Her face was swollen and out of shape from crying. But then she really scared him when she began to laugh and cry at the same time. He couldn't figure out what to do. Her laughter went on and on. Finally, it was a relief when Charlie came home and insisted she take a sedative.

The house got quiet. Charlie made scrambled eggs for dinner and David thought they made a surprisingly good dinner. He enjoyed the quiet little shuffling sounds of footsteps inside and cars going down the street outside, everything in relief in the silence. Charlie said, "What's the matter with her?"

David thought. "I don't know. Did you have a fight?"

Charlie laughed a little. "Probably. We bicker. We don't get along. I'm sorry about that."

Did it mean Charlie would leave? How could it be both a relief and *not* a relief if Charlie left? He felt both feelings.

The next morning, Charlie was gone early. His mother seemed dazed, but she was kind to him, spoke softly, asking him what he wanted for breakfast. He couldn't think about food. "Anything," he said. She made him scrambled eggs. He thought it was sort of funny to have them again so soon, but he just ate them. She kept tousling his hair, a move that irritated him.

He ran off to school. Did he forget about his mother's grief on that day? Probably. There was enough shoving and pushing and insult at school to occupy any thirteen-year-old. Did he shove harder than usual? Maybe, probably.

When he got home from school, his mother was dressed in her best clothes, a dress, a coat, nylons. She said, "I need for you to go with me somewhere."

"Where?"

She said, "I like to think I can be strong. I have to do something difficult." He thought of courts, filing for divorce, but she wasn't married to Charlie, so that made no sense. They drove into the city. His mother's face was swollen, determined. He thought they were going to Charlie's house, the one he kept in the city but rented out so he could stay with them. Soon enough, he saw they were going somewhere else. She took another exit, drove past a cemetery, down a nice street with beautiful houses David wished were his, big city houses with perfect lawns, good paint jobs; then she drove into a poorer district, which got more dilapidated as they drove. He saw some signs that told him the name of the neighborhood; it was a name he recognized from the news: Homewood. One of the high crime areas.

"Where are we going?"

"You'll see."

"Who lives here?"

"People who can't pull themselves up. No will. Losers."

He thought she sounded kind of crazy. "Then why are we bothering?"

"There's a woman I want to talk to. Has her hooks into Charlie. I wouldn't, except . . ." She fought off tears.

"I don't see why you need me." Had he said that? Yes, he thinks he said, "I don't see why you need me."

"She'll be embarrassed in front of you."

"Maybe it was better before he came to live with us." He didn't mean this; he didn't want it to be true. "You don't get along."

"He still thinks of himself as a free man. I guess that's how he thinks."

"I wish it would just stop."

"What?"

"All the fighting."

"Well, maybe other people are responsible for that. We're going to meet her."

To fend off his discomfort with a confrontation, he scrunched up his body, took the sullen pose of a teenager who had to be somewhere he didn't want to be. I'm disappearing, he said with his body. I'm not here.

He stared out the window. She was slowing down, then parking on a street with one small frame house after another, each seriously run-down. Railings and window wells sagged. Torn window shades, half up, half down, reminded him of eyes shutting in spite of themselves. The houses looked tired, sorrowful.

"I'm sorry," she said. "I don't want to be weak. I guess I'm scared. I'm sorry I made you come along."

Up ahead, he saw Charlie's car. She was staring at the house and she wasn't aware of it.

It felt like the end of the world. It was going to be embarrassing. It was going to bring shame, he thought. What happened was much worse than that.

"I'm going up to the door. If you could come with me, I'd appreciate it."

"How'd you know about this place?"

"A woman called. She called and said, 'Do you know where your husband goes?' And I told her I didn't. She gave me this address."

Oh man, David thought, This is bad. But whose fault was it?

He followed his mother in her nylons and heels down the bumpy sidewalk to the house. He was afraid to look around toward Charlie's car. Maybe he'd been wrong. Maybe it was someone else's.

To his surprise, his mother opened the door and went in. There was stuff everywhere. The house was dark inside, because even though the drapes were half off the hooks, they obliterated most of the light. In the dimness, he made out something that might belong to a car engine. Mostly parts of things. Leftovers, remains. Plates hadn't been picked up. There were several with bits of food left on them.

He shivered to think people lived like that.

The staticky sound of radio—almost all static, only a note or phrase here and there—led them toward the kitchen. David followed his mother through a hallway where a trash can overflowed; the first look at the kitchen showed dirty dishes and pots making precarious pyramids in and on the sink.

At first, there was only the sound of the radio. Then there was another noise from somewhere. Another room. The room with the door closed.

David said, "No, Mom, let's go."

She said, "I'm here. I might as well finish this."

"Please," he said, "please." He tried to linger in the kitchen, looking at the terrible sink. He wasn't sure if he should call out and give Charlie a warning.

"Come with me," his mother said decisively. She took his elbow and started toward the door.

The little girl's room wasn't so bad, not as much litter, not as much maddening noise. She lay on the bed. He couldn't see her that well, but he could see she didn't have much on. Charlie jumped when they came in. The girl rose to a sitting position. The springs creaked and creaked and creaked with each small movement she made. Charlie put an arm around the girl and whispered in her ear. She nodded.

His mother froze. For a minute, she didn't move at all, just stared.

David could see the girl better as his eyes adjusted to the darkness of the room. She was pretty, a delicate blond child, but there was something wrong. She had a funny look in her eyes, as if she strained to listen to music three houses away. She was only about eight.

Charlie handed her a small T-shirt. She didn't react. He put it on her; then with rougher movements he pulled on her cotton trousers. The trousers had an elastic waist, so they could be pulled and tugged and pulled until they were on. "I take care of her," he said. The lie swirled all around the room.

David can still smell the warm animal smell of the room. In his dreams, it comes to him.

Lines almost come to him. Things that were said afterward. But mostly the rest of that day and the next disappear in a haze. He was aware of Charlie packing things up, putting them into his car. He found Charlie in the garage before he left. He had the hood of the car up and was checking the battery.

"About the other day? It's a very complicated situation," Charlie said.

David said, "I shouldn't be here. . . . Mom doesn't want me to talk to you anymore. She says you're leaving for good. Are you?"

"She's asked me to leave. It's best. I have my own place, after all."

"She says she's going to report you if we talk. If you talk to me at all. So I can't. I just wanted to explain that before you leave. I wish it didn't have to be this way."

"Maybe it's best."

"The woman at the supermarket, remember? She said I looked just like you." He waited for an answer.

"The world is full of shit. And secrets. All kinds, all kinds, all kinds. Don't dig 'em up, kid; they're never good."

Then Charlie left, and he kept his word that he wouldn't get in touch. In secret, David kept wishing he would. His mother moved them from Monroeville to Sewickley. One day in summer, David took a series of buses into town to try to find Charlie, to talk to him, to understand. When he got home, his mother asked him where he'd been and he made up a line about having gone to the museum. His mother studied his face and then started asking him directly if he had seen Charlie. She got the truth by quizzing him and reading through his denials. Even though they'd only been in the new house in the new neighborhood for a short time and even though she liked it out in Sewickley, they moved again. She took him with her to West Virginia.

WHEN COLLEEN LEFT THE restaurant after her dinner with Hoffman, she drove for a few blocks, waved off the police following her to let them know she was all right, then realized there was something she still wanted to do. She drove straight back to the restaurant, hoping the table hadn't been bused yet. When she got inside, the waiter said an automatic "I'll seat you in a minute," but she was already checking the table she'd been at. It was empty. The waiter realized he'd seen her before. "Forget something?"

She moved toward the kitchen.

"Hey, that's the kitchen."

"I know. It's important."

He followed her through the door. The cook looked up, then back down at what he was cooking.

She showed her badge. "I have to locate our dishes and take the fork and the glass of the person I ate with," she said as forcefully as possible. She saw their things. Not in the dishwasher yet. The waiter and cook watched, fascinated, as she picked through the dishes. She lifted a wineglass carefully by the base and saw lipstick on it. Hers. She chose the other one. "I need a clean napkin and a paper bag."

"I could get you plastic."

"Paper," she said. There was no telling how much the dishes had been touched and whether they would be useful. The cook came up with a paper bag. She put the wineglass in it. She identified which plate was Hoffman's and thanked her stars the busboy had left the dirty dishes intact with knife and fork, just as they'd been at the table. To be sure, she compared the forks. One was more oily with red sauce. The other more creamy. His. She put it in the paper bag. In a pinch, they might yield something.

"Do I need to tell you how confidential this has to be?" she asked.

"I don't *think* so," the waiter said.

"Well, let me try to explain. If anyone, anyone at all, should ask you if I came back or what I took, you would be in great trouble by seeming to know. I suggest you erase this completely. Don't tell even your mother or your girlfriend. It's confidential. Period. A leak would endanger people and you'd be liable."

The cook and the waiter looked sober enough, appeared to buy her lie. Still, two people were two too many.

Carrying what looked like a take-out bag, she got into her car once more and drove to Headquarters. She felt proud. She'd initiated something. She hurried up to her office, still wearing the gauze skirt and fancy tank top she'd fetched for dinner, but carrying a pair of jeans and a shirt along with the bag from the restaurant.

Christie was standing in the hallway. "Greer, you look great."

"For a person who hasn't slept for a long time. Thanks. Well, I have a present for you."

"I ate."

"It isn't food. I ran back and grabbed his fork and glass."

"You found him shaky? Suspicious?"

"Shaky, yes. Suspicious, I don't know. He seemed completely shocked about Jamilla. But I thought getting his DNA sooner rather than later could be useful."

She waited nervously for a reaction.

He said thoughtfully, more evenly that she liked, "It was smart. It was a good idea. Very good. Lab is overworked, of course."

"Of course. But—"

"And you had a reason for getting a DNA sample, I'm sure?"

She counseled herself to wait in future for a compliment instead of asking for it. Calling the evidence a present was a mistake, too. She plucked off the large earrings she wore and took a breath. "Okay. It was weird. He asked if I was wearing a wire. He spoke pretty much only what he might want us to hear."

"Is that all?"

She hesitated. "That's all. Except he mentioned his mother liking

Laura. I asked if she was coming up for the funeral and he waffled. So I'd like to make an excuse to go talk to her, that's one result of the meeting."

"Where is she?"

"Somewhere in West Virginia."

"West Virginia is big."

"I know, Boss. It's just on my list of possibles. I'll find her. Not something tonight or even tomorrow."

His phone rang. He put a finger in one ear to hear better. From his replies, she couldn't tell who it was. Her watch told her it was nearly eight o'clock. Christie nodded slowly, listening. He started toward his office and indicated with his head that she should follow him in. After a series of thank-yous, he hung up and turned to her, saying formally, "Almost certain they're park bags. We have to go over there tonight, examine the place. Depending on what we find, those of us who go over there may be going past eleven tonight. We, you and I, need to be there at, say, six tomorrow morning. And I want to be at the school at seven or eight, when the administrators come in. Just so you know." He noted the jeans she carried. "You went home? In between?"

It might be a criticism, she thought, time spent badly.

She blushed to think of the shower she'd sneaked in before dinner. "I went home to change for dinner. These . . . I had in the trunk of my car."

"Can you be ready to go to the parks buildings with me in, say, ten minutes?"

"Got it."

He started to walk with her toward the ladies' room. "You ever noticed any park workers around when you run over there?"

"All the time. Well, usually I go a bit later than I have the last couple of days. I only went at the crack of dawn today because I couldn't sleep."

Christie looked serious. "That's a shame about sleep. Some people are lucky. Dolan sleeps. Tell me about the park workers."

"Oh. I see them a lot. They—well, you know how it is—they talk a lot among themselves, don't work all that hard. Take their time. Blue-collar mentality. Every time I see them, it seems they're in a different vehicle—tractor, cart, truck. They do different jobs on different days, you know. I've seen them do a routine garbage bag pickup and replacement. One drives; the other hops off and does everything else. Sometimes they rake. Sometimes they spray."

"Their ages?"

"Mostly older. Fifties, sixties. One youngish guy, maybe thirty. He's the one who gets to change the garbage bags."

"We'll talk to all of them tomorrow." He nodded toward her jeans. "Meet you here in a few minutes. Tonight, we'll just see what we see."

When she did meet Christie and they were walking out to the parking lot, he asked, "Your boyfriend's place is close to the park?"

"Just across from the park," she said simply. And because she said it this way, to spare him the bother, the breakup seemed for a moment not to have happened.

"It could be useful, since you have the energy for that kind of thing," Christie was saying, "for you to do your usual in the park tomorrow morning. See what you see."

"Sure," she said. "Happy to do that assignment."

Christie checked the rearview mirror on the way. There were two other cars going to the Park Center. When he got there, Dolan and McGranahan pulled up in one car and Potocki and Hurwitz in another. The supervisor, Vernon Gabig, let them into the office and garages. Christie asked Gabig to stay outside.

There were ten vehicles inside—three flatbeds, three carts, three tractors, one van. Christie said, "No way to tell which one has been moved—if one has. What I really want is the ideal old lady who had nothing better to do than look out her window all night and could tell us exactly what she saw."

Dolan said, "I must have asked a hundred perfect old ladies everything about their window habits and cars coming and going, but so far, nada."

McGranahan kept yawning. Colleen thought he yawned bitterly, as a performance. Later, she heard him ask Christie, "She still partnering you on this one?"

"Yes," Christie said simply.

HURWITZ USED A VIDEO CAMera, while Potocki worked the digital one. Colleen wasn't sure why they'd added the video; maybe it just happened to be available. Christie called them together and cautioned them, "Watch what you say. Video's rolling."

"Oh shit," said Potocki.

Christie laughed before he said, "That's what I mean. Exactly. Language and whatever would show us in a bad light in court."

They scanned the floor with bright lights. An earring, that'd be a find. But no, Jamilla had had both earrings on still. A little purse, the teensy things teenagers carried—something like that'd be great. But nothing that obvious came to them. Shoe print? Maybe. There were shoe prints, but too many of them. That was clear when Christie shone a light at an angle on the floor.

If it was going to come down to trace evidence again—hairs, fibers, prints—more delay.

Colleen began to flash her light on one of the open-backed pickup trucks. She pictured a body lying in the bed of the truck. Feet might not touch. But if they did, if the body got jostled at all, they'd hit cab or sides or back latch.

Her first reaction upon seeing what she saw was that her eyes were deceiving her, giving her what she wanted, about to take it away again. She looked more closely, taking her time. Her flashlight caught a shoe print on the back latch of the truck. A dainty print.

"Boss," she said. "Here. I think she was here."

Christie clapped her on the back and said, "Good work, Greer." Then he called the crime lab. "Hi," he said. "It's me. I'm afraid so." And he began to give directions.

They were there for hours more while the lab printed the place and combed the truck for hair and fibers and smears of blood. Then they had to go over everything that might have been used to strangle and smother the girl. There were no pillows around, but there were a couple of jackets hanging on hooks.

Christie's phone rang constantly. Colleen had time to wonder what John was doing, if he was home, what he was thinking. She went to a corner and returned his earlier call. No answer. A deep sadness settled over her as the phone rang and she caught herself wishing for the simple press and warmth of him.

THIRTEEN

WHEN COLLEEN GOT HOME, she felt a jolt of wide-eyed energy. Fear. The willies. She turned and scanned her block. Nothing. No one. She felt danger, but it made no sense. Ghosts and demons were peopling her thoughts. Passing her neglected front yard, she felt jangled with all kinds of feelings. For Jamilla, for herself. She needed to sleep deeply tonight to make up for the last two nights.

Her house had a distinctive smell—her shampoo, things she had cooked, and, who knows, maybe even things the previous owners had cooked—deep in the walls. Home. Time to get used to it again. She flung the bag holding clothes, a hair dryer, and a second set of makeup items on the bed. She sat on the edge of the bed, then slowly lay down. How could she have been so unaware it was falling apart? John had spent just about every day with her, talking, confiding, sharing meals, making love. Companion and bed buddy—that's all he'd wanted.

Call again? She picked up the phone, noticed the time, and let the phone rest on her stomach, a small pressure, like the weight of a hand.

Lying there, she realized she was starved again, but she was too exhausted to get up. Finally, her stomach insisted, and she went to the kitchen.

Refrigerator was nearly empty. Cupboards, empty. Some pasta, yes, sauce, yes, sort of decent stuff from the market in the strip, but no, not in the mood. She made two pieces of toast and slathered them with peanut butter and jelly. When she finished eating, she made two more and did the same.

Then she took a quick shower and hit the bed. She lay there with her mind whirling. The clock ticked off 12:40, 12:50, 1:00. She was due back at six. And no sleep potions in the house.

She went into her study and worked on her notes. All she'd gotten down so far about the afternoon was that she'd gone to Mindy Cooper's house and found out there were never evening or weekend hours at the Center, that Cooper had never noticed evidence that anybody came in late, that even cleaning people came in the daytime, and that Jamilla Washington's parents had come in *once* about a year ago. Now Colleen wrote, *I showed her Jamilla's picture and asked if she had ever seen her around. She hadn't. I asked if she had noticed her in the park. She said she never much looked around when she was going to her car. Note: I didn't tell her I'd once worked at the Center*. She thought for a moment and added, *I asked if Hoffman had ever talked about Jamilla and Cooper said no*. There. That interview was pretty much recorded.

The thing that didn't go into the notes was the fact that Cooper seemed so lonely as to be grateful for the police visit. Or that she lived in a place of lacy doilies and family pictures. Everything at Mindy Cooper's house was perfect. The air conditioner whirred, the woman wore a lightweight version of a pink sweat suit and pink back-less track shoes. She served hot tea in a china tea set. Colleen felt sad for her and admired her too. Lots of people were lonely. Some kept up their dignity, as Cooper did.

She still had to write about Hoffman, but there was no way she'd forget a moment of that visit.

She searched the shelf for something to put her to sleep. Aha. A novel she'd tried to read twice before. *Coal Deep* had done the trick when she didn't want it to. Give it a shot.

Forty minutes later, she drifted into dreams. At 2:55, she woke up wide-eyed and picked up *Coal Deep* again. It didn't work the second time. Seventy-five pages later, she wasn't sure what she'd read, but still she was awake. She *should* have done the Hoffman notes. All the while, her mind was whirling, replaying her conversation with him, his nervousness about certain subjects. There was a secret there. What was it?

She got dressed in her sweats and carried a second set of clothing once more. This clothes-changing on the hoof was getting to be a habit. She started out for Headquarters and was in her office at four in the morning. Janet Littlefield was on duty again. At Christie's orders she'd gone home to get some rest, but now she was back. And asleep, head down on the desk, on top of papers.

Colleen tiptoed around to make coffee.

The noise, minimal as it was, wakened Littlefield. She dredged herself up from sleep, studied Colleen. "You okay?" Her voice was thick with the cold.

"Yeah."

"Why don't I believe you?"

"Okay. Not great."

"Understandable. I hear you knew both victims. That has to be weird."

"It is. I know it is." And because Janet Littlefield was one of the nicest people she had ever met, she said, "And my boyfriend picked yesterday to break up with me." There. She had needed to tell someone to make it official.

"Oh man. I'm sorry."

"Yeah, me, too."

"It came as a surprise?"

"Yeah, it did. So I feel stupid on top of whatever."

"You'll be okay. Just doesn't feel like it at the moment. My guess is you'll be better off, soon as you come to realize it. If it isn't working for both people, it isn't working. And you've got everything on your side. They'll be beating down the doors."

"I doubt that."

"I promise you."

Sure didn't feel like it. "Why didn't I see it coming?"

"You were busy looking at something else." Littlefield checked her watch. "When are you supposed to be here, officially?"

"Christie and I start at six today. Couldn't sleep."

"Hmm. Man, nobody can sleep tonight. Assistant chief came in a while ago, too."

"Who?"

"Dun. It's one of those nights."

"I guess."

"Hey. We have to have a girls' night out someday soon, when these cases let up. Get you feeling better."

"Thanks. What are you working on?"

"I'm supposed to find out a couple of things about Hoffman. See if there were any old newspaper articles, whatever, about the center where he worked." Littlefield knocked at her computer as if a grinch might come out and tell her what she needed. "You go eat something now. You'll feel better. The guys brought in some Panera last night. Just eat and catch up on your work. Sometimes we just need to be around people."

"Thanks."

She got a coffee and a fruit/nut bread from the bag and came back. Littlefield was trying to stay awake, staring at the screen.

"One thing I wanted to ask. Have you found Hoffman's mother?"

"Yeah, I have. Mother is Eileen Hoffman. Lives in Charleston, West Virginia."

"Could you get me an address and phone number for her?"

"Could do. That's good. Keep asking me to do things. You're keeping me awake."

Colleen took the address moments later, mapped it to see how long it would take her to drive there. Not bad. Under four hours. Three if she drove fast.

"Who was this guy you were seeing?" Littlefield asked.

"Just a guy. A regular guy."

"Maybe you need *not* regular. Maybe you need special."

Colleen felt bad that she'd made John sound boring. He'd been so much fun at first, anything *but* boring. He'd bought her a helmet, encouraged her to drive his Vincent while he rode the Triumph. Then one day, together on the Triumph, clothing billowing out, John shielding her from the wind, they'd gone up to Lake Arthur to sail. He'd balanced on the boat, talking nonstop. And he was a great hugger. She wanted to let Littlefield know it had been good for a while, but Littlefield was working again.

At five o'clock Colleen decided even though it was early, she would go run in the park. She stood up from her desk.

"Oh. If you get any facts about his grad school days, let me know. I'd like to track down some friends he had then, maybe a roommate."

She shivered inadvertently, aware of someone behind her coming into the room. She turned.

Assistant Chief Dun stopped in the doorway.

His eyes, a very pale blue, frightened her. Her first thought, a flash, was that he found her inadequate on the job, but no, that couldn't be it, because she didn't answer to him anymore. He was in charge of the patrol officers and she was past all that.

But his eyes. For some reason unknown to her, he didn't like her. She got the message, in her gut, and that was always accurate—"the brain in the abdomen," they called it these days. She forced herself to be polite as he came forward into the room. "Hello, sir."

"Hello." He smiled. It was as false a smile as she had seen.

She almost talked about how she'd mistaken him at the picnic yesterday for someone else. She felt she needed to say *something,* just to be civil. She grabbed her bottle of water and said, "You're gracing us in our quarters this morning. Or more like middle of the night."

He didn't answer. He walked toward the barred window, looked out, then moved off again toward his office.

And then this and that little piece came together and she knew. She just knew.

FOURTEEN

IT IS MONDAY MORNING.

A whole bottle yesterday evening, but he can hold it. He can hold it better than anyone he knows. And after a bottle, and it took a bottle, he could think straight. For some people, it works that way.

Walk the straight line every time, he can.

What to do, that's the thing.

He has made errors. Rage is a terrible thing. He is not himself; the simplest phrase gets it right: "not himself." He has behaved as if he knows nothing, knows no better.

No connection must be found. None. Nothing. Whatever he has to do.

He is a man in charge. His car, unscratched, new, clean, even waxed. Orderly. He sits at his desk, reading the in-house mail. Once again studies his computer, clicking through sites.

Erase certain things or no? No. He can give reasons for everything that's there. All pictures, all texts, explainable.

And never again, of course. Never again must he let himself go.

Hangover, his form of it, comes with brushed teeth, clean skin, sparkling clothes. He moves through his day, doing his work, greeting people, growling and demanding, teasing, and none of it seems real, neither what happened before nor the day he is living.

HEAT IS ALREADY THREATening, traffic sounds starting to pick up, people crowding in on the day. A siren, a horn, a copter. The world is awake. The ground is dry, grass parched, but the air is humid, skin-glazing wet.

Colleen has lost her conviction that she knows what's going on. She will say nothing until she has more to go on. There are enough people waiting for her to do something wrong. She's got to think clearly.

Christie is all out of sorts, too. "We gotta look at these people," he says. "Logic dictates. Why is my brain not coming around to it?" He shakes his head irritably.

A hapless bunch of men stand before them in a line, looking for all the world like a row of servants in a period film or a play. Put lace at their necks, boots on, tattered service doublets, and they easily migrate to another century, another situation.

Vernon Gabig is the supervisor and they talked to him last night for a good long time. The few wisps of hair he has lift up over his ears with the single breeze of the morning. His face is red. He asks, "What about our routine?"

"Your work?" Christie asks.

"We're supposed to empty garbage. Then there's other stuff."

"That has to wait."

"This was none of my men," he said last night when they questioned him. He answered most questions willingly—only he and the second in command had keys to the building, but there was a third set kept in the drawer, and a fourth somewhere downtown in the mayor's office or some other city official's. He never saw the one in the drawer missing, but he didn't check it regularly. He'd never seen Jamilla in the park offices, or around them, or in the park. The only time he got twitchy was when they asked him when he was last in the office. "Friday at three," he said.

"Exactly three?"

"More like something after two."

"You left early?"

"The work was done."

"Everybody left early? You dismissed them?"

The man looked as if he might cry. "It was Friday and they got done early. Please," he said, hoping no doubt that the Commander in Homicide would forgive him for shaving some time off the work clock.

"I'm not here to report you," Christie said briskly.

Finally they got him to admit they'd gone home at 1:00 P.M.

Now Christie sits at one picnic table and Colleen sits at another questioning the other park workers. Joggers stop by the patrol car to ask what's up.

Colleen removes pictures of Jamilla from her briefcase. "Have you ever seen this child inside your building? Outside near it?" She sees that across the way, Christie is also showing a photograph. Each of the workers says no.

Finally she and Christie come together again and he calls over the supervisor once more.

"You ever seen any porn around the place?"

Gabig pauses, embarrassed. "Once, couple of years ago."

"What sort?"

"A magazine."

"You remember the name of it?"

"*Penthouse*."

"Who had it?"

"Jimmy Vento."

He is the youngest employee. Married. Two kids, pretty young kids. Not the brightest dime on the sidewalk.

"Did you ever find anything else around, any pornography that had images of children?"

"No."

"You're sure."

"Yes."

"Let's us three take a look inside," Christie says. He escorts Gabig to the crime scene, Colleen following. Gabig studies it for a good long time before saying, "Nothing out of the ordinary."

Christie asks him to study the large boxes of garbage bags. "Tell me, were both boxes opened before the weekend?"

"Yeah. Yeah, they were, best I can recall. There was no good reason for it; we just sometimes open a box when we're standing there, just because, no good reason."

"Some of the guys take a couple of bags home? Yard work and that? Storing summer clothes, winter clothes in mothballs?"

"Maybe. I don't look. I don't count. If they do, is it a terrible crime?"

"Crime, yes. Terrible, no."

"Maybe someone else will notice something. I sure don't."

"Ask Jimmy Vento to come in."

Jimmy Vento is a tiptoeing, guilty-looking young man, eyes darting away, odd smile. But what is he guilty of? He is eager to find something amiss in the garage, but he leaps with ADD inefficiency from one thought to the next, beginning sentences he has no intention of finishing. "So you guys are—" "You want me to—"

"Do you notice anything different?"

The guy thinks hard. "Police tape is all."

A COUPLE OF HOURS LATER

Christie and Colleen are at the school, trying to learn about Jamilla, any friends she had who haven't been named yet. Christie has Potocki back at the office checking for priors on all the park workers. He checks in regularly but so far Potocki has found nothing. This afternoon they will check alibis. "Petty blue-collar theft is the only thing we'll have on them by the end of the day," Christie mutters.

Everything about the case is still locked, unyielding. Colleen's crazy thought of the morning stays with her but she doesn't say anything about it.

"You checked with Mindy Cooper this morning?"

"Yeah. Hoffman tried to come into work. She sort of gently sent him home. He didn't want to go. There's a guy named Michael Craver taking over Hoffman's clients this morning. Apparently, Hoffman was all exercised about making sure everyone who showed up was seen, and Craver was willing to fill in. She made us an appointment to talk to Craver at noon. He's a regular counselor there."

"Good."

Heat keeps creeping into the day.

"My mind keeps going back to Hoffman," Christie says. "He has an alibi and he has nothing to do with the Park Service. I feel nuts."

"I know," Colleen says. "Ditto."

Christie goes back to the office for half an hour to catch up on messages. Colleen uses the time to run the fork and glass to the lab.

ASSISTANT CHIEF DUN SITS IN his office, calling up the computer program he put into effect, the KID Pages—Kids In Danger. None of this could have been possible a decade ago, or even years ago, not to this extent. Digital cameras have made it possible to keep photos of every child in every family whose homes police are called to for abuse, neglect, domestic disturbances, anything that makes the patrol cop think the children are at some risk. This includes felony and misdemeanor arrests of one parent or the other, leaving the child in a home often unsupervised.

He studies the pages. This is a good thing he's done. It's good.

Such victim's faces most of the kids have. You can see all the trouble off the bat, at first glance. He never likes the victimized look. He likes the ones who are brave or happy beyond their circumstances. Medical scientists and social scientists will have a lot to study one day from these photos alone. There are indications beyond bruises: the way the eyes fall, skin eruptions, weight problems—too skinny or overweight.

The things that happen to people. Some of these kids go hungry.

Jamilla was one of the pretty ones, one of the kids who have rough situations but somehow do not end up looking like victims. She's in the system because her parents were always in trouble. Battery was the last thing Deon got tangled in. Before that it was always drugs or alcohol and whatever they led to. Jamilla is in the KID system, smiling. Age seven, then eight, then not again for a while, then eleven years old. And there's her brother at a couple of ages in the computer files, too.

He stares at the pictures.

COLLEEN FINDS MICHAEL CRAVER

a perfect companion, a fit with the people in the park. In this film the police have landed in today, Craver is the nobleman—odd, damaged, genteel and gentle. Suspect the gentle ones? She's heard that.

She, Christie, and Craver sit in one of the family counseling rooms.

Craver is dressed in what could very well be his grandfather's well-tailored twills. He wears hard-soled shoes. And his hair is unusual too, parted and wavy, but pressed down over his ears. He has a sweet inquisitive face.

"Please, go ahead, eat your lunch," she says, fascinated, studying him.

He smiles benignly, unfolds his brown bag carefully, takes out what looks like a ham and cheese sandwich, placing it on the table in front of him. Then he removes an apple, then a small waxed-paper package that holds (clearly) two cookies. Classic child's lunch from a decade ago. No spinach pies or Thai chicken for this guy. He pushes the food aside.

"Go on," Colleen says. "We know you only have so much time."

"I couldn't eat in front of people," he protests. "I just—it isn't right. Unless I had enough for you."

"Oh, I don't need anything," Colleen says just as her stomach growls loudly.

Everybody laughs.

"Maybe you'd better share with Greer, here," Christie jokes, but the man takes him seriously and slides his sandwich over.

"No, no, really, this will only take a short while," Colleen says. She can feel the hunger headache taking the pathway up her neck, to the back of her head and somehow—although the path it takes on these occasions she doesn't understand from a physical point of view—as always, ending up at her eyeballs.

So, basically, nobody gets to eat.

Christie takes the bulk of this interview. He is mild at first. "What are your hours?" "How many people do you see?" Then he starts to press. "Have you ever come in at night? After hours?" "Do you recognize this picture?" "Did you know her yourself? Ever work with her family?"

Craver says a quiet, "Oh, oh goodness." His thin body, knees tight together, continues to suggest he is the kindly aristocratic landowner in a small English village.

After the questioning is done, Christie and Greer leave. Going to the car they brought, he says, "Unusual man."

"Different. I liked him."

"I did, too." He laughs.

"I'll try to learn more about him. Couple of phone calls."

"Right. Speaking of, I have about a hundred to make. Would you order lunch for me? Anything. You take the car." He tosses her the keys. "Drive. Drop me off at Headquarters, then get us some lunch."

"Other way around if you're willing. Drop me on Western, where I can order something. You keep the car. I need the walk." She tosses the keys back.

"Fine." He lifts his phone as he starts the engine. "Autopsy ought to be done soon. I kept expecting a call while we talked to Craver."

"We're going to hear she was pregnant," Colleen says sadly.

Christie sighs, nods. "I've been factoring it in. In spite of the fact that she looks like a little kid. She was very slight."

Slight, she thinks, slight. On Western Avenue, she hops out of the passenger seat and he drives on.

Ordering takeout, she uses the time well. First she calls the Lutheran church to thank them for the first round of groceries to the Washington home. Then she leaves a message with the McCalls that she's willing to talk to them about the funeral if they want. Finally she gets hold of the counseling program at Duquesne University in order to talk about Craver. While waiting to be connected to someone who knew him, and while also waiting for the sandwiches to be made, she manages to scarf down a cup of soup, no matter that it's hot out. She has to get something into her stomach fast, get rid of the headache.

The woman at Duquesne promises to call her back when she finds a contact.

As soon as Colleen hangs up, her phone rings. It's John.

"Hi, John."

"Working?"

"Yeah. I am. How's the dating going?"

"Give me a break."

"I thought I had."

"I don't like it when you sound bitter."

Truth is, she doesn't like it either.

"I'm just checking in, checking on you," he says.

"Nobody's taken a pop at me yet," she says. She promises him that as soon as she can find the time—and she isn't lying—she will have the sit-down he wants, the polite undoing of whatever it was they had.

"Hey," he says, "hey. Take care." His voice is raspy with some sort of emotion, and she begins to cry.

Work is a salvation, anyway.

The order is put before her in bags—two side salads and two sandwiches, one tuna salad and one chicken salad. Each sandwich comes with chips. Police get lots of potatoes in their diets one way and another.

She hates to cook for just herself, but she has to turn that around, she tells herself on the walk back to Headquarters.

"Which do you want, Boss?" He chooses the chicken and she goes off to her own office. Just as she sits down and aims for her first bite of the tuna sandwich, her phone rings. It's a guy from Duquesne who supervised Craver. "He is an odd bird, isn't he?" the professor says. "And you know what? When it's all said and done, we pretty much ended up wishing we were all a bit more like him. He's serious, he's smart, and he's good in the clinic. We never had a word to say against him."

"You don't see him as someone who's harboring unexpressed anger or any of that?"

"Not a bit of it. What do you suspect him of?"

"We don't. It's a routine screening. But I do have a case," she says, "that you might be able to help with." She knows this stuff, after all, but to keep this guy on the phone a bit longer, she pretends to not knowing.

"What's the most current profile of pedophiles? Anything new in the findings?"

"Pedophiles. Craver is not your man. Good heavens, I wouldn't think so. Okay. Let me think if I've read anything new lately. They're single usually. Sometimes family men. Caucasian more often than not. Good chance they were abused. Often not very well educated. Often have job problems. That's the bulk of them. As research has it. But you know there are exceptions to most rules. The only certainty really is that there's some secret somewhere. A place. A time. A pattern of behavior when they go off and do what they do. Most of them keep that secret pretty well. And there's access. They usually find ways to be around kids. Men looking for boys end up being coaches, Scout leaders."

"How about men looking for girls?"

"Access is not *as* easy. I don't think *different* in too many other respects."

"Ever run into a case of a well-educated, well-employed predator?"

"No. But then I don't do much counseling myself anymore. There is stuff in the lit about it, though."

"Could happen?"

"Oh sure.

"Right." She knows this, just by knowing human nature doesn't always run to statistics and studies. She hangs up and has her sandwich and chips, thinking. If she breathes deeply and asks herself if she is going nuts or if she's onto something, she finds herself leaning toward the latter.

Moments later, Christie calls a catch-up meeting in the conference room, and she, it turns out, is the star witness.

"Autopsy report is in. She was strangled, she was smothered, she was pregnant. No rape at the time of murder. I want to keep the pregnancy out of the papers, understand?"

The detectives mumble and nod that they will keep this fact among themselves.

"We're thinking predator. Nobody so far knows a thing about a relationship with a boy her age, and there's the odd fact of her getting a phone call from an older person. So, until somebody shows me differently, that's how I'm thinking. So we need backgrounds on anyone we look at, because there's usually a history."

"We find anything on Hoffman in this regard?" Potocki asks.

"Not so far. Greer used to be a counselor; she's trained in all this. And you all are more or less caught up to current thinking, I know that. And we all watch TV. So, Greer? What do the counselors say?"

"There's nothing new." They continue to look at her, so she explains, "The grooves are cut early in the way we think about anything, and the predator's brain has a certain pathway of thoughts that spells excitement, a certain sequence that brings pleasure." She hesitates, wondering how clinical her terms should be. 'Baseline masturbatory fantasy' is what the books would say. "Once that's established—and the pleasure might be very intense—it's very difficult to shake it or to cut another pathway to pleasure. So the predator may *learn* there's something wrong with the pathway his brain—or her brain (since, there are female predators)—has chosen, but then they have to choose either no pleasure, no excitement, or they sneak back to the thing that works. That's why they almost never heal."

"Thank you," Christie said. "So it would take a strong person like a successfully recovering alcoholic to fight the old pathways. It would take concerted effort to cut new pathways."

"Yes. In counseling, we were always taught that healthy play or experimentation in childhood leads to healthy adults—I know you all kind of know that."

Potocki is nodding.

"So what's Potocki nodding about?" McGranahan says in a joking tone that falls flat.

"I was very lucky," Potocki says good-humoredly, "to have a neighbor girl who liked to take her knickers down for me. We were the same age and we were consensual."

Colleen smiles. Potocki is up to speed on the theoretical thinking.

McGranahan continues his attempt at levity. "Potocki doesn't say when, notice. This could have been last year."

Potocki shakes his head and surprises them all by not joking. "What Greer is telling us is these guys are like addicts."

"Exactly," Greer says. "They *are* addicts. And . . . they tend to think someone else's life is less important than their pleasure. And they learn an absence of soul." Too serious, too high horse.

"Soul!" McGranahan says under his breath.

Soul, a word she wishes now she had not used.

FIFTEEN

HE TURNS ON HIS TELEVISION, turns it back off. He walks out his front door into the day, which has grown gray with steamy air. Good for the skin, his mother used to say, moisture, however you get it. And now he just stands there on his front doorstep.

He lives in a row of town houses, where he lived with Laura, too expensive for him alone, but he'd kept it, needed to feel something was right in his life after Laura left.

Dead. He is still trying to get used to the idea. Stabbed. Dead.

A man carrying two grocery bags is coming up the sidewalk to the house next door. The man looks away, pretending he doesn't see Hoffman. His own voice, which he would like to summon, is stuck. He can't think how to say a simple hello. The neighbor man goes into his house, afraid, almost dropping what are probably eggs and bacon in his bags. The smell escapes each morning, always the same: eggs, bacon, toast of some kind.

A thought edges in that's too terrible to know. So he watches a red convertible go down the street, thinking, Is that an Audi, like a small comma, or something else? Thinking, Is it going to rain? Will the convertible driver put the top up in time? Thinking anything but what he knows and what is coming at him if he doesn't drown himself in television or work or sleep.

He is going to have to talk. This can't go on. He is going to have to find out and then . . . and then talk.

He goes back into the house for his keys and locks the door. The keys jingle and the veins stand out on the back of his shaking hand. Palsied. Like an old man. As if he's lived more than double his years and come to the age where he thinks daily about cashing out.

In his car, he changes his mind a thousand times and just keeps driving. At one point, he drives the whole way to the Police Headquarters on the North Side and looks at the barred windows of the imposing building. Should he go in, talk to the people on the case? Would Colleen be there?

He drives away, going the whole way out to Sewickley, where he once lived, long ago, briefly.

He finds the house they had for six months or a little more—he thinks it's the one. Everything looks different now. But maybe it's just that he can't remember things from that time in his life. The edge of madness is not so far away. He's there. Right, right at the very edge.

A pay phone is what he needs now, and they're not so easy to find these days. The country club is a possibility. But he might be turned away or, worse, remembered. The hospital, yes. He pulls in, parks the car. A hospital will always have a pay phone.

No quarters in his pockets. He stops at the gift shop, gets himself a bag of M&M's, paying with a five, asks for quarters in change. The woman at the register makes a show of looking under and behind for a reserve roll of quarters, then, not finding them, turns down her mouth as she counts out some fourteen disks from the change tray.

"Thank you."

She doesn't respond.

He finds a phone down the hallway. Thinks, This is as anonymous as it gets, isn't it? Thinks, Why does it always have to be a pay phone? He presses the numbers, hearing a melody, not exactly familiar, but not totally foreign, either. The gruff voice answers, "Yep?"

"It's me."

"I'll call you. One hour." The call cuts off.

Half a second. No tracing that call. When he turns from the booth, he stumbles, dizzy. He hasn't eaten today yet. It could be plain hunger. He opens the packet of M&M's and eats a few. The sugar courses through him, making him not exactly less dizzy, for as he walks back and forth, it's as if he steps uncertainly through a bed of cotton candy. He can't wait at the pay phone for an hour. He keeps at the M&M's on the way to his car, in his car, and until he has driven to a restaurant, where, the only person there, he orders a burger and fries.

An hour goes by with him doing nothing but thinking, eating. The heavy meal sits like a squirrel in a snake's stomach. The muscles of his shoulders and arms droop with sluggishness. His cell phone rings.

"I told you not to call."

"You did this."

"I didn't."

"I'm not taking the heat for you."

"You're not taking the heat for anyone. You'll come out okay."

"How do you know?"

"I know. What do you think? How do you think I know?" Think? He can't. The voice says, "You should go away for a few days."

"You've got to be kidding. If I leave, they'll think I did it for sure. I'll never be able to turn it around."

"You ever want to just leave? Just start out somewhere new? Job, money?"

He has. Often enough.

"You haven't been happy."

"But it's crazy to think like that."

"A name is gettable."

"But I didn't do anything."

"It doesn't matter. I'm talking about cutting losses when things are bad, starting again. A whole new life. I just want you to imagine it."

In spite of himself, he imagines it again.

"If it looks like they're going to pin you on circumstantial, I'll get you out. You won't be sorry. It'd be nice. Some little town in Indiana, or go more south if you like. See, it's my own fantasy. Perfect small-town life."

"Plenty of little girls."

The line goes dead. Elated that he's talked back, defeated that he hasn't listened more closely, or asked questions, he sits for a long time at the restaurant, waiting for the phone to ring again. But it doesn't. He carries his cell phone, ready, open, hoping to hear something. He drives for a long time, hours, filling up his gas tank and laughing to think he is the last man in America who drives for therapeutic reasons. What's forty-five dollars when you need to be moving?

He keeps waiting for the phone to ring.

Nothing.

After a while, he thinks about an imaginary other place, a small town, a new start. Because if he talks, it will be bad, bad.

SIXTEEN

IT IS MONDAY NIGHT AND ALL of them have been given a dinner break. Colleen is on the phone with John, about to take him up on meeting at the pub, when Christie comes up to her, waving a hand for her attention. "Couple of us are going to Tessaro's. You want to come?"

"Rain check," she says into the phone. "A working dinner. I really didn't have very long anyway. In a day or two."

She feels a little relief that she's put it off again. It's not going to be easy, John trying to be nice, her just wanting to get away. Tears, self-doubt, anger, depression, the whole ball of wax waiting for her. She picks up her purse and follows the others out.

It's Christie, Dolan, Coleson, McGranahan, Potocki going to dinner. They start toward two squad cars and McGranahan opens the door for her as she's heading to Christie's car. Christie looks over, says, "See you there." Colleen looks at the situation, which is really kind of funny. The adult detectives are somehow jockeying for position to ride with the boss. "Hey," McGranahan says to Coleson, opening the back door of his car. "Want to jump in with us?"

"That's okay," Coleson answers. "I was just telling Commander something." Potocki is already getting into Christie's car. Then Coleson does a silent head count. "We've ridden five plenty of times. Actually, we could probably all fit in one car if we wanted."

"Look real good if we get called out on something," McGranahan says. "You want to?" he asks Colleen.

"Greer can sit on my lap," Potocki calls back.

She suspects Potocki has done his little act to defuse the car-riding arrangements. "It's okay. We're fine." Still, riding with McGranahan feels like being banished to second or third place.

She loves Tessaro's, the place the detectives haunted most when the Investigations Branch was located in East Liberty; they get back there when they can.

"This is the part I hate," McGranahan is saying. "All we can do now is interview the same people for the sixth time and wait for the labs."

When she sneaked over this morning with the DNA samples for Hoffman, she took one guy, Jack Higgins, aside, explaining what she needed. He listened to her pitch—was it because she was new, fresh? At first, he repeated that they were all getting evidence ready for the DA for a court case midweek. She fully expected him to say he wouldn't get to her DNA sample for a month, but he said instead that he would personally get going on it right away, in and around his other work.

True? He seemed nice enough.

It's crazy to want everything so fast. Computers that were state-of-the-art two years ago, faster than what she could have imagined, now seem like lollygagging children when she pushes them for what she wants.

What about old-style detective work, good old footwork?

Still, to have the technology in place and not have the money to hire enough people to get to it in a timely manner—maddening.

They pass the park where Jamilla was found, take the Sixteenth Street bridge, make their way over to Liberty Avenue. Colleen watches the other car up ahead, making it through the light just as McGranahan's car has to halt near the warehouse building being renovated with new fancy lofts. At each new place she encounters—city or neighborhood—Colleen asks herself, Could I live here? The place they're passing would have no trees, no grass. She imagines a life in the warehouse loft. Probably beautiful inside, but nothing much *outside* except traffic, concrete, and wholesale foods.

McGranahan adjusts the air conditioning, which is already doing a good job of pumping frigid air into the car, to an even lower setting. Colleen's skin has gone from damp to plain cold. Soon she will have goose bumps. In three miles or so, they'll get out of the car, sweat in the heat of the street, go into Tessaro's, and start the cooling process all over again. No wonder Littlefield got sick.

McGranahan says, "You seem sad. You sad?"

"Just tired. I didn't sleep again last night. I'm going to have to take something tonight. I went to the drugstore earlier. I hope to turn it around."

"I know the feeling. My wife can't sleep if I can't. So I give in half the time and take something the doctor gave me, Flexerol or something. Only it makes me feel awful the next day. Things that relax your muscles supposedly relax your brain, too, my doctor said. So then what good are you?"

"I know. I know." She's glad McGranahan is trying to be friendly, personable. It doesn't come easily to him.

She has got to sleep tonight, but her mind is buzzing buzzing with ideas she can't talk about. What if, what if, what if.

The streets of Bloomfield burst with color, signs out for pierogies and kielbasa at the Bloomfield Bridge Café and for hot dogs and kielbasa on sale at the Sure Save.

"A person can definitely get kielbasa in this hood," she says.

Traffic is heavy and parking is, as usual, impossible. They drive around and park two blocks from the restaurant, then start walking back. The smell of grilled meat and fish fills the neighborhood. "I detect a restaurant," McGranahan says.

Colleen smiles. It's a tired joke among police. "I couldn't live here, in these blocks," she says. "I'd be hungry all the time."

too bookish. And wondering what the hell she's doing in the middle of their boys' night out.

Coleson tilts a nod toward Colleen. "The kid's putting us down."

Christie smiles, points to his temple. "She's got kidneys."

Another old joke, but they laugh agreeably.

Potocki starts by ordering a rare burger. With home fries of course. Everybody at the table goes for a side of home fries. Dolan orders a burger too, asks for bacon and cheese on his.

"What are you having?" Coleson asks McGranahan.

Coleson and McGranahan fit in their odd-couple way. Contrasting the convex chest and good-boy personality of Coleson is McGranahan's concave chest and a habit of saying the wrong thing. McGranahan could eat no fat, Coleson could eat no lean. Coleson gets a burger, McGranahan a skewer of chicken.

Colleen orders the steak she's been wanting.

Christie hesitates and then goes for the chicken sandwich. Doesn't he get tired of chicken sandwiches?

"Peccadillo," Christie says, trying the word again. "Politician had a hell of a one. Poor bastard."

"What do you mean?" Coleson grunts.

"You have to feel bad for the guy."

The others nod into the idea. Guidance lessons for the troops. She finds that so interesting, that thing Christie has, a kind of sympathy for people in trouble. He'll laugh, he'll joke, then he'll remind you of the sad part of things.

He looks at his watch when they've finished eating. "We all have things to finish up tonight. Tomorrow—same long hours. I know you're tired."

"So tired," Potocki murmurs, "I made a big mistake the other day and I'm still paying."

"What?" Christie looks alarmed.

Potocki grumbles, "No, at home. I wasn't paying attention and she was saying all her clothes look dowdy and out of fashion. I was on automatic pilot, and I said, 'Come on now, honey. You know you'd look good with a bag over your head.' " The others start to snicker. "I meant to say with a gunny sack on, but I got my clichés mixed up."

The others shake their heads in sympathy, but they're laughing. Colleen tries to remember what Potocki's wife looks like, but she can't remember having met her.

"She said it was a Freudian slip," Potocki murmurs to Colleen.

She throws her hands up and tells Potocki to listen better to his wife next time.

The others are laughing and muttering, "Bag over her head. Whoa, that was not too smart."

Later, walking to the cars, she manages to get Christie alone. "Request permission," she says, "to go to West Virginia to talk to Hoffman's mother tomorrow."

"Why?"

"I know there's something. Something up close to be had there."

"Anything you want to tell me about?"

"No. A feeling. Four hours to get there. Four back."

"Okay. You've called? She's there?"

"I've called. I pretended it was a wrong number. She's there. I could start out early. Five, six, use my own time if need be."

"Okay. Go. But you don't have to go that early."

"I might want to so I don't miss what's going on back here."

"How's your fellow taking all this? Homicide schedule." Waving a hand as if to erase, take back, the personal question, he keeps moving.

Colleen answers it anyway, keeping up with him. "He's not."

"I beg your pardon."

"He's not in the picture anymore. I mean he's almost out of it. We're unraveling the last strands."

"You broke up?" Christie stops, looks disturbed, then—damn, damn, damn him—he gets that sympathetic look. It makes tears sting her eyes when he asks, "How'd that happen?"

"It just did. Sort of."

"The work?"

"I don't know what it was. Me. Just me he doesn't want. He wants to date others. I think a specific other, but it doesn't matter."

"What kind of jerk is he?"

"Thanks."

"We'll talk." He shakes his head, moves off to his car, turning back to get everybody moving. She thinks he looks kind of like a boxer, sturdy, very physical. Dresses well.

"What was that all about?" McGranahan asks.

"Nothing much." She shrugs. "Just small talk."

SEVENTEEN

CHRISTIE AND DOLAN WERE sitting across from Shoemaker in one of the small interrogation rooms at nine on Tuesday morning. It was good to be working with Dolan for a day. They were used to each other. And Dolan could cut through a lot of crap fast.

They were focusing this morning on the McCall case, and Christie held open the possibility that the two cases might be connected.

They had Shoemaker, Amy Rosenstein, and Hoffman—bam, bam, bam. Maybe something would happen.

Shoemaker looked around worriedly. He had got himself a haircut. He wore a shirt and tie and carried a sports jacket. The shirt and pants were in the gray range and the jacket and tie were navy, making him look uniformed.

Christie figured the guy was rehearsing his funeral clothes. "Detective Dolan and I have a few more questions for you," Christie said.

"Like what?"

"She had to have talked about her husband with you," Dolan began.

"Sure, some."

"Now is the time to be completely forthcoming. What did she have against him? Private stuff. Could be helpful. He was premature, he was inconsiderate, he was impotent, he was rough—these are all the kinds of things people go through and tell us about all the time. What was it in their case?"

Shoemaker looked uncomfortable. "I would say she found him mechanical and . . . and kind of . . . tense?"

"Violent?"

"No. More desperate."

"That makes sense," Dolan said easily. "So you two had a good sex life."

"Yes," he said, "but it seems wrong to talk about it."

"Why is that?"

"It's personal. She's dead. She wouldn't have liked it. She was shy."

"I'm sorry," Dolan said. "I understand. But I'd be lying if I didn't tell you sex is usually at the back of a crime like this. That much anger—you know. It's related to passion. We have to look into personal lives. So you two were fine—"

"Look, we were probably just ordinary. Nothing wild, no screaming. But we liked that aspect of our lives. We had pleasure."

"Sounds good to me," Dolan said. "Respect and pleasure."

"Yes. That was part of it. Respect. Thank you."

"What caused the tension—I know you had to give this some thought along the way. He was what? Gay? Closeted, did she think?"

Shoemaker appeared surprised by the easy classifications. But he said, "No, she didn't think he was. She thought he was straight. But hurt in some way."

"Hmm. She sounds smart. And sensitive. It must have been hard on her to leave him."

"It was. It took a lot out of her."

Dolan nodded. "Her parents liked you?"

Shoemaker nodded. His eyes reddened even more. "Her parents are good people, honestly. They're very messed up about the funeral arrangements. But through it all, they've kept their relationship with me."

"So. You were loved, accepted. You had something very good."

With that compliment, Christie knew Dolan was just about to corkscrew his way into something more difficult.

"See, the husband tells us he was supposed to go over there. Now this is a little odd. Was she still seeing him?"

"No," Shoemaker said. "No. Not that way. But he wanted to talk to her—well, he always wanted that. She let me know. She didn't hide it."

Dolan nodded. "So you believe she agreed to this meeting?"

"The truth is, I don't know. Okay." He sighed. "She was doing something odd. I know I have to tell you. I don't want to tell you, but I know I have to."

"What?"

"She was watching him. Trying to."

Christie and Dolan tried not to look at each other. Each felt the other almost gasp. This was good. This was good stuff.

"How do you mean?" Dolan asked.

Shoemaker shook his head.

"A detective? A PI?"

"I think, I think *she* was the PI. Acting like that."

"Something really disturbed her."

"Yes."

"What? She must have said something." Shoemaker shook his head again. "Indirectly? You must have a hint, man. What could it be?"

"Once, she asked me if I'd ever had any attraction to children."

"To children?" Dolan almost dropped off his chair. "What did you tell her?"

"I said no." And in the quick glint of his eyes, Christie saw a man who saw sex everywhere and didn't know what to make of the fact that he could *see* it, even the wrong stuff.

"Did that seem like an ordinary question?" Dolan asked.

"It's just that when she heard of a case, it upset her terribly. She just thought it was the worst thing ever."

"Most people would agree," Dolan said evenly.

Dolan spent twenty more minutes angling this way and that, but even he couldn't get anything else out of Shoemaker, so eventually, they let him go.

They watched him shuffle out.

"Children," Dolan said.

"I hear you," Christie said. "Ready? We have Amy Rosenstein next."

"Trick here," Dolan said, "is to keep me from leading the witness."

AMY ROSENSTEIN WORE HER blond hair past her shoulder blades and stick-straight. It moved when she did. It reminded Christie of a curtain.

Dolan was gritting his teeth to keep himself in check. "Was she happy romantically, sexually, with Shoemaker?"

"Yes, I suppose."

"Do you think he was kinky at all? Unusual?"

"No, I think more the opposite."

"What's the opposite?"

"A little bit dull, maybe, but not . . . kinky."

"So, now think about the husband for a moment, David Hoffman. What kinds of things bothered her about him?"

"They didn't click."

"Was he kinky in any way?"

"You keep asking about sex. Things aren't always about sex."

"No." Dolan looked thoughtful. "Not always. But in a murder case of this sort, ninety-five percent of the time, yes, so, you see, we have to check it out. Somewhere, sometime, she suggested to her best friend what kind of thing turned her off. Use of force, for instance. Did you get the impression David Hoffman could be rough?"

"I . . . didn't get the impression he was rough, no."

"And what else? Anything that slipped out from her. What freaked this friend of yours out?"

"Well, things that would freak anybody out. Bad behavior."

"Like what?" Dolan looked to Christie. He couldn't help himself. He said, "Like being inappropriate with children?"

Rosenstein looked surprised. "I never heard her say that about her husband. But when she first started to see Shoemaker, she said she hoped he wouldn't turn out bad and end up liking little girls or something."

"She said it that way? Casually? You're having coffee or what?"

"We were walking down the street and she was happy about meeting David—Shoemaker, I mean. She was all excited. Getting to know him. They'd been out twice, I think. She said, 'I really like him. He feels right. And I think he's a good person. Oh God, I hope he doesn't turn out to like little girls or something.' "

Dolan said, "You know, the reason I find that so interesting is that every woman I know who said such a line always ended up with 'I hope he's not an ax murderer' or 'I hope he's not a serial killer.' It's just sort of specific in an interesting way."

Christie acknowledged Dolan's observation with a nod. Then he jumped in. "Shoemaker thinks Laura was trying to find out something about her ex. Trying to resolve something. Do you know if she ever hired a private detective?"

"She talked about it once, but just about how expensive they were. This was a long time ago, before they separated."

"What was she looking for?" Christie tried to appear objective and calm.

"Evidence of another woman, I thought."

"She mention a specific detective she *wanted* to get?"

"She never gave me a name."

"What a shame," he said. A long silence elapsed. He watched Dolan's foot tapping. Both of them stood at the same time. Christie released her to her waiting boyfriend. "If you remember anything, let us know."

Did they have something? Or did they have a puff of smoke?

How did an amateur like Laura McCall *watch* somebody?

Christie said, "I'm thinking we get Laura photocopied and start showing her picture around where he lives, where he works, anyplace he goes to regularly. See if anybody saw her hanging around. Think she ever had a key to his workplace? Skulked around, raided his desk?"

"Looking for?"

"Porn? Porn. Kids."

ABOUT TEN O'CLOCK ON TUESday morning, Colleen tapped on the door of a well-kept frame house in Charleston. The woman who answered the door dropped her smile when she saw Colleen's briefcase. "If you're selling something—" she began.

"Mrs. Hoffman. May I come in? Police. Detective Colleen Greer."

The woman grabbed the door frame. Colleen was afraid she was going to faint.

She hastened to add, "I'm also a friend of your son's. I had dinner with him on Sunday night."

Eileen Hoffman studied her carefully but didn't open the door. Colleen smiled. "We always talk to in-laws. They're interested in clearing their own family members, and they often have excellent insights. May I come in?"

"You had dinner with my son?"

"Yes. We went to an Italian place. Maybe he told you. I imagine you are on the phone to him a lot. He needs support through this, and we used to work together." Colleen tried the door handle, turning gently, and the door opened slightly. "May I?" she asked.

Eileen nodded, backed up. "At first, you said police. . . ."

"That's my job now. I was one of his employees a few years ago. I remember Laura from social gatherings, parties. She was a lovely woman. I am very sorry for your loss."

"Yes. Thank you."

"I thought you might be coming up to Pittsburgh for the funeral, but David didn't say, he didn't seem to be sure."

"No. I don't handle things like that too well."

"Well, I'm not sure most people do. It's very upsetting."

They continued to stand in the front hallway. Eileen Hoffman said, "At any funeral I've ever gone to, I can't stop crying. I mean, when I start, it's rivers. The tears just keep coming. And this would be much worse."

"I understand. The tears are for all kinds of things, all kinds of memories. I do understand."

"I think maybe you do."

"I hate to trouble you, but if I could have a glass of water, that would be just great."

"Yes, okay." Eileen went to the kitchen, looking back over her shoulder.

"Do you mind if I go into the living room?"

"Yes, it's okay. You want ice?"

"Yes, thanks, ice would be great." She stood in front of a framed photo of David, probably his high school class picture. His mother came back into the room wiping the bottom of the glass with her hand. She was still rattled.

"Good-looking kid," Colleen said.

"He was always smart in school, too."

"He continued to be smart out of school. I mean at work. We all thought so."

Eileen handed over the water. "I don't know what you want. You drove all the way here?"

"I like to drive. May I sit?"

"Yes. He didn't do anything bad. If that's what you're here to ask."

"I was hoping you could help fill in his history. I hope you kept photos and report cards and all that. My parents did."

"Why would you need that?"

"If there's circumstantial evidence against him, then it's helpful to have all the good history to put next to it. To give an accurate portrait of him. I know I sound a little like a defense lawyer, but the police have to think like that in case a thing goes to court."

"Court?"

"I hope it never comes to that. We have to cover so much ground."

"You just want to see his school things?"

"Things like that, yes. I'll help you sort through, see what would be useful."

"I did keep everything," Eileen said uncertainly.

"Are they handy? It wouldn't take long for me to see what's useful."

Hoffman's mother went upstairs and came down only two minutes later with two boxes of things, the most interesting of which was a school scrapbook.

Colleen said, "Aha. I knew you'd keep everything neat like this. You seem like a person who cares for things."

"I do. I try."

Colleen looked at the *A*'s and *B*'s David had earned. There were no reports of behavior problems as far as she could see. "Excellent grades." She smiled. "*And* perfect scores on attendance, conduct." She pretended after a few minutes to lose interest in the scrapbook before her. "Anyway. Did Laura keep contact with you? After the split with your son?"

"A Christmas card and a birthday card. But nothing much written on them. You know, getting a little distant."

"People do that."

"I still don't know what went wrong between them."

"These things happen." Colleen casually turned back a page in the scrapbook and noticed something. The address on the report card had changed. Pennsylvania. The later report cards came from West Virginia, but this earlier one came from Sewickley, near Pittsburgh.

"I keep getting distracted by the scrapbook. I love things like this. Watching someone grow up." She kept leafing back in the book, and saw the address change again, this time to Monroeville, a suburb of Pittsburgh. "There's a whole life in records like this. Pittsburgh's a great city, isn't it? David told me he always loved it."

"I never got to know it well." The change of expression on Eileen Hoffman's face told Colleen there was something to go after.

"How long were you there altogether?" Her voice was steady, but her heart began to pound as she thought of the possibilities of the connection she hoped to make. She closed the scrapbook but marked her place with a finger.

"Not long. We moved there for a couple of years, two and a half or something like that, then came back here."

Her heart thumped harder. She was going to leap, to gamble. She opened the book again and kept leafing backward. "Yes. I see. Good. That would have been when you were with his father." She looked up.

Aha. Yes. A hit. Eileen's face was so pale, she looked sick. Her voice was wisp-thin when she said, "What do you mean?"

"He told me you lived with his father for a while."

"Oh."

"Didn't work out, he said."

The woman tightened both fists until the knuckles showed white. "We were happier down here."

"I see." Colleen continued to study the book as she hurtled forward. "Interesting, though, his grades went down during the time with Charlie." She looked up.

Charlie. She'd said it, just like that.

And Eileen Hoffman didn't say *I don't know what you mean.* She didn't say, *I don't know anybody named Charlie.* Her eyes glazed over and her face went still.

Colleen wanted to ask a million more questions, but she knew she had gone pretty far.

"I don't know a Charlie," Eileen finally said weakly, her voice almost inaudible.

Colleen's spirits sank. She couldn't afford to be wrong. She thought she'd had it right in her hands.

"See, David's father died in Vietnam two months after we got married."

"I'm sorry. How awful for you. What was his name?"

"Peter. Peter Hoffman." Eileen reached forward and took the scrapbook. "Why do you need all this? Why am I talking to you?" The voice of the woman sinking into the sofa cushions came at her in the unmistakable high tones of fear.

Colleen had gotten somewhere, but she wasn't sure where it was. "Because I'm trying to help you. Because I'm trying to help your son."

And as she said it, she realized it was true.

IN THE CONFERENCE ROOM

where Christie and Dolan were meeting Hoffman, the blackboard held the ghost of Christie's map from Sunday afternoon. The windows had safety bars on them. The whole building, in fact, had barred windows. The police had thought it was impossible in their new quarters for anybody to escape, particularly from holding cells and interview rooms where there were *no* windows, but someone *had* gotten away, last summer. A little Houdini act. Fellow broke his shackles, went up through the ceiling vent, got away. An amazing testament to the wish to be free.

Start with the easy stuff was Christie's and Dolan's motto.

"We know about the trouble with the funeral," Christie began.

"Either Colleen will budge them or the judge decides."

"What place did you choose?"

"Near where I live. Freyvogel."

"Very reputable. I'm sorry things are rough with the family. Do you—I have to ask this—do you have anyone else in your life at the moment? Someone you see?"

"I just had that one dinner with someone on Friday night."

Christie consulted his legal pad. "Paula Conti."

"Yes."

The woman had corroborated Hoffman's account. She said she'd liked him and was shocked when she saw the news.

"Anybody else?"

"The last woman I dated was, say, four months ago or so. Joanna Nazeem. If you want character witnesses, you could go to her. And Colleen Greer, I hope. She knew me. Then there's Mindy Cooper, who works for me. And the therapists on staff now—Andrea Colum and Michael Craver."

"Right. We are planning to talk to Andrea when she gets back from vacation. We met Michael Craver, as you know. What do you think of him?"

"A good therapist. And a kind soul."

Christie smiled. "They still make kind souls? I like to think so."

"I know. He has an odd manner. But he's gold."

"We were there about Jamilla Washington. Did he treat her?"

Hoffman twitched. "No, he's not been there long enough."

"Did you treat her?"

"No. But at the Center, we treated her family."

"Do you have any idea who killed her?"

"I have no idea."

"But you remember the family?"

"Oh, yes, definitely."

"And what do you remember?"

"Anything I know would be confidential."

Christie said abruptly and irritably, "I understand there are some things you can't say. But this is a murder investigation. And a child is dead. And we had a murder two days before that. And a lovely woman is dead. And unfortunately for you, you knew both of them. Is it too much to ask you to cooperate, to bend any rule you have as much as you can?"

"I'll try." Hoffman mopped his brow. "Believe me, I see that this is a special condition. I'll try."

"Well, let me help you out a little. We know Deon Washington and his wife drink."

"They did."

"Well, they still do. Big-time. Did you know that?" Hoffman sighed, shook his head. "Our records show he was arrested again six months or so ago, but charges were not pressed. You know anything about that?"

"No."

"He didn't come in for therapy?"

"No."

"Why the hell were charges not pressed?" Dolan asked.

And Christie answered him in the little play they were enacting. "Because the guy he beat up didn't press them. Because Deon was scheduled to go to AA and to go to therapy."

Hoffman looked surprised. Was he acting, too? "I never saw him again. It never came to me. It's a ball that got dropped."

"Or he came in and you released him?"

"That didn't happen. He did come in once a year ago, not six months ago. Ask anybody at the office. Go on."

Dolan said in his mildest tones, "Well, you have to understand we have to ask you your whereabouts on Saturday night and Sunday morning. You hearing me? The time of Jamilla's disappearance."

Good word, Christie thought. *Disappearance.* How many ways they found not to say *murder, killing*.

"Look, all I know is that I've been at home watching television and sleeping ever since . . . what happened to Laura."

"Nobody saw you?"

"Nobody saw me."

"Did you see Jamilla Washington on Saturday or Sunday?"

"No."

"Did you know she was sexually active?"

"No." Seemed genuine. They let a silence go by.

"She would have been thirteen now," Dolan said. "Did you know the molestation apparently goes back, way back?"

"What do you mean?"

"When your people were treating the family, didn't it come out that she was abused in this way?"

"No. It's always a possibility. But I didn't know that."

"Who do you think did it?"

Hoffman's hands went to his face, over his eyes, up his forehead into his hair. He looked like a man in terrible grief. "The father," he said, "is the obvious choice."

"Do you believe it?"

"No. I don't know."

Christie slid a legal pad over. "Okay. Okay. Write down everything you can think of from the TV on Saturday night. TV is your alibi. Write it down."

While he wrote, Christie and Dolan went into the hall. "What do you think?" Christie asked him.

"Man, you want my gut or my brain?"

"Gut."

"The man is a mess. He knows something. He doesn't know the nitty-gritty of what happened."

"Go on."

Dolan chose his words carefully, evidenced by the slow way he pronounced them. "He didn't do it himself."

Their gut reactions matched. They went back into the room.

"I thought of some other things," Hoffman said before he turned over the legal pad. "I was on the phone—with the funeral home, with

Laura's parents, with Shoemaker, with my mother, trying to work out the details. Laura's parents wouldn't actually talk to me, but they got their lawyer and Shoemaker to call back a couple of times."

They already had an order in to get his phone records. They could check it out.

"Write it all down for us."

Hoffman wrote for nearly an hour before he left.

COLLEEN STOPPED ON THE WAY back from West Virginia at a place just outside of Wheeling. She needed fuel—for her brain and her car. Only a muffin and a cup of coffee earlier that morning stood between her and a massive headache. She parked and walked back around behind the big trucks to unhinge her knees, then went indoors.

The woman Colleen had questioned all morning was a combination of steely and weak—victimized, but not letting anyone in, either—the kind of person who was hell in family counseling, defended to the teeth. What was her history? Hoffman said she was a single mother. But he didn't say, "I had a father who died before I was born." Interesting omission. Fifty-eight, sixty, Eileen Hoffman still looked good, in a pale, bottled-up sort of way. Had Peter Hoffman existed? Yes, Colleen guessed. Eileen did not seem the sort of woman to have a child out of wedlock, even granting it would have been the late sixties. She seemed more the type to abort.

Colleen had tried her trick. She had said the name Charlie as if she knew something, and she had seen alarm, or what looked like it, on the woman's face, but after that, only denial. So. Was it her imagination? And was her imagination so active it bordered on crazy?

The menu at the truck stop presented her with delight and despair. Almost everything was substantial. The special was roast lamb, of all things. For lunch. In summer. You had to feel sorry for the cooks in the kitchen no matter what kind of air conditioning system they had. Shoring up her resolve to get a little discipline back in her life, she ordered the Caesar salad with chicken on it. Dull, but not self-destructive.

Once the order was in, she went to the ladies' room, washed her face with a quarter-size piece of complexion soap she carried with her, reapplied lipstick and blush, fluffed her hair. Things she would revise if she could: more height; lower jaw retracted by a little; eyes larger. Oh well, it didn't matter. She was beyond all that foolishness, right? And beyond expecting life to work out in all those conventional ways. She had plenty of evidence that it wasn't going to.

The truckers—she assumed they were truckers—appeared to give her a nod of approval as she slid into her booth. And she had a moment of feeling grateful they approved. Silly. Silly.

When her phone rang, she saw it was the McCalls' number. She walked outside into the sunny haze and humidity to take the call. She'd managed to get the McCalls last night and done her best to move the funeral along by suggesting they divide everything down the middle—time, cost, decisions. She was surprised now to hear Mrs. McCall say, "Your plan. How would that work if we wanted to go ahead with it?"

"I'm glad you want to go ahead. Just call your lawyer. He'll help you divide the time."

Good. Now the police could work the funeral. The *funerals.*

The viewing for Jamilla would begin tonight. Lots to do. Lots.

She peered inside the restaurant. Her food was not at the table yet. She made another call. The Lutheran church had come up with more food deliveries to the Washingtons. That, plus the kindnesses of neighbors, would hold them for a few days.

She called Headquarters.

Christie, who had been in interviews all morning, answered. "Greer!"

"I stopped for lunch. I wondered—" She could hear voices in the background.

"We'll catch you up when you get in. The mother?"

"She lived in Pittsburgh for a couple of years. And seems to want to hide it. There might be something there. She has a very obscured history. Why she does is the question. And also—"

The airy sound that punctuated their conversation told her he had an incoming call.

"Can it wait till you get back? I have to get this."

"Sure."

And so she went inside and ate her salad, thinking, I have to say the words, let him laugh at me if I'm nuts. I have to take the chance.

Driving back, she felt such longing—for what? Everything, all kinds of things, everything she didn't have: autumn weather, the roast lamb, a changed John.

When she finally got into Headquarters, she went to Christie's office. Dolan was in there and the two of them were talking quietly and going over reports on the two cases. They indicated with a look that she could come in, but they kept talking to each other. Dolan was saying, "Hoffman is cooperating. Why don't we get him back in for a polygraph tomorrow? See how he reacts to doing one?"

Christie said, "Yeah, let's."

Dolan wrote it down on his legal pad.

"We can talk tomorrow morning, decide what we're asking him. Both of you." Christie nodded to include Colleen.

Dolan's phone rang and he took the call. As soon as he said "Hello," Christie's cell phone rang. It was clearly his wife—or seemed to be. He said, "I know, honey, I know. Okay, I can do that. Give me five minutes." And before he could say more, his landline phone rang. He held a hand up to Colleen and answered it.

Fifth wheel for sure was what she felt like. She waited for a pause. Dolan ended his call. Christie ended his. She tapped her legal pad, said, "I'll write up what I did today. I want to follow up the years in Pittsburgh, what relationships the mother had."

"Okay. Good."

"And when you have a moment, I'll come back. There's, um, something else I want to talk about, maybe check."

Christie looked harried. "Okay. Come back in five minutes."

She left, trying not to feel foolish.

"SO," DOLAN BEGAN. "HERE'S the next question. What—"

Christie's phone rang again. He picked up. "Oh, damn, oh, damn, oh, damn," he said. Then he listened some and said, "If I read all night, I couldn't be caught up. Okay. If I have to, I have to." When he got off the phone, he said, "I have to be in court tomorrow. I heard they were delaying. I thought I was getting out of it for a couple more days. Lousy timing. You were saying?"

Dolan had been elaborating on the earlier idea of a hit man. "What if there's a mysterious third factor, a *voluntary* hit man?"

"I get you. Same theory you had about the Chandra Levy case, right?"

"Right. Listen. A man complains to a friend that his career is about to be ruined by a woman, and the *friend* hires a thug—so the man with the problem doesn't know how his problem got solved. The guy at the center is innocent so long as he doesn't figure it out. So he tries to put away the ideas hitting him; he doesn't want to know. Who would, huh?"

Christie had to admit that was the kind of expression he thought he'd seen on Hoffman's face. "Maybe," he said. "Maybe. Could be. Greer has some ideas, too."

Dolan tipped his head toward where Colleen had left. "How is Greer holding up?"

"Fine. She's doing fine. Her relationship—maybe she told you—started falling apart right about when all this started, but she's hanging tough."

"She didn't tell me."

"Well, I'm sure it isn't something she'd talk about much."

Dolan's eyebrows went up. "But she told you."

"It sort of just happened."

"Well, it's clear to anyone who looks at her that she has a crush on you."

"I'm mentoring her. It doesn't mean anything."

Then Dolan smiled and seemed more himself for a second. "Well, everybody needs a crush now and then. It's sweet."

"I don't know about that."

A tap at the door and Colleen came back in. "Ready for me yet?"

"I have to go to the john," Dolan said. "I'll be at my computer after that."

He left and Colleen sat. She looked very serious.

"I know this sounds wild," she said. "You know how faces look alike in some families? I mean, you could look at Kiefer Sutherland and if you didn't have his name, you'd still be saying, 'He reminds me of someone.' You know?"

"Who's Kiefer Sutherland?"

"Actor. Donald Sutherland's son. You look at him and it makes you think of Donald Sutherland."

"Who's . . ." It was half a joke, half serious. Christie always told people he paid no attention whatever to popular culture.

She laughed dutifully. "Okay, never mind. Let me start again. You know who Hoffman *looks* like? I mean, I keep jumping when I see this guy."

"What? Who?"

"Assistant Chief Dun."

Christie thought about it. "They look kind of alike, I guess. Yes, I see it. You have anything else?"

"Nothing more concrete than a look on Mrs. Hoffman's face when I kind of passed his name by her, first name only. But I'd like to check it out. Check out his history. I realize what I'm saying. I mean, I know I don't have anything real yet. It's a feeling."

He did what he always did with rookies, gave them room when they had a suggestion, so as to build self-esteem, or at least not damage it. "Well, sure, check it out. Get back to me."

"Intuition," she said. "I believe in it."

She left and he sat down, hauling the files he needed for court toward him.

A look-alike kind of thing. He tried to summon the two faces. Yes, there was a resemblance. Not enough to get a jolt in the gut, as Greer no doubt had. But something.

Well, she'd check. She might be intuitive, and, Lord knows, that could be an excuse for just about anything, but she also had a decent logical side.

His phone rang again, and this time it was his wife. "Sorry I didn't get back to you," he said.

For almost the first time in his marriage to Marina, he heard the policeman's wife in her voice. She fought it, all right, but the way she asked, "Do you have to read the reports there? Could you bring them home to read?" made him feel guilty.

"I'll split the difference. Read some here, bring some home." He'd probably be a snarling dog around the house.

"We can have a late dinner," she said. "How about that?"

"I'll start out from here at, say, seven-thirty. Promise."

He read for two hours or so before Colleen came back in. She said, "Boss, I've done everything I can on the computer. At least Dun, one *n,* is easier than all the two *n* Dunns. There aren't as many. But if I'm going to run with this, I need to get into the files at Personnel."

Dog on a scent. He nodded. She was dead serious. "Because they look alike?"

"It's more than that. He came in at four-thirty in the morning the other day—well, yesterday, Monday. I didn't have time to tell you. Then I told myself it was nothing. But the look on his face is still with me. I have to check him. How do I talk to Personnel so they don't alert him?"

"I'll go with you. Tomorrow morning. At nine. Before I go to court."

"And they won't leak it? I mean, this is . . . just the fact of checking a superior, it's explosive, I know that."

"I'll talk to Personnel," he said. "Go home. Get some rest. You did good today."

She hesitated. "We were scheduled for the funeral home tonight. First viewing for Jamilla."

"Oh. Damn. Right. Can you do that on your own? That would be a big help."

"Sure. Anything else I can do?"

Christie thought about it. He handed over the files on predators. "Match what you see here to anything you know. Do your little lecture thing to the troops tomorrow."

He watched her walk off with the files, hauled up his own paperwork, and went home.

MARINA GREETED HIM AT THE door with a wry smile. "I never thought I'd be one of those wives." She took his hand.

He kissed her.

She sat him down, saying, "I'll let you work. I do intend to feed you, though."

He closed his eyes. Marina kissed his eyes, his forehead. He felt so sad, so sad.

"You need sleep," she said.

"Everybody needs that." He heard himself using Dolan's phrasing. *Everybody needs a crush.* Except it wasn't true. It made life confusing. "I like working a case hard," he said. "The only problem is . . . failing." He laughed. "Failing kind of gets in the way of the thrill."

"You're not failing."

"Feels like it at the moment."

She slid down to the floor next to him, head on his knee. Kissed his knee.

Sweet.

She had time on her hands; that was part of the ache. Rehearsal hadn't started up yet. Her job as artist in the schools had been over since June. She was meant to be onstage, tackling something difficult.

"I'll put dinner on. How long do you want to work before we eat?"

"Ten minutes."

"Good, ten it is." She stood and got ready to move off.

He grabbed her behind the knee, brought her back to him. "I love you."

"I know."

EIGHTEEN

HOFFMAN GOT THE PHONE CALL he wanted when he least expected it—at one in the morning. He was groggy. He could hardly understand what he was hearing. "Find a pay phone. Call me. My cell."

Click. Dial tone.

It took him only a few minutes to get dressed, get into his car, and drive downtown, where he knew there was at least one pay phone that worked. The thought that his father had something to hide came to him, sickening him. He pushed the thought aside, hoping there was a way for it not to be so.

When he made the return call, his father answered before the first ring was complete. "You have gas in the car?"

"Yeah."

"Take Seventy-nine south. Head to Morgantown, through it, then ten miles the other side, you'll see a sign for Cooper Road, right off the highway, then a sign for Smiley's restaurant and truck stop. Got it?"

"Yes."

"Go to the truck stop. Wait for me if I'm not there. I'll probably be right behind you. Stay in the car. On the road, check behind you every sixty seconds or so. Make sure you're not followed. Except by me. At some point, if I hit it right, you'll see the Buick. You see me, you just keep going. I won't show if you're followed by anyone else. If you are, go back home."

Followed. Surveillance on him? Fear was inching through his body; he felt it in his gut, down his left arm; he was a suspect, it was real. "What's going on that you—" he began. "Are you there? Hello?" Only dead air. He looked at his watch. He thought, I won't do this, yet he was leaping toward his car, starting it up. He'd been here before. Going toward, terrified, and wanting to go away.

As the buildings on Fifth, then Smithfield, disappeared behind him, he had to caution himself to drive more slowly. He didn't stop for a bathroom or gas. Every sixty seconds, he looked left, right, in the rearview mirror, but he saw nothing that made him feel he was being followed. There was hardly any traffic on the parkway. The only cars he saw pulled off at exits or passed him, going fast, maybe airport-bound. Nothing, nothing. But as soon as he left 279 for 79, he saw the Buick van. The night and the glare on the windshield glass obscured his father's face. He couldn't tell if the face was kindly, impassive, scowling, but he kept looking back every sixty seconds, as if he would finally be able to see it.

When had he eaten last? Couldn't remember.

The truck stop, when he came to it—and he wondered if his father would zoom ahead and lead him there, but it didn't happen—was easy to slip into, a huge parking lot that went way beyond the yellow-brick building that held the restaurant. He fancied he smelled trucker food—sausage and bacon, maybe biscuits, gravy, potatoes—but he was the whole way out in the parking lot, so it was probably imagination.

He pulled around to the car-park area, not too many autos there, maybe forty trucks, most of them eighteen-wheelers. The Buick pulled way over near the trucks. He didn't know what he was supposed to do next, so he waited. After a while, his door partway open, the sounds of nothing but motors humming, he got out of the car and walked toward the Buick, head down, grateful for the slight breeze in the night air. The pools of oil on the concrete made dark stains, like blood, he thought. He stepped carefully, as though he might slip on the oil.

His father got out of the car and started walking around behind the parked trucks, motioning to him with the slightest tilt of the head. He realized now where the sound was coming from. Many of the trucks had their motors running to cool the cabs or cargo containers. Dinosaurs breathing, ready to leap at a moment's notice. Some probably had drivers sleeping inside, although none were visible.

The air was hotter again back around the trucks.

His father wore a polo shirt, jeans, looked casual, like a regular guy. They walked a little, in shadow, then in a spill of light.

The sight of his father's face was unwelcome, welcome, frightening, comforting—all at once. Meeting with the old man was dizzying every time. Were they alike, as his father had so often said? It didn't seem so. "You look like him," Laura had said when she finally met the old man, the time she'd followed him, thinking he was meeting a woman. She'd found him instead having a burger with his father at a Denny's. Did they look alike? His father was florid, light hair gone gray, blue-gray eyes, not the startling blue of some, but almost colorless. His father was getting heavy, yes, a good twenty pounds more since he last saw him, but he carried it well, with that sense of authority that put a positive stamp on his weight.

Charlie, he called him. Always called him by that name.

Charlie said, "I want you to go away for a while. Tonight."

At first, he almost laughed. It was one thing to fantasize, another thing to do it. "I can't."

"You can. You have to."

"You don't understand. The private viewing is tomorrow night at the funeral home."

"Listen to me. I'm taking a big chance here. I'm taking a big risk even coming to talk to you. They're going to put you on a polygraph tomorrow. They're going to get you on circumstantial evidence. I read the reports."

"But I didn't do it."

A long pause. "Maybe not. But you've heard of an innocent man going to jail, eh? And I don't think you'd handle a polygraph well. You don't bounce back from a thing like that."

"And if I'm gone, what does it look like?" Again, the conversation he meant to have got right out of his grasp and he was having a different conversation.

"I'm taking a big chance here. It'll be fine if you go away. They'll find someone else to blame it on. Or it will go cold. An intruder—that's hard to pin down."

"You're talking about Laura."

"What else?"

"The girl."

"What girl?"

Of course his father knew. And so the lie said what he feared. There was no other explanation.

"Don't treat me like I'm stupid. I know."

His father looked at him for a long time, a deep, studying glare. Finally, tears welled in his father's eyes. "All my life, I never could trust anybody. It's funny it should turn out to be you. The only person I could turn to for help. It's funny." His father was laughing and crying, wiping the tears with the back of his hand. "We have to get out of here. Bad enough we could be seen talking."

Hoffman felt sick because now the answer was yes. Questions buzzed in his head. But he knew he wouldn't get answers.

"I don't understand how—"

"There's no time for that now."

"Are they after you?"

"No. They're going after you, and I think I can deflect the investigation if you stay away."

"I have a job."

"People fall apart. People go away. Leave a message, say, 'I have to go away for three days.' "

"Three days?" Hoffman asked hopefully.

"You'll be gone longer, but they need to be thrown off, not know."

"They'll find me."

"No. No. I've brought you cards, identity cards, everything you could possibly need. Money. Plates. You get out tonight, go to a small town. Rent a place—stay out of hotels. Eventually, you'll get some work."

Anger surged in him. This was what it felt like to be erased. His father was suggesting, ordering, a whole new identity, as if— "You know goddamn well I have a job. I have a profession. What do you think I've worked for all these years?"

"I'm telling you something important."

"Damn you. This time, *this time,* I can't do what you want."

"You're not letting me help you."

"Who's helping? Who's doing the helping?"

"For a while, then. Buy me some time. You talk about reputation. Do you want to bring me down? After all the good I did. All the years of good I did."

One of the trucks fifty feet ahead of them went into gear, wheezed, rumbled, and started out. Both men froze, watching the driver curve around to the gas pumps.

"He could have seen us," Hoffman said.

"He could have. Might have." A silence came over them. "You have to go," his father said finally.

"Why?"

"Because I know better and I said so. I know how these things work."

"I never actually get any answers from you. Well, I have some questions. You're asking me to do something, so I have a right to some answers. What did Laura do? To you?"

"She was playing detective again."

Hoffman tried to catch up to what this meant. Laura had followed him a couple of times, right before they broke up. She'd assumed there was another woman, and, looking for that common thing, she ended up finding out about their crazy family arrangement. A father he met for a meal every once in a while, not the sort who came for visits or to Thanksgiving dinner or who called on the phone. Nothing much he could explain to her.

His father said, "She was a nosy bitch. She endangered us, you and me, both our reputations."

"How?"

"Snooping around the North Side office."

Jamilla. It was his father and Jamilla, then. That's why Laura had called him.

"Do you hear me? I'm talking about both our reputations."

His father had a key to the Family Counseling Center, and he'd given the key out himself when his father requested it. That made him an accessory. He didn't ask how his father used the place. He knew. How could he say he didn't if he had thought it and feared it?

Hoffman's hands came up to his face, covered his mouth. Finally, he let his hands drop. "Couldn't you stop yourself?"

"I made a mistake," his father was saying. "I cared about her. I loved her. It wasn't simple. It wasn't anything you could understand. It was something that happened over time."

Hoffman let himself fall against a wire fence, groaning. There was nothing at all he could do. No way to save the situation.

"Who's going to understand? You see, even with all your degrees, you don't understand. You won't let yourself understand. Every day in the paper you find this coach or that doctor or that father is arrested for what happened between him and someone young. Right? When are people going to say, Hey there's something we don't want to admit because it doesn't fit how we think things are, but it's there, it happens, it happens all the time."

"Not all the time," Hoffman said weakly. "Don't give me that." He pressed away from the fence and began walking. He was sick, and one of the trucks leaked fumes so putrid, he was nearly overcome.

Flashes of a court case came to him as he walked. He could feel his father walking behind him, but he kept going, walking into the future, his father on the stand, him called in to testify, cameras going. He stopped, held on to the fence again. It was unbearable. He had given his father the key to the place. He had asked no questions.

He didn't know what to do.

"We're alike, you know?"

He shook his head. "No. No, I never—"

"They're going to keep calling you in. They'll be relentless." His father paused. "You had dinner with a detective, right?"

"Yes. As a friend. I knew her."

"Right. That's where you're dumb. See. They'll question you until you break. You have to be gone."

"I don't have anything with me."

"I told you: I have everything you need."

"Clothes? I don't have clothes, papers, money, nothing."

"You can't take the time to go back. I have twelve thousand in the package, not to mention some charge cards. Two names. You'll see. The card I mainly want you to use says your last address was Lexington, Kentucky. Head that direction. You buy a set of clothes one day in one place, another day in another place. Stay modest. First couple of days, treat it like a vacation. Go to Mammoth Cave. I can get more money to you in time. I wish it were me. I wish I were on the road."

Why not you? he asked silently.

But his father answered as if he'd heard. "They're not looking at me. They're gunning for you. You don't want to go through an interrogation. You don't want to. That son of a bitch Christie will get you saying anything."

Hoffman took the package.

His father grabbed his hand, squeezed. "Thank you. Go now. Please."

Hoffman walked to his car and started out.

Ten miles from the truck stop, he found an empty lot and changed his plates. He was supposed to get rid of the old ones and his wallet and identity cards—that was the last thing his father had told him—but he couldn't make himself do it. He put those things under the passenger seat, deciding he would find another way, a place to hide them. He didn't want to be someone else forever.

He called work and left a message: "I'm not doing well. I'm taking a couple of days off. I need to get away, clear my head."

It was too late to change his mind; he was already driving toward Lexington, new plate on the car, new wallet in his pocket.

He was Patrick P. McDonough, forty-two years old. Married, divorced, two sons. He'd gained four years, a divorce decree, and two kids in a couple of hours. He had several copies of a work résumé that said he was an insurance investigator. Well, his father could get anything. But he was a counselor, and a good one. There was no way he could imagine himself using the résumé. He'd be better off washing dishes.

He drove south, wondering how long he could stay awake. Forever perhaps. Keep driving. End up someplace he hadn't ever been. Where it was hotter and more humid, where the flies buzzed and the kudzu grew, and the earth steamed up.

He had to take action. He had to. He couldn't. The car hummed along, taking him with it, somewhere.

NINETEEN

WEDNESDAY MORNING, COLLEEN appeared in his office, paper Starbucks cup in hand.

Christie told her to sit for a moment. "Funeral home?" he asked.

"The way Jamilla is laid out, they have her looking like an underage bride, which, I guess, is ironic."

"Sad," he said. "And? Talk?"

"Lots of it. Nothing new. I'll go back. And to the McCall viewing tomorrow."

Christie said, "Right. I hope to get to some of it."

"Funny. Jamilla will be buried tomorrow, before people even begin to pay their respects to McCall. Reverse order of the deaths. Oh." She dug in her bag. "Here are your files."

"Anything jump out?"

"Two more possible than the others. I've made some notes." He looked at her notes as he phoned Personnel and asked for Elizabeth Thuma. When she came on the line, he said in a voice hinting at warning, "I need to see you. Can you spare me a few minutes this morning?"

Thuma said she could in tones that picked up his hint.

"Let's go," he said to Colleen.

Thuma met Christie, followed by Detective Greer, at the door to her private office. He indicated with a thumb that he wanted Greer to come in, too. Thuma backed up; he motioned Colleen in ahead of him, then closed the door. The three sat down.

"There's someone I need to look at," he said simply.

Thuma didn't say she'd figured as much, though she surely had. She, like Christie, chose words carefully. "Tell me what you need," she said.

"I want Detective Greer to do the reading of the files. Whatever she needs. Is there a private room here she could use?"

"Yes. I can make space."

"Thank you. The files she needs to read would be for Charles Dun. Assistant chief."

He had to give Thuma credit. He saw her eyes waver, he heard the inner "Oh man, oh no," but all she said was, "I'll get it, Commander."

COLLEEN HAD FOUND DUN'S address, phone number, home ownership, tax status (he paid regularly), and financial records (he had an excellent credit rating) on the Internet. She'd even found a couple of newspaper articles that mentioned him. But it didn't take real work; you could get that kind of stuff on anybody.

"Is this everything?" she asked Elizabeth Thuma when the Personnel woman brought a thick file in a hanging folder to the table of a small interview room.

"No. There's another folder. The earlier years."

"I'll want that one, too." Maybe especially that, she thought.

"I'll get it."

So as not to lose any time at all, Colleen began reading the folder covering the later years. One positive letter after another suggested Charles Dun took his job seriously. Disappointment and a tinge of shame came over Colleen. What did she think she was up to? A junior, a rookie, going after an assistant chief because she thought his cheekbones and the angle of his eyes and something about his jaw reminded her of the current suspect. And because he so clearly didn't like her. Chief liked him a lot. According to these letters, Chief thought he was top-drawer.

But then she noticed what he was doing before he became assistant chief in charge of patrol officers five years ago. He'd been commander in charge of the Family Crisis Division. That squad had also come to include sexual assault.

Yearly evaluations. She began to skim faster, until one paragraph caught her eye. A commendation for starting the KID Photo File. She backtracked. She knew about KID—patrol officers called to domestic disturbances had to take and file photos of children in households marked by abuse or neglect. Also, they were supposed to make recommendations for psychological or—*bingo*—family counseling. Various counseling centers were mentioned as part of the recommendation. One of those was the one on the North Side. She didn't know Dun had initiated this system ten years ago. Colleen could feel her heart pounding. Blood rushed to her head.

Before she finished the folder she was working on, Elizabeth Thuma came in with the early materials, nodded curtly, left.

Christie had trusted her with this. She couldn't screw up. Facts. The house number in Highland Park. It stayed the same through the first and second folders. Guy hadn't moved all of his life. She looked to the earlier folder. Same address, and not an address in Monroeville or Sewickley. So she was wrong. Or was she? Police weren't allowed to live outside the city. So maybe . . . Phone number. Same. Unlisted. Cell phone in more recent years, different numbers. She got them all down.

She shivered, as if someone, Dun, looked over her shoulder and saw what she was doing.

The older folder went back another twenty years. It yielded a different kind of thing: people. She went through it fast, looking for names. His partners when he was a detective. She jotted the names. One of them might be an old friend of Christie's, someone he could have a *sotto voce* with. She went the whole way back to the beginning, Academy training. There were people who had gone through training with Dun and were still around. McCallister. Still on the Robbery squad, if she remembered correctly. And Evans on Narcotics. Old guys, creaky, but still on the job. And James Picarelli, who had just retired. Dun came off as younger than these others—he had energy.

Then she saw it. For the years 1979–1981, a different phone number was listed, described as an alternate phone number. *Bam,* her heart hammered now. Monroeville. This was definitely a Monroeville exchange.

He couldn't have resided somewhere outside of the city officially because of the residency requirement for police. But he'd hung out somewhere else often enough to give that phone number.

To quiet her heart, she started again slowly through the early yearly evals. Things had not always been rosy. One letter referred to an earlier letter of reprimand, but that letter wasn't there. Another letter referred to excessive force. That letter suggested he'd been drinking at the time.

And a couple of years were missing. The letters had been removed.

She used her cell phone to call the phone company while she continued making notes. Insurance policy—nothing changed on that over the years, only a cousin listed as beneficiary. That made her spirits dive again. No wife, no son. If he had a wife and son, wouldn't he have made them beneficiaries?

After a dizzying round of recorded messages from Verizon, she spoke her problem into the phone in such a way as to confound the computer waiting to hear "bill" or "out of service" or "dial tone" or any of the ten things that were programmed in. She said, "I need access to phone company archives. I need the number for corporate offices." And that, to the computer, was an unintelligible message, which got her transferred to a live human being. Unfortunately, the live person was also confounded by the question.

While waiting, she went through the folder on the later years again. Another mention of drinking—a report that someone had smelled liquor on him and been bothered enough to mention it. She jotted down the name. Hrznak. Homicide detective. Christie could talk to Hrznak.

The confused person at Verizon returned to the line, asking Colleen to start over.

"I need to trace a number that was used between 1979 and 1981—find out who it belonged to."

"Oh. That isn't possible. We don't keep records like that. See, you could call us every day and change your phone number if you wanted. Thirty days goes by and we can give your old one out again."

"Who has those records?"

"Let me see."

Another couple of minutes passed. The same woman came back on to say, "You'd have to go to the library."

Right. Colleen blew out a big frustrated breath. She'd thought of calling the library in the first place, but if the number was unlisted, she'd be nowhere. She prayed it would be listed. She'd have to check name to number instead of the other way around, which felt purer.

She called the library and, after another round of recorded messages, got a librarian she would have liked to kiss. He was clear, sane, full of information: Yes, he had the 1979 Bell Telephone directory. It was on microfilm. The old phone company, partly because of deregulation, had just taken all their archival phone books from a records office downtown and dumped them on the public library, where nobody could decide what to do with them. The directories sat around for a while; then finally they were microfilmed.

That was the good news.

The bad news was that he had no staff to do research; she'd have to go through the microfilm herself.

Colleen liked libraries, hated microfilm.

Poking her head out the door, she was glad to find Elizabeth Thuma in sight. Colleen stepped toward her. "Do you want the folders? Or should I leave them?"

Thuma looked around, checking that everyone was acceptably busy. "I'll return them," she said. Again, that flicker in her eyes. To know something and button it in. Yes, she was good. She'd carry the folders out as she carried them in, with the name obscured, half under the summer sweater she wore, needed in the frigid air conditioning.

Colleen slipped out of the Personnel office, trying to look as if she had just been by to change her benefits, something routine.

By now, Christie might be in court. She decided to just make a run for the library without bothering him.

She signed out a car and was on her way.

The morning had started out hazy and was getting grayer by the minute. When it stormed later in the day, it was going to be a downpour. The old parking lot near Carnegie Library had been dug up to make a park. There was supposed to be an equal amount of street parking, but it just didn't seem true. She kept doing U-turns, and finally she drove up into Carnegie Mellon University, found a meter there that she had to duel for, then realized she had no quarters. She also had no umbrella. Thunder rumbled. She trotted down the hill to the library.

Then, fifteen minutes later, in the Pennsylvania Room, she watched the microfilm being threaded through the machine by an assistant librarian.

It took awhile for her eyes to adjust to the movement of the material on the screen.

Ho, Hof, Hoff, Hoffman. Hoffman, E. She took a big breath and let her finger slide across the column.

Her heart almost jumped out of her body. The number matched.

It was true. She was right. Dun once knew Hoffman. That's all she can prove right now, but they *look* alike, and if she can find some neighbors who knew them both back in 1979, maybe she'll soon be able to prove more than that.

And why didn't Hoffman call Dun for help when he was at Headquarters being questioned? If he did call, Dun didn't show up to give support.

She hopped through the first drops of rain. Two seconds before she got to her car, the deluge began. In those two seconds, she was virtually soaked, but her hand wouldn't work faster to get the door open. Air conditioning came on with the motor and sent a chill to her wet skin.

The dashboard clock said it was noon.

No ticket. Rain scared away the meter maids. Good. Luck.

Little gift of sorts to take Christie. Cat drops a dead bird on the bedspread. Not all gifts are welcome.

COLLEEN GETS BACK TO THE North Side, parks quickly, and makes her way rapidly down the hall to find Christie in his office, eating lunch. "What happened? Court is done?"

"Delayed. I got a couple of hours back here. Brief me quickly," he says.

She drops the dead bird on the bedspread. She can't read his expression as she explains the addresses, phone numbers. She hands over a list of names of people who might be useful. The muscles of his face tighten. He studies the names soberly. "Evans maybe, Picarelli definitely. Hrznak definitely. I'll see what I can do later today." He looks up. "You want to check the Monroeville neighborhood?"

"Yes."

"Okay. Give it this afternoon, but be back to check with me around five, say." He crumbles his sandwich paper, tosses it to the wastebasket. He walks to the door of his office and says, in tones heavy with caution, maybe even with disappointment, "This is something else, this idea of yours. Keep it to yourself for now, outside of what you have to do, eh?"

"Of course."

He doesn't say, "I believe in intuition and I believe in you." He doesn't say any of the lines she's written for him.

But she knows she's right, she knows it. Almost jumps up and down behind Christie's departing figure to think of it. Then sobriety sets in.

TWENTY

HOFFMAN SITS ON A HOTEL BED, staring at the nightstand, which holds a phone and an envelope with ten thousand dollars cash in it. Cash. It's ridiculous. More to come. Doesn't everyone use ATMs and credit cards for everything? On the other hand, if someone happens to call out "Mr. McDonough," it will take him a long time to realize he should be the one answering to the name. "Pat, call me Pat," he says to himself.

Cash. He can at least get himself a change of clothing. And so he studies the phone book for stores, deciding to buy everything he needs in one place.

The feeling that washes over him is dread. There is no way out. Each way he turns, no way out. And even now, even now he doesn't know if his father loves him.

The phone beckons. He would like to call Colleen Greer to say quickly, "Whatever it looks like, I didn't do it. I want you to know that." But phones talk; they tell about place. Sadness, memory, fills him as he stuffs his pockets with cards, cash.

He sinks back to the edge of the bed, remembering. He is ten and his mother is going on a date. The relatives always talk about how lovely she is, and he thinks so, too. She wears a flowered dress; her hair is permed—large, loose with curl. The man who comes to the door stares at him, saying, "Well, let's meet him finally."

"This is David," his mother says. "David, this is Charlie."

How clear the memory is.

From where he sits, he can see outside the motel window. His car is in the lot. Nobody is looking at it. Charlie knows about things like this—running from the law, how people hide from the police.

"This is Charlie," his mother had said. "Charlie, this is David. You see what I mean?"

David had no idea at the time what it was his mother had already said about him, but whatever it was made Charlie look hard at him, he knew that much. Years later he understood Charlie was his real father and that others had suspected it, seen the stamp of proof in his face.

"So, we'll have to do something together, Sport, maybe a poker game, or maybe one day I'll take you hunting. You like that kind of thing?"

"I don't know."

"Well, we'll see, then."

"Charlie is a policeman," his mother says. "He arrests the bad guys."

"Sometimes I do," Charlie says. "Sometimes I play cards with them." His mother's eyes get wide and Charlie winks at David.

So, his mother and Charlie sit for a while in the kitchen, drinking bourbon while they wait for the baby-sitter to arrive. David is supposed to be watching television in the living room, but if he works hard at it, he can hear them underneath the dialogue and music coming at him from the tube. It's a question and answer session mostly, Charlie asking, his mother answering brightly, sometimes hesitantly. Finally the girl from down the street arrives breathless with apology for her tardiness. He doesn't *need* a baby-sitter. He's old enough to take care of himself. His mother and Charlie go out to have something to eat.

It's funny the way people get used to things, slowly, gradually, and the way the mind changes. He hadn't wanted his mother to like anyone, to be gone from the house. But he got used to her going out, and he got used to Charlie. Soon Charlie stayed late, long after David went to bed. Then, months later, he was there in the morning. Then most mornings.

They no longer spent time with the relatives they'd been close to. He missed them, but on the other hand, his mother was happy.

Charlie took David in a police car once, showed him a gun, gave him a shooting lesson—he hadn't liked it, but he thought he should pretend he did. He wasn't particularly good at either shooting or pretending, the buckled face of the man he called Charlie told him.

Then, just as slowly, and in the same way, gradually, his mother began to show unhappiness and things clearly changed again, going in the other direction.

Sometimes, when Charlie went to a ball game with a group of men, his mother suggested David go with them. Charlie said, "Nah, that wouldn't work out."

"Why?"

"They get rough. Rough talk."

"And drink," she said bitterly.

"And drink," he said. "You got that right."

By the end of the first year, there were arguments, his mother saying Charlie should move in, Charlie saying he couldn't because of work. Then his mother insisted they should move to Charlie's house in the city.

"Change schools and all that? Kids hate that. We're doing okay the way we are."

More tears. At the end of the second year, David's mother confided to him that she had put her foot down and Charlie would let someone stay at his place—no lease, kind of on the sly because of police rules. If anyone asked, David must say, she explained, that Charlie still lived in Highland Park. But he'd be with them.

"Do I still call him Charlie?"

"Yes," she said vaguely.

"But if people ask who he is, do I say he's my father now?"

"Say . . . say he's your stepfather."

Though his mother wasn't as happy as she had been at the beginning, and though he often did things badly, in a way that didn't please his new stepfather, David remembered the feel of the man's hand on the top of his head or over his shoulder. He remembered the cheerleading way his stepfather, as he thought of him, gave him a wink or a punch and told him to do this or that.

He'd felt the absence of a father all his life, and the photo of the soldier on his mother's bureau only made him envy the kids who had fathers *around.* Now he had one of his own. A man who told jokes—one after another, some nights—and got angry sometimes, but the anger was part of a sense of drive, of purpose. It seemed part of his importance.

The high school photo of the man he thought was his father moved from his mother's bedroom bureau to his. It had a small snapshot of a young man in uniform tucked into the corner of the frame.

His grandmother and aunt Susan didn't come around, but one time they invited him and his mother to visit them. David listened into their conversation and he caught a reference to Charlie as a teenager, as a young man.

Later, when his grandmother and aunt walked them out to their car, he asked, "How did you know Charlie *before?*"

They told him stiffly—he was twelve, thirteen, maybe, some time not too long before he and his mother left Charlie—they told him, "Charlie and your father were best friends for a lot of years."

Around Charlie, his stomach twisted and he felt he needed to prove himself, and yet he sought him out. He liked listening to Charlie talk. And one time, when Charlie wept, he felt heartbreak for him.

It took a long time for him to understand the soldier had been the understudy, the stand-in husband, and not his real father. Finally he got the picture. Eileen had been pregnant, Peter Hoffman liked her, maybe loved her, and flung himself on the altar to do something his pal Charlie was unwilling to do. A nice guy, probably, Hoffman senior. Might have made a good stepfather if he had lived. And so the real father acted the part of stepfather and the stepfather, just a man in a photograph, had seemed all those early years to be the real father.

"Why did you never tell me the truth?" he asked his mother when he was in his twenties and had the courage to bring it up.

"It was hard to explain," she said. And after mother and son discovered

Charlie had problems—"a sickness" was how his mother put it—she didn't want him to know. She decided cutting ties was the solution.

David remembers that long bus ride he made into town. It was a hot day and most of it was spent searching out his father, whom, of course, he thought of as his stepfather. What he wanted to know was, what had happened to the little girl he saw his father with that day in the awful house in Homewood. He dreamt about her, worried about her.

His father had wept when he asked.

The next day his mother told him they were leaving town.

Years later David spent some time trying to track the girl down. He discovered she'd been found dead of an overdose of sleeping pills when she was sixteen. In Texas. She'd run off with someone, ended up in Texas.

He moves in a daze now, gathering his few things, checking out.

He is in his car again, safe with the new plates on, and somehow it's afternoon and he's at a mall buying underwear, jeans, two shirts, socks, another pair of shoes. Toothbrush, toothpaste, electric razor, comb and brush, hair dryer for the thin hair Laura once explained needed to be fluffed up. This can't go on. And yet he buys what he needs, taking a step away from it all, from the funeral for his wife, from his job, his home. For some reason, abandoned as he is, he can still distinctly remember the heartbreak he experienced for Charlie when he found him that day in Pittsburgh, when he talked to him. How could he explain this to anyone? Charlie was a monster, but he was not a monster. Both were true.

TWENTY-ONE

COLLEEN RANG THE BELL OF A house in Monroeville, the sixth she'd tried.

A dog went crazy inside. A woman's voice said, "Okay, boy, that's nice. That's good. Very good." The door opened, revealing an old woman wearing shorts and a T-shirt, her gray hair every which way. The ropy veins of her legs stood out and her expression was what she might have worn if she were saying, "This body. What do I do with it?" If dogs spoke, hers, panting at her side, would have said, "This energy. What do I do with it?" The woman said, "Yay. A visitor. Just kidding. You're selling something?"

Colleen laughed. "Insurance. Just kidding. I'm police. I'd just like to talk to you for a moment."

"Oh, my, did I do something?"

"Probably. Wouldn't surprise me."

"Well, come in. I'm caught. Here, boy, you sit with me." The dog obeyed. Very impressive.

Seated, Colleen said, "Unfortunately, I have to get serious. I'm on the clock."

"Ah, the clock."

"Would you please write down your name, address, and phone number so I don't have to come back and bother you again." She handed over her small notebook.

"Come back anytime." The woman squinted through her glasses and began to write.

Colleen read the writing upside down. Jolene Fowler. "How long have you lived here in this house, Mrs. Fowler?"

"Jolene. Jo. Forty years. I'm letting it fall apart along with me."

"Forty years is just what I need. How many other families around here go back several years, do you know? Say back as far as 1978?"

"That wouldn't be too many. The houses on this street are for sale every two years, it seems. People come and go. That's the world these days."

"It is." Colleen had guessed as much, but here she had one long-term resident at least. "Now I need to ask if you remember a family named Hoffman, lived at twelve twenty-seven?"

"When?"

"Let's say from 1978 to 1981."

"Oh my. Give me a hint."

"You don't remember?"

"My mind doesn't do well. Give it a nudge, it comes along."

"Nice-looking woman named Eileen. Blond. Fashionable. Would have been about thirty years old. Had a son of ten, almost eleven, with her, stayed here until he was thirteen." She was reluctant to give more information; police were trained to get it, snatch it, trick it, win it.

Jolene Fowler dipped her head forward in a large nodding motion, encouraging her memory to kick in. When she stopped moving, she said, "Got a picture of them. Yes. Yes. Got it."

"Did you actually know them?"

"No, sad to say, I didn't."

"Think for just a moment. Can you lead me to other people they knew?"

"Hoffman or something else? Did she ever get married?" Hopefully to someone named Hrznak or something easy to trace.

"Yes, that's why she moved. Married a guy who already lived up there."

"You know his name?"

"I don't. I could call someone if you want."

"Someone who would know? You can just give me the name."

"Let me think. Fran. Frances. Frances Morgan. That's right. Used to bring her mother to bingo. Friend of Susan's."

Colleen hurried to her car, dialing. She caught the secretary at St. Regis before she left for the day and soon had Fran Morgan's address. She saw it was only two miles away and drove there. She knocked and rang the bell for ten minutes. Nothing. Damn. Probably at work.

A neighbor watched from her window. Colleen went to the neighbor's door and showed her credentials, which the woman studied hard for about five minutes before saying, "She went to the beach this week."

Summer. Damned summer.

"If it's important," the neighbor ventured, "I could get you a phone number for her."

"It's important."

The woman withdrew into her house, moments later emerged out the back door, went across the lawn, and into Morgan's back door. A few minutes passed. Then the woman reversed directions, taking the long path to her own front door again.

But in the end, Colleen had a phone number in hand. "Virginia Beach," the piece of paper said. Would she get a hotel, a house, or an apartment?

While she drove back to Headquarters, she pressed in the numbers and waited.

A woman answered. The connection was terrible, filled with static, but speaking over the noise, she established the fact that she had Fran Morgan on the line.

Morgan was as careful as her neighbor. "I'd want to check your credentials first; then I'll have Susan call you. Is that all right?"

Funny how nobody trusted the police.

Traffic was dense. She sat in it, then crawled forward in it. The strange slow movement made her sleepy.

Jo Fowler said she was going to be married in two years. To whom? To whom?

Nearly forty-five minutes later, pulling into the lot at Headquarters, Colleen took a phone call from Susan Hoffman, sister-in-law of Eileen, aunt to David.

She'd had the door of her car half open, but she closed it again as she stated her business carefully, generally. "You could be helpful if you would just answer a few simple questions. We're interested in checking out some family details for David Hoffman. We're making inquiries about the man your sister-in-law married sometime after the death of your brother."

"She never remarried. Not so far as I knew. Just took up with the guy again."

Again. "Would you explain?"

"What?"

"You said 'again.' "

"Apparently, she was seeing him about the time she was seeing my brother, back when they were all young. Personally, I hope he's the one who's in trouble."

"So you knew this man?"

"Yes."

"Would you tell me his name?"

"Yes. Charlie Dun."

Colleen almost fainted dead away to hear it like that, so clearly. She was right, she was right. She took a deep breath, trying to hold steady. "He was friends with your brother and Eileen?"

"Yes."

"Are you in touch with him anymore?"

"No, absolutely not."

"You didn't approve of him?"

"No. No, I didn't."

"Can you tell me anything else about him?" There was an uncomfortable silence. "Did you disapprove of how he treated David?"

"I don't know about that. I kind of had a bad scene with him at one point and I didn't like him at all. I don't know why my brother liked him, but it was something to do with, I don't know, power or charisma or one of those things. And he had it."

"What sort of bad scene?"

"He was being sneaky with me, sort of sexual. I was just a little kid. I . . . you know, I was younger than my brother."

"Did you ever know him to prey on other children?"

"Not that I heard. I figured it was just to do with some meanness toward me."

"He was mean?"

"I think so. The mother and son left him. They must have had reasons."

"Did you or your mother keep in contact with Eileen or David?"

"We didn't. I sometimes thought I should, but my mother . . . was too hurt. I mean, my brother *died* in Vietnam, and this woman had used him just to get married."

"Your brother wasn't David's father, is that right?"

"We didn't think so."

"And Charles Dun probably was."

"Yes. We thought so."

"But Eileen never admitted it?"

"No."

"My records show she moved back to West Virginia. Is that correct?"

"That's correct. She had her own mother there."

Colleen sat for two full minutes before pulling herself together to go into Headquarters. Christie wasn't in. They said he'd be back in a few minutes. She felt she would explode holding on to the information she had. In her nervousness, she kept looking around, expecting to see Dun, but she didn't see him.

A cluster of detectives stood in the hallway, discussing the cases. It was the dinner group, the inside six. McGranahan called to Greer, "What's up?"

She shrugged.

"We're catching up here. Christie said he had you checking out some men with priors outside the target areas."

"Yes," she said carefully.

"Anything?"

"Eh, maybe," she said. Dolan caught her eye. So he was in the know. Christie had talked to him.

McGranahan continued: "I talked to two of the men today with backgrounds of assault. In the target area. One raped a teenager; one raped a young woman. We're bringing in both tonight for more questioning—just in case. But we can't make any link to the park workers or the truck."

"You had the park workers in again?" Potocki asked.

"Yeah, we're not getting anywhere with them. They all had alibis. Somebody got into the garage. That's all there is to it."

Colleen could have lectured. She could have told them that since, in Jamilla's case, the abuse went back to when she was a child, the man who did it was not someone with a Lolita complex, but a pedophile, one who liked preadolescents. And she knew who it was. Dolan caught her eye again, reading her expression.

"I wish we had the manpower to put surveillance on Hoffman," Coleson was saying. "You going to talk to him again?" he asked Colleen.

"Tonight. I'm going to try tonight."

"She should wear a wire this time," McGranahan offered. "I wish she had the first time around."

Potocki said to her, "Don't let him bug you. You have to trust yourself on these things."

She nodded.

"Well, one more thing while we're at it," McGranahan said. "Really, I don't mean to come down hard on you, Greer, because it's mostly that you're new. But you're a little bit sloppy. You put down the DNA sample as 'to be identified' and you called him Jeremiah Doe. What was that all about?"

"It didn't feel . . . public yet."

"If you don't do things by the book, there's always trouble later. You should get the name down. And, besides, you typed it up, but you never entered in to the hard drive. I saw it today and I entered it."

Colleen felt herself go pale.

Too late. It was done. There was no calling it back.

There was nothing she could do. Dolan was watching her closely, saw her blanch.

"You could thank me," McGranahan said.

She nodded vaguely.

Christie arrived and came up to the group. Before anyone could ask him about court, he said briskly, "I need to see Dolan and Greer about the funerals. My office."

McGranahan held Christie back. "You want me to shadow Greer on any meeting she makes with Hoffman tonight?"

"Maybe. Let me see."

Christie unhinged himself, but Potocki followed them a little way toward Christie's office. "You need someone to go with Greer if she meets Hoffman, I could do it as well. Just so you know."

"I'll remember."

"My concentration on the computer is shot. I don't know what I'm seeing anymore," Potocki said.

"You need a break of some sort, huh?"

"Yeah. Like a movie. Or a ball game." Potocki made a wry grin and headed off.

Finally, Christie, Dolan, and Greer were in his office, the door tightly closed, and even so, they whispered. She made her report.

Christie said, "Nobody, but nobody, but us three, you understand?"

Dolan said, "Nobody knows but us three. I agree."

Colleen said, "Look, do you think Dun reads our files, our daily reports?" Supposedly, only Homicide detectives could see them, but that early morning at the office gave her the impression Dun was snooping, however he could.

The two men each nodded slowly.

Colleen swallowed hard and pulled herself up straighter. "He's going to know we have his son's DNA if he reads the files."

Dolan explained to Christie how McGranahan had entered Colleen's report about the DNA.

"I didn't want him to be able to see that."

"I know what you were trying to do," Christie told her soberly. "McGranahan couldn't have known what you were thinking. In the long run, McGranahan is right. We have to keep records, and up-to-date ones. This is a once-in-a-lifetime situation."

"Better be," Dolan said. He rapped his fists against the table.

"How fast can we move, then? Tomorrow morning, Greer combs the files from Personnel all over again; tonight or tomorrow morning early, I talk to Hrznak and you talk to Picarelli. Okay?"

"Okay by me," she said. "I wish I knew what was in the missing year-end evaluations. Susan Hoffman told me Dun messed with her when she was a little girl. There might have been similar charges and . . . he either removed the pages or somebody did it for him."

Christie said, "I'll try to get the copies from the ex-chief's files. Could be delicate. I'll try sometime tomorrow." He seemed to consider another possibility. "Eileen Hoffman probably wouldn't talk if we tried her again."

"She wouldn't," Colleen said.

Christie said, "Listen. I'm going to type in tonight that we're stepping it up with known sex offenders in the North Side neighborhood for Washington. That might throw him off some. It isn't exactly a lie. Meanwhile, let's see if we can connect with Hrznak and Picarelli. Greer keeps after Hoffman. Go ahead. Call him. You're calling as a friend."

She picked up her cell, scrolled for Hoffman's number, and pressed the SEND button. Christie made a list as Dolan watched. Both listened as she left a message, saying, "David, I've wondered how you're doing. I was thinking . . . you might need some support tonight. I could do dinner if you could. I'm going to head to Alexander's in case you get this message and just feel like joining me. I'd be there around seven-thirty. I know you have the funeral home sometime tonight, the private viewing, but if you need a break, give a call or meet me at Alexander's." She hung up.

Christie said, "Good. I'll get pictures of Dun made up. And after we do the early stuff tomorrow, the three of us will hit the Washington funeral in the morning and the funeral home for Hoffman in the afternoon."

They told him they would be ready.

"I'd better head to Alexander's," Colleen said.

"Dinner!" Dolan exclaimed. "I knew there was something I wanted."

In the end, Christie and Dolan got takeout from the Pleasure Bar and ate in the car, talking on their cell phones, making appointments with Picarelli and Hrznak, while Greer ate at Alexander's all alone. Hoffman never called back.

TWENTY-TWO

THE FUNERAL HOME WAS A neat, sober brick building among the row houses. A TV camera crew was there. But the family hadn't arrived yet. Dolan, Christie, and Greer sat in the car for a while, watching arrivals.

Dolan said, "According to Picarelli, Dun got into trouble a couple of times when he was a young cop and also when he was a young detective. A. It was drinking. B. There were some anonymous calls about him, something murky, allegations about something sexual, but Picarelli wasn't sure what the details were. Just that there was something."

Christie said, "Got the same from Hrznak at breakfast. He told me Dun still hits the bottle like a champ. Only thing is, he seems to be able to do his work without a hitch. He didn't know about what was in the early reports, but he figured there was something, some kind of trouble. I haven't gotten to the missing letters."

Colleen said, "I must have combed the files well the first time, because I have nothing to add."

"Let's go inside," Christie said suddenly.

It was the first Christie and Dolan had seen Jamilla in her white lace dress, holding flowers. Dolan, taking a long look at the coffin, buttoned his lips tightly.

Finally, the Washingtons arrived. In their finery, and beautiful as they were, they were heartbreaking. The boy wore a suit and the baby a dress. The clothes, Jamilla's included, must have cost the family more than they could afford.

Something about the parents—they weren't quite conscious yet.

Dolan whispered to Christie, "I want to talk to the boy. You have that picture of Dun?"

Christie palmed it over carefully.

"How you doing?" Dolan asked Greer.

"I'm kind of nervous, if you want me to be truthful. The ball I started rolling has me scared."

"It ought to," he said simply. "I got to go talk to that boy."

DOLAN FOUND THE BOY ALONE in a hallway outside the room with the casket, crying.

"Come here," Dolan said. He put his arms around the boy, hugging hard. The sobs racked against his shoulder. "You should cry," he said. "This is sad. It makes me cry. Go on. It shows you're a good person."

People passed. They noticed the man comforting the boy and they left them alone.

When the boy stopped crying, Dolan said, "Look. I'm supposed to be working another case, but we all break some rules here and there. What's happened is . . . I ended up thinking about your sister. And I ended up feeling like I want to be the one to find her killer. So I came here instead of doing my other work. You understand?"

Kameen said he did. His eyes searched Dolan. He was interested.

Dolan said, "I know guys sometimes know secrets about their sisters. She probably told you things, right?"

Kameen said, "Not secrets, no."

Dolan said, "Even if she didn't, you probably figured some stuff out. Your father said he didn't know what she was up to, but I figured you're the kind of kid who notices things. I told my other detectives, 'Somebody somewhere had to care about Jamilla, and I'm thinking it was her brother.' "

Kameen nodded. Dolan sat with him, rubbed a hand on his back. "Funeral homes are pretty. Isn't that weird?" he said. "Brocade padded bench. All this fancy stuff. It's strange." He kept rubbing the boy's back. He felt the muscles change a little. He knew he was seducing him, that his manipulations were not all that different from those of priests and coaches and other predators, but what he wanted was information.

He took out the picture of Dun. "You ever seen this man around?"

The boy studied the picture. "No, huh-uh."

"Sure?"

"Yeah."

The two of them sat there for a considerable amount of time. When there was a pause, and then a hush coming from the other room, it was clear the preacher had come in and was about to speak to the mourners.

Christie and Colleen had disappeared for a while, gone outside, then come back in. Dolan saw them look at him questioningly. He was about to give up, when the boy spoke.

"That lady in the picture. The picture they showed us at the station?"

"Yes?"

Kameen said, "She maybe was the lady that bothered my sister one day."

Dolan kept still except for the hand that was rubbing the boy's back. "Tell me about it," he said. "You saw her?"

"No. Just got it from Jamilla."

"How did the lady bother her?"

"Followed her. Talked to her."

"About what?

"She didn't say. She just didn't like it that the lady asked her so many questions."

"Where was this?"

"Somewhere in the hood."

"When was it?"

"Couple of days ago. My sister had to go somewhere, and when she was on the way home, the lady started following her."

"Where'd your sister have to go?"

"Don't know. Someplace she had to be for something. She always had stuff she needed to do."

"Which day?"

"I don't know."

"Think now. Before you hurt your foot or after?"

"I don't know."

"Same day maybe? Or next day?" Dolan asked gently. "Close your eyes. Think."

"Some day. Yeah. I was laid up and didn't go to the window."

"That would be Thursday. Right?"

"I guess."

"What time?"

"Like maybe seven."

"You didn't see this woman?"

"No. I had my foot up."

"Did your sister describe her?"

"Nope. Except she was white and asked questions. That was all."

Dolan gave the boy a hug and told him it was a small thing but that small things, like who talked to whom, could be helpful. He led Kameen into the funeral parlor, where the service had begun. Before the preacher had uttered too many sentences, his ringing tones drove Artie Dolan up the wall. Artie didn't like anything canned, and this was a *canned* speech. It was to the preacher just another young black death. He found Christie. "I'm ready to get out of here. Where's Greer?"

"Talking to a little girl. Little girl was crying pretty hard and Greer zeroed in on her."

COLLEEN HAD SEEN THE YOUNG girl crying at Jamilla's casket and she had known immediately she wanted to pull her aside. She got the girl's father's permission and then, like Dolan, found a quiet place away from everybody—in this case, a viewing room that was empty. The girl's father came along, too, and she knew she couldn't stop him.

"I knew Jamilla," she said to both of them. "I'm working to find out who killed her."

"She can't help you," the father said. "She doesn't know anything recent."

"Why can't you help?" Colleen tried to direct her attention to the girl, whose name, she had learned, was Vanessa Walker.

"We wasn't best friends anymore."

"Used to be," the girl's father said. "Used to be real close."

"A long time ago," the girl said. "When we were little."

"What happened?"

"I don't know. She got funny. But I still liked her."

"How did she get funny?"

"Just always busy."

"How long ago were you best friends?"

"When we were little." The girl thought. "Maybe nine. I don't know."

"Do you know, was it around the time she was going to the Family Counseling Center—it's a center over on Arch—does that ring any bells?"

Vanessa nodded, alert now. "She used to have to go to sign in. That's what made her secret."

"Sign in how? Can you explain what she did?"

"I think she just had to sign in that her family was doing okay and nobody was in trouble and all that."

Colleen closed her eyes for two full seconds to compose herself. "Why was that a secret?"

"I don't know."

"How often did she sign in?"

"I don't know. I think it was Thursday nights for a while, then on Saturdays."

"Night? How late?"

"I think her appointments were like six or seven o'clock. I don't mean night exactly. You know what I mean."

"So they were appointments?"

"She said just to sign in."

"Who did she sign in with?"

"I don't know. Some guy. I got mad at her because she stopped telling me things. I yelled at her real bad." Vanessa's lip trembled.

"Hey, honey," her father said, "these things happen all the time. People fight. That's what they do." He turned to Greer, saying, "They were just in third or fourth grade." He turned back to his daughter. "You're doing okay," he said, putting an arm around her. "You're helping."

The girl was crying again, pure grief for a friendship she could not repair no matter how long she lived.

EACH OF THE DETECTIVES HAD lunch alone over paperwork, typing up what they had learned.

Colleen looked behind her three times as she wrote her report, fearing Dun would somehow appear at the door, walk right into the room.

A little before two, the three detectives drove to the Freyvogel funeral home.

There were five cars in the Freyvogel parking lot when they pulled up. Soon several more cars arrived. Christie said, "Good. Couple of people we haven't seen. Might be something good to be got here. Besides our boy Hoffman, who will definitely be interesting on a polygraph now that we know to ask about his pops."

They went inside and straight to the funeral director to ask what time they should expect Hoffman, given the particular strains associated with this funeral.

"Hoffman skipped the private viewing last night. The parents have the first hour this afternoon. They agreed to share the second hour with Hoffman and to give him the third hour. I hope they can all handle it. The second hour, that is."

An hour to wait. Colleen's heart twinged a warning. *He won't be here.*

Christie and Dolan looked around for people to question, and found them. Colleen found herself with the parents and David Shoemaker. Mr. McCall had taken a liking to her. Now he held on to her hands, as if she were a longtime friend of his daughter. She tried not to show too much resistance when he guided her to the coffin.

Everything about funeral homes horrified her. Coffins, embalming, the overabundance of flowers. Cremation gave her the willies. The only solution was not to die.

Laura Hoffman was a wax doll whose expression, no matter how serene they tried to make it, spoke of suffering. A flowered dress draped the body; a filmy scarf covered the neck.

Colleen stood politely, looking. All the while, she was working the puzzle. How had Laura McCall known about the Washington girl, or had she?

Had she gone to talk to the child or did that happen by accident? She had probably called both father and son. The son didn't know the father had been there. What was the *story*? Only David Hoffman could help, and he was terrified.

Thirty minutes went by. Then another thirty.

No David. She caught Dolan's eye. He nodded slightly. Yes, he was thinking the same thing. Then she caught Christie's eye. He winced. They were worried now.

When Mindy Cooper arrived, Colleen caught her at the door. "Have you seen Hoffman today?"

"No. He called yesterday. He left a message at the office—said he wouldn't be coming in to work right away. He shouldn't have tried when he did." She looked around. "He'd be coming here, though."

Colleen, heart sinking, searched for Dolan and Christie and found them in the parking lot, talking together.

"Something's up for sure," Dolan said before she could say it.

"You hang here, we'll check his house," Christie told her.

Thanks a lot, she said to herself. Why couldn't she be the one to go to the house? A funereal type she was not. The hush, the murmuring voices were killing her.

She took a walk around the parking lot to clear her head. Then she went back in and found Mindy Cooper.

"What is 'signing in'? At the Center?"

"I don't know what you mean. You mean signing in when they arrive, like in a medical office? We don't do that."

"No, I mean something where a client has to come in just to sign in. Like at night."

"I don't know. Definitely not at night. We never have night hours."

"And no Saturday hours?"

"No. Huh-uh. Not in my time. I think I told you."

"Have you ever seen any sort of sign-in sheet?"

"No."

"Heard anybody use the expression?"

"No. You're really taking me by surprise."

He must have waited for Jamilla outside school, outside therapy, showed his badge, made her meet him. Jamilla and how many others?

THERE WAS TWO DAYS' MAIL in the box. Once they got into Hoffman's house, and they got in so easily it made them laugh—a key under a flower pot, so stupid, and in Shadyside, of all places, where every resident had electronic equipment the urban burglars wanted—what they found was evidence of a man who had left hurriedly. Phone pulled toward the side of the bed that was open. Lamp still burning in daylight. Closet door ajar. Aircon running, pajama bottoms on the bed. No evidence of a breakfast. No coffee made. Drawers full of clothing. Electric razor charging away in the bathroom.

"Oh man," Dolan said. "This is good."

"You bet."

"Went voluntarily or not?"

"Can't tell."

"And what are we doing in here exactly?"

"Well," Christie said, "we came by and the door was open and we got worried, got suspicious, peered in the window, where the shade was up—"

"Was it?" Dolan said, yanking the bedroom shade up.

"We saw an open drawer—"

Dolan opened the drawer on top.

"Came in, took a quick look around, made sure the door was locked again on the way out. Wouldn't you think?"

"I would."

They started to their car. "And now what?" Dolan said.

Christie said grudgingly, "We spare someone to watch this house and someone to keep an eye on Dun. The first one is easy, but how the hell we do the second when he knows most of us, I don't know." He called Colleen's cell. She answered right away. "He didn't show, right?"

"Right," she said.

"He's not home. Looks like he hasn't been there."

"I knew it."

"You ready to leave?"

"Get me out of here."

"We'll be there to pick you up in five. Make sure—"

"Funeral director calls if Hoffman shows."

"You got it."

AT SEVEN THAT NIGHT, COLLEEN is on her dinner break, sitting across from John at the Pub, both of them cutting into their meals. How odd. It feels *old*, just like other times, perhaps times when one or the other of them was miffed or overworked, quiet, and now here they are again, together. He looks good, tanned, fit, in his olive green T-shirt, shorts. She could reach out and touch him, easily, easily.

His eyes cast up toward the television. Baseball. He looks back at her, smiles. "So. Finally," he says. "I tried hard to get a meal with you. Tried since last Sunday."

"It's only Thursday."

"It seems like a long time."

Long and short, both, depending on perspective. And now she has an hour to give him, no more.

"I've been following your cases on the news. No arrests yet?"

She thinks to joke: "We lost our best witness. He was more or less my responsibility and he blew town." But she isn't in the mood to joke.

John smiles. What is this thing he so much needs to say to her? He puts down his fork and knife, seems hesitant. Now. Whatever it is, here it comes. *Thanks for the memories*. "I like you a lot," he begins. "Always did. I want you to know that. And that I took you seriously. And that I tried. I've thought a lot about this. We were both trying to make it work. It's as if we were good friends, but without that spark, and that's the—"

"You'll have to speak for yourself. I got the message last weekend at Lindo's. You like me but you don't love me. Okay."

"I am speaking for both of us," he says in a low voice. "That's the thing. You tried hard. You don't love me, either. And you didn't."

"That's not true."

He makes a face, picks up his fork again. She expects him to say, "Wow. I'm sorry then," but he doesn't. His face is still frowning. He cuts a bite of steak, eats. "It isn't a logical thing," he says finally. "I know you'll know I'm right in a week or two, as soon as you get some rest and get some peace back in your life. You're in love, I think, but not with me."

"What!"

"You're in love with your commander. Christie."

There it is. Said. She's already untangled the idea herself, looked at it this way and that. "Everybody has a crush on him. He's one of those people people get crushes on."

"I saw that. I saw it. I saw the way you reacted when he talked to you."

"Well, it may please you to think my attentions are elsewhere now—"

"*Have been* elsewhere. And I'm not saying what happened to me is any kind of reaction or rebound. I think we both sensed it wasn't the big IT with us."

"No. I accept that you are onto something else. But a crush, a work crush, is not the same thing as being in love."

"Okay. I've said my piece. I want to be on good terms with you. If you'll let me. Christie is probably a great guy. I don't know, but I'm willing to grant him that."

"He's also very married."

"Doesn't seem to stop people from getting crushes."

"Well, no, because it's pressured work, and I'm dependent on him. The feelings are strong feelings in a situation like that, but they aren't love."

John frowns again, thinking. "Well, you're the shrink. You know about these things. Just . . . I hope you won't always blame me. Enough said."

Underneath her brisk replies is a memory of the Monroeville seer's prediction that she is on her way to a marriage. In spite of herself, and she does have a mostly rational mind, she feels a sort of tug, a foolish fantasy, that Christie might choose and requite her crush above all others.

Silly. People are silly. She sits there looking at her salmon and mashed potatoes and back at John who seems still sad and nervous about ending this well. And she thinks if they both just turned this little page or that little page, she could easily sleep with him tonight, but it wouldn't blot out the crush, either.

"I wish you luck," he says. He reaches over and touches her hand, lightly at first, then clasps his over it. "And love. You deserve it."

The condescension, or pity—whatever it is—stings her with tears.

When her phone rings, she fumbles for it, relieved to have something to do. Automatically, she reads the screen. The area code is unfamiliar and so is the number. What is it, Indiana, Illinois? A thrill goes through her.

"Yes, hello," she answers.

"Colleen, I know how it looks," David Hoffman says. "I just want you to know I didn't do it, any of it. I need for you to know that."

"I *do know*. But don't hang—" Too late. She stares at the phone for a second, then asks the screen for the last incoming number, reaches around in her bag for a pen, and writes the phone number on her napkin, just in case, hard copy, just in case. She tries to dial it back. No answer. Without stopping to explain to John, she calls Christie and reports the call.

"Good. He wants to keep contact with you. I'll find out where this phone is."

"The area code is Midwest—Indiana, I think."

"What does it mean, huh? Is he ready to talk?"

"Not ready. But he wants to be found," she says.

"I think you're right."

TWENTY-THREE

COLLEEN'S UNCLE COMBED HIS straight dark hair backward. It always looked wet. His forehead was high. His eyes were large. He was tall, of medium build. Something about his cheekbones intrigued her. They were especially prominent, reminding her of something—American Indians perhaps. He didn't look particularly like her father. She realized he was probably considered handsome. He was highly physical—body-aware. He didn't mind being studied; he certainly gave her plenty of opportunity.

There was a week one summer in which she and her brother were staying with her aunt and uncle. The days were hot, humid. "You're sweating," her uncle said. He touched the moisture on her upper lip. She looked around, but there was nobody watching. Her brother had found some boys his age who played baseball all day; he was never anywhere when she wanted him. And her uncle was everywhere around her all the time.

"I'll let you read." He sat across from her, a few feet away, watching her. Colleen dipped back into *Cannery Row,* some of which she didn't understand, some that she did. Something about the book cheered her, the men drinking and being buddies; it made her feel better about her father's reliance on buddies and barrooms. She liked the character Doc.

When she looked up, she saw her uncle was staring at her, down between her legs. "I can see up your shorts," he said, "and I love it." She pulled her knees together and didn't answer him. He leaned forward to take the book from her hand, making her lose her place. She reached forward to get it. He lifted her T-shirt a little. "Belly," he said.

"Quit it."

"Okay, tell me about the book."

She wasn't sure what to tell him. She tried to explain it was about a place, a community. But he was reading the back jacket; his eyebrows went up. "Is a bordello what I think it is?"

"Probably." She tried to get her book back, but he held it away from her.

"You read stuff like this? I knew you were a hot one. I knew it."

"Come on. You don't know anything about the book. It isn't like that."

He laughed.

She tried reading outdoors, indoors, in front of the house and out back. He always found her.

On the fourth day, she was huddled indoors on the sofa, where she slept at night. Her aunt started vacuuming around her. There is nothing quite like the sound of a bumping whining vacuum cleaner to let you know you're in the way. She asked directions to the park where her brother played baseball, got them, and started out the door. Before she left, she thought to come back and ask her aunt, "Is there a neighborhood pool I could walk to? Or even take a bus to?"

"No, nothing like that." More vacuuming. Her aunt was a sour thing.

It was another steamy day outside. The air tasted wet. Moisture glazed her skin. When she passed a tiny neighborhood grocery store, she smelled Popsicles and strawberries. Summer was her favorite time and this was a vacation, supposed to be, she thought irritably, though not a word had been said about going to see the Liberty Bell or driving to the beach. She wanted Popsicles, strawberries, ice cream, swimming, fun.

The bleachers were under construction at the ball field. She sat on the grass, her back against the fence, watching the game. The grass around her was newly mown and damp still. Bees buzzed. One of them landed on her arm and investigated, reluctant to leave. Don't move suddenly, she told herself. Finally, it flew off.

The grass was sticking to her, but it smelled good, like summer.

A car drove right up to the fence. The gravelly sound of an old motor was followed by her uncle's voice. "Hop in. We're going back for your bathing suit. I heard you want to go swimming."

"Oh. Let me get Ronnie. Where are we going?"

"To a pool." He shrugged. "That's what you asked for, right?" He was leaning way over to talk to her out of the window on the passenger side. She saw the landscape of him, eyes, cheekbones, chest, thighs.

"Ron! Ronnie!" she called.

When the batter who was up singled, Ronnie said, "Hold on, guys." He ran toward her. "What? Lunch?"

"We're going swimming. Uncle Hal's driving us."

"I don't think I want to go. Maybe tomorrow." Ronnie started back to the outfield.

"What's up, Pittsburgh?" one boy called.

"Hey, Pittsburgh. That your girlfriend?" another shouted.

Her uncle said, "Are you getting in or what?"

"I'll wait till tomorrow," Colleen said.

"Come on. Get in. I came all the way to get you. We're going today."

The car smelled strongly of gasoline. A worn-looking scrap of cardboard in the shape of a Christmas tree swung from the rearview mirror, doing nothing to improve the smell of the car. The exhaust fanned hot air tinged with fumes back into the car; the heat, the smell made her head light and her stomach queasy. "How far is the pool?"

"About four miles."

Four miles. Her aunt could have told her. Not impossible to walk it. But it was so hot, so—

"This is a stinko day," her uncle said. "I'm drenched already. A pool is just the right thing."

They drove back to the house and she packed her suit, her towel, her shampoo, her books. When she got outside, her uncle was pacing back and forth, car door open, motor still running.

She hoped he would just drop her off, but he parked, paid admission, and went through the gates, too.

He didn't touch her at the pool, but she knew he watched her the whole time.

She finished the Steinbeck and started on *For Whom the Bell Tolls.* Her uncle took her Steinbeck and tried to read it.

Then back in his car, the sound, the smell.

How clear the memory is. Fresh. To be lived again if she lets it in. . . .

She notices they are not going back the same way they went to the pool. The trees are different. The streets are different.

"Where are we going?"

"Hey, do I know what I'm doing or what?"

"I don't know."

He laughs. "You don't know! I'm going to show you something."

The car creeps into narrower and narrower roads until they can only be called paths. She says, "No. No. I don't want this. Let's go back."

"Don't want what?"

"I don't want to be here."

"Don't be stupid," he says. "You're not stupid. You're not like your hopeless mother and father. You're more . . . you're smarter," he finishes.

"Don't talk like that. Against them. They're smart."

"Well, if they are, they wouldn't be surprised, then. You're that age. You look like sex. You're aching with it. I've had a boner for a week. Is it fair to come invade our house, to do that to me? Huh? What did I do to deserve it?"

"We'll be gone in a couple of days."

"It's nice here, isn't it? Cool. Shady. Leaves are pretty."

She tries to look at the scenery. It is. It is pretty.

"Let's . . ." he begins, but doesn't finish. He brushes a hand over her and groans. "At least that."

She can't remember the exact words that got her through it and back to the house, the backyard, her book. She thought, there, that's it, I'll just hide from him tomorrow.

The sixth day, her aunt says, "Go to the store for me and get me what's on this list. We keep running out of everything. Your uncle will drive you."

"I can walk."

"No, you couldn't carry all that back. What's with this walk everywhere thing?"

"I don't mind walking."

Uncle Hal is lying on the couch, a hand over his eyes.

Only two days to go. Colleen's head feels as if eight manic buzzing flies are circling it. The air vibrates. She wants to close her eyes. She wants to get back home, safe, with her flaky parents.

She can almost hear her aunt thinking, *Trouble, she's just trouble, just like the rest of her family. You want her, have her, it's the least she can do.*

Colleen is once more in the passenger seat of her uncle's car.

"I know you were thinking about me. Had to be. I was thinking about you. All night. Up all night with my boners. I'd jack off and I'd picture you and there'd be another one. You had to be thinking about me."

"I was sleeping," she says, affecting a sleepy manner even now. It helps to close her eyes against the sun, against him.

"It's natural," he says. "Natural as breathing. People are doing it all the time everywhere. In the books you read. Down the street. Up the street. It's what you do as soon as you can attract someone. It's just how it is."

The eight buzzing flies are with her all the time now. What he says seems true, sounds true, but she doesn't know why.

He reaches over and puts a hand on her thigh. Soon the hand creeps into her shorts. She pushes him away. "Don't do that."

"Why?"

I don't like you, is what she wants to say. He's mean. She knows enough to know that. "You're driving," she says.

"That I can stop. The other I can't stop." He pulls over to a strip mall and his right hand makes its way back to where it has been.

She pushes at his hand harder. "Someone will see you. Quit it."

And he starts driving again, fast.

"I didn't mean that. Turn back. I don't want to do this."

"Why?"

"I just don't want to."

"Yes you do. Your body tells me you want to."

They are driving toward the woods where he took her on the way back from the pool. "Stop, please. Go back. We have to get groceries," she says.

He laughs. "Such a do-gooder. We will. All we have to say is, 'The store was busy. It took a long time.' Don't worry."

"Please. Please don't do this. Let's go back." She says it again and again. She is ready, if he slows down, to jump out of the car.

"We're almost there." He drives much too fast over the rutted road. "My little spot. Pretty in here, isn't it?" The trees, the woods, peaceful and sun-dappled, come into view. "This time no excuses, no tears." He tries to unfasten her shorts even while he's driving.

"No," she says. "I won't. It's wrong. I don't want to." She pushes hard at his hand until she can see his knuckles turning white.

The car jerks to a stop. "What is the fucking matter with you? You've been asking for this all along." His face is so close to hers, she smells the ripe hotness of his breath. "I'm going to show you what you want to know. Don't be a liar. Don't lie to yourself."

She hits him in the face, a good solid slap with the right.

He's as surprised as she is.

"Little bitch," he says, grabbing at her arms. He tries to climb on her to pin her down with his body on the old bench seat. She brings a knee up hard. His face tells her he's in pain before he yelps. He tries to catch his breath. "Bitch, you fucking bitch."

She feels for the door handle, pulls out from under him, opens the car door, and starts to run. She can't believe she got away. Rejecting the path behind the car, she goes for the woods because the trees are thick enough that he can't bring the car in after her. Her feet slip on branches and leaves, but she keeps running. Behind her, the sounds of his feet coming after, spur her on.

"Hey, stupid," he calls. "Where do you think you're going?"

But she keeps going until it seems she can't breathe any more. She turns back. He's not in sight. The rattle of a motor in the distance gives her hope that if she stays where the car can't make it, she'll be okay.

She isn't sure how long she's hunkered down in the woods, trying to breathe again. After what feels like a long time, she starts moving.

Finally she hears and then sees traffic way ahead.

When she gets to the house hours later, she's a mess from walking, running. Her aunt looks at her with disgust. Her fault. Something she's done.

Her uncle hardly speaks to her. He acts as if he's been wronged by his minx of a niece, and her aunt likes the lie. Prefers it to the truth.

Her parents pick her up and she says nothing. They don't ask about the new silence that's come over her.

Worse things happen to people every second. She knows that. And, besides, she got away.

TWENTY-FOUR

FRIDAY MORNING, CHARLIE DUN looks into the mirror, trying to read his own face. Can a person see he has not slept well? No. His eyes are worried, *he* can see that, but would anyone else notice anything different?

The thing that worries him most, that he can see in his own eyes, is the thought that something has changed in him. He never lost control before, not like this, only at the beginning a little, the early years on the job. Rage, yes, at the start, but not a problem after that.

His body catalogs the worry. He's swallowing differently. He can hear a rattle in his breathing. And his forehead is producing sweat that he is constantly mopping.

Laura's face keeps coming to him now. Didn't know the woman, hardly spoke to her more than twice before the other day. But he sees her now. When she called him, he knew it was trouble of some sort, even before she said, "I want to talk to you about David. And about a young girl he hurt. I need your help." His mind did somersaults. He wasn't sure what she meant, but he rushed to her house. He asked for a bourbon. That part he can remember. He tried to make things friendly. He can still see her questioning look. He called for a second glass for her, poured, insisted she drink with him. She thought it was David who'd got the girl pregnant. The girl, she said, was named Jamilla. The news came at him too fast. And when she saw his face, she figured out her mistake. He was the one. Her face keeps coming to him, the way she was saying, "You, it's you. Oh my God, he's been protecting you."

She was very dumb. She told him she was not going to let it go. She said it was wrong and she would tell anyone who would listen.

He threw a glass of bourbon in her face. . . . The part he isn't sure of starts here. He must have grabbed her. . . . Nothing stopped her insisting she would tell. Then he had a knife in his hand.

A whole life of doing good, and she—

How he hated her. She was one of those people who had to know things.

He cleaned himself and got out, carrying two big trash bags. He drove to West Virginia, to a dump, where he tossed the bags. Then he collapsed, sat in his car like a dummy, and wept. Wept. Went to a bar, got liquid courage, and drove home. And the phone rang. It was his not very bright son calling him.

"I don't know nothing," he said, and it seemed an honest answer, as if someone else had done it. He took a two-hour shower, then scrubbed his car and took the last bits of his clothing and cleaning rags to a Dumpster. When he could think of nothing else he needed to do, he erased the day as if it hadn't happened. About four in the morning, a good bottle of bourbon in him, he fell asleep. Sleep is something he values. There's so much purity in it. He usually can carry that into part of the day. But that Saturday morning, he woke up with the thudding realization that he had to talk to Jamilla.

He reads the paper, drinks coffee, looks out the window at his trim backyard. Life, normal daily life is what he wants. The same birds coming to the bird feeder. He can't get a deep breath, and when he forces it, there's a rattle in his breathing.

Retire. Put in for early retirement and leave town. Oh, he's thought of it many times. Now, it's what he *has* to do. But how, when? And there's the house. . . .

Jamilla, he thought mistakenly, would be easy to control, for she always had been. He went crazy.

Did he know from the beginning what he would have to do? Sometimes, now, it seems he must have. But he didn't plan it.

All the violence in him, all the anger that sat under his heart for so many years, controlled, erupted at once last weekend, and he couldn't catch it or stop it. Reckless, reckless. Jamilla died so quickly. A few seconds and . . .

Go away, out of town. Slowly, carefully, so as not to arouse suspicion. A medical condition would do it. A heart problem discovered while playing golf in—pick a place he's always wanted to go—North Carolina. Under doctor's care. Told he needs to take it easy. Can't come back to work just yet. Medical leave. Leave of absence, whatever they call it. Then the retirement. It's all in the cards and all possible, if only he can catch hold of things now. First, he must get into the lab and get the sample out. Because he knows enough about DNA to know that the lab will take a look at his son's wiggles and lines and spots and they will compare those to the child found in Jamilla and they will write up a report that says: "DNA shows David Hoffman is not the father, but someone in his family is, someone related." Then people will dig, search, figure it out.

The only comfort he can take is that labs are notoriously slow and falling behind. DNA testing takes a long time.

Stupid, stupid woman, meddling where she had no right.

He does all the usual things. Has breakfast, talks to people on the way in, jokes, locks the door, gets on the computer.

All the while, he's thinking, figuring.

FRIDAY MORNING CHRISTIE calls Dolan and Greer into his office and says, "Lab called. Higgins tells me he'll get us DNA results by Sunday, Monday."

"*That* is the fastest turnaround time I ever heard of," Dolan says, eyebrow cocked.

Colleen feels a blush cross her face.

"Our Greer made a hit with Higgins, I guess."

"Oh ho," Dolan offers admiringly.

"We'll know if David Hoffman *or* someone close to him is the father of the baby."

"It's going to be Dun," Colleen says. "He has the history."

"I agree," Christie says.

"And all the while, the KID program was his. Hundreds of pictures of kids in danger. But who was the danger coming from?" Colleen fumes.

"I want to get to his computer," Dolan says. "See if we can figure out who he looks at, that kind of thing. Is he in yet?"

"Came in all cheery. He's in there."

"We can't let him on the loose for much longer," Dolan says grimly.

Christie furrows his face, thinking. "Are we ready to tip him off just yet?"

Colleen just wants to see Dun suffer and die. "He'll try to get out of it," she says angrily. "Most pedophiles are callous. They have no remorse. None. They lie, you put them on the stand—"

"I know," Dolan says. "No expression on their faces. They're gone, been long gone, nobody home there."

Christie appears to consider this. "If he did two murders, he's living with chaos now, no matter what kind of act he puts on. We have to be ready. I'll try to get to his computer when he's not there. In the meantime, other evidence we can marshal?"

"What I'd like to do," Colleen says, after a shadow of silence, "is trace the key to the Park Center. Gabig says he doesn't know of anyone who has a key, right? City Commissioners say they don't give out keys. But if I can find out who had the job before Gabig, who had charge of the keys in the mayor's office, like, ten years ago, what if then . . ."

"Good, follow it up."

Dolan says, "Why'd Hoffman cut out?"

"Afraid of his father . . . protecting him," Colleen suggests.

"Families," Christie says quietly. "Doesn't matter if they get along or not. They won't turn each other in. It's amazing. It must be physical, genetic. It goes beyond logic. They can't do it."

Love, she thinks. It's a version of love.

"Hopefully, you'll hear from Hoffman again soon. Lots is in your hands."

"Funeral time," Dolan says. "Let's go kiddo."

"I can make the calls about keys on the way," she tells Christie who nods but doesn't say anything about what a great, efficient worker she is.

A few minutes later, Colleen has the names of two retired men who had the jobs at the Park Center and at the mayor's office. One is still alive, one gone. She stays on the phone in her car, Dolan listening as she makes inquiries, and as they drive to the funeral of Laura McCall, windshield wipers flapping. She leaves messages, accompanied by rain and road noises, at the homes of the retired park worker and at the home of the widow of the other man. "Why aren't these people at home?"

Dolan chuckles. "Fear the all-day shopping trips."

"Yeah," she says, as if she's been at this for fifty years.

"Damn rain. The grass needs it, but I don't."

They park and sit for a moment, looking at the black-clad people going into Laura McCall's funeral service, black umbrellas aloft like something out of *Our Town*.

TAP ON HIS DOOR. HE GOES TO open it. He knows the knock. Chief is his buddy.

"You want to go over to East Ohio at lunchtime?"

"Sure. Yeah. That'd be fine."

He does some work. He writes up a report on a patrol officer who used excessive force on a drunk guy.

Before twelve, he and the chief go over to one of two places on East Ohio where they can have a drink with lunch—drink, or two or three in his case—in the dark bar with the pinball machines going and the TVs on and the chief bitching about this and that, where everything seems just right, everything in its place.

HE KNOWS HE'S SUPPOSED TO stay in a motel room and watch TV all day, but he can't do it. Instead, he waits for an hour at a pay phone outside the library of a small town, the name of which he can't even remember, but his father doesn't call back.

It's the day Laura is being buried. Right now. Everyone is talking about him, surely, thinking he did it, because he's not there.

Last night, he said, "I didn't do it." And Colleen said, "I *know.*" Was she lying? What do the police know?

Restlessly, he gets into his car, picks a road without knowing where he's going, and drives. It's the only thing that feels right, moving.

His mind leaps ahead to a courtroom scene. "And when did you give your father a key to the Counseling Center?"

"Several years ago."

"How long is several?"

"Five."

"And what did he say was the reason he needed the key?"

"He just wanted to have a place to sit, put his feet up, every once in a while."

"And you believed that?"

"Yes."

But then the other lawyer would ask, "You knew your father's history?"

No. He would say no.

You didn't know how he was using your office?

No.

You didn't suspect?

He would try to say no.

Is the title of your thesis *Early Sexual Aggression: Childhood Backgrounds of Pedophiles*?

It's a subject out of many I could have chosen.

Why did you choose it?

I wanted to understand.

You have a tendency toward pedophilia?

No. No, I just wanted to understand.

Why? Who did you want to understand?

They would make him say it.

Would he go to jail for giving the key? Because he should. That's the truth, he should. Thinking about what must have happened, imagining it, it feels exactly as if he committed the crimes, all of them. Driving along again, he tries to concentrate on what he's doing, but thoughts rip through his head. Jail would be nothing compared to a trial, newspapers, reporters. It's the shame he can't handle.

He looks at his watch. Past lunchtime. He must find a phone and try again. It could be that his father was completely unable to call him back. When his father doesn't answer the phone, he hates him. When he answers, he loves him.

A sign tells him he is headed for Muncie, Indiana. For a moment, he's cheered, because the song with that town's name in it is comic. Ahead of him, in a truck, a woman cuffs her husband lightly. He can tell by the movements of the two of them that they're laughing. It goes on and on, a good old joke. He can't remember the last time he experienced anything like that. The truck with the two happy people takes the next exit.

At one o'clock, he calls his father from a truck stop near Muncie. His father answers. "Call you back in an hour. I'm in a meeting."

Didn't sound like a meeting. Sounded more like pinball machines.

The rain starts to come down, not heavy at first, just a warm, humid spray that won't do the crops much good. But the sky is dark and he doesn't feel like waiting in the rain near an outdoor phone for the callback. He goes inside for a soda. After forty-five minutes, he decides he can't sit still any longer, and he is halfway out of the parking lot, leaving, when he forces himself back. His father might know something.

He parks again and loops his way back through the warm rain to the phone. At exactly an hour after his own call, it rings.

"Yeah," he says.

"Hold steady. Call me tonight. Of course they'll search some for you, because they have to do something, but they don't know beans yet. Just keep the car out of sight for a while, just hole up somewhere and I'll get back to you."

"Okay."

"Where the hell are you?"

"Muncie."

"Indiana. That's good. That's very good. Just the right-size town. Hang in there. Call me tonight. I can't talk any more now. I have almost everything taken care of."

Click.

The old man is nuts. David goes into the truck stop again, studies the map on the wall, and heads back out through the rain. He looks at his watch. It's two o'clock.

DUN DROPS INTO THE CHIEF'S office around three to say he's taking off early for the weekend to go play some golf. It's a long drive, but he's got a favorite course in North Carolina he's eager to get back to.

"Probably got a willing woman near the green, too," Chief says.

"One or two." He laughs.

CHRISTIE AND DOLAN AND GREER meet in Christie's office again at three.

Dolan reports. "I came back here, but Greer did the whole number—Butler, the gravesite."

"And?"

"Sad," she says.

"I need—" He stops, sneezes, shakes his head. "Damn. Littlefield is sick. Maybe it's going around. What I was saying, I need soft undercover surveillance on Dun. We can't go whole hog. I can't let that many people in on it. There's a coffee shop across from his house. We could get some comings and goings from that. Hoffman might show up at his father's house for instance."

"I'll do it," Greer says.

"Sure? You need to be invisible. Scarf on your hair, dark glasses, newspaper."

“I’ll do it,” she repeats.

“I need one other person and it can’t be Dolan. Too visible.”

“Skin color,” Dolan notes, with a little bite. “And they say we all look alike.”

It isn’t just his skin color. He’s small and well built to bursting. Memorable. Has star quality. Colleen wants to tell him that, but now isn’t the time.

“Potocki,” Christie says. “I’m going to give it to Potocki. He can be a block away, ready to move if Greer calls him.”

LATE AFTERNOON, HOFFMAN IS making his way through Ohio rain, not very different from Indiana rain, same storm, moving. In a sense, he guesses how the police are working, though he can’t make himself behave accordingly. By now they would have information on his car make, they would have checked rental agencies, airlines, put a watch on his house and all that. Yet he drives through the rain feeling invisible.

OVERNIGHT CASE, A FEW SHIRTS, gun, phone, cash, cards. Golf clubs. Ready for anything. Ready for everything. He turns back at the door, kisses his fingers as if saying goodbye to his house. He goes out into the gray gray summer rain to his car. A neighbor waves.

“Golf?” the guy calls.

“Yep!” What does it look like, asshole? He smiles, nice broad smile, in case anybody ever asks the jerk.

He drives, parks, dips through the scattered raindrops to an early dinner in Shadyside—gourmet pizza, couple of drinks. Five o’clock passes, five-thirty, six o’clock. He’s sitting there like a regular person, but he is so far inside himself, he doesn’t remember who was in the next booth earlier or who waited on him. He will give up whatever he has to give up—but his house, that’s hard, that hurts. He’s lived in the same place for forty years, except for one little blip on the screen, and if he loves anything, it’s the house.

"Another bourbon?" A woman, young, dressed in a tank with spangles. Is she the one who waited on him before? Sassy. He doesn't like her. "Or something else?"

"Another."

"Bourbon all the way," she says with a lilt.

These kids today are so confident, it's disgusting.

Two more and it's six-thirty. The rain has let up. Sun is coming out. Waiters are wiping off the outside tables. People tilt their heads toward the TVs, catching the news. He, too, looks from time to time, sees only stories on politics, graft, sales, weather, sports. If one of the channels covered the funeral, it's been there and gone, a brief farewell.

Seven, eight minutes to get to downtown. Time to take his chances.

He drives to the crime lab, hits the buzzer. A voice squawks at him, asking him to identify himself.

"Meeting Joe Vesterlund at eight. I'm way early."

"He's not on tonight."

"I know. We're just meeting here. I left him a message."

"Oh. Well, okay."

And he's in. A young man pokes his head out to the waiting area. "You're meeting him here?"

All he has to say if he's ever asked about this is that he left a phone message for Joe. When Joe says he never got the message, he can mutter about having left the message at a wrong number. Happens all the time.

"Yeah. I'll just sit out here and read the paper." He picks up a *Post-Gazette,* its tattered appearance clearly indicating it's been handled all day. *I haven't had a tour of the place in ages, he can say. I'm just going to look around.* With the right line, at the right time, he can get back to the lab shelves. Somewhere, there is a container with his son's DNA samples in it. Got to get it before it's enzymed and incubated.

CHRISTIE HAD BEEN HOME with Marina and the kids from five-thirty on because he wanted to see them, but also because he was feeling sick. His throat was scratchy, his head felt full and foggy. And the whole way home, he'd had a sneezing fit. He needed a long, long sleep.

The rain sprinkled everything for a while, then let up. Marina lighted the grill, wiped off the table on the back porch, gave the chairs in the yard a swipe. He changed clothes. He thought, This is right, this is good. He went downstairs and a little bit later was having dinner in the backyard, just burgers on paper plates, the kids all sweaty and talkative, when Potocki called about Charlie Dun.

Earlier, Greer had called to say Dun was leaving with golf clubs and a small satchel and that Potocki was taking over close watch. She'd be a block away. It turned out Dun didn't go far. Potocki followed him and reported that Dun had been sitting in a bar in Shadyside for some time. And Potocki had a good view. He'd placed himself at the same bar, but in the upstairs area, where he could look down.

"He using his phone much?" Christie had asked.

"Not at all. He's eating. He's drinking. He's drinking a lot."

"And you?"

"Not to mention. They'll remember me as the hip guy who had three gallons of diet Coke at a hot spot."

Potocki had been discreet, not asking *why* he was watching the assistant chief. Still, there was excitement in his voice.

"He didn't see you?" Christie quizzed.

"I don't think so."

"And he has a satchel?"

"In his car. And a golf bag."

"Might he be waiting for someone?"

"Might be."

"Where's Greer?"

"Block away. Holding till she's needed. She's fine. She's being real steady."

"Can you mark his car?"

"Can't. It's right outside where he's sitting."

"Check back in a quarter hour."

Marina had brought him a cold remedy—a gel for his nose, supposed to head off the sneezing.

Now she sat across from him, asked him if the gel had done any good.

"Can't tell," he said.

She touched his leg, frowned, leaned forward and touched his forehead. "Hmmm, you might have a little fever."

"I feel shitty." Summer colds. They were simply *wrong.* "You should stay clear."

"Is the case about to break?"

"Maybe." He'd confided in her his suspicions about Dun, murmured them in bed last night. Rules were meant to be broken.

"Dolan and Greer still your only confidants?"

"I've added Potocki—didn't tell him everything, though. Potocki may be thinking Dun is protecting Hoffman; or he may have stumbled on the idea the rest of us have."

"I like Potocki."

"I do, too. You have any feeling about Dun?"

Marina gave it some thought. "Never paid attention to him. I always thought of him as a good old boy, a little hearty, too macho, whatever. False. I can see the other in him now that you say it. I can."

"Women have Geiger counters for certain things."

"Probably."

"Greer is absolutely sure. I suspect she has some kind of bad history with someone. Little things she says. As if she knows Dun from her own experience as a victim."

"Is the guy in her life okay? The one at the picnic?"

"They broke up."

"Oh."

"Just your usual asshole, I think."

"So she's achy." She pats his knee. "You don't have to solve it."

"What?"

"Your propensity to fix everything, fix everyone."

"Fix you," he said, arching his eyebrow.

She laughed. "I think you're too sick for that now. Besides, you told me to steer clear."

"There might be things we could do later. You look delicious." But he was forcing it. He didn't have the energy.

His phone rang again minutes later. This time, it was Greer. "He's at the crime lab. I lost him for a while. Potocki gave me the word that he was starting out and I followed him, but traffic lights got me and I had to stay behind. But then I kept looking ahead and I got a feeling—you know, downtown, time of day, and . . . and my own paranoia. So on a hunch, I drove to the crime lab and, voilà, I saw his car there."

"Good work. Where is he now?"

"This was, like, a minute ago. He must be inside."

Ten seconds later, Christie was on the phone with Jack Higgins, who was doing the DNA testing. "I understand the assistant chief has some business over there. Don't let him near anything from the cases I'm working on. This is strictly *strictly* confidential. Preserve anonymity of the samples and preserve the samples. Please. Make sure nothing is switched or traded."

Jack Higgins's shaking voice said, "Okay. You couldn't switch it, though. I mean, I've got the argarose soaking right now. I was going to do—" Higgins went quiet for a moment. "I hear him out there asking questions. He says he's meeting someone here at eight."

"Wonder who."

"I didn't hear."

"I'll hang up. Protect the test."

"Will do."

Christie hung up the phone. "I've got to go," he told Marina. His head felt foggy, terrible.

His daughter, Julie, said, "See, I told you."

Her brother, Eric, said, "I am not going to get into a fight with you. All I want to know is if we're ever going on vacation or not."

Christie went upstairs, unbuttoning his khaki shorts, kicking off his sandals, and grabbing a pair of jeans and a pair of solid shoes. His heart was pounding and his stomach decided to tumble dinner around.

His phone rang again. "Lost him," Greer blurted, distraught. "He came right out *right* away. I *had* to hide. I couldn't follow. And I was getting an incoming call at the same time and—"

"He left the lab?"

"Yes. I'm so sorry."

"Not your fault. Where's Potocki?"

"He lost him, too, so he went back to Dun's house in case he—"

The call was interrupted by an incoming call. It was Higgins, saying, "I was locking the lab door when—well, I'm told he sat down at one of the computers outside and started fiddling around and, like, reading what was on-line. Then he just up and left."

"What would he have seen? About your work, I mean."

"Just that the testing was in progress."

"Thank you. Lock the doors. Don't let Dun back in. I'm going to send over some extra protection. This is absolutely confidential."

"Right."

Seven o'clock, a few minutes after. He clicked back to Greer, but she wasn't answering. She was on a call, too. She came on the line moments later.

"I got a call, Boss. Widow of the man from the mayor's office said her husband complained that some guy had pushed him around and insisted on getting keys he wasn't supposed to have."

"Did she say who?"

"No name. Just that the person was police."

"Good work."

"It isn't hard evidence."

"No, not yet. But we're close. Go home. You've put in eighteen-hour days for a week. Go home. I'll call if you're needed. Rest."

He sat on the bed. Five minutes past seven, the bedside clock said. His daughter crept into the room. "Are you okay?"

"It's just a cold."

Marina came behind her, stood at the door. "You don't have to go?"

"I do. I just don't know where."

MARINA WENT OUT INTO THE yard to pick up whatever plates or napkins had been left lying around. Julie and Eric were pretty good, trained to pick up after themselves. Thanks to her, not their mother, they were becoming small good citizens.

"Hey, know what we need to do after we clean up?" she asked.

"What?" Eric was a bit cross still about losing his father one more time to work.

"Drive over to Fox Chapel, get your dad a bag of peat—"

Eric looked curious as to why this was going to be fun, but Julie was already expectant that something good was coming.

"Then hit the Baskin-Robbins for some ice cream."

"Yay."

"We'll bring some home for your dad. Hand-packed. Special."

"If he has a cold," Julie observed, "he shouldn't be eating cold things."

"Right. We'll have to hold his till he's ready. Meanwhile, lots of hand washing, okay? Might as well start now, since I don't remember who touched what."

They lined up at the sink. She knew their mother was always bad-mouthing their father. He had faults, sure. The worst of his faults, the need to be special to everyone, scared her plenty. A person who belonged to everyone belonged to no one. Everyone fell in love with her husband and nobody got enough of him.

"Your dad is really good at what he does. That's why he's high up in rank and it's why he has to run off when he's needed. He doesn't let anything go. I admire that."

The kids were listening, pretending to be more interested in pumping the hand soap and getting a good suds going than they were in listening, but she knew they heard her.

"It's the same in everything. Every job. The really good people, whether we're talking about football or surgeons or whatever—actors are the same—don't let go. They give all of their energy to each second."

Eric, frowning, said, "But not every minute every day. A football player doesn't run out and play a game at midnight."

She handed him a hand towel. "Well, probably not. But the great ones have that energy. They use the practice time, they use the video study time, they use the warm-up time. They're focused. And when they play, they're concentrating every second, not letting any possibility get by them. That's what the magic is. Concentration."

"Polamalu?" Eric asked.

"Absolutely right."

She was looking at Julie's beautiful dark hair. It was almost straight and her own was very curly, but more than once people had assumed Julie was her natural child. Marina moved forward and gently pulled the girl's hair back, lifting it for a moment off her neck. "You're hot? You want a haircut?"

"Huh-uh. I like it long."

She loved the kids and they loved her now. It had happened. They trusted her. She made a difference in their lives. She let Julie go.

The kids ran out to the car.

Gathering her purse and keys, she allowed herself to think about why the new detective, Greer, might be attractive to men in general and to her husband in particular. Colleen Greer wasn't especially young; she was in her thirties, as Marina was. But she was a rookie, and something about her newness—as well as something in her personality—made her appealing in the way youth was appealing. Men were always looking for daughters who were not literally their daughters. And women who were unfinished, who were still in daughter mold, were dangerous.

GREER KNEW REST WAS NOT what she needed. She'd be able to sleep when they were booking Dun.

Being related to someone who knew two victims. Not enough. Not enough. Filching parts of his file, a bad history, estrangement from family, possibly the possessor of illegal keys, innovator of a program to do with kids in crisis. Messing around at the crime lab. All suspicious, not enough to *get him on.* Should they consider going back to West Virginia and openly confronting Eileen Hoffman?

She wandered around her house. The rain had stopped. Cold air blew in from the vents, but there was an almost chemical tang in the air from its being closed up with the air conditioning on for so long. She threw open the back door. Good, the sounds of children playing on the street.

She threw open the dining room windows. Hot air made its way in—bad for the energy bills, but maybe healthy in terms of air circulation.

Music, not too loud, not loud enough to drown out the kids on the block outside, music was what she needed. In the smaller bedroom she'd outfitted as a study, she found the last few CDs she'd played at home, still out of the rack. Cuban music. Okay, that.

Still she had the willies, felt unsafe.

She tried to sit in her living room, just relax. "Rest," he'd said. It was . . . impossible. She felt if she didn't move, she would die. It was the microversion of how she'd felt as a counselor, sitting, talking to kids and families in trouble. Her body wanted to be up and doing, fixing. She leaped up, filled a bucket with Spic and Span and hot water.

Her phone rang. Potocki, speaking very quietly. "He didn't come home yet. I'm so sorry I didn't get downtown fast enough."

"I'm the one who lost him. I got sent home."

"I don't think it was a punishment. Do you think so?"

"It felt like it."

"No. Not your fault. It's . . . it was a weird assignment."

She wasn't sure how much Potocki had guessed about what was going on.

There was a funny silence on the line and she kept expecting Potocki to crack a joke. When he didn't, she asked, "You're still watching his house?"

"Yep. Sitting in the coffee shop you sat in earlier. I'm the goon with the laptop and the dark glasses and more caffeine in me than I can stand. You take care now."

"You take care, too."

Nearly eight o'clock. It took only five minutes to scrub the kitchen counters and cabinets, and she was half-finished attacking the kitchen floor when the phone rang again. It was Christie saying, "I'm in Oakland with Dolan. We three ought to talk."

"I'll be there. Where?"

She could hear him consulting with Artie. "Can we come over? That's the most private."

"Sure." She gave directions. Police driving—it would take them four minutes. She would have liked a shower, but she settled for washing her face, brushing her teeth, finishing the floor. And then there was the sound of two cars pulling up and the noise of footsteps on her front porch.

She was nervous in a way she wouldn't have been if they'd done the meeting in Oakland. Having them in her home—superiors—was making her self-conscious. "I haven't spent much time here. Place needs a good cleaning."

"Looks fine to me," they both said in unison. "Real comfy," Dolan added as he plopped on the couch. "Oh man, remember this feeling?"

Christie sat in the large chair that faced the couch. He looked funny, strained and frowning. "Got the cold I was fighting," he said. "Littlefield's cold."

"Oh, sorry," she said. "Who needed that?"

"You two don't, so don't come close. Thanks for letting us meet here. Nice place. Really nice."

"You're welcome. Water, beer, Coke, wine, that's it. Unless I brew some tea and cool it down fast."

Water was all they wanted. She came back with three tall glasses of water and took a seat on the sofa.

Christie said, "We have no way of knowing what Dun is thinking. He took a small satchel with him. Told a complete lie. There was no plan to meet Joe Vesterlund. Now we have something on him—though it isn't much in the big scheme of things. And we don't have him."

"People come back to their houses," Colleen said. "Their jobs. Eventually. Right?"

"Not if the satchel holds enough cash," Dolan said.

"He might be gone." Christie nodded. "He's got a cell, probably has more than one, but he might not use them. He knows enough to know we could get him that way, eventually, with everything in place. I hear there's a TV show that has everybody thinking every single cell works as a homing device just like that. If only."

To get a warrant, they'd have to talk probable cause to a judge. If they went that far and if Dun used his cell, they could get a general location.

"Where will he go next?" Christie asked. "He got jumpy at the lab. Think."

"See his son?" Dolan suggested. "Wherever the hell he is."

"Maybe."

Dolan said, "By the way, anybody hungry?"

Colleen was. She had eaten a sandwich at the coffee shop across from Dun's place, but that was it, and she didn't feel like cooking pasta.

Dolan said, "I really want a pizza. Anybody mind if I order one?"

Christie looked amused.

Colleen said, "Get an extra-large. I'll pay."

"No need for that." Dolan made a call, put in an order.

How odd to have the people from work here in her house, just hanging out. Colleen felt both violated and accepted, too much known and also released from the usual polite strictures. While waiting for the pizza, she searched her kitchen, found a pretty full container of ice cream in her freezer. "I have dessert," she announced.

They looked utterly comfortable.

Pals. They were pals.

DAVID HOFFMAN IS IN HIS CAR, outside the gate of the cemetery in Butler where Laura is buried. It's locked now; he cannot get in. And he cannot go home. He is an hour from every destination that occurs to him—where he lives, where his father lives, where his father works. He looks around. Don't the police watch cemeteries? He half-expects to be picked up, but nothing happens, and he leaves.

His car has a mind of its own. It does not want to go to Canada or Iowa, even though he has promised his father he will be far away, helping by staying out of reach.

The new cell phone he bought with his alternate name is so small, he can't find it in his pocket. When he does, he clasps it before pulling it up to tilt it toward the light. While driving, he attempts to get the feel of the tiny buttons. Are they monitoring the land phone at his house? Who might call? His mother? He presses in her number.

"I just wanted to tell you very quickly I'm okay. I'm not at home."

"I think there are police watching my house. Why is this happening to me? Did . . . you do it?"

"No. Please don't ever think it."

"I told that detective you couldn't have."

"What detective?"

"The woman. Your friend. Colleen Greer."

"She called?"

"She was *here.*"

"When? Yesterday?"

"No, beginning of the week. She kept asking about . . . him."

At first, he thinks he heard wrong. "Beginning of the week? What are you saying?"

But she's talking over him, saying, "Tuesday. And she mentioned Charlie."

He can't think. He sees an exit, pulls off, but even as he does, he's asking, "How did she know about him?" He needs to stop. He needs to think, to listen in *stillness* so he can understand.

"I didn't say anything. I pretended I didn't know what she was talking about. You're not in touch with him, are you? I don't think I could forgive that."

"Just a minute. I'm driving. Just a minute until I pull into a parking lot." The phone drops to the floor. He makes his way down the exit ramp, past a stop sign, to an abandoned paint store that once advertised boldly that they had absolutely every color known to man in stock.

He catches his breath, picks up the phone.

"You should have called me," he whispers.

"I didn't want to know . . . if you did it. Or if you're like him after all."

He thinks of things he won't say: that his father did it; that the man is unraveling; that his father wants the police to think he's the one. All he tells his mother is, "I didn't think they knew anything about him."

"I wanted him out of our lives," his mother says. "And here he is again."

In that moment, sitting in front of the defunct paint store, David sees himself clearly as a product of his parents—his mother too afraid of everything, preserving herself in plastic, wrapped and clean and unknowing. His father with a horrible secret and a position to maintain. Himself struggling away from them, trying for a decent life, for dignity, always being pulled back into the moment when he was a boy, attached to his father, falling in love with his father, finding him more human in some way than his mother. But she had got him to shut up then, and after. He is like her in some ways; the thought makes him . . . not hateful, but sad.

"David? What's happening?"

"I have to go now," he says. His phone-clock tells him it's nearly eight-thirty. Then he dials another number.

COLLEEN'S CELL PHONE RINGS. She reads the number before punching the button. She has time to tell the detectives, "Indiana area code. Different number. This might be what we're waiting for."

They stare at her for a second, then begin making hand motions—keep him on, keep him talking, do a miracle.

"You said you knew I didn't commit any murder."

"Yes," she answers. "I said that. I do know. I know you must be suffering. Where are you? Is he . . ." She almost asked if Charlie was there, but she caught herself in time. Better not give away what she didn't know. She recovers with, "I hope he's all right."

"What do you mean?"

"Running. It's . . . horrible."

Christie and Dolan stand in front of her, listening.

"The funeral was dignified. I think you would have approved. I know it must have been hard to stay away."

"It was." His voice breaks.

"Tell me what I can do. Tell me how I can talk to you."

"I'll call you back." The line goes dead.

She tells Christie, "He's crying. He may try to harm himself. I can't tell. He's at the end of his rope, though. He says he'll call me back. I don't know if he will."

Dolan says, "I can have the number traced. Write it down for me." She does. "Sure it's not the number you gave us yesterday."

"No. Same area code, both numbers. Land phone yesterday—pay phone," Colleen says. "Boss checked it out."

Dolan and Christie make lots of phone calls, maybe forty. Eventually they agree to put on the TV to watch the ball game, remote at the ready to mute it when they have to. Dolan carries the second handset from Colleen's home phone so that if her landline rings, he can coordinate and pick up just when she picks up her living room phone. Christie looks worried, paces, sometimes to the front yard, sometimes down the hall of her little house to the bathroom. The pizza arrives.

DUN LOOKS AT THE GOLF BAG, thinking to remove the bottle of bourbon he has in there. Decides, no save it. He pulls up to a bar, seedy little place, goes in, orders a drink. Then a few more.

DOLAN TAKES A CALL FROM HIS contact at Verizon while winding a string of pizza cheese back onto his fourth slice. His contact gives him the first bit of information and he relays it to the others as he gets it. "Cell phone number. Huh. Okay. Now. If you could just tell us where the calls are being made from. Global positioning. Yes. You are fantastic. I'll be at this number or . . ." He gives Colleen's landline, as well.

Christie paces. Colleen waits expectantly for instructions.

"She'll come up with location."

It's almost dark out now. The sound of kids playing vanishes from the street. Colleen wonders how long Christie and Dolan will stay at her place.

"Call him," Christie tells Colleen.

She calls, leaves a message, saying, "Please call. I want to help you. I know what's going on and I want to help."

"I'm going over to see Judge Martin," Christie says abruptly. "He only lives three minutes from here. Wants to socialize unfortunately. So if I go there and schmooze, and Artie gets down to Headquarters for the paperwork we need, delivers it to me in, what, forty-five minutes tops, we're clear to use whatever we get about Hoffman's cell. Completely legal. I hate it that he's still in Indiana or God knows where. I hate sending someone else to talk to him." He turns to Colleen and says, "You'll have to wait here. He might call you back."

"Something else I can do?" she blurts. "Besides waiting?"

"Waiting is important."

HOFFMAN MAKES HIS WAY PAST Pittsburgh, close enough to graze it, stopping twice, calling his father's two numbers from a pay phone each time, but the old man doesn't pick up. Charlie could be anywhere by now. On a plane, on a train, driving to Indiana to be with his son, not knowing, of course, that his son is only twenty-some miles from home. David can't go home and he can't stop moving and the only thing he's sure of is that he must find his father. The messages he leaves are simple. "I have to talk to you. Call me."

Once he's in Bridgeville, across from the strip of motels—foam pillows, stiff mattresses, bad morning coffee (but free!)—he calls from a pay phone at the corner BP, wondering which motel he will crash at. Oh, how he wants to be in his own house, to grieve, to arrange his possessions, to go into work, where he's useful.

No answer. Nothing.

Night falls in earnest. He crosses the road to the Holiday Inn Express, plunks down his second fake ID, and some cash, and he's in for the night. Tonight, he's Robert Parrish.

He orders a pizza. He puts on baseball. He can't bear to go out again in search of a pay phone, so he tries one more time from the room phone to his father's cell and this time leaves a more complex message. "I'm at the Bridgeville Holiday Inn Express. Room Twelve. I'm not going to stay away any longer. I can't. So I'm going to try to get some sleep and then go in tomorrow. I wish I could talk to you before I go in."

COLLEEN PACES HER HOUSE, feeling suddenly very alone. Ten minutes, twenty, thirty click slowly by. When her phone rings, she jumps, startled.

It's Artie Dolan's friend from Verizon asking for him.

"It's okay. You can tell me. He's talking to a judge, making it official," Colleen says. "I'm supposed to take the information if you have it."

Colleen is expecting to hear the woman refuse, so she's surprised when the Verizon rep tells her easily, "Cell phone was purchased by a Patrick McDonough. Calls from the cell used several different towers today, from places in Indiana, Ohio, then Pennsylvania. Once in Pennsylvania, the towers used were in Butler, and, let's see, something that just says Pittsburgh. Last call used a tower in Bridgeville. As of a couple of minutes ago."

"Bridgeville!"

"Yep. He would have been somewhere at, say, Route Fifty and Washington Pike."

Twenty minutes away.

She slams into her car and gets on the road.

THE PIZZA IS FINISHED, JUST a few crusts left, and David sits at the small table in his motel room, making notes on the notepad provided by the management. Isn't it cost ineffective to make notepads with only four sheets of paper on them? When you figure in manufacturing time, cardboard backing, all that?

He will go in to Headquarters in the morning, when he's rested and able to talk. Right now, his jaw drops with an exhaustion he can hardly describe. It seems, sometimes, he has never rested at all in his life, always been waiting, nervous, worried about the next moment. What he did wrong—jots it down as if he will forget it. Did not tell police what he suspected a week ago, accepted a stolen identity—two in fact—accepted fake plates, charge cards. Protected a suspect. Will anybody understand he couldn't think what to do? "You let him have the key, you asked no questions?" There it is, his real crime. Digging a hole and hiding knowledge from himself. How can he explain? Who will ever forgive him?

ON THE PARKWAY, SHE DIALS Christie's cell number. He doesn't answer right away. Talking to the judge, can't be rude, she thinks. If he tells her to go home . . . if he does, she will have to go home. Five minutes later, he calls back, and when she explains, he says, "Keep going. We'll catch up with you."

Then Dolan is in one car, Christie in another, all three using their various phones to review motels and other possible spots in and around Bridgeville—and to figure strategy.

At one point it's just Colleen and Artie Dolan on the line.

"If he didn't book into a motel," Dolan says, "we'll be tromping to every business, every restaurant. And maybe nothing will come of it. I hate nights like that. All we have is the phone tower."

Greer asks, "Will your contact call you back if Hoffman makes another call?" Hoffman, alias McDonough.

"Yep. She will."

"Good."

"Right. This woman . . ." Dolan chuckles. "In case you're wondering, I don't go the distance with her. I flirt. I suppose I always seem possible, if you know what I mean. I strongly suspect she likes possible and favors it over the real."

"I understand."

"We do what we can."

"Yes, thanks."

"You're already good at it."

"What?"

"Suggesting the possible."

"Thanks, I guess."

Christie's call interrupts them, so Colleen cuts the call with Dolan. Christie sneezes twice and says in a muffled voice, "I'm not going to bring in state or local people. I'm guessing we can get Hoffman to co-operate." He sneezes again. He sounds as if he's been crying when he says, "Show us to his father."

"Boss, you sound awful."

"I get such bad colds."

"Every time?"

"Yeah. My body has one of those pathways cut. The germs just run right in like a bunch of hoodlums."

"About like that, if I remember any science."

"Greer?"

"Yes, Boss?"

"I'm thinking about how sure you are about Dun. I'm sorry if I'm prying. I've been wanting to make sure you're okay. I just got a feeling that maybe something bad happened to you—beyond what you called 'flaky parents.' "

It comes out of her so easily, she can't believe it, as if it's been written on her forehead all along. "I had an incident with an uncle. It was violent. And I more or less protected myself. I mean, I ran away and got away. The trauma was . . . well, probably worse because I never told my parents. They couldn't have handled it."

"I'm sorry."

"Yeah. It's nothing, really. In the big picture. I got away."

"You have to take yourself seriously. If you've been hurt, you're carrying whatever you got. Well, you know that."

"Oh, sure. I know that. I told a couple of people later. In therapy school."

"We'll talk. When it's a better time. I'm going to pass this idiot in front of me. Ohio drivers."

"Where are you?"

"Close to the Bridgeville exit. Three minutes from it. Where are you?"

"Three minutes ahead of you."

"Dolan will take the Knight's Inn, I'll take the Rustic Inn, and

Greer, you take the Comfort Inn. Check the parking lot first," Christie says. He reads out Hoffman's plate numbers. He tells Colleen he's had Potocki calling Indiana motels to see if Patrick McDonough registered at any of them and what plate numbers he wrote down on the registration—not that he holds out much hope. Nor does Colleen, for, as he says, "What motel staff actually goes outside to check plates? You could write down any damn thing."

She has just taken the exit and now looks ahead to where there is one business and motel after another. Hoffman is here somewhere. She drives fast, looking for the Comfort Inn, but she doesn't see it from the road.

"I can't see the Comfort Inn yet. I'm looking."

"Good." Christie loops back to their previous conversation. "Maybe your parents would have, you know . . ."

"What?"

"Handled it. Better than you think."

"They were big on denial."

"Consider it."

There is a long almost silence when the only sound is Christie trying to blow his nose without hawking a big one into the phone.

HE HEARS A KNOCK AT THE door. He looks to the pizza box. More of a tip wanted? The pizza man back with a complaint? Management arriving with feather pillows and a substantial notepad?

He opens the door.

There is a long, still moment. Then his father is in the room, closing the door behind him.

"I thought I'd never see you again."

"Here I am. You knew how to get me here, too. What are you thinking? *What are you thinking?* You can't go in. You can't turn me in. You would do that to me?"

Hoffman sits at the edge of the bed. His father stands near the doorway. "It's that I need to clear myself. This isn't me, running, pretending to be someone else. I had a life."

His father walks to the table, picks up the notepad, puts on a pair of glasses, and reads what's there. "What you did wrong. Like a little boy." He lifts the first page and reads the second. The color leaves his face. It's the part about the key. His father rips off the pages, crumbles them, looks around, goes into the bathroom and flushes them down the toilet. "We're going to talk," he says when he returns to the room. He sits on the second bed, across from his son. "You didn't have any kind of life. Who are you fooling? Where were your friends? Huh? Couldn't keep a wife. Counseled riffraff day in and out. What was that? Status? You can do better. I'll help you do better."

A small crack appears. He can see the bluff. He can pick apart the words and find his own truth. His work life is not negligible. The part about Laura, he hasn't sorted that out yet. "I might like my own life. I might need it. I won't drag you in. I'll let you go where you go. I'll . . . hope you get away and go somewhere and don't hurt anyone ever again. I won't drag you in." He shakes his head to get rid of the repetition, steps toward the next thought. "I just need to separate myself from you. I'll take my punishment. For my part."

"You'll go to jail."

"I'll probably go to jail."

His father is up, pacing. Hoffman realizes, belatedly, the television is perseverating, obsessively and dramatically dispensing CNN news. His father waves irritably at the television and gropes for the remote to shut it off. "You say that as if you can handle it. You have no idea what you're talking about. You won't be able to handle it. Jail."

"I'll have to. Listen to me. Charlie? Here's the truth. Are you listening? They know about you. One of the detectives went to West Virginia. Talked to . . . Mom. About you."

"How do you know that?"

"I called Mom."

"Who went? Christie? Son of a bitch? It wasn't in the records. I read the records."

"Detective Greer."

His father spits out, "Her. I knew her in training. A cocktease and an uppity bitch. You like her? She's your friend, huh? Guess what I found out. She took a sample of your DNA, and you think she's your friend?"

"She did?"

"Yeah."

"They know about you. She must have figured it out. You're going to run, well here, take the money you gave me. They must be looking at you, too. You want to run, go ahead. Keep making it worse for yourself, for everyone." He throws a wallet thick with bills onto the bed. "I'm done. I'm not going anywhere."

"Except jail. You're a coward."

"I'm not running."

COLLEEN PULLED INTO THE BP lot to ask, "Where's the Comfort Inn?"

The man at the next pump pointed across traffic to the Holiday Inn Express. "Used to be Comfort. Not any longer."

"Thanks." She crossed the road, parked, and got out of the car. She was about to go to the registration desk to ask about a Patrick McDonough, but she remembered she was supposed to check the lot first. She started to walk around.

She had jotted the plate numbers down. David Hoffman was not a person she would have guessed would use fake IDs, fake plates, but so much for guessing.

It was night now, ten-thirty. Mostly, the place was quiet. People were sleeping. Some rooms didn't even have lights on; many had the tiny glow of televisions. Cars were not coming and going; people were not carrying takeout. That hour was past. A person could stay invisible at this time of night.

She dialed Christie.

"Anything?" he asked.

"I'm at the Holiday Inn."

"Oh. I saw it from the road. I was going to—"

She stopped in her tracks. "Uh-oh."

"Greer?"

What she saw in front of her made her breath catch. She dropped the phone to her side. She was staring at a silver Honda CR-V, the same make and color vehicle that Hoffman had driven away in from Alexander's. Wrong plate, but— "I've got him," she said. "Found him."

"What do you see?"

"His car. I'm pretty sure. I'd say room twelve, thirteen, fourteen, one of those."

"Stay in your car. We'll be right there." He hung up. She didn't tell him she wasn't in her car.

She leaned against the building, trying to get a deep breath. Go to her car or not? It would mean losing her view of the room. She decided to stay where she was. It was only a matter of minutes until they got there. All the rooms had the curtains drawn. She tried to peer through the crack of the curtain in room fourteen. Saw very little. Heard a TV. She moved on to thirteen, where she could see a woman moving about. Probably not that one, then. Twelve. Two men's voices, raised, the sound of one of them familiar. She froze. She was about to reach for her phone again, when the door opened. It took her a moment to realize this was it. She was standing there face-to-face with Charlie Dun. Past the open door behind him, she could see David.

"You! What the—" Dun choked.

His face went red with blood and his eyes were so full of rage, she almost couldn't look at him. She tried to head off his fury by talking. "I came to see David. I understood . . . I thought you were golfing somewhere this weekend." Surprise threw him for a second. "I need to see David," she repeated. She stood in his way, counting seconds, wondering how long until Christie would get there.

He must have read her thoughts. He said, "Excuse me. Let me pass or you're going to get hurt."

"I'd say it's the other way around." She pulled her gun. "Stand or you will get hurt."

"Don't, please," David cried out.

"Just back into the room," she said firmly.

"What will you do? Shoot me?" He tried to laugh.

"If I have to."

"For what? Going to my car? You're out of your jurisdiction here."

"I'd be very careful if I were you," she said. "Move backward slowly." She watched him thinking, trying to figure out how to turn it around. She saw him curse himself that he had not brought his own gun into the room. He backed up and she advanced. The door slammed shut behind her. Dun stepped backward right into David, but she kept her grip and the gun didn't leave her hand even as she watched Dun collide with his son. Both men lost their balance and fell toward the nightstand; David tried to right his father. Dun said, "Stop. Wait." He shuffled awkwardly, then sat on the edge of the bed. "Hurt my arm," he said. "Let's just see what's going on with you. Put the gun away. You have no jurisdiction here anyway. As I said." He laughed a little more successfully now, at her eagerness, it would seem. "Let's talk."

She didn't put the gun away. "Let's talk."

David began to move forward. "I was going to come in tomorrow, talk to you. You can put the gun away."

"For now," she said, "I'm going to ask you to move over that way. Keep your hands where I can see them." She backed up to the door and opened it a crack, kept the side of her left foot against it to keep it open. "You were going to come in, David, and you were going to be able to tell us something. . . . What?"

He spoke slowly, looking toward his father nervously. "That I didn't kill anyone. That I knew I was a suspect. That I knew running looked bad. That I was admitting to using a fake ID and that . . . I don't want to be on the run or away from home. I wanted to say that."

"What else?"

"I'm not sure what else."

"Where did you get the ID?"

He hesitated.

"It sure casts suspicion on you." She saw Dun's face light with hope, but his face also showed something of his craziness. He looked odd, tense, of course, but odd. Was it because he'd been drinking? The thought made her aware of the smell of liquor, or perhaps it had happened the other way around, just as she saw in her peripheral vision the bottle of bourbon on the table. She worked to keep eye contact with Dun. His face was the face of a man in turmoil, breaking apart. His eyes were darting this way and that; he was still looking for a way out.

There was no real proof yet. And he could walk away. And if he tried it, would she shoot him to keep him there?

The sound of a car pulling up raised her spirits. Then she heard a second car. Yes, there were the recognizable door slams. How strange that she could recognize the metal-on-metal production of sound, like a car's fingerprint.

"Commander," she called. Her voice had a streak of hysteria in it that she despised. "Twelve."

She hardly had the word out before Christie was in the door and beside her. Then she heard Dolan come in behind.

"You!" Dun said. And he didn't try to disguise the scorn. He looked at Christie with the same kind of look he usually gave Greer. *Not interesting,* not worth regard.

Colleen saw now that it wasn't a charge of incompetence so much as a charge of something like ordinariness. The assistant chief's eyes flickered at Dolan. For some reason, Dolan passed muster with him.

"If you don't have a weapon," Christie said, "we can just talk. That would be better. All around."

"I told her you have no jurisdiction here. *You* must know that much, huh?"

"She knows it. We all do. We were glad to be able to find you here and to be able to talk; we prefer it this way. It's . . . to our advantage and yours. Dolan is going to search you and then we can relax."

"I need a drink." Dun swabbed his brow and hairline. He was sweating profusely.

"Okay."

Dun stood, weary, amused, as Dolan searched him. Dolan did a thorough job of it, taking longer than usual, turning out the pockets. Nothing small, no razor blades or surprises. "I think you just want to spend time with me," Dun joked.

"I tend to get up close and personal," Dolan said.

Colleen watched Dun's face, trying to understand him.

Christie said, "Dolan, if you'd do the same for Hoffman?"

Hoffman came forward cooperatively. His father snuffled and spit out derisive sounds, the words not quite intelligible.

After Dolan stood away from Hoffman, Christie said, "Now, pour him a drink, a nice stiff one."

Dolan looked around for a cup or glass. "This it?" He held up a plastic cup.

"That's all they provide here," Hoffman said.

"It's not usable as a weapon," Dun said dryly. "At least pour me the damn drink."

Dolan did. He put it on the nightstand and let Dun pick it up himself. Dun drank the liquor down in five or six big swallows, looked at them, and said, "You going to have Annie Oakley put away her gun?" He put down the plastic glass; it made only a feeble plunking sound in punctuation.

Christie said, "I think that's okay now."

Colleen tried not to rush herself, carefully holstering her gun, aware she might want it again. She took a long, deep breath.

Dun said, "I could use another." He held his glass toward Dolan.

Christie said, "In a couple of minutes. We need to talk for just a bit before you get superrelaxed."

"I don't get 'superrelaxed.' Ever."

"More's the pity."

Dun laughed disdainfully. "You have some funny expressions. Somebody told me you almost became a priest. Is that where all your guff comes from?"

Hoffman stood near the bathroom door, tense. "Are you doing okay?" he asked his father.

Dun made an awkward wink. "Not sure, not sure."

"How about you have a seat on the other bed?" Christie suggested to Hoffman. "I'll use the chair. That's about all we have to sit on. You two okay?"

"I'd rather stand," Dolan said.

"I'm fine," Colleen said.

"We just need a couple of minutes," Christie assured Dun.

Again, Dun looked hopeful. Colleen couldn't imagine how Christie could mean what he said, that they only needed minutes, but she figured the time for lies was upon them.

"I'm glad we're out of our jurisdiction," Christie said again, nodding to Dun, "for your sake. We're looking at you, as I know you know. Got to the point where we knew we had to call you in, and if we did it around home, around the office, word would get around so fast . . . even if we took you in this time of night. Well, you know. It'd hit the papers before we had any control of it. I, for one, take it pretty hard when the police are in trouble. So, here we are. We're safe. We can sort it out, see what we have."

"You have nothing," Dun said. "Nothing."

"Not true. We have the lab reports. More coming in all the time. Right after you went down to the lab, they called me, wondered about what you were up to there. They gave me the DNA results for Jamilla's baby and the matches they were working on."

Dun blanched and looked toward the bourbon bottle. "I know police bullshit when I hear it. DNA takes much longer."

"In this case, they were on it straight off. Higgins was amenable. Right after you left, they gave me the preliminary findings they'll confirm tomorrow by noon. The father of the baby was not David here, whose DNA we have, but someone closely related to him."

Dun pursed his lips. "And that's who? I'm Dun. He's Hoffman. We're friends. That's it."

"He's called you his father."

"Stepfather."

"Look at the two of you. Lab will confirm the relationship soon enough, but we don't even need it that way, do we—science? Just look at the two of you. Greer saw it straight off the bat. And then she talked to your ex, David's mother, and family, neighbors in Monroeville, got the whole sequence. I'm afraid we're right around the corner from proving it."

"You don't have my DNA." Dun's eyes glanced off the plastic cup.

"We do. We picked it up from your office. Prints, hair."

This was a lie, but they could get it easily enough, Colleen knew.

"So it's a matter of time," Christie said.

"I'm sure I can prove this was mishandled."

"I'm sure you can't. We've been especially scrupulous. So you see, we know your relationship with David, and we have this question about your relationship with Jamilla—to start with here."

"Let me give you an idea that should have occurred to you. David here . . ." He paused. He stared at his son, looked up to Christie, said calmly, "David has a son of his own from when he first started working at the center, when he was a pup out of school. He took up with a woman he shouldn't have bothered with, okay? The son is fourteen now, right?" He looked back at David. "And they don't have much contact, but he protects the kid. That's who got Jamilla pregnant."

The surprise on David's face was evident. It wasn't a look of guilt so much as of amazement.

Christie said evenly, "Tell us your son's name."

David shook his head.

"You refuse to?"

"I never had a son. I'm sorry." He looked sorrowfully at his father. "I'm not in this with you."

Dun's expression turned venomous. He said tightly, "We'll see who's right."

Colleen tried her best to send David a sign of encouragement.

"We will," Christie said simply. "That's the thing. Everything surfaces in time. We had questions about why certain parts of your employment portfolio were missing, but we got the copies and we were able to fill in what wasn't there. We know you had some bad history, accusations of alcohol abuse—"

"I like the stuff. I can handle it." Dun picked up the plastic glass and nodded toward Dolan and the bottle.

"Not yet," Christie said. "Not if we want to have this conversation now, swiftly, without going in to Headquarters. Accusations of other kinds of abuse, as I was saying."

"You have nothing on me," Dun said almost gleefully. "I could walk out right now and you'd have nothing, really."

"Not true," Christie said. "We have people explaining how you got a key to the Park Center."

This was a lie, too. Again, the word might come in at any time, but Christie's claim was unsubstantiated as yet.

Christie continued. "And David has given you a key to the Counseling Center. That piece of information came from one of the counselors who went back one night and saw you use it."

A lie, a bold lie. Colleen watched Christie, fascinated.

Christie continued smoothly, as if he were telling the truth, "So we know you could get in there."

"I'm sorry," David said. "I never should have allowed it. He said he needed a place to put his feet up."

Dun gave a pained smile. "You see, he is very stupid. No offspring of mine would be that dumb."

Christie said, "So we know your use of places. We know from one of Jamilla's friends that she used to go meet you there years ago, that it started years ago. And that she didn't want to go but thought she had to. She was only eight, nine years old."

"She wanted to meet me. We talked about how her family was doing. I was helping them."

"She most definitely didn't want to. She told her friend that."

Colleen tried to figure out what they had on him when the lies were erased. This was a case of nothing concrete being made to sound like something.

David had begun to cry at the mention of Jamilla. "How could you, how could you?"

Dun yelped, "Whose side are you on, boy?" He seemed different somehow, not laughing and not as angry. He kept holding on to his left arm.

"Your arm? What is it? Dad?"

"You ought to know. You slammed me into the table here." He knocked at the bedside stand, winced.

"I was trying to catch you. Are you okay?"

"I'll be okay when we're done with this ridiculous conversation." He looked back to Christie.

Christie sounded like a cop testifying calmly in court—simple and exact. The calmness seemed to permeate the room. "We've put a wide net out to children who went to the Center. We intend to find out how widespread your meetings with kids were. We know there were meetings."

"How could you?" David said again, addressing his father, then looking away. "How could you?"

"You knew how I was made. You knew." Dun said this simply.

David said, "You did this? To kids? Again?"

Dun looked at his son as if he pitied him. Hoffman lunged toward the bathroom.

"Stay with him," Christie said to Dolan, who was there with Hoffman in a shot. The room went silent except for the sound of Hoffman's retching.

"I'm sorry," Hoffman was saying. "I can't help it."

"No problem," Dolan said.

"You could help us, you know," Christie said to Dun. "You could tell us who you saw, what kids you saw, how often. You tell us and we don't have to make so much publicity about it, it's less public. You don't tell us and it's the kind of thing that's on the news and in the papers for months on end as we get the kids to come forward."

"Why would I help you? I should have a lawyer here. Why would I help you?"

"Well, our work, loyalty to it, our reputations. You've worked hard, you've stayed a long time in the job, you've come up in the ranks, you've made friends, the Chief among them, you've done a lot of good."

Dun's face changed. Christie had hit a nerve. Christie saw it, too, and pursued this thread. "The good part of your history, your work, is going to get buried if you make us drag this out. That's all. I can't help it if you let it go that way. I can only hope you don't. Chief thinks a lot of you. He's . . . very upset, very, but he knows you . . . lost control lately. He didn't know why before we showed him what we had, but then it made sense to him. He's distressed for you. And for himself and the whole force."

Dolan and Hoffman came back into the room.

"That's what you're looking at, my meetings with kids? Because I can give you a little bit on that, if you can help keep it quiet, but I didn't do anything else."

"What do you mean? Anything else?"

"Homicide." He raised his eyebrows. "Murder."

"The murders are going to talk and they're going to talk loud. The prints in the shower at McCall's house, the trace evidence in the tub trap, the reports of neighbors—"

A lie again. No neighbors had seen anything.

"And"—Christie sighed—"what McCall told her boyfriend about you coming over to see her and about what she saw when she followed you to the Family Counseling Center." Christie shook his head. "There's a lot coming in on the murders."

Christie sounded so believable Colleen almost bought the whole package—but she knew no neighbor had reported *seeing* Dun.

"And," Christie continued, "we have hairs, fibers from the Park Center, and we have prints on the plastic bags, and shoe prints in the dirt."

True.

"We have a resident of one of the Allegheny apartments ready to say what car she saw parking that night Jamilla was killed, and how she saw a man and a girl go into the building and the man drive one of the trucks out in the middle of the night, and how she saw the man return the truck and get into his car."

No such resident. A wished-for resident.

Dun was smart, so it was no surprise that he asked, "Then why didn't you come for me earlier?"

"You know why. You're a detective, a good one. You know perfectly well why. And you know how we were feeling, how we held out every hope it wasn't true."

"You're arresting me for murder?"

Christie scratched his forehead as if an answer might be there. He sneezed twice. "Sorry," he said. "I keep avoiding calling in the Bridgeville police or the state police because it's going to get ugly. I was hoping you'd see the wisdom of telling us everything, going in with us, nice and peaceful, letting us help."

"Help how?"

"Keep it moderately quiet. Dignified."

"Could I have another drink?"

"How are you feeling?"

"I don't feel all that well."

"You're used to drinking a lot?"

"A lot more than I've had today."

Christie shook his head. "It can't be good for you in the long run, but if you're used to it . . ."

"I need it."

"Go on, then, a little. Go ahead, Artie, and pour him a short glass." There was a silence. During it, Dolan poured a drink and Dun gulped it down but kept the glass close to his chest.

Hoffman said, "Go on, Dad. Let them take you in. They know. Greer knew from the start. She was asking about you way back to last Sunday."

She was asking even when she didn't know she was.

Suddenly, Dun roared and threw the plastic glass at Colleen. It didn't go the distance, but fell on the floor, weak, a weak sound. He got up from the bed and lunged toward her and swung at her. Christie and Dolan pulled him back before he could hit her.

Even though Christie and Dolan had hold of Dun, he was still trying to press forward. Hitting her was all he wanted. From the time she entered the room, she'd been afraid he'd come at her whether she was armed or not.

Dun was still looking at her, trying to intimidate her. Shaken, she held his gaze. He sputtered and collapsed back on the bed, "What do you know? Huh? What do you know about me?"

"Lots. A whole history."

"Fucking bitch."

She could have told him he'd no doubt been molested by a woman, probably his mother, that he felt inadequate, that he had developed a huge ego to make up for the hurt, that he had a fury against adult women. Instead, she just nodded at him and let him hate her. She hated him, after all.

Hoffman went to his father and touched his knee. It was one of those strange, awkward gestures that held some kind of power. Even Dun stopped staring at her and looked at his son.

The detectives went silent, watching.

"Will you go in with me?" Dun asked Hoffman.

"Yes."

"Don't let them write things about me."

"I won't be able to stop that."

"I can't stand it."

"You have to stand it."

"I can't."

"I'll try to stop them," David said helplessly.

"What do you need from me?" Christie asked. "To make it easier? What I need from you is . . . a couple of sentences. Just something very short." He grabbed up the notepad that came with the room. Only two sheets on it.

"I got you covered," Dolan said. "Lots of paper in my car." He went outside.

Christie was saying, "Just something simple so we can close the case as quietly as possible."

"Go ahead, Dad. Write it. It'll help."

Dun looked helplessly at the two small pieces of paper. Dolan came back with a legal pad and handed it over to Dun, who took it but leveled a gaze at Christie. "I want you to find me a way out. You understand?"

"I think so."

Colleen was surprised at Christie's quick answer. Was Dun asking for an insanity plea? Or a gun and a car and a satchel of money? Why did Christie seem to agree?

Dun started writing. His handwriting was tiny, his face folded in a grimace. Dolan tried to read over his shoulder; Hoffman tried to read upside down. As he wrote, Dun winced again. His face flushed. He sweated. His eyes became unfocused. He squeezed his face and kept writing, but his hand opened and the pen dropped.

"Say it," Christie said. "Say it, then. It's the right thing to do."

"I did what you said," he growled.

"He's choking," Hoffman said. "Is he choking?"

Dolan grabbed up the pad and studied it, tilting it under the lamplight. "'*Stabbed Laura McCall to death and strangled Jamilla Washington to death.*' He wrote it. We have that part."

Dun held his left arm.

"Say it. Please. About the children. Boys, girls, both?"

"Girls." His voice was almost a whisper.

Hoffman said, "He's not okay. Something's happening. It's his heart. Dad, is it—"

"How many?" Christie asked. He didn't sound gentle now. Colleen heard the voice of a prosecutor, a voice she was unfamiliar with when it came to Christie.

Dun fell to a knee. Both Dolan and Hoffman moved toward him, but he waved them off. Colleen took her jacket off. She knew CPR, they all did. But he might be faking, he might have a gun under the bed. She watched, trying to figure it out.

"Maybe twenty over the ye—"

"Twenty? Is that a real number? Or more?"

"Nineteen, I thi—"

"How many from Family Counseling?"

"Four. Four. I tried to stop."

"What ages?"

"Eight, mostly. Jamilla was the only one older. We had a . . . friendship. She liked me a lot. She wanted the . . . the friendship. There were times—"

"She didn't want it," Colleen said. Christie looked at her, but he didn't reprimand her for speaking up. Instead, he changed again, said, "You son of a bitch piece of scum. She was a child, a baby." He looked at Colleen. "Tell him."

She said tightly, "Jamilla kept the appointments out of fear. She didn't want them."

"You can't know."

"I know."

"I know this much," Christie said. "You took your problem and you landed it on an innocent child. I swear to you, I can't think of a punishment bad enough for you."

Dun reached for the bourbon bottle, but a spasm of pain hit him and he went down. There was no reaching under the bed for a gun, only pain on his face and gasping.

Hoffman held his father in his arms. "Leave him alone now," he whispered. "Leave him alone."

Christie said, "We still have questions. Nineteen. Do you have a list somewhere?"

"No."

"Can your son help us trace them?"

"No. He doesn't know."

Dolan moved forward and asked, "Were they all black kids?"

"No."

"Black and white? Equal opportunity? You know what black guys in jail do to white guys who did what you did? 'Cause, see, black guys know about power, they know when a thing is unfair."

Hoffman rocked his father. "He's . . . really sick. He's having—"

"I can do CPR," Greer began. But so could Hoffman, surely, and Christie and Dolan certainly could. She felt Christie hold her back firmly.

Dun was dying. All of them understood that and they weren't moving.

"We're going to have to call nine one one." Christie made a gesture to Dolan that seemed to mean "very, very slowly." Dolan left the room.

Dun clutched at his chest, letting out a cry of pain.

Christie moved forward and held Dun's pulse. "We'll get nine one one for him," he said to Hoffman.

"Let him go," Hoffman said. "I understand. Let him go."

"And I understand what you're saying," Christie told him. "But I have to behave in a certain way. I'm sorry."

He beckoned to Colleen and they went just outside the motel room. A man from another unit was parking, going to his room. He hardly seemed to notice them.

"You're slowing it down?" Christie asked Dolan.

Dolan whispered. "I've dialed the nine. I could put the first one in any time."

Colleen's head spun. They were just letting him go. He might live, he might die.

"You don't plan these things," Christie said quietly to her. His voice was hoarse, almost nonexistent, broken by the cold and whatever else he was feeling. "But I think it might be a blessing. If it happens, the case'll go away more quickly, quietly."

"It shouldn't go away. There are two women dead and a lot of kids—"

"It won't go away, right. It'll just hurt less."

"I dialed the one," Dolan said. "One more number to go."

"Don't hurry the rest," Christie said. He looked up. "Damn towers take such a long time to process the numbers. Come on, Greer, we're going back in."

They slipped back into the room. Hoffman still cradled his father, who lay limp in his arms. "I can't explain it," he said. "He did terrible things, but I still loved him."

"He did terrible things. He must have been a very tortured man."

"Tortured is right. I think he was. I think he's gone. I hope to hell he has some peace now."

Christie nodded. "I don't know why I'm not hearing a siren yet. Some of these outlying areas take so long to respond."

Colleen looked behind her to Dolan, who punched in the last one, then walked away to disguise the fact that it was the first time he'd talked to a dispatcher.

All of that, all of that *show,* in case Hoffman changed his mind later and wanted to blame them, in which case they'd have a partial cover. Lies everywhere.

She wanted Dun alive, in prison, having to face what he'd done. There were nearly twenty victims of sex abuse, and two women dead, and the man wasn't *paying* for any of it.

After the paramedics came and took Dun away, after two hours of phone calls back and forth to the chief, to the Bridgeville police, after they'd gotten everything on record, showed the legal pad with its written confession, talked to the son, heard his corroboration, done their own note taking on the verbal confession, after all that was squared away, it was two-twenty in the morning.

It was the end of a long week in summer, in which they'd both gotten and lost their man, but the books could be closed now on two cases.

Christie's eyes and nose were streaming now, and when he spoke, his cold was on him in such full force, he could hardly make himself understood. It was as if he'd backed it off for as long as he needed to and now had to take the balancing consequences.

Through Christie's muffled vowels, Colleen made out that they would now be released to get some sleep and they would meet in the morning. Yet the three of them stood, leaning on Christie's car, talking as if it were midafternoon.

"Some first case," Dolan said to Greer. "You've been initiated all right. Better or worse."

"Yeah." Tell a lot of lies and let them die. "What about Hoffman?"

Christie pulled his jacket tightly around him and said thickly, "He'll stick around. He'll be planning another burial. Then we figure out if we're going to charge him and with what exactly."

"Boss, you are so sick. You're shivering. And it isn't cold out. Not even near cool."

He nodded. "We'll have to explain all of this. Answer what we did right and wrong."

Colleen blanched.

"Speaking of," Dolan said, "I saw after the fact you didn't report your West Virginia visit. Same as the DNA sample? Tricky business. I wasn't reading the reports closely—okay, I admit that—but Commander'll tell you you can't leave things out. I know McGranahan was being a jerk, but it all comes down to how we back ourselves up in court."

"But . . ." She looked to Christie. "I had Dun in mind from the start."

His face became long, sober. "I can finesse the fact that you didn't keep the reports—and I'll do it this time. That's it. Never again. You went after your guy; you wanted him. Okay. You wouldn't have shot to kill, but you wanted him bad, and in a way, you killed him."

Colleen felt doubt welling in her. Pushing him into the room *had* started something. It only took reviewing the scene to see that when he fell, he'd hit, if anything, his right arm, not his left. She'd seen him nursing his arm the whole time. He must have had a smaller heart attack, then the big one.

"We killed him," Christie said. "All three of us. We all said things. We made it happen; then we let it happen. We're going to have to live with that, square it."

Colleen shivered.

"You going to be okay?" he asked her.

"I guess. It's all . . . murky."

"Let's all get to our beds." Christie looked around, puzzled. He was looking for her car. Colleen had never had a moment to explain.

"My car is up around the building. See, I found the room on foot. That's how I got myself into it. Dun ran smack into me because he was leaving the room. I couldn't let him get away, so I made him go back in."

"Oh," Christie said. "That's why you had a gun pulled. Explains a lot."

"Well," Dolan said. "And we thought you were trying to be a star. Though there is a little bit of that in you. Go on, admit it." He gave her a nudge on the upper arm. She wasn't sure if it was a friendly nudge or not.

"I guess."

Christie reviewed everything they would need to do the next day. It got to be three o'clock and they were still there. It was as if the whole last week were lifting off reluctantly, a dream hanging on.

Christie said, "With all the overtime, I just about bought myself enough time off to get rid of the cold. Then I'm back a week, then family vacation."

Colleen pictured him going on vacation with his family. She tried to imagine what he was like away from work, how he spent his time, what he ate. "Let me know if I can do anything to lighten your load. Like . . . write up your reports for you," she said, with as much whimsy as she could muster.

"I might just take you up on that."

Again, they stood around, didn't move off. "Thank you both for everything."

Dolan tipped his head, finally looked at his watch, whistled, studied the stars.

"Where the hell *is* your car?" Christie asked, looking around.

"Up at registration."

"I guess I ought to get going," Dolan said.

"I'll walk her to her car," Christie volunteered.

They bid Dolan good night. They walked slowly, watched Dolan drive off, waved, kept going.

"Glad to know what happened back there at the beginning. You probably couldn't have done anything else."

"Didn't seem so. I'm sorry about my mistakes. Things just happened, running into Dun that morning, knowing, then running into him trying to leave. It all sort of *came* to me."

"This one had your name on it. But you aren't always going to be this lucky. Probably never again."

"That might be okay with me."

Her feelings were tumultuous still. If Christie weren't there, she would kick something, hit something.

He saw that. "What? What?"

"It isn't enough. He got away with it. He never got punished. When I let myself feel the anger, I feel like I'm going to explode."

"I get it. I could tell even while we were in there. It's . . . well, I feel the same way. Don't you know that? I was worried I could have killed him some other way, hitting, choking. Then it happened the way it did. Oh, I don't look forward to talking to journalists on this one. I put them off. I have to call one guy back."

"You probably have to if you want to control how they hear it."

"I do." When they got to her car, Christie said, "So, overall, the whole case, you did good. You were instrumental."

"Thank you." She felt enormous relief at getting the compliment she so much wanted. She opened her car door but didn't get in, let it sit ajar. Christie leaned his elbows on the roof of her car, as if he had all the time in the world. She rested against the back fender, aware, after a while, that the stars were out, shining brightly.

Christie rapped the roof of her car, a little rat-a-tat.

Colleen thought she might always want to be up at this time of night. The silence, punctuated by a car motor here and there, was something wonderful.

"Do you always lie so much?"

"Yeah." He laughed. "Have to." He reached over and hugged her. It was a comradely hug. It felt wonderful, and she held it a moment too long because she didn't care, she just wanted it.

He pulled away firmly enough that she felt awkward. But then he started talking. "I'm thinking we need to . . . make everything as normal as we can. See, Dolan and I are used to each other, so I have to try to make sure I partner with him again. You were good, you were real good, so you should know it's no criticism of you if I don't take a case with you in the near future, and maybe at some point in the *far* future, we'll work something together." He stopped, suddenly aware his words might have a double meaning. "Ah, I'm blathering. When I get one of these colds, they last me three weeks and I have no mind. Anyway, I have to put Coleson back with McGranahan. They kvetch all the time, but they suit each other. So, I'm thinking, thinking, Potocki is bouncing around ever since Picarelli left. I'm thinking you might work well together. He's top-notch. People don't always know it, because he cuts up."

"He's funny."

"He's funny, he's smart."

"Okay. Whatever you say. I know I'm not the only person who wants to work with you. The whole squad likes you. That's a pretty good trick."

He deflected the compliment with a shake of the head. "I'm not a very exciting guy, so if people like me . . . I guess I feel lucky." He shrugged. "You possibly have the same disease. People want to work with you, too."

"They do?"

"I think so."

He started to back away. "I'll follow you back. I'll keep an eye on you."

She didn't want to get into her car and end it, the case, the week, the night, but there was no getting around it.

Her car motor started up almost too eagerly. "Peppy," she always said of it. Christie motioned to her to lock her doors. She watched him walk toward his car, then followed slowly and waited for him to start up before she moved ahead of him. When she was in position to be followed, she started driving fast—police speed—toward home, as if she might shake him off, as if she wanted to.